A Little More Primitive

by Josh Langston

DEDICATION

This novel is dedicated to Shasta and Bailey, two of my closest and dearest friends -- on this or any other planet. Though they don't know it, and I have no way of conveying the message, these two ever-young ladies provided a wealth of inspiration, an abundance of love, and some incomparable nuzzling, without which it's unlikely this book would ever have been written. Thank you, girls. Please know that you are adored, honored, and even from time to time, obeyed.

Meet me in the kitchen where we keep the treats!

--Pop

Chapter 1

It's always the little things...

Tori focused on the computer monitor in front of her. The wide, flat screen was a thank you gift from her friend and editor, Cassy Woodall, whose life Tori had saved by providing a blood transfusion. Tori considered the gift extravagant, but Cassy insisted she keep it. Now, Tori couldn't imagine working without it. She didn't, however, feel quite the same way about the other new additions in her life, a pair of young lovers for whom the word "civilization" remained a mystery.

Tori had typed and retyped the same sentence several times, her concentration derailed by the intimate sounds coming from behind a makeshift screen on the other side of the one-room cabin.

Why the hell couldn't they do it when she wasn't around?

Though she couldn't see them, she easily imagined the two diminutive bodies writhing on the little mattress she'd picked up at a yard sale in Ten Sleep, the nearest town of any size. She had no idea how old the lovers actually were, but they had the stamina of teenagers on Viagra: steam-driven and drip fed. It made her so jealous she could spit, not that she'd ever admit it.

"I'm takin' the dog out," she said, mostly for her own benefit, then snapped her fingers to summon Shadow, a gigantic animal of questionable lineage and occasional loyalty. The big, black Rottweiler/Lab/bison mix trotted over and rested his massive head on her thigh. She scratched him behind the ears as he turned his soulful brown eyes in her direction and wagged his tail. He was likely just as horny as she was, and neither would be getting lucky any time soon.

"Out," she said. The command sent the dog thundering toward the door. Tori opened it and followed him into the bright sunshine. "Don't eat anyone," she said as he took off across the top of the bluff on which her cabin stood.

She'd come to Wyoming primarily to avoid her ex-husband; she'd stayed primarily because of the view. As Shadow plunged through the brush chasing butterflies, prairie dogs or buffalo -- anything in roaming range would do -- she was content to just stare at the mountains.

In all too typical fashion, however, her reverie was trashed by the buzz of her cell phone. She fished the tyrannical device from her pocket, stabbed the Answer button, and held it to her ear. "H'lo?"

"Mizz Lanier?" a male voice asked. The accent was thick as grits -- heavy, with a touch of Cajun flavoring. *Nice, actually*. But then, she knew the man behind the voice, and whatever mystery there might have been, fled.

"Whatcha got, Dallas?"

Dallas drove the UPS delivery truck and had never worked up the courage to attempt the obstacle course Tori euphemistically termed a driveway. She wasn't entirely unsympathetic. One section in particular worried her as it ran alongside the base of a steep incline. Winter weather often loosened the grip of rocks and boulders on the hill, and the ground through which Tori's "drive" meandered was littered with huge stones that had broken loose. A wash on the opposite side of the narrow trail prevented her from making wide detours. She'd dealt single-handedly with most of the debris, although her friend Caleb, a retired rodeo cowboy turned grocery merchant, had helped her nudge a couple of the largest boulders out of the way.

Maintaining the route between her cabin and the highway was a pain, but she managed. It helped that she drove a little Nissan pickup with better than average ground clearance. Dallas drove one of the ubiquitous, boxy, brown UPS trucks, about as far from an off-road vehicle as one could get. As a result, Dallas called when he reached the turn-off to let her know she had a package.

She'd made the mistake of driving out to accept a delivery she'd been anxiously awaiting, and he'd been smitten. Who knew cupid wore cowboy boots? She'd noticed his name neatly embroidered on his brown UPS shirt and made small talk about it while he recovered enough to get her signature on his snazzy computerized delivery pad.

Since then he found something to discuss with her on every trip. She suspected he broke up multi-parcel deliveries just so he'd have extra reasons to drop by, though God only knew how he could justify driving umpteen miles into the boondocks just to chat her up. Evidently, loneliness could drive a man to do extraordinary things. Too bad navigating her driveway wasn't one of them.

"It's pretty big," he said, "but not too heavy."

"Who's it from?" Tori hadn't ordered anything

lately. She could only stretch her royalty checks so far. Living off the land was not an option. That sort of thing was fine for outdoor types, but not for Tori Lanier, novelist and unofficial guardian of two very small Indians. Oh, and a sacred hole in the ground.

"It's from New York," Dallas said. "Can't make out the name."

"Why don't you just leave it?" She glanced skyward. It didn't look like rain, but she knew from experience that could change with little warning. "I'll pick it up later."

"I dunno," he said. "I really hate to leave stuff out. Ya never know who might drive by."

"On that road?" She laughed. "Nobody."

He didn't say anything, but Tori could sense his disappointment. "Okay. Lemme grab my keys. I'll be there in a minute."

"No hurry," he said. "I've got time."

Shadow spotted her when she fired up her truck. She slowed to a stop so he could jump in the back. She doubted Shadow got out any more often than Dallas did.

The UPS man was sitting in the high seat of his huge vehicle when she bounced across the last set of ruts which marked the end of the driveway. He left his vehicle and approached hers with a large box in his arms.

"Told ya it was big," he said when he handed it to her.

She put it on the passenger seat where Shadow wouldn't attack it, or worse, then turned to conclude the transaction by signing his computer thingy.

"You ever been to the music festival in Ten Sleep?" he asked.

4

"The woodchuck thing?"

He took on a pained expression. "It's called 'NoWoodstock.' You know, like the big hippie concert in New York? 'Cept it's not like that at all."

"Right," she said, slowly. "I missed it last year."

"I was thinkin'... You know, maybe you and me--"

"It's mostly country music, right? I'm not much--"

"It's blues, too. And some rock. Lots of different stuff. Gospel."

Swell. "I dunno," she said, stalling until she came up with a plausible excuse for shooting him down. The last UPS delivery guy never called. In fact, she'd never met him. He'd just leave her stuff and drive away, even in the winter. Some deliveries sat for days. Since he was no longer around, she assumed he'd been canned for forging her signature on the delivery gizmo. In any event, Tori had no desire to make her way onto the new guy's shit list.

"There's always a crowd," Dallas said. "Lotsa food and stuff. C'mon, it'll be fun. My treat."

She smiled. He wasn't unattractive. Get him out of those silly brown shorts and he might even look like an adult. *Hmm.* "How old are you?"

"Twenty-two," he said, a streak of uncertainty shading his answer.

"Wouldn't you rather go with someone uhm... a little younger? I'm--" she coughed, "almost thirty." She covered her mouth to keep from giving herself away. She'd been on the wrong side of thirty for a couple years. Okay, four years, but who was counting?

"No," he said, grinning like a medal-winner at the Special Olympics. "I like older women!"

She fixed him with a stare. "Do I look like an older woman?"

5

"No, ma'am," he said.

"Ma'am?"

"I mean, no. You're... You know. Kinda pretty."

"Well, there's a ringing endorsement." She walked around to the driver's side of her truck and got in. "I'll have to check my schedule. When's the big do?"

"Second weekend in August."

Surely she could find some sort of commitment by then. "I'll let you know."

He tapped his phone. "I'll call ya, okay?"

"Right," she said, starting the truck's engine. She pulled out onto the paved road to turn around, narrowly missing the bumper of the big brown truck. She waved as she drove back to the house.

"Kinda pretty," she said -- out loud -- then yanked down the sun visor and checked her reflection in the vanity mirror. Okay, she admitted to herself, she wasn't likely to end up in the Sports Illustrated swim suit edition, but she was still a damn sight better than "kinda pretty," and if Dallas the delivery dude didn't recognize it, he needed glasses. Big time. The more she thought about it, the more she looked forward to turning him down when he called back.

She made a rare shift of gears, higher speeds not being desirable on her private version of the Oregon Trail. That and a sharp turn while negotiating the cliff passage caused the package to lean, teeter briefly, and then fall toward her. She shoved it back in place, then stared at it in curiosity. From New York. Had to be Cassy. She didn't know anyone else who lived there.

The box appeared big enough to hold a lamp, assuming the shade was shipped separately. Which, if true, meant yet another encounter with the love struck UPS driver. "Kinda pretty," she muttered, urging her subconscious to get over it and move on to the package. Her conscious mind made the effort, but there was interference.

Christmas in July!

Zzt... Date with Dallas.

Brown paper packages tied up with strings!

Party with Dallas.

Package!

Party.

Package!

Party? *With Dallas?*

Oy.

~*~

Jarred Carter, MD, sat in the fifth floor nurses station reviewing a file on Brooklyn Memorial hospital's patient database. Though merely a first year resident, Carter had been working at the hospital long enough to recognize when something -- especially the recovery of a critically ill patient -- went well beyond the ordinary.

There were plenty of staff members eager to chalk up such rare occurrences as the work of the divine. Carter wasn't so sure. A confirmed agnostic, he had no problem taking credit for any such cures which occurred on his watch, although to date, there had only been two. Still, it bothered him on several levels that he couldn't pinpoint what had triggered the reversals.

Turns for the worse were far more likely, especially considering cost-conscious administrators, lowest bid contractors, and overworked staff. A hospital was a terrible place to be sick. But, that's where the experts were, so what choice did anyone have?

The record he found so interesting concerned a patient named Cassandra Woodall: single, late thirties, no unusual medical history. Woodall had been delivered to the emergency room barely alive. Whoever had administered the beating she'd suffered had surely intended her to die. That she survived at all was nothing short of a miracle. She had been consigned to intensive care, and while a number of surgeries had been discussed, she was in no condition to undergo any of them.

Carter, on call at the time of her admission, had been assigned to her care, though no one really expected her to live through the night, much less the week which followed. He had looked in on her as often as required, but when her condition varied at all, it was inevitably for the worse. She was, prognostically speaking, a loser.

And then, in the space of 24 hours, everything turned around. It happened so fast, he almost didn't notice. Cassy Woodall was going to live. And not just as a shell of the woman she'd once been. Cassy's injuries were healing in ways that defied medical experience.

Carter wanted to know why. He needed to know why. What made this woman different? What made it possible for her to survive a beat down on the order of the worst he'd seen in two-plus years of ER night shifts in one of New York's shittiest locales?

The pictures scrolling on the screen in front of him suggested but one possibility. Someone had entered Woodall's room and administered a treatment of some kind. The public wasn't supposed to know about the in-room video hospital administrators had installed in the wake of a much-publicized string of mercy killings the previous year. The resulting video database was enormous, and combing through it would take a lifetime, unless one knew what he was looking for. Carter did.

Though grainy, the picture on the screen in front of him revealed enough detail to satisfy him that Cassandra Woodall's miraculous recovery was linked to a visitor rather than to anything done by the staff at Brooklyn Memorial.

He needed to know who the visitor was, and what -- exactly -- she had done.

~*~

Mato rolled onto his back. A light sheen of sweat marked the passing of his lust. And not just his. Reyna shared it. She had the usual glassy eyed look of the recently sated, her head resting on Mato's arm. She, too, looked up at the ceiling of the giant's cabin -- their home the past several weeks.

"Do you think we've pleased the Spirits?" he asked.

She smiled. "I'm pleased. Is that not enough?"

He rolled toward her and smoothed a long, dark hair from her forehead. "That's more than enough. I just hoped...."

"You want a child, of course. I'm not stupid, Mato. But I wonder, is this the best place to have one? What would Winter Woman say?"

Winter Woman was Reyna's grandmother, a person of vast respect among The People. Mato could have no greater ally on Earth. Still, the woman could be unpredictable. He couldn't be sure she would welcome the news that Mato and Reyna had added yet another generation to her pedigree.

"She will be pleased," he said, though caution tempered his certainty. "And if not, she'll get used to the idea. What choice does she have?"

Reyna curled toward him, her hand doing delightfully casual and deliberately carnal things. "What if she's angry? Do you think she's ready for a great-grandchild? The child of two dreamers?"

He smiled. *Two dreamers.* That would be the issue most on Winter Woman's mind. The tribe needed dreamers -- those who glimpses of the future often meant continued life for the tribe. The Old Ones sang of times when there were few such gifted members of The People, and those times had been difficult indeed. Still, there was no certainty that if Mato and Reyna produced a child, he or she would have the gift. Winter Woman would know, of course. She might wait until she held such a child in her withered arms before she even decided if she would welcome it, or not.

"I would rejoice at the chance to present a child to her," he said at length. "Nor would I care if our child knew the gift of dreams. I would be proud, and I would challenge any who dared find fault."

She hugged him. "You make *me* proud."

"I am Mato!" he said, as if he had just entered a room full of warriors who didn't already know him. "I am a hunter. I am a provider!"

She pinched a recently evolved roll of flab around his middle. "I fear someone has been providing for you, too much."

He pulled away and took to his feet, embarrassed. The door to the cabin burst open and Tori, the she-giant, entered along with her dog. Mato and the dog had long ago achieved an understanding based on mutual admiration and respect. Shadow, while clearly the physically superior member, was also the junior member, intellectually. The great animal shuffled toward them, his nose busy with the scents their love-making had painted in the air, then collapsed beside their bower. Mato dug his hands into the thick fur of the dog's neck and rubbed him diligently. Both Shadow and Tori approved.

The she-giant placed a huge box on the table in the eating area of the cabin. She stepped back and contemplated it in silence.

"What is it?" Mato asked, concentrating on the words to get them right. The past several weeks had been spent in concentrated study of the giant's language. He was getting reasonably good at it, owing mostly to his superior memory. Tori still struggled with the speech of The People, and they both knew he needed her language more than she needed his. Still, he often had trouble finding the right words, especially for concepts outside the normal experience of The People.

She shook the box and shrugged. "It's from Cassy."

Mato and Reyna had met the woman. Yet another she-giant, Cassy had traveled an unimaginable distance to visit with Tori a few weeks ago. Tori had tried to explain, pointing to the sky and telling him how her friend had ridden in one of the giant's machines that traveled through the air. Reyna assured him it was all nonsense, a boast by the giants meant to demoralize them. Mato knew better. He had learned that much of what the giants took for granted, he mistook for great magic. Reyna had yet to make the logical leap needed to discern the difference. The giants were incredibly clever, but what they had at their disposal wasn't magic. They had something Tori called technology. He had thought, at first, that it was just another word for magic. But it wasn't. It merely referred to cleverly designed machinery.

The revelation had brought him great solace, but he had yet to convince Reyna. She was still held in the grip of superstition, and a lifetime of teaching focused on the evils of giants. Such a background was not easily changed. But, in time, he knew she would recognize his superior wisdom.

Tori plucked a knife from a drawer and made several cuts through the thin, almost invisible membranes, which held the box securely closed. They parted easily under her skillful hands, and she unfolded panels of the thin brown container.

She stepped back, clearly surprised. "What the hell?"

Mato and Reyna scrambled out of bed to get closer. Mato reached the giant-sized chair first and reached down to assist Reyna. They stood side-by-side gazing in wonder at the contents of the box.

~*~

Carter gripped his phone lightly as he spoke into it. "Ms. Woodall?"

"Yes?" She sounded less than thrilled.

"This is Dr. Carter, from Brooklyn Memorial."

She didn't respond immediately. "Is this about my bill? Because my insurance is supposed to cover everything. I--"

"No," he said. "It has nothing to do with that. In

12

fact, I couldn't care less about your bill. I just wanted to check up on you."

"You did?"

"Yes. I try to follow up on all my patients."

"Oh. How nice. I didn't think doctors did that anymore."

"Well," he said, breathing a subtle sigh of relief, "my folks were old school. They thought it would be a good habit to get into, and I have to agree. Although--" he laughed "--you'd be surprised at how many think I'm trying to pull something over on them."

"I hate to hear that," she said. "There's so little trust in the world these days. How can I help you?"

"Actually, that's my question," he said. "How're you doing? Your recovery was nothing short of miraculous. I couldn't help but wonder about you."

"Why's that?"

"Well," he stumbled, "it's not every day one is presented with a miracle. Either as a patient or a physician."

Again she didn't respond immediately, and he wondered if he'd overplayed his hand. "Ms. Woodall?"

"I'm still here," she said. "It's an unusual situation. Perhaps we could discuss it."

"Over dinner?" he asked.

"I... Uh, sure."

"Would you care to suggest a place?"

She mentioned a restaurant not too far from the hospital.

"That'll work," he said. "My schedule is crazy; I can't plan more than a day or two in advance. So, would tomorrow evening be too soon?"

They sealed the deal and Carter hung up. Could it really be that easy, he wondered. Then he smiled. A little charm could go a long way.

~*~

Tori stared at the contents of the box. What had Cassy been thinking? Or, perhaps more apropos, what had she been smoking?

Mato and Reyna were equally transfixed by the sight, standing shoulder-to-shoulder on a kitchen chair. "Nekkid as newborns," Tori's mother would have said, shortly after she'd run screaming from the room. Though still not at all comfortable with their casual attitude about clothing and hygiene, Tori refused to let them ruin her consternation over Cassy's gift.

Inside the box, cushioned with a more than generous supply of bubble wrap, stood a two-foot tall doll. The fully clothed, more or less adult-looking male figure stared at her from a face so lifelike she half expected it to step forward and introduce itself. Thankfully, it didn't.

"Jesus, Mary and Joseph," she muttered as she reached for the envelope taped to the doll's abdomen. Once she'd removed it, the libido twins advanced, poking the helpless figure and examining its stylish attire.

Tori removed a note from the envelope and scanned it quickly:

> *Allow me to introduce Lance. He's*
> *a ball-jointed doll, custom made for my*
> *friend, Rachel, who was with me the*
> *night of the attack.*

Tori remembered the chronology all too well. Cassy's friend had died trying to defend them from Tori's insane ex-husband.

> *I've known about Lance for years. He was one of Rachel's prized possessions, and according to her, was the only male she ever loved. Rachel's mother insisted I take him, as if I wouldn't remember Rachel all on my own. Anyway, I couldn't help but think about Mato and Reyna and how hard it must be for you to travel anywhere with them. I thought if people grew accustomed to seeing you with Lance, they might not even notice if one of your little friends took his place.*
>
> *I don't really have any use for Lance, though I'm sure he's a great guy and will never promise more than he can deliver. If you decide not to keep him, please let me know, and I'll arrange for an adoption. You can't imagine how expensive these things are!*

What intrigued Tori more than the doll was its wardrobe, which Cassy had included in the shipment. Although the clothing reflected some odd notions about male fashions, Tori chalked it up to Rachel's sexual orientation. Cassy had often commented on their relationship, though without providing any significant details. Tori had always been thankful for that.

Reyna had both of her hands on the doll's face, a look of sheer wonder on her own. She exchanged a few hurried words with Mato, who then asked, "Is toy?"

Tori pursed her lips while she pondered her response, then smiled and nodded yes. She removed Lance from the box and stood him on the table. Mato leaped up beside him. Reyna motioned for him to stand tall, then put her hands on her hips and appraised them both. Mato had begun to look a bit peeved when Reyna finally smiled and said something to him that relieved the tension.

"Mato more pretty," he announced, dropping lightly down to the chair to hug his gal.

Tori would have agreed, but Mato's ego was sufficiently inflated.

Encouragement? No way!

She looked back at Lance. He had the same dark hair as Mato, and it was nearly the same length. His complexion was considerably lighter than Mato's, and while someone had airbrushed a five o'clock shadow on his sharply defined jaw, it didn't do much to alter his basically androgynous features.

Reyna whispered something to Mato, in deference to Tori's feeble grasp of their native tongue, and the two chuckled. Tori suspected Reyna had already determined that Lance was anatomically correct, though undoubtedly not in the same league as her paramour.

Tori handed them both a few items of Lance's clothing. Reyna was quick to try things on; Mato was reluctant. Lance, it seemed, had never spent any time in the gym, while Mato's life in the wild gave him a

musculature most jocks would admire, despite his
minimalist frame. The end result being that the
clothing fit Reyna better than Mato, and she clearly
enjoyed strutting around the cabin. She had the poise,
presence and exotic good looks to be a runway model,
albeit on a significantly smaller runway than usual.

The more Tori thought about it, the more pleased
she became with Cassy's gift. Well, she thought,
Rachel's gift, and she made a mental note to phrase it
that way when she penned her Thank You note. She
resumed her place at the computer and had just begun
to compose an E-mail message to Cassy when her
phone rang again.

"I haven't checked my schedule yet," she said by
way of a greeting, assuming Dallas to be on the other
end of the line.

"Excuse me?"

She didn't recognize the voice.

"Sorry," she said, clearly embarrassed. "I was
expecting someone else."

"This is Nate Sheffield with the Washakie County
Sheriff's office."

Wonderful. "How can I help you, officer?"

"It's deputy, not officer."

"Okay then, how can I help you, *deputy?*"

"May I speak frankly, Mizz Lanier?"

"It won't hurt my feelings."

"We aren't gettin' anywhere with our
investigation. We know a little more than we did the
night your husband attacked you, but since then he's
disappeared without a trace. There's no sign of him
anywhere."

"I'm inclined to take that as good news," Tori said,
knowing precisely what her former husband was

17

doing -- decomposing.

"Unfortunately, ma'am, it suggests to us that he could show up just about anywhere. He might possibly try to come after you again."

She wondered if she ought to feign a certain level of fear, just for the benefit of Deputy Sheffield, then opted to go with frontier bravado, a decision made much easier knowing that Shawn was at the bottom of a deep crevasse which ran through a cave beneath her cabin -- a cave which had remained a secret from the world outside Mato's tribe for generations beyond count.

"I'm honestly not worried," she said. "I've got a great big dog and a shotgun full of buckshot. If he's stupid enough to come back, I'm still pissed enough to put a bucket-sized hole in 'im."

"I can appreciate that, Mizz Lanier, I surely can. But we'd like to avoid any further bloodshed if at all possible. This really isn't the wild west anymore."

Fearing she may have gone a little overboard, Tori tried to show some remorse. "Of course," she said. "I wouldn't *really* kill him if he came back. I'd be satisfied just takin' off one of his legs." She didn't volunteer which one.

"We try to discourage violence," he said.

"A girl's got to protect herself. I don't have any neighbors I can call on."

"That's what's got us so puzzled. We don't understand how your husband--"

"*Ex*-husband."

"Yes'm. How your ex-husband managed to get clean away without leaving any tracks. It's like something swooped down out of the sky and hauled him off."

She chuckled. "I seriously doubt he has any contacts among the angels." His contemporaries occupied a much less desirable realm.

"We'd like to take another look around your cabin, in case we missed something."

"And you need my permission?"

"It'd save us the trouble of gettin' a warrant."

She didn't like the idea of folks poking around her cabin. Granted, the entrance to the cavern was cunningly disguised, yet she had found it. Who could say some enthusiastic crime fighter might not stumble onto it as well?

"I don't want y'all to think I'm trying to hinder your investigation," she said at length. "You're welcome to come out and have a look around, but I'd appreciate knowing when you're coming. The place is a mess. She suddenly realized she'd begun to turn into her mother, unable to resist the urge to straighten up the house before the cleaning lady arrived.

"Would this afternoon be too soon?" he asked.

~*~

Chapter 2

How will we ever keep 'em down on the farm?

Tessa Bidford, sole heiress to the Geoffrey Day Bidford estate, sat behind the wheel of an exquisite, jade green Mercedes Benz SLS AMG. The soft leather seat cradled her petite curves as if it had been handcrafted exclusively for her. Which, of course, it hadn't.

The car belonged to Tessa's boss, Jerry Bernstein, CEO of Bernstein Labs, a biotech firm once the darling of Wall Street's most astute traders. Bernstein was married, had three children -- all older than Tessa -- and would have disinherited every one of them for the chance to sleep with her.

Not that she'd ever let that happen, though the temptation grew with every day the balance sheet of the Bidford fortune took another hit.

Unlike the moderately repugnant Bernstein, who actually produced something other than offspring during his lifetime, Tessa's late father had occupied himself with the goal of spending the entire family fortune before his daughter could get her hands on it. The last vestige of the once considerable family wealth, a summer home in the Hamptons, was soon to go on the auction block. Sadly, for Tessa, she lacked anything like the financial means to bid on it.

She down-shifted and pressed the accelerator to the floor, the wheel requiring but the lightest touch. The engine responded instantly and sent her hurtling past the vehicles clogging both southbound lanes of I-

87. The Mercedes rode the shoulder as if it were the autobahn, and the sudden snarl of the finely tuned German engine barely registered within the nearly sound-proof interior.

Desperate for something to lighten her mood, Tessa turned on the radio. Bernstein had set every button to some variety of news or talk station, forcing her to scan for something, anything, that had a beat. Lyrics didn't matter. Nor did melody, or even familiarity. She needed something percussive to match her mood.

Bernstein, the pot-bellied, bull-headed idiot, had forced the FDA into rendering an early decision on the company's latest product, a cure for androgenic alopecia, better know as male pattern baldness. After the months of mind-bending effort she had put into hyping the product's potential, Bernstein armed himself with overwhelmingly inconclusive test data and presented his case to the feds. Not surprisingly, they shot him down. Bernstein Lab's share price dropped like the blade on a guillotine, loping off Tessa's dreams for the future like Marie Antoinette's head.

Her employee stock options worthless and her portfolio a smoking ruin, Tessa somehow maintained her composure when she confronted Bernstein.

He merely shrugged and said, "It's not the end of the world. There will be other products. I've been through this scenario before and will surely go through it again."

Assuming you survive. Barely keeping her temper in check, she asked, "You've done this *before?* More than once?"

"Oh my, yes. Several times."

"And just when, exactly, did you plan to learn anything from these disasters?"

"You're still young," he'd said, as if that explained something. "What you don't understand, is that the product sucked. I knew it months ago. I waited until the price was right and started unloading my shares."

"You *what?*" Breathing had suddenly become difficult.

"I have an overseas broker who buys and sells for me all the time. Confidentially, of course. Been doing it for years. You didn't think I survived on my salary, did you?"

"What if the SEC finds out? Geezus, Jerry, that's insider trading. You could go away for years."

"Nah." When he shook his head, the fat under his chin did the Jello dance. "They'll never find out."

"Why didn't you tell me?"

He laughed. "Tell you? Are you kidding? You're the last one I thought needed a warning. You're the sharpest person who's ever worked for me." He paused. "And I don't mean that just in the physical sense."

She had been completely flummoxed, unable to respond.

"Listen," he'd said, "I can make it up to you."

"How in hell are you going to do that?"

That's when he tossed her the keys to the Mercedes. "Take a few days off. Drive down to the company condo on Virginia Beach. Let off some steam. You've got a company credit card. Use it. Buy yourself something nice. Relax. When you come back, we'll figure out what our next big thing will be. I know there's not much in the pipeline, but I've always been able to come up with something. It won't take long, you'll see. You'll get it all back, and more. Just stick with me, kid."

She'd taken the keys and left without another word. Sticking around would only have brought her closer to committing homicide, and she had too much living to do to waste time in prison.

But Virginia Beach was not her destination. She had her sights set on New York City. There was a young doctor living there whom she hadn't seen since her undergrad days. They had some history, a little of which she recalled fondly, and although it had been years since they last saw each other, she knew they'd find something to talk about.

And if not talk, well....

~*~

Mato was grateful for Reyna's sexual appetite, and the arrival of Tori's disturbingly lifelike toy. Both had distracted him from thinking about the dream he'd had the night before. For the most part, Mato had no trouble determining whether a dream was ordinary or not. Though neither the common variety nor the portentous ones came with any sort of logical context, he knew which was which. That, and the pronouncement of The People's Spiritual leader, had earned him his title. His real name, Black Otter, he saved for only the most intimate of his contacts. Everyone else called him by his title: Mato. Dreamer.

Reyna, too, had experienced ominous dreams, though not nearly as often. She, however, had the additional skill of interpretive ability. When confronted with a rendering of something a dreamer had seen, she could often find the meaning behind it long before real world events made such knowledge obvious.

In this case, however, Mato was reluctant to sketch what he'd experienced while in the realm of dreams. Not only was he loathe to dwell on it, he feared what it might mean, especially since it involved Reyna. He had seen her in some sort of cage, her arms outstretched defensively as a giant dressed all in white came for her. Somehow he knew, even without seeing the giant's face, that it wasn't Tori. It wasn't any giant he'd ever seen before.

He glanced at Reyna, still glowing with satisfaction. What might such a vision mean if she carried their child? Would the giants care? He took a sharp, involuntary breath. What if their *child* was what the giants sought? How could he protect Reyna, or a baby? How could he possibly defeat an opponent three times his height and many times his weight? How could he pit his puny stone-tipped weapons against their -- what had Tori called it? -- technology.

His mind was still spinning with unanswerable questions, or questions he wanted no answers for, when Tori called him. She had found something among the clothing that had come with the doll. She referred to the toy as "Lance," for reasons he could not fathom. The toy had no need for a name! One never called out for a knife as though it would grow legs and deliver itself. One might as well cry, "Shirt!" or perhaps, "Meat!" as if such things required the type of distinction the Spirits vested in their chosen among all living things -- The People. If the giants observed such a convention, he was unaware of it.

"Try these on," she said, handing him blue leg coverings similar to the kind she regularly wore, except for their size. "I can't imagine Lance in jeans," she said, as if that resolved some mystery. Mato had never heard of jeans, let alone visited the place.

He slipped the pants on but fumbled with the fastener. Tori quickly solved the problem, demonstrating a clasp that snapped into place, securing them around his waist. A gap in the front of the garment had been thoughtfully provided should he need to relieve himself. He reached through the opening and arranged himself more comfortably. Tori watched him with an odd smile on her face, but he ignored her. She often looked at him that way. Reyna said it meant nothing, and he was content with that.

He had felt the heavy fabric Tori wore, and doubted anyone could fashion something comfortable out of it for someone his size. Fortunately, his new leg covering was made of a much lighter fabric, though it certainly looked like the real thing. He was grateful for that, too.

"I'll take Lance with me wherever I go from now on," Tori announced.

Ah! If the doll represented some sort of totem, that would explain much, but he didn't know how to word such a question. He settled for, "Why?"

"If people see me with Lance all the time, they'll think you're a toy when they see you."

"Lance is doll," Mato said. "Not move like Mato. Fool no one."

"You would have to become stiff. Pretend to be like Lance."

Reyna gave him a little shove, obviously annoyed that he wasn't interpreting for her. He quickly shared the details, and she looked at Tori with the same sort of suspicion he felt.

"I don't want anyone to know about you, yet. When you're ready for the world to know, you can tell me. Until then, I want to keep your existence a secret."

Mato struggled with the concepts, and their conversation -- marked by frequent interpretive asides for Reyna -- went on for quite a while. Eventually everyone agreed to the wisdom of Tori's pronouncement. Both Mato and Reyna were eager to see more of the giant's world, but they had no idea how they could if they had to remain hidden. Lance represented a possible solution.

"Doll too much like woman," Mato said, making no effort to hide his disdain.

Tori smoothed the toy's hair. "Yeah," she said, "he's not a tough guy like you."

Reyna held up her thumb and forefinger, then laughed.

"And you measured him at his best," Tori said with a giggle.

Mato merely crossed his arms on his chest and smiled.

Deputy sheriff Nathan Sheffield arrived late in the afternoon. His dusty, white Ford F-150 pick-up rolled to a stop beside Tori's much smaller truck. Shadow announced his arrival and begged to act as official greeter. If the cop was good with dogs, Tori thought, his chances of not being eaten would improve dramatically. If, on the other hand, he looked or acted like he intended doing harm to any occupant of the house, Shadow would not hesitate to engage his impressively crocodilian jaws. Shawn, her late and unlamented ex, most emphatically did *not* get Shadow's seal of approval. The memory still made her smile.

She looked through a modest window in the cabin's only exterior door. "Good," she said to herself. "He's staying in his truck."

"Mizz Lanier?" Sheffield called, only too aware of Shadow's steady alarm.

"Hush," she said, wagging a finger at the dog. "It's a friend."

Shadow sat on the floor, unconvinced, but no longer raising hell about it.

"At least, I hope he is," she added to herself, then opened the door.

Shadow exited the building at roughly Mach two, though the distance he traveled was short. He halted at the driver's door with his paws on the window and his nose pressed into the glass.

"Back off, Shadow," Tori said, but without conviction, a point not lost on the man sitting alone in the vehicle.

When the dog dropped down on all fours, Sheffield opened his door and called to him. Shadow's tail began to wag, and he advanced in a much less aggressive manner. His approach, in fact, bordered on obsequious. Tori frowned her disapproval, but Shadow was too busy having his noggin scratched to pay any attention.

"Good thing I'm not one of the bad guys," Sheffield said.

"We've still got some work to do on the whole 'protect the homeland' thing." They watched as Shadow ran off to find an exciting new place to pee, a never-ending source of canine joy.

"Is there anything I can do to help you?" Tori asked.

"I'd just like to look around, if that's all right."

"Sure, sure. I'll be inside. There's a bourbon in there with my name on it. Lemme know if you'd like one."

He touched the brim of his Stetson like a Hollywood cowboy, then set about touring the area immediately surrounding her cabin. Tori went inside to get her drink. Mato and Reyna were safely hidden away beneath the fireplace. Though the dirt-floored foyer to the cavern where they were hiding was pitch dark, she figured they'd find something to occupy their time while Sheffield made his rounds. She prayed they would resist the urge to grunt, groan, or scream in ecstasy while they were at it.

She sat on the stoop, drink in hand, and waited for him to finish. It didn't take long.

"Find anything interesting?" she asked.

"Not yet," he said. "May I look inside?"

She waved him through the door knowing he'd soon be asking questions.

Her recollection of the night Shawn had crawled through the tunnel and back into her life, remained hazy. At least, the part which occurred immediately after he stabbed her in the stomach with one of her own kitchen knives. Somehow, Mato had subdued him while she dragged herself to safety. By the time the paramedics arrived, she was too delirious to know what was happening. Her friends, Caleb and Maggie, who had arrived on the scene in time to summon help, had filled her in on the details later.

When the police visited her in the hospital and inquired as to Shawn's whereabouts, she was honestly able to say she had no idea. Could he have crawled out like she did? It didn't seem likely. Neither Caleb nor Maggie had seen him, but that, in itself wasn't utterly conclusive. It was only later, after she'd healed, that she went back into the cavern and located his footprints. He had evidently stumbled around in the dark until he stepped off the edge of a deep crevasse. Tori had shined the most powerful light she had into the fissure, but it wasn't enough to reach the bottom. Anything that fell into that hole wasn't going to be crawling anywhere.

Sheffield's examination of the cabin was cursory at best, but he came to a complete halt when he spotted Lance stretched out on the baby bed mattress so recently occupied by Mato and Reyna.

"Okay," he said, a look of bemusement on his tanned face, "who's this?"

"That's Lance."

"Right. No last name?"

"Uh, no," Tori said. *Last name? Are you kidding me?*

"I can honestly say I've never seen anything like it. Him. Whatever. He looks a little, you know, girly. May I pick him up?"

"Sure. He may look like a lightweight," she said, "but deep down inside, he's a real bad ass."

Sheffield chuckled as he picked up the doll. "I can see that." He moved the figure's arms and legs, clearly intrigued by the flexibility.

"He's a ball-jointed doll, or BJD, according to what I read on the internet. Also known as an ABJD for Asian, ball-jointed doll." She paused. "So, do I call you sheriff, or deputy, or--"

"Nate," he said. "The folks who aren't shooting at me call me that." He glanced toward her shotgun which he had already inspected, and nodded appreciatively. "You can, too."

"Well then, you can stop calling me 'Mizz Lanier.' I prefer Tori."

They shook hands as if meeting for the first time. Nate seemed reluctant to let go when the time came, but neither made anything of it.

"I guess old Lance here is your only roommate?"

"No, there's Shadow." She spread her arms in a gesture meant to include all of the one-room cabin. "It gets pretty crowded in here with the three of us."

"But Lance doesn't complain."

"And I respect that," she said. "But more importantly, he's never lied to me."

Nate looked at her from beneath the brim of his hat. She noticed that it bore some of the same reddish dust as his truck and reminded her of her native Georgia.

"Have you lived around here long?" she asked.

"All my life. Went to school in Ten Sleep."

Suddenly, they'd run out of things to talk about. "Can I fix you a drink?"

He looked at his watch. "Why not? I'm off the clock 'til sunup."

"I've got bourbon and..." She looked in the 'fridge. "Tea."

"Not my favorite combination. What're you havin'?"

"Bourbon and Coke." She pulled the corners of her mouth down in an exaggerated frown. "But I used up the last of the Coke."

"Got ice?"

She nodded.

"That'll do nicely."

Tori poured a generous helping of Wild Turkey into a glass, then added a pair of ice cubes.

Nate removed his hat and pressed the cold glass to his forehead. "I could get used to this."

"Bourbon, straight up?"

"Bourbon, straight up, with a pretty girl."

Though she lived in the middle of nowhere and had no prayer of fending off an unwanted advance if Nate tried something, she wasn't worried. He had the look of a western gentleman, and something in his manner suggested he wasn't anything like the asshole she had married and divorced some ten years earlier.

"So," he said, obviously intent on ruining her mood, "why don't you tell me the truth about what happened the night you got stabbed?"

Well, just shit. She faced him squarely, though she couldn't help but notice how funny his hair looked after being confined by a cowboy hat all day. The pale band of white skin near his hairline didn't help. "Y'know, I'd rather talk about dinner. My memories of that night aren't very coherent."

"Maybe I can help. I got there right after the chopper landed."

"All that's a blur," she said, honestly.

"I believe you. But I want to know about what happened earlier. Tell me about the stabbing."

"Ugh. Bad memories. Seriously."

"I know it's tough thinkin' about it."

"You have no idea."

He shook his head. "You'd be surprised. I've dealt with some pretty strange stuff."

Not this strange, pod'nuh. She exhaled in resignation. "Okay. My ex-husband showed up. He wanted money. I didn't have any. We argued. He

31

stabbed me and ran away. End of story."

"Why'd he leave his car behind?"

"I didn't know he had," she said. "At least, not until later."

"And why couldn't we find any tracks anywhere?"

"Beats me," she said. "Who looked?"

"I did. And I'm a pretty good tracker."

Not as good as Mato, I'll bet. "I don't know anything about tracks," she said. "Really, I don't." She hoped she appeared sincere.

Nate took a sip of his drink, then gave her a long, penetrating look. "You and I both know that's bullshit."

"Oh? Really?"

"Yeah."

"I don't know what you want from me," she said.

"Sure you do. Just be honest with me. It's not like you're in trouble or anything. Somebody stabbed you. My guess is, whoever did it--"

"My ex-husband did it. I already told you."

"Okay. Your ex did it, and I'm thinkin' now, he's dead. I think you killed him in self-defense, and Lord knows, you've got the scars to prove it. Why you're afraid to show me where his dead, worthless body is remains a mystery."

You don't know the half of it, Sherlock. "I need some time to process all this," she said.

"Okay. I'm good with that. How much time do you need?" He tossed back the rest of his drink and swallowed.

She shrugged. "I dunno. Can I call ya?"

He smiled. "I've got a better idea. Why don't I come back out here next week, pick you up, and take you to the music festival in Ten Sleep? We can have a good time, and when you're ready, you can bring me up to date on what happened out here."

She felt whipsawed. What kind of game was he playing? First he accuses her of killing Shawn, then he asks her out on a date, then he says she can confess whenever she freakin' feels like it?

"Well, what d'ya say?"

"I--"

His smile was really quite appealing. Maybe it was the bourbon.

"I like music," she said at last.

"Me, too."

"Okay." *Now what do I tell Dallas Doormat, the luv-muffin of UPS?*

~*~

Jarred greeted Cassy Woodall as she entered the restaurant a few minutes behind him. She offered a firm handshake and backed it up with a broad smile.

"You look a lot better today than when I first saw you," he said.

Her laughter was forced. "That wasn't exactly my best day."

After they were seated, he tried to be reassuring and smiled as brightly as he knew how. "I'm really quite stunned by your recovery." Though he'd thought he could resist the temptation, he stared intently at her face anyway. The woman had suffered one of the worst beatings he'd ever encountered, and yet she bore only the faintest of scars. On the outside.

"I would love to examine you more closely."

"Here? I doubt the management would approve."

He sat back in his chair, slightly flustered. "No, of

course not! I'm such an idiot. I didn't mean to embarrass you."

"You didn't, and I'd be more than willing to let you examine me -- in a more clinical setting, of course."

"Of course. May I arrange something at the hospital?"

"That would be fine."

They both fumbled out day-planners and agreed on a day and time for the exam.

"What is it you're looking for?" she asked. "You weren't very specific on the phone."

"Well, that's the thing. I'm not really sure what I'm looking for. Your recovery was simply amazing." He gestured at her face. "If there's any real scaring, it's very hard to see."

"I could be wearing heavy make-up."

He leaned closer, his eyes scanning her cheeks, chin, and forehead. "No. That's not it. You're actually wearing very little make-up." He grinned. "You don't need that stuff anyway."

"Flatterer."

He asked the waiter for a wine list and looked at Cassy with pleading eyes when it arrived. "I've been on call for the last 36 hours. If I get a bottle, will you help me with it?"

"I'd be honored," she said.

They made small talk during the meal. Jarred learned that Cassy had been a book editor for ten years. She lived alone and had suffered more than just a dreadful beating the night she arrived in the emergency room at Brooklyn Memorial.

"Rachel and I had been seeing each other for over a year. We were... very close. She tried to protect me, but--"

"I heard," he said, reaching for her hand.

She withdrew it and sat back, her lower lip trembling. "I still can't believe she's gone. We--"

"I've reviewed your record very carefully," Jarred said, intent on changing the subject. "You were given all the standard protocols. There were notes in your file about the need for plastic surgery. Only--"

"Only no one expected me to live. Right?"

He nodded. "But there was nothing in the file to suggest you'd been given any extraordinary treatments. And that's what's been bugging me since you left the hospital."

"You think I'm special?"

"Absolutely."

She looked away, her eyes still a bit misty.

He plowed ahead. "If I knew how you managed to recover so quickly and thoroughly, maybe I could use that knowledge to help someone else."

"Well, that's noble."

He couldn't tell if she was teasing. "It's just... I get the feeling there's something you're not telling me. Something you did, or had done, that made the difference."

"Some secret treatment? A voodoo ritual in the dead of night when no one was looking?"

"There's a lot of people who believe in that stuff."

"Are you one of 'em?" she asked.

"No, but that means nothing. There are lots of things I don't know. People have been practicing medicine for thousands of years. I've only been at it for a few." He shrugged. "I need to know more."

She appeared indecisive, as if there was something she wanted to tell him, but couldn't.

He stared into her eyes until she looked away.

35

"There *was* something, wasn't there?"

"Maybe."

"Maybe? You arranged for some sort of treatment that helped you survive, and you won't tell me about it?"

"It was pretty... unorthodox."

"There was a time when sterilizing surgical instruments was considered unorthodox." He refilled her wine glass.

"I'm sorry," she said. "I promised not to say anything."

"But why? What could be wrong with revealing something with the potential for so much good? Will it work on children? I have patients who--"

"Stop," Cassy said. "It's not something you can duplicate. It's not a medicine or a ritual. It's just-- I can't talk about it. I promised."

He tried not to look sour. He'd gotten so close. Had he pushed too hard? "I'm sorry. I overstepped my bounds."

"It's all right. I understand where you're coming from. If I were a doctor, I'd want to know more about it, too." She closed her eyes and shook her head as if to lock in her decision. "But I won't break my word."

"That's okay," Jarred said. He took a stab at smiling but knew he hadn't pulled it off very well.

Cassy smiled back. "You make me feel guilty."

"I didn't mean to, but I confess, I'm even more intrigued now than before."

"I've already said too much."

Yes, dammit, I did push too hard. He raised his hands, palms out. "If I've caused you any aggravation, I apologize. It won't happen again."

He put the bill on his credit card and walked her to

the door, still apologizing.

"There may come a time when I can tell you," she said, squeezing his hand. "If so, I'll do it gladly. But until then...."

"Right," he said. "I get it."

She turned to leave.

"Only--"

She stopped. "Only what?"

"Only, how do I explain that to the families of my sickest patients?"

~*~

Chapter 3

Music makes the world go 'round, and 'round, and...

Both Mato and Reyna understood why Tori asked them to hide in the stone-walled space beneath the hearth when the new giant came to the cabin. Had they encountered him on their own, outside, the great lumbering human would never have seen them. Never had known they existed. And they agreed with Tori that such a state must be maintained. It was dangerous enough that four giants knew about them. Thankfully, all were friends, though the concept of friendship with giants was still new to them, especially so for Reyna.

They stood, holding hands, before the entrance to the tunnel leading to the cavern of dreams. It loomed before them like the mouth of a toothless monster. Mato flashed the beam of his hand-held light into the hole. Reyna refused to touch the device.

"A torch with a flame would do just as well," she said.

"Except for the smoke. And when it's all burned up, what do you have left?"

Reyna sniffed at him, her antipathy plain. She pointed at the LED flashlight, a gift from Tori. "The same as when the magic in that is all used up. Will it be any less dark?"

"Of course not."

"But," Reyna said, a look of superiority on her beautiful face, "we won't have angered the Spirits in the process."

Mato took a deep breath, then exhaled, unwilling to have another argument over the Spiritual downside of using the giants' tools. As far as he knew, there wasn't one. At least, he had yet to experience any in all the time he'd spent with Tori.

"I'm going down into the cavern," he said calmly. "Would you like to join me, or would you prefer to stay here?"

"I'd rather go outside." She tapped lightly on the metal door, disguised from the outside to look like part of the rock wall supporting the cabin's fireplace.

Mato smiled wickedly. "But that would require you make use of a tool built by the giants! Aren't you concerned your soul will shrivel up like an old snake skin?"

"A door is not a tool!"

"Of course it is." He brought his light to bear on the portal and the mechanism which allowed it to be locked and unlocked from either side. "Could The People have built anything like this?"

She pursed her lips, steadfastly refusing to answer him.

"Do as you wish," he said at last. "There is much of the cavern I have yet to see."

Reyna called after him as he began to march down the steep slope into the Earth. He knew better than to rub his little victory in her face, and merely offered his hand and held on while they journeyed underground.

"I had a vision," Reyna eventually said as they walked.

"Good or bad?" he asked.

"Definitely not good."

Mato gave a quick silent prayer that her dream was unlike his own. "And what did you see?"

"Someone -- a giant, certainly -- will hold me against my will."

Mato's stomach tightened. "Do you remember anything else?"

"That was enough. Once I awoke I could not go back to sleep."

He squeezed her hand. "It may be just a common dream and not a vision at all. I often have such dreams. Bad dreams. I think it has something to do with life among the giants. It's stressful."

"All I know is that I'm frightened," Reyna said. "I think we should go home. We can tell The People what we have learned and then help them move away as we planned in the beginning."

"But we haven't learned nearly enough! Think how much knowledge we can bring back. The lives of everyone will be better for it."

"You put too much faith in the giants' magic. The old ways are safer."

"The old ways won't work much longer," Mato said, his tone one of resignation. "The giants will find us eventually, and when that happens we'll never know peace, ever again."

"They've already found us! Or had you not noticed that Tori isn't the same size as you and me?"

"She's not like the other giants," he insisted. "And neither are her friends. We can trust them."

"I do not share your faith, Black Otter. You know I love you, but you make too many decisions with your heart and not your head."

"I think you have it backwards," Mato said. "Perhaps when you know as much about the giants as I do, you will feel the same way."

Reyna shook her head. "Please don't stake our

lives on it."

~*~

Tessa had reconnected with Jarred Carter via computer, on a social networking site she had been using to promote Bernstein Labs' cure for hair loss. A mutual acquaintance saw their names and suggested they contact each other -- become network "friends." An odd choice of words for a former couple who would most likely be coupling again, soon, she thought. Or would if Tessa had anything to say about it.

While not clinically obsessive compulsive, Tessa was passionately single-minded. The trait had been of great help in college, and resulted in a tenacity about her work that led to rapid promotion. Those at Bernstein Labs who dismissed her as "just another pretty blonde" usually ended up reporting to her, if not the unemployment office.

She had been scrupulous in limiting her social contacts with those connected to the Labs or its namesake. And, since her life over the past two years had revolved almost exclusively around her job, she had few social outlets, though she had received an invitation to join the company softball team. To that she had famously replied, "I'm good at playing games, but geekball isn't one of 'em."

Bernstein evidently wasn't aware of the quote as he frequently wondered, out loud, why such an attractive young woman had no social life.

Tessa didn't believe Jarred would change all that. In fact, her expectations were quite modest. Much as she hated to agree with old man Bernstein, he was right about one thing: she needed to get the hell away for awhile. Get her head straight. Figure out where she was going -- whether it was back to the grind, or in a whole new direction. The fact that Bernstein was unclear on what products he intended to develop next didn't inspire great confidence. She knew the contents of the company's R&D pipeline as well as anyone, and it was pretty thin. Pathetically so. What they needed was something new. Something beyond special. Something totally freaking *out there!*

And she wanted to be in charge of promoting it.

Sadly, she had no idea what that might be.

~*~

Ever since her meeting with Dr. Carter, Cassy had been unable to concentrate. Previously she'd been able to dive back into her duties at the publishing house as a convenient way of forgetting the attack, and more specifically, Rachel's murder. Now however, Jarred Carter, MD, had screwed all that up. *Damn do-gooders!* One earnest Samaritan in her life was more than enough, and until the appearance of Carter, Tori Lanier had the job locked up.

Carter's parting query, about how he might explain Cassy's refusal to help him, left her with a load of guilt the nuns at Saint Margaret's would envy, and they were masters of the craft.

His previous shot -- about sick children -- had been an even lower blow. Kids got sick all the time; it wasn't her fault! She gave to all the appropriate charities: March of Dimes, Save the Children, Cystic Fibrosis, Jerry's Kids. The list was endless, and as much as she would have liked to support them all, she only had so much to give. Now Carter wanted more! It would have helped considerably if he'd been a bastard about it, but every damn word he said was reasonable. How was she supposed to deal with that? What would Tori say?

Well, no, there really wasn't much to worry about there. Tori would simply remind her that she'd sworn to be quiet about anything that might lead to the exposure of Mato and his people. Or tribe -- or whatever he called 'em. But she knew, if word got out about their healing ability, wherever Mato and his two-foot-tall super hottie girlfriend came from would suddenly become ground zero in a manhunt the likes of which no one had ever seen before. Yet, the more she thought about it, the more she realized it was just a matter of time. The secret would come out. It had to! Eventually.

Meanwhile, how many innocent, or presumably innocent, people would die because she kept her mouth shut?

Damn that miserable, holier-than-thou Carter!

Well, she thought, pouring herself another martini -- was it her third? -- she might give him a little more information, but he sure as hell wasn't going to get it for free.

~*~

Nate called when he reached Tori's driveway. "I'll be just a few minutes," he said. "I'm turnin' in now."

"Right. See ya!"

Tori had agonized over her wardrobe. Jeans or Daisy Dukes? There was no question she sat on her best feature, and she wasn't about to wear something frumpy. When it came to shakin' it, she had no intention of covering up her best asset. Jeans she decided, but tight ones. Jeans made sense; it might get cool at night, and one could never tell about mosquitoes. The park was right next to the Nowood river, so the little bloodsucking bastards would probably be out in force. That's how it worked in Georgia, anyway. And if she was any judge of men, tight jeans would appeal to Nate.

She chose a short-sleeved top that accentuated the positive and kept her make-up to a minimum, then checked herself in the full-length mirror in her bathroom, turning to inspect all angles. "Damn," she said, winking at herself, "you're hot, girl!"

Standing in the bathroom, she considered her options and the potential for this outing. After a brief hesitation, she grabbed her toothbrush. It would fit nicely in her purse. One decision led to another and she left extra food out for the dog. The Energizer Bunnies could fend for themselves.

After waving goodbye, she waltzed out the door and waited for Nate. He didn't disappoint her, sliding to a dusty stop only moments later.

He gave her a much-appreciated wolf whistle when he got out of the truck and actually took her hand to walk her to the vehicle, as if she might trip on the hard packed soil in the intervening fifteen feet. Not that she cared. It was the thought that counted. Nate was decked out in a black cowboy shirt, with -- thankfully -- very little trim. His jeans were worn in all the best places, and the cuffs concealed most of his boots.

She was halfway into the truck when she froze, her derriere aimed squarely at Nate's chin.

"What is it?" he asked.

"Forgot something. I'll be right back."

Tori darted into the cabin and grabbed Lance. When she returned to the truck, Nate looked at her as if she'd sprouted boobs in the middle of her forehead.

"You're bringin' a doll?"

"Yeah."

"But, you're a grown woman."

"I'll take that as a compliment." She settled Lance on the console between the front seats and slid in beside him. She buckled her seatbelt while Nate stood outside, looking in. He hadn't moved.

"You comin'?" she asked, putting Lance in her lap. "Or do you want me to drive?"

He closed her door, then walked around to the driver's side and got in. He paused to look at the doll sitting between them, then let his gaze wander up to her face. "He's like a... a chaperone?"

She grinned. "Do I need one?"

"Don't know yet," he said. "Maybe." He started the engine. "At least he doesn't talk much."

They drove in silence except for the rumble of the oversize truck tires negotiating the deep ruts in Tori's drive. Compared to the ride in her Nissan, this crossing was blissful. She made a mental note to price new shocks. Nate took his driving seriously, and kept his attention sharply focused on reaching the highway in one piece.

"I'm really not a lunatic," Tori said when they finally found pavement.

"That's a relief."

"I brought Lance mostly just to see how other people reacted to him."

"My reaction wasn't good enough?"

"No. Yes! There's more to it than that. I want to see how crowds react."

Nate chuckled. "Right."

"It's hard to explain."

"Then don't bother." He flipped on the radio and found a country western station that wasn't too bad. Tori had a limited tolerance for twangy music, but she actually liked the tune they were listening to. After a while she asked, "Do they line dance at these shindigs?"

"Depends on the music," he said. "Line dancing to 'Amazing Grace' can be tricky."

Tori groaned. Her tolerance for gospel matched her taste for country.

"That's some piece of road leadin' to your place," Nate said. "Great way to see if your fillings are loose."

"Nothin' says 'out west' like a crappy driveway," she said, still thinking about gospel music.

"I know a guy that owns a scraper," he said. "You oughta talk to him. Smoothin' out that stretch might not cost too much, and he could straighten out the part that's prone to rock slides."

"And give up my only security feature?"

"You've still got the dog."

"Maybe you didn't notice how much he wanted to climb in your truck and go home with you."

"Can't fool me. Right up 'til you gave him the All Clear, he was only interested in sending me home alone."

She enjoyed the drive to Ten Sleep and vowed to herself to get out more often. The existence of Mato and Reyna didn't mean she had to become a hermit.

When they reached Vista Park, Nate found a shaded spot at the back of the parking lot. A band played in the distance, and Tori couldn't help but feel energized. When Nate offered her his arm, she grabbed ahold and they walked toward a huge canvas pavilion erected for the performers.

The crowd consisted of about a thousand people, or roughly three times the population of the town. Tori didn't recognize anyone. Nate didn't seem to know many more than she did, but occasionally tipped his hat one way or another. People were clearly more interested in her than him, but mostly they just stared at Lance. There were more than a few giggles and hurried whispers partly hidden by hands over mouths. A couple youngsters dared approach her for an introduction. She was happy to oblige, mostly to satisfy concerned parents that she wasn't there to lure away their offspring.

Suddenly, a face appeared which she did recognize. "Damn. It's Dallas."

"Who?"

"A guy I know who drives a UPS truck. He asked me to come here with him."

"But you were holding out for me?"

She looked at him as if he were deranged. "I'd never heard of you."

"You didn't stand him up, did you?"

"No. He called, and I told him I had other plans."

She ducked away in hopes of avoiding contact. Still, she couldn't help but peek to see if he had a date. Sure enough, he did, but she didn't look old enough to attend a PG movie without a parent.

They worked their way toward the front of the crowd, though the task wasn't difficult. Most everyone sat in lawn chairs and rows were more or less orderly, not that anyone cared. Nate was about to settle them into a spot well to the side of the stage when Tori saw Caleb and Maggie waving their arms like shipwreck survivors hailing a rescue craft.

"Over there," she said. "Let's sit with my friends."

"Nate Sheffield, you sonovagun! Look at you with Charm's resident author," Caleb said when they arrived.

"I thought she was Ten Sleep's resident author."

"She's closer to me than you, pard," Caleb said.

"In miles, maybe."

Tori gave Caleb a quick hug, then turned to Maggie. The trim, off-duty park ranger nodded in Nate's direction and gave her a conspiratorial wink. "Nice catch, hon. Hope you can land him."

"It's our first date, Mags. I'm not looking for a proposal."

"Yeah," she said. "I've heard that before."

Caleb introduced Nate to Maggie and eventually the four of them settled down on a timeworn bedspread the older couple had brought. Tori propped Lance in front of their cooler while Caleb poured drinks.

The retired cowboy-turned-grocer stared at Lance for a long time before saying anything. "Y'know, he's about the same size as--"

"The other doll Cassy has," Tori said, turning to give him an Are You Nucking Futs glare that Nate wouldn't also catch.

"Right," he said.

"Yep, he's sixty centimeters tall, exactly."

"What's that in a real measurement?" Nate asked.

"Two feet," Tori said.

Nate pushed his hat to the back of his head. "Fascinating."

They stayed through two performances and most of a third before Nate suggested that he and Tori take a walk. "The river's quite nice this time of year, and we can still hear the music."

"Can I put my feet in the water?" she asked.

"You're a big girl. If you want to dangle your toes out there for the trout, you go right ahead."

She gave him a worried look which he rewarded with a smile and the two of them turned away from the pavilion and a trio cranking out a bluegrass tune Tori remembered from when she was growing up. Her grandparents listened to the Grand Ol' Opry. A lot.

When they reached the river bank, Tori decided it looked a little too murky for wading. They both sat down in the grass beside the water. It wasn't moving very fast, and they could still hear the bluegrass band quite clearly.

"Thought you were gonna stick your toes in."

"Maybe next time."

"Where's your sense of adventure?" Nate asked.

"Guess I lost it somewhere along the way."

"Like the night Shawn Dunlevy stabbed you?"

"Man," Tori said, shaking her head. "You're nothin' if not subtle."

"I told you I'd be asking you some questions. This seemed like a good time."

"We went over all this before. Nothing's changed."

He plucked a long slender stalk of something green and started pealing it, his brow wrinkled in concentration. "How 'bout I try some different questions? Stuff I've been thinkin' about since I came out to your place to look around."

"What kinda stuff?"

"I noticed some things that struck me as a little

odd."

She frowned. "I've been called worse."

"I've been in a lot of old cabins, and yours has the cleanest fireplace I've ever seen."

Crap. "Okay, I confess. I'm a neatnik."

"I also noticed several plates in the dish rack by the sink. Big ones and little ones. Cups and glasses, too. But what got my attention were the four shot glasses. Who uses four different shot glasses?"

"Somebody who likes bourbon?"

"You use a shot glass to make a bourbon and Coke?"

"Maybe I like to be precise."

"So, you're a *precision* neatnik."

"Yeah."

"But you didn't bother to fold the doll clothes lying on the floor next to the little mattress."

Crap, crap, crap!

"And I noticed that Lance wears shoes, and there's no dirt on them anywhere."

"So?" She had no idea where this was going, but tried not to look overly concerned.

"So, who's feet left the dirt smudges on the bed covers?"

She shrugged. "Shadow? He tracks stuff in all the time."

Nate remained quiet for a while as if considering how to ask his next question. "See, that's what I thought, too. A smudge is just a smudge. It's not like the kind of print a foot would leave in the dirt." He paused to drop the remains of the shredded leaf. "I saw lots of footprints on the ground outside. Mostly between the cabin and the end of the driveway."

"And around the big rock slab where I barbecue."

"Right."

"And?"

"And under the cabin."

Oh, shit. "Under the cabin?"

"Yeah. But those were different. As if made by tiny little feet."

Tori couldn't resist looking down at her own.

"Smaller than yours," he said. "Much smaller. I'd say about the same size as Lance's."

She tried to laugh, but it didn't work. "Who knew he was wandering around down there?"

Nate fixed her with a deadly serious stare. "Tori, are you hiding a child somewhere out there? Is that what Dunlevy really came looking for? Is that what you two fought over?"

He waited for her to say something right away, and when she didn't, he asked, "Is that why you killed him and hid the body?"

She stared back into his eyes, the intensity of his gaze all but overwhelming. Could she trust him with the truth? Did she have a choice?

"You can relax," she said at last. "I've never killed anyone, and there aren't any kids out there. Never have been, as far as I know."

"Then who made the prints? It sure as hell wasn't Lance."

"That's true. It wasn't Lance."

He was sitting cross-legged on the ground, his boots scoring little creases in the dirt. She wondered how far she could run before he caught up with her. She used to jog pretty regularly. *Maybe I could get Cal and Maggie's attention. Hide in their car, or--*

"You aren't gonna make me chase you somewhere before you answer me, are you?" he asked. "I wouldn't appreciate that. No ma'am, not one little bit."

~*~

Jarred Carter had been thoroughly confused on more than one occasion, but he couldn't recall a time when his confusion had reached the level he was experiencing now that Tessa had dropped back into his life. He'd been delighted when she first contacted him on-line, especially since he never really understood why she steered their relationship from romantic to platonic while they were in college. Had he said or done something to make her see him more as a sibling than a soul mate? If so, he dearly wished she would tell him about it, preferably in detail, so that he could have the offending tendency surgically removed. And if that wasn't possible, he was more than willing to pursue other treatment methods, including post hypnotic suggestion or possibly even satanic ritual.

But, while her on-line contact had been pleasantly suggestive, everything since her actual appearance on his doorstep had been utterly orgasmic.

He had asked her in, apologized for his lack of housekeeping skills, offered her a drink, and in what had to be world record time, found himself in bed with her. Their first night together was a sexual marathon compared to his relative celibacy during and after med school. Other staff members at Brooklyn Memorial, especially the nurses, had commented that he looked much more chipper, though his energy level seemed to flag by shift's end. Was he getting enough sleep? Was he taking vitamins?

While he appreciated their concern, he opted not

to mention he was having his ashes hauled on an incredibly regular basis. Instead, he focused on his own reaction -- a typical ballplayer's response to the sudden appearance of good fortune -- when things are going well, don't change anything! It was the only way to ensure that whatever he'd stumbled into doing properly wouldn't get screwed up simply because of a change in routine. This outlook, however, did not extend to his wardrobe. His regular change of socks and underwear achieved an almost ritual status.

For her part, Tessa was sublimely unruffled. She spent her days shopping, reading, cruising the internet, and waiting for him to finish his shift so she could ball his brains out. After just over a week of it, he was seriously wondering if he should propose. The idea so obsessed him that when Cassandra Woodall arrived for her scheduled exam, he barely recalled why he had arranged it.

"I've been thinking a great deal about our conversation the last time we met," she said as she joined him in a tiny, curtained sanctuary amidst the general clamor of a busy general hospital's emergency facilities.

"You're here," he said, "so I presume you're still willing to allow me to conduct an examination."

"Yes, yes, of course. But things have changed a bit."

"How so?" he asked.

"I've been through a great ordeal, as you are well aware. No one, myself included, expected me to survive."

"We always had faith."

"Bullshit."

He smiled. "You're right. But don't expect us to admit it."

"I don't." She smiled back. "But don't underestimate the profound impact this whole nasty business has had on me."

"I don't! Not for a minute."

She nodded her head, but it was impossible to tell if she believed him.

"I lost someone very dear to me," she said. "That's something I'll live with for a long, long time. And it's forced me to consider what's truly important. What in my life could possibly replace the love and trust I lost that horrible night? How can I honor the sacrifice Rachel made for me?"

Carter held up his hands, palms out. "Miss Woodall, this probably isn't the best place for--"

"Hear me out, please. My life has been turned upside down. If you want to examine me, then you're going to listen to what I have to say first."

"Certainly," he said, trying to back away both physically and emotionally. "I understand."

"I don't believe that for a moment," she said. "But I don't care." She shook herself, as if to announce to their secluded world that she had it all together, and screw any random observers who might choose to think otherwise.

"I want to have a child," she said. "Preferably female. I'm going to name her Rachel."

"Whoa," Carter said. *I may be in my sexual prime, but--*

She reacted to the look on his face, then laughed. "Relax. I didn't have you in mind as the child's father."

Thank you, Jesus! "Good," he said. "I mean--"

"No. Aside from the ethical issues, it wouldn't... I mean... I'm not...."

He made what he hoped was a dismissive gesture.

"I'm cool with it. Really. I'm sure you've got someone more appropriate in mind."

"Actually, no." She regarded him closely, as if in an entirely new light. "To be honest, I hadn't given it a great deal of thought."

"I, uh--"

"I was thinking about just going to one of those clinics. Getting a... Having an anonymous donor."

"Right!" he said. "I can totally see that."

"But that's rather stupid, isn't it?"

"Excuse me?"

"I mean, why pay to have some stranger's sperm clinically injected into me, when I could go out and select someone with the kind of intellectual and physical traits that appeal to me?"

"Y'know, Ms. Woodall--"

"Cassy."

"Right. Cassy." He groped for a way to proceed. "No. It needs to be Ms. Woodall. Listen--"

"You're feeling very uncomfortable."

He looked at her in relief. "Actually, yes. I am. Very."

"Do I repulse you?"

"What? Good God, no! You're an attractive woman."

"A bit older than you, certainly."

"Well, yeah. But in this day and age, that's not--"

"Relevant?"

"I'm in a relationship," he said at last.

"I was, too."

Silence descended on the room and lasted for a long, awkward moment. "I'm looking for a suggestion," Cassy said. "A recommendation, actually. If I can't find a suitable donor on my own, I need to

find a good fertility clinic. Do you know of one?"
    "A clinic or a donor?"
    "Either."

~*~

Chapter 4

Look deep into my eyes.
You are getting very sleepy...

Mato had visited the cavern of dreams so many times he no longer thought about what a great thing he had accomplished for The People by rediscovering it. Reyna was certainly proud of him, but she, too, had grown so accustomed to standing in the holy place she no longer spoke of how difficult it had been to find.

As they had done so many times over the past few weeks, Mato and Reyna walked among the images painted on the walls by untold generations of dreamers. Those paintings closest to the ground Mato assumed were the oldest, since they were the easiest to reach.

He had added two paintings as well. The first was of a man he later learned had been Tori's mate. Mato had foreseen his death in a dream, and depicted the last moments of the desperate man's life as he groped blindly in the dark before falling into an opening in the cavern floor.

Mato had not understood his second painting until Reyna explained it. The image he had left on the cavern's ceiling recorded the last moments of two other tribe members. Young warriors like himself, they had also been searching for the cavern. A great brown bear had taken one of them; the other had ventured too far into hostile lands and died from thirst. His sun-bleached bones would soon be scattered by the winds.

Though saddened by the deaths of two warriors with whom he had grown up, Mato knew they would merely rest in the land of the Spirits before returning to The People as newborns. No doubt they would be stronger and wiser as adults owing to their sacrifices for the tribe.

"I would rather not paint my dream on these walls," Reyna said. "I fear it foretells my death."

Mato stretched his arms wide. "Look about! How many deaths do you see recorded? Very few. Most are of the good times to come: days of plentiful game and peaceful living."

"I see only one painting of a giant, and none of their magic."

"They have only clever machines," he assured her for at least the thousandth time. "They have knowledge, not magic. Only The People have magic." *Pitiful though it is.*

He put his arms down and pointed toward a shadowed wall. "There are renderings of giants over there." He hoped she would not examine them too closely, for one showed giants feasting on ancestors of The People.

"There is too much sadness here," she said. "It is not good for our baby."

Mato brightened. "You have missed your moon time?"

"No, but I fear your seed will not take if we remain so far from home."

He recognized her ploy but did not make an issue of it. "We promised the elders we would learn as much from the giants as we could. We'll go home when that is done and not before."

Reyna did not answer, but Mato suspected he

would not be welcome in her bed that night.

~*~

"It would be much easier to show you than try and explain," Tori said.

Nate still hadn't relaxed the fierce expression on his face. "And I'm guessing this little 'Show 'N Tell' exercise can only be conducted at your cabin."

"Pretty much."

"Well then, let's go."

"But there are still a couple more bands set to play."

"They'll get by without us," he said.

"Caleb and Maggie will be suspicious."

"Of what?"

"Of us leaving early. It sends the wrong message."

Nate got to his feet and offered his hand to assist Tori. She ignored it and rose in a single fluid motion, compliments of two years of yoga. He wasn't overly impressed.

"Would you rather I tell them I'm considering arresting you for obstruction of justice? Would that be a better message?"

"You don't have to be an asshole about it," Tori said. "Once you see the whole picture, you'll realize I didn't have much choice."

He shrugged. "I'll keep an open mind. How 'bout that?"

"Careful now. Someone might get the idea you're being reasonable."

"I'll get over it."

He guided her back to the crowd where they reconnected briefly with Caleb and Maggie. Tori retrieved Lance, and they walked back to Nate's truck.

"Could we at least stop and get some dinner?" Tori asked. "There's not much left to eat in the cabin, and I'm not really feelin' the love for cold cereal."

Nate finally softened. "I guess I at least owe you a dinner, this bein' our first date."

"You say that like there might be another."

"We'll see."

Nate pulled to a stop in front of the Crazy Woman Cafe. "Let's not make a production out of it, okay?"

"No problem. I'll just order something cheap, stuff it down my throat and run back out to the truck. God knows I wouldn't want to do anything that might slow down your hectic crime fighting schedule."

"You don't have to be sarcastic."

"Actually, yes. I do. It's either that or just shut up, and I've never been real good at that. Ask my ex."

"I'd like to."

Keep it up, buster, and you may get the chance.

Once inside the cafe, they ordered sandwiches to go. Nate chatted up the staff, since everyone seemed to know him, and then they left. Dinner was consumed en route, and Tori felt better by the time they pulled to a stop near her cabin.

Nate hadn't questioned her during the drive, which gave her time to think about finally being able to unburden herself about Shawn, Mato and the cavern. She considered trying to swear Nate to secrecy when it came to Mato and Reyna, but she decided that would have to come from him. He'd already sworn himself to a different cause -- law enforcement -- and it didn't seem likely he'd disavow one to adopt another.

He polished off the last of his sandwich and wiped

his mouth with a paper napkin, then sat back and looked at her. "Where do we start?"

"Inside, I suppose." Shadow had been oddly quiet until she heard him bark as he ran toward them from the far end of the bluff. Tori dropped to one knee and hugged the big dog like a long lost friend. Shadow shoved the top of his head under Nate's hand to reseal the bond they'd formed earlier.

"This way," Tori said, opening the door to the cabin.

~*~

"The thing is," Jarred said as Tessa poured him a second glass of wine, "the test results didn't show anything out of the ordinary. She's as healthy as you or me."

"This patient of yours... What'd you say her name was?"

"I didn't. Patient confidentiality, y'know?"

Tessa exhaled and looked up toward the ceiling. "I'm not a district attorney, for cryin' out loud. I just wondered."

"Why are you interested? I mean, I only mentioned it because it's so odd."

"Well, there you have it," Tessa said. "Why wouldn't I be intrigued? I work for a company that specializes in finding ways to help people, to cure dreadful health problems."

"Like baldness? Not exactly a life-threatening issue."

Her frown suggested he'd truly hurt her feelings. "Sorry. I-- Never mind."

She popped back quickly. "So the results didn't

61

show anything. What did you expect?"

"I thought her blood tests would reveal something. After all, she said the reason she recovered so quickly is because she received a blood transfusion from a friend."

"You're still doing blood transfusions? I thought everyone got blood from, I dunno -- the Red Cross. Some kind of common pool."

"We do. This one wasn't authorized. Nobody on our staff typed the blood or had anything else to do with it. The hospital would've fired 'em if they had, so that's no big surprise. When I asked the patient to describe the procedure, she couldn't."

"She was there, wasn't she?"

"Of course, but she was in and out of consciousness for a long time. She'd been so badly beaten we didn't expect her to survive."

Tessa squinted at him as she considered his words. "So, who gave her the transfusion?"

"She wouldn't give me the name. Said it was a friend of hers from out west."

"Who just happened to pop in and donate some of her magic blood?"

"Pretty weird, huh?"

"Yeah." Tessa tapped her front teeth with the tip of a brightly polished fingernail. "How did the new blood test results compare with those from when she was admitted? Any differences?"

"Not really."

"Any chance there might be a sample of her post-transfusion blood lying around somewhere?"

"No such luck. I already checked." He paused as if lost in thought. "There was a note in her file about a non-standard bandage on her wrist. A nurse assigned to change her dressings noticed that the incision under it had almost healed by the time anyone thought to change it."

"So, how long had it been there?"

"I can't be sure. All I know is that it's highly unlikely any hospital staff member gave it to her. What makes it significant, is that if she had a transfusion, that's where it would have been administered. And yet...."

"What?"

"There was no sign that anything like that took place."

"But you just said--"

"A transfusion takes time, even if it's administered via conventional methods. I got the impression from Cassy -- I mean, the patient -- that she and her friend had merely cut both wrists and pressed their forearms together. Not only would that be terribly inefficient, it'd take ages for any real blood exchange to take place. The donor would likely get as much as the recipient."

"But some sort of exchange would have taken place, right? Even if it were minimal."

"Well, yeah. But--"

"And that was enough?"

"Seems so."

Tessa sat back, a look of amazement on her face. "Far out."

"No kidding."

"We've gotta find the friend."

"We?" Jarred gave her his best "are you insane" look, but Tessa proved immune.

"Seriously," she said. "Whoever gave her that transfusion is a walking medicine cabinet, and not just your everyday, garden variety aspirin and vitamins kind of medicine cabinet. He or she is the holy fucking grail of medicine cabinets. We've got to find 'em."

Jarred held up his hands, palms out, in protest. "No," he said. "We don't. In fact, it's none of our business, yours or mine."

"But--"

"This is a done deal. It's over. There's nothing more to be learned. Okay?"

She squinted at him as if he'd just belched in four-part harmony. "Are you crazy?"

"I'm actually quite sane," he said. "But I'm beginning to worry about you."

He slid a little closer to her on the sofa and set his nearly empty wine glass on the low table in front of them. "I was thinking we might get a little sushi tonight and then maybe do some shots. I know this place--"

Tessa got to her feet. "We have work to do."

"And later we could... Y'know...."

She gave him a puzzled look. "I have no idea what you're talking about."

"Huh?"

"How did you leave it with your patient?"

"How did I leave what?"

"You said she asked you to suggest a fertility clinic or a sperm donor, right?"

"More or less, yeah."

"So what did you tell her?"

"I told her I'd look into it."

"And then what?" Tessa asked.

"Then I sorta hoped she'd forget about it."

~*~

Tori followed Nate into the cabin. Shadow bolted ahead of her, but remained strategically located between them. *You havin' second thoughts about this guy?*

Nate quickly reached the middle of the one-room cabin and turned to face her. Shadow parked himself in front of the lawman, looking up intently.

Tori started in on her explanation of events. "I moved out here and restored this cabin because it once belonged to my great uncle. I based my novel on his life, and I used his journal as the source for most of the story."

Nate crossed his arms and listened. He appeared interested if slightly impatient.

"A year or so after I moved in, I found an Indian under the house."

"An Indian. A native American type Indian? Like an Arapahoe?"

"Yeah. Dressed like he'd just come from the Little Big Horn, only without war paint."

"He was alive?"

"Yes, but just barely. Or so I thought. So I--"

"How'd he get there? Where'd he come from?"

It was her turn to look impatient. "Bear with me, okay? It's complicated."

"If this is going to take a while, maybe we should sit down." He eased toward a kitchen chair.

"Suit yourself." She dropped into the room's only easy chair and continued. "He was so small, I thought he was a doll at first."

"Like Lance?"

"Exactly."

"You're telling me you found a two-foot tall Indian

65

under your house."

"Well, I'm trying to, but you keep interrupting me."

"Sorry," he said, without appearing so. "Go on."

"His name is--" She stopped, wondering whether to go into an explanation of his names, then thought better of it. "I call him Mato. And yes, he's small. Very small. He doesn't suffer from some kind of glandular condition or anything like that. In fact, he's quite athletic. Amazingly so. He can jump from the floor to the chair you're sitting on without a running start. That'd be like you or me jumping up on something chest high."

"Good trick."

"And he makes it look easy. Reyna does too, for that matter."

"Reyna?"

"I'll get to her in good time."

"There's two of them?"

Tori exhaled wearily. "Are you going to let me finish?"

"Of course. It's just-- You've gotta admit, this all sounds a little odd."

"You have no idea," she said. "So, at first, it was just Mato and me. I didn't know anything about him. He couldn't speak English, and I sure couldn't speak his language, so we weren't able to exchange a whole lot of information. But, we've both learned a lot since then.

"Anyway, it turns out he was searching for a cavern that's very important to his people."

Nate's eyebrows went up. "And that's significant because...."

"Because my great uncle built this cabin right on

top of the entrance to it. The only entrance, as far as we know."

The deputy sheriff swiveled his head around to scan the room, his focus clearly on the floor.

Tori stood and walked to the fireplace. While Nate watched, she removed one of the stones which surrounded the hearth, then pulled the remaining stones, which were attached to jointed arms, out to either side. She glanced at him over her shoulder, pleased to see the look of surprise on his face.

When she grasped the handhold in the metal floor of the hearth and dragged it out from the fireplace, it gave a squeal suitable for summoning demons.

Nate was out of his chair and across the room before the sound stopped rattling around the room. He leaned over the resultant opening and stared down into the little dirt-floored chamber that fronted the narrow tunnel leading down into the ground.

"And that's the entrance to the cavern?"

"Yep."

"Why's it so small?"

"'Cause it was never intended for people our size."

"You've been down there?"

"Sure."

He looked from her to the tunnel opening and back again. "That's a damned small hole."

She shrugged. "I got through it. So did Shawn. He's still down there."

Nate grimaced "Dead?"

"Very."

~*~

Mato put his arm out to stop Reyna, but the effort

67

was wasted. She already stood still. Someone was coming down the tunnel, and they weren't being discreet about it.

"I'm sure it's just Tori," Mato said. "The only other giants who know about the cavern are far away." He glanced at her with uncertainty. "Aren't they?"

They both listened intently as the sounds of descent grew. There seemed to be two voices, though the second was muffled and indistinct. They reached a simultaneous conclusion: even if it was Tori, she wasn't alone.

They turned and hurried back to the cavern. Mato flashed his light from one side of the great space to the other hoping to find a spot where they could hide. None of the sharp, upward pointing rock formations was large enough to shelter them both. They separated, but remained within whispering distance.

Mato knew that he and Reyna shared the same fear. They had both dreamed of Reyna's imprisonment, though neither had gleaned enough detail to be sure when it might happen, or if Tori were somehow involved. Mato couldn't believe she would ever betray them, but Reyna had made it clear she didn't share his faith.

Mato grimaced at his own lack of preparedness. Other than his knife, he had no weapons at all. His belt pouch, which contained the sleep-inducing paste he smeared on the tips of his arrows and spear when hunting would do him little good if he had to battle a giant with nothing but his wits and a paltry stone blade. He felt the chill of the cavern for the first time, and wondered if the Spirits stood beside him. And if so, could he count on them for assistance, or would they merely laugh and mock his death.

With a nod to his life-mate, Mato clicked off his flashlight, and the two waited in utter darkness for the arrival of their fate.

~*~

"Because it's my time, that's why," Cassy said, her voice breaking up slightly over her cell phone. "You said you'd find a clinic which could take care of me. You said--"

"I know what I said." Jarred held the phone away from his ear as if it had teeth.

Tessa squinted at him. "Who is it?"

He covered the mouthpiece with his hand. "It's her."

"Who?"

"Cassy!"

"Dr. Carter? Are you still there?"

"Yes, of course," he said, signaling Tessa to be quiet. "What do you mean, it's your time?"

"I'm talking about my fertility window."

"Oh. Right. Listen, are you sure you've thought this through completely? I mean--"

"I've thought of little else," Cassy said. "My mind's made up, and my body's as ready as it's ever going to be."

Tessa crowded Jarred, pushing her ear as close to the telephone receiver as she could get it. Jarred tried to push her away gently, but she frowned and pushed right back.

"Dr. Carter?"

"Yes, I'm still here."

"Did I interrupt something?"

"No. Not at all," he said. "I'm just-- I had to finish

up something I was doing."

"So, which is it?" she asked. "Clinic or donor? And, just so you know, I'd prefer a clinic, even though I know it'd be expensive."

Tessa motioned for him to cover the phone.

"I'm sorry. Can you hold on a minute?"

"Sure."

Jarred covered the phone and hissed at Tessa, "What?"

"You can do it. You can be the donor."

"*Me?*"

"Sure. You're in good health, and you made it through med school, so you're no dummy."

"So what?"

"So that's a hell of a lot more than she'll ever known about some anonymous donor at a clinic. God only knows what kind of weirdoes sign up to make those -- ick -- *donations*. It's just creepy."

Jarred uncovered the phone. "Miss Woodall? I'm sorry to seem so distracted. I'll be back with you in a moment." He slapped his palm back over the mouthpiece.

"Are you nuts?"

Tessa pressed on. "Don't you see? You can trade your uhm... services for the name of her friend. She'd do it. She's desperate."

"Can you even spell ethics?"

"Oh come on. Cowboy up! You'd be helping her. She'd be helping us."

"There's that 'us' again."

"Call it *quid pro coitus*." She giggled. "Do it. Make the offer."

Jarred stared at her. "You honestly want me to make love to her?"

"No, I don't want you to 'make love to her.' I want you to knock her up."

"But--"

She wagged a finger in his face. "But you don't even drop trow until she gives you that name."

Jarred exhaled to clear his head then put the phone to his ear. "Miss Woodall?"

"Yes?"

"I think I know a way to resolve this."

"I'm listening," she said.

Tessa waved him on.

"Okay," he said, "here's the deal...."

~*~

Tessa thought about phoning Jerry Bernstein, but decided against it knowing he'd have questions she couldn't answer. At least, not yet. But if she had any hope of finding out if Jarred was on to something -- and it certainly seemed like he was -- then she needed more time to figure the angles. She had no qualms about taking charge if anything did come of it, but Jarred seemed to be sprouting reservations like an airline call center. If she could just keep his head in the game a little longer, she'd be able to smell the payoff.

She would almost certainly need some assistance from the eggheads at Bernstein Labs. Sadly, there weren't any she felt she could simply talk into helping her. Either Jerry would have to point them in whatever direction she had in mind, or she'd have to come up with a less direct alternative.

There was one guy -- really more of a lab rat than a man -- who might prove pliable enough, assuming she hadn't completely burnt the bridge he tried to erect by inviting her to join the company softball team. The mere thought of donning a T-shirt with the company name on it, like some sort of gas station attendant, made her queasy.

What the hell was the guy's name? Morlund? Moribund?

She'd figure out his name eventually, and until then she contented herself fantasizing about how she'd get him to do her bidding. A glance at Jarred assured her she definitely had what men wanted, not that it came as a surprise. The real issue was how easily she could put her physical assets to work without suffering any emotional distress. It required simple discipline, much like investing, though neither the capital nor the dividends were the kind one could tally on a monthly statement.

~*~

"How much farther?" Nate asked.

"Quit complaining. You were the one who insisted on finding Shawn's body. I was all about just letting it go, but no...."

They crawled on, Tori leading the way, until the ceiling leveled out while the floor continued to drop. Tori stood up as soon as she could. Sheffield, taller by several inches, ducked his head to keep from scraping it on the rough limestone. He walked a few more paces, then stopped and stretched.

"Man, that's a killer," he said. "You need to have someone come in and dig a proper tunnel."

Tori pointed to the kneepads she'd put on before they began their descent. "These help," she said.

"Besides, it's not my tunnel. I don't have any say over it or the cavern it leads to."

"It's on your property, isn't it?"

"In my mind, that's not enough. All I invested was money; the real owners invested a hell of a lot more."

"We'll see."

Tori pointed her flashlight down the ramp-like path. "Consider yourself one of the lucky few."

Nate brushed dirt from his hands, then from his jeans. "Lead on."

Though she wasn't positive Mato and Reyna were in the cavern, she suspected they might be. If Mato had gone hunting -- Reyna had trust issues when it came to the contents of Tori's refrigerator -- then she would have stayed in the cabin. The two Indians got along famously with Shadow, but Mato complained the huge dog frightened the game away before he could get close enough for a shot. And, since he employed stone-tipped arrows and a bow shorter than Tori's arm, getting close was imperative.

Hopefully, if Mato was indeed in the cavern, he hadn't brought any of his weapons with him. The last thing she needed was a medevac team to come after Nate if Mato got testy.

They paused when they reached a spot where they could shine their lights through openings in the stone wall on their right.

"Holy cow," Nate said, his voice barely above a whisper. "This is incredible."

Tori pulled him on. "It hit me hard the first time I saw it, too."

"Look at all the paintings!"

"Let's keep going so we can see them close up."

As they neared the end of the path and the

enormous chamber beyond, Tori stopped. She put her arm out to halt Nate. "Mato?" she called out. "It's just me, and a friend. Kindly don't kill him."

Nate swiveled his head sharply to look at her. She smiled back. "Did I mention he's a little uhm, unrefined?"

"You didn't give me too many details. Is this guy armed?"

Tori shook her head. "Beats me. I'm sure he's got his knife, but he's way more deadly with his bow and arrows."

"Oh, well, that's great."

"He's got a nasty spear, too," she added cheerily. "You'd be amazed at how accurately he can throw that sucker."

"I didn't bring my gun."

"And I appreciate that. I hate it when guys brings guns on dates. Ruins the mood."

"So, it *was* a date!"

"Best I've had in... I dunno. Months." *To say nothing of being the only one.*

"Is he down here, really?" Nate asked. "I don't see anything moving."

"I doubt you'd see anything until it was too late. You laughed when you saw Lance and said he looked girlie. Mato's a whole different deal. Short as he is, he's quite a hunk."

"You worry me," Nate said. "Sometimes it's hard to tell when you're joking."

"Bummer." She called again, "Mato? Come on out. Please?"

They both saw a glow appear behind a stalagmite. Two small heads rose slowly from behind a pair of jagged rock formations.

"Mato, Reyna, this is Nate."

Mato stepped out in the open. Reyna joined him, but stayed slightly to the rear and looked over his shoulder at them. Neither smiled. Mato pointed at Nate. "Why bring here?"

She pointed at the painting Mato had done of Shawn. "He wants to see the body."

Clearly unhappy, Mato made a statement that began, "Cave belongs" but Tori couldn't understand the rest. She presumed it was the name of his tribe, about which he'd volunteered nothing.

Nate only stopped staring at the Indians when Tori elbowed him in the ribs. "Wake up!" she whispered.

Scowling a bit, and rubbing his ribs as if she'd hurt him, Nate stepped closer to Mato's painting.

"He did it before Shawn got here," Tori said.

"He *knew* your ex-husband?"

"Saw him in a dream. The likeness is uncanny, though I don't ever recall seeing Shawn scared shitless." The visage on the ceiling radiated terror. "But, honestly, I like him that way."

Nate turned away from the painting, pointed his light at the wide crack which ran through the cavern. "And he fell in there?"

"I tried not to obscure his footprints when I was last down here," she said, pointing her own light. "They're over there."

Squatting, Nate inspected the thick layer of dirt and the tracks which marked Shawn's passage. "You're right," he said at length. "They go in, they don't come out."

"Like a Roach Motel," she said.

"At least they don't come back out *right here*."

"Feel free to look around," Tori said. "Because I seriously doubt Mato's going to extend an invitation for you to come back."

Nate looked her in the eye. "He may not have a choice."

"In case you hadn't noticed, this is like a church for him."

"Yeah? Well, when people get killed in churches, we still have to investigate."

Tori frowned. "Please tell me you aren't going to let the whole world know about this place."

He glanced at Mato who hadn't moved since their arrival. His hand was on the knife at his belt. "That's a really bad idea, pal."

"I think we should go now," Tori said.

Mato pointed toward the way out.

"Looks like your friend does, too."

~*~

Chapter 5

*The bigger they are, the more space they need
when they hit the ground.*

Mato watched Tori and her friend as they talked.
Her attitude about him continually changed from one
of subservience to one of equality. The speed with
which she made the transition was dizzying, but he
focused on his anger at her betrayal. He never
dreamed she would reveal the secret of the cavern to
anyone else. Had she not told him the cavern and The
People must remain a secret?

"Why is she doing this?" Reyna asked. "You said
we could trust her."

"I thought we could. I never claimed to understand
giants."

Reyna gave him a glare so cold he felt icicles
forming on his manhood.

"Will they never leave?" she asked.

"He's looking for the dead one." Mato nodded at
his painting of the giant who had attacked Tori. "See
how he keeps shining his light down in the opening."

"It has no bottom! How does he expect to see
anything?"

"I can't explain all the crazy things giants do."

Reyna squeezed closer to him as they watched,
and he put his arm around her shoulders. "I thought
you were mad at me."

"I don't blame you," she said. "It just makes me
sad. The giants come and go as they please, and we
can't do anything to stop them. The Spirits will be

angry with us."

"Giants aren't invincible. One day I'll have the answer; they'll give it to me themselves."

Reyna simply shook her head. "What are they doing now?"

"Tori?" Mato called. "Do you leave soon? The Spirits grow weary."

"I cannot speak for him," she said, gesturing at her companion.

"What he want?"

"He seeks the dead man to see if I killed him."

Mato frowned in exasperation. "He fell in hole! Alone."

"Nate is a good man. He only seeks the truth."

Mato pointed at his artwork on the ceiling. "Truth there! He blind?"

"In a way," she said. "He has no faith."

"I'm right here, y'know," the man said. "It's not like I'm deaf. Or blind, for that matter. Just tell your friend I'm a lawman."

"Why don't you?"

He straightened up from the edge of the crevasse. "I'm a deputy sheriff. It's my job to investigate crimes, especially murders."

Mato had no idea what the man was talking about. It was hard enough to keep up with Tori, and she tried to speak slowly and simply. The language of the giants had too many twists and turns. Words that meant nothing. Names for things that didn't deserve names. Multiple names for the same thing. It was terribly confusing. He didn't blame Reyna for not trying very hard to learn it.

"Mato not understand," he said. "Truth is truth. Man fall in hole. Die. Smell very bad! Dead man live with Spirits now."

Tori nodded. "End of story."

"I need a stronger light," the male giant said. "I'll have to come back. Maybe bring a hoist so I can go down there and look around."

Tori tugged his sleeve. "We need to go."

"But--"

"Now. I'll explain topside," she said.

He sighed and stood. "Yeah, okay." Looking straight at Mato he said, "I'll see you two later."

Tori smiled and waved at them then ushered the man back to the path. Soon the sound of their footsteps dwindled in the distance.

"What are we going to do?" Reyna asked. "We cannot have intruders roaming around in our most sacred place. We can never bring The People back here with giants all around."

"I know, I know! If only there were some other way in and out. Then we could seal the tunnel. Hide the old entrance as if it never existed."

Pulling Mato with her, Reyna walked slowly toward the long treacherous opening in the floor. When she reached the spot where Tori's friend had spent so much time, she urged Mato to shine his light down the hole.

"We know the hole is deep," she said, "but do we know if the crack goes through to the outside?"

Mato followed the jagged opening with his light. Both ends of the seam continued under the enclosing walls of the cavern. If one could somehow travel the length of it without falling in, there might be a way to reach through the wall to the valley beyond. But unless he turned into a bird or a bat, it wasn't likely that he would ever make such a trip.

"It's hopeless," he said.

"Hope ends when life ends." She put her arms around him. "And we're still breathing."

~*~

"Gosh, that went well," Tori said when they returned to the cabin. "Compared to... Oh, I dunno. Custer at the Little Big Horn?" It felt good to stand up again, knee pads or no knee pads.

"I'm going to need more than footprints, y'know," Nate said as he boosted her up onto the steel plate that sealed off the antechamber. He climbed up beside her and they swung their legs in opposite arcs to face the room, then slid forward until they were free of the fireplace.

Tori began to close the opening, but Nate intervened. "How will your two friends get out?"

"Side door," she said, pointing to the mechanism built into the stone walls supporting the chimney.

"You did all that? Impressive."

"My great uncle did it. Over a hundred years ago. He's the impressive one."

"So, obviously, he knew about the little Indians, too."

"Well, yeah. He did. My new book is based on his life after the Civil War. I'm changing the details, of course. It's supposed to be fiction. I have no intention of giving away the secret of Mato's existence." She reached for his arms, gripped them hard and looked deeply into his grey eyes. "I'm begging you to do the same. If people found out about them, they'd never have another day of peace."

"I understand."

"Do you? Think about it! Imagine how many tourists would show up to see the tiny, primitive people, not in some jungle in a country they wouldn't visit in a million years, but right here in Wyoming! Some asshole will set up a trashy roadside stand where people can have their photo taken with the cute little Indian, and buy some tacky souvenir frame to go with it."

"Tori--"

"I'm on a roll here, okay? The science types would flood the area looking for the rest of the tribe. They'd be all over the place, unless of course, we told them about the cavern. Then they'd be lined up outside, demanding that I allow them to trample the holiest place in Mato's life. How would that be? Pretty cool, huh? You wanna explain all that to Mato?"

"Of course not."

"Then what the hell are you smiling at?"

"You," Nate said. "You're all worked up. It's... cute."

"I'm serious, damn it!"

"I know you are."

"And it's not because I'm trying to hide anything."

He held his hands up, palms out. "I believe you. Honest!"

"Then, what's the problem?"

"The law is the problem. I have to fill out a case report. The sheriff will read it. Probably not right away, if no further action on the case is required, but sooner or later he's going to read it."

"So why can't you just leave out Mato and the cave paintings?"

Nate appeared to be mulling the idea over. "Well, for openers, it wouldn't be completely honest. I've never fudged a report before. It's one of those slippery slope things. Once you start--"

"I get it. You leave out a few details in one report, and before you know it, you're completely making shit up on all your other reports."

"You're exaggerating."

"Ya think?"

"Tori, listen. I don't want to ruin their lives. I really don't. I want to protect folks, and I take my job seriously." He looked longingly at the bourbon on the kitchen counter. "You want a drink?"

"Yes, but don't change the subject. If you're all about protecting people, then protect Mato! What's the big deal?"

"The truth is the big deal. I need to see the body."

"Assuming you could even get to the body, are you qualified to examine the remains?"

He shook his head. "I'd have to take them to the coroner."

Tori tried to recall if there was anything odd about Shawn's body that a medical examiner would find. She couldn't think of anything, but it didn't mean there wasn't something there. Shawn was such a sneaky bastard, she wouldn't put anything past him. In the last miserable seconds of his useless miserable life, he might have figured out a way to point a damning finger at her. Or worse, at Mato.

"Do you think you can do it by yourself, or are you going to call in a crew?"

"I can try to do it by myself."

"I'm willing to help," she said.

"The sheriff's going to want to know where the hole is that Shawn fell into."

Tori looked at him in complete shock. "Nate, this is Wyoming. Look out the damned window! See any canyons out there? Are you telling me you can't find one that'd be convincing? Is the sheriff even likely to follow up with a personal visit?"

He laughed. "Okay, okay. I get it. I'll have to use my imagination. But what about the lack of tracks leading away from the cabin?"

"It's been weeks since the incident. They wouldn't likely have survived rain and wind, and there's been plenty of both."

"I tell you what. You help me recover the body, and I'll do my best to keep the cavern and your little pals out of my report. Fair enough?"

"And if the coroner decides I'm the one who killed him?"

"Did you?"

"Hell no! He tried to kill *me*, remember? And he almost succeeded."

"Then it'd clearly be a case of self defense."

"Nate, I swear the only thing I tried to do was get away from him."

"And how'd you do it? What made him stop attacking so you could run?"

Tori bit her lip. "Mato. And Shadow. They sorta ganged up on him."

"Well, I've seen the dog, and I sure wouldn't want him comin' after me. But the little Indian dude? What could he possibly contribute, short of a sacrifice?"

"I already told you about his bow and arrows."

"Yeah, but how lethal could they be? I mean, c'mon. His bow would be like a... a toy."

"He puts something on the arrows. Once it gets in the target's bloodstream, it's lights out."

"Poison?"

"No! Not at all. It's like knock-out drops. It puts 'em to sleep. Only, real quick."

"And you know this because...."

"My great uncle wrote about it in his journal. I asked Mato about it, but he didn't want to say anything. He's pretty tight-lipped when it comes to revealing anything about himself, or his people."

Nate scratched his jaw in concentration. "If Shawn fell into the hole because he was drugged, it wouldn't look so good for Mato."

"Whatever happened to the self defense thing?"

"Well, that was before you mentioned the poisoned arrows."

"It wasn't poison!"

"Whatever. Right now, it doesn't matter. The big challenge is going to be finding the remains and hauling them up here. I've no idea how I'm going to manage that."

"I'm sure you'll think of something," Tori said. "You want that drink now?"

"Yeah. That'd be great."

"Then don't try any funny stuff. I haven't forgiven you yet for screwing up my first date in... in a while."

"I find that hard to believe. I thought that guy you saw in the park was interested."

"Dallas? I could get arrested for going out with a guy that young, couldn't I?"

"Maybe not, if you considered it a rescue."

"You want Coke with your bourbon?"

"Ice," he said, his voice low. "I could use a piece of ice right about now."

"I have a gun y'know."

"Me, too." He grinned.

"Seriously," Tori said, "if you want to have any chance with me, you're going to have to be nicer to Mato and Reyna. Especially Mato. Can you do that?"

"Be nice? Sure. I thought I had been."

"Only if your definition of nice means not arresting him. I'm talking about friendship."

"He's a suspect, Tori."

"Well then, I guess I am, too."

~*~

"Well, how'd it go?" Tessa asked.

Jarred plopped down on a sofa, the centerpiece of his Spartan apartment. "Not so good."

"What happened?"

"Nothing."

"She backed out of the deal?"

"Not exactly."

Tessa struggled to maintain her composure, a task growing increasingly more difficult where Jarred Carter, MD, was concerned. "Either she did or she didn't."

"It wasn't her. I couldn't--" He coughed. "I had a little problem."

She gave a snort of laughter. "You're some stud, you are."

"Evidently not."

"Amazing. This is the one, tried and true method for continuing the species. Horny guys have perfected it over thousands of years. It's cheap, simple and reliable."

"You sound like an ad for a bicycle."

"Bikes are way trickier than sex."

He left the couch, poured himself a stiff drink and offered her one. She declined.

"It's not like she's exactly into men," he said. "She plays for the other team."

"I picked up on that. But it doesn't change anything as long as she was willing."

"She was willing, but not eager. It had a definite effect on me. I needed a little, you know...."

"Foreplay? Oh, come on! You want me to go with you next time? Get you started?" She paused as if struck by a sudden revelation. "That could be a little kinky."

His eyebrows drew down in a tight V. "No. That would be weird. Way too weird."

"I thought it was a fantasy all guys had."

"Will you just stop? I'm not going back. I gave her the name of a clinic. I was so embarrassed--"

Tessa stared at him in disgust. "But she didn't give you her friend's name?"

"No."

Tessa stood up and walked slowly to the two-person table that represented Jarred's dining room, in reality, little more than an alcove. She picked up the stack of papers he had brought home and thumbed through them. "Is this the whole file?"

"You're not supposed to look at that!"

"Right. The confidentiality thing. Gotcha." She found a grainy photo of a woman in a hospital room, but most of her face was turned away from the camera. She put the page aside and continued scanning the other documents until-- *There it is!* She closed her eyes in an effort to commit the snippet of data to memory. Maybe there was hope after all. Come morning, she'd have to make a phone call, but it was a call that could change everything. She dropped the stack of papers back on the table and folded the single sheet she'd extracted in half, and then in half again. It fit neatly in her pocket.

Jarred called out, "That whole 'confidentiality thing' you take so lightly is important. I could get sued if anyone found out I copied that file."

She stepped close to him and gently patted his cheek. "Relax my little stud muffin. I'd never turn you in." *Unless maybe there was a reward.*

~*~

Tori offered no explanations when she snatched up Lance and announced she was off to get food. How Lance could possibly be of any use in such an endeavor was not discussed. Shadow chose to stay outside though it would clearly be a hot day. Mato liked the cool interior of the cabin, even if the machine which kept it that way did so with an unending stream of clunks, rattles and buzzing sounds.

Mato called to Reyna and bid her sit beside him in Tori's big chair. The two fit comfortably side-by-side, and Mato enjoyed both the chair and the proximity of his dark-haired beauty.

In his lap he held a device that once awed him, for it seemed capable of magic on a scale he found unimaginable. Tori had shown it to him during his early days with her, and though she had been amused by his initial hesitation to go near it, or the larger one it controlled, she eventually helped him understand they were merely two more of her clever machines. They contained no more magic than Mato's moccasin. But while he knew everything there was to know about his footwear, he feared the other devices would forever remain mysterious.

The smaller device consisted of a flat rectangular unit covered in sharply defined raised surfaces. Tori called them "buttons," though they fastened nothing. *Giant words were terribly confusing.* Each button bore a symbol which held a specific meaning for her. She tried to explain them, but there were simply too many to remember, and though she promised to teach him to interpret the symbols -- and many others -- he would have to master her language first. Mato hoped Reyna would stay long enough for him to do that.

The larger of the two devices was similar to what Tori labored over daily, only the controller she used had even of the more of the mystifying buttons bearing even more complex symbols. Touching those buttons caused marks to appear on a flat, lighted plate which sat in front of her.

She called the device in his lap a "shooter," which term made absolutely no sense. But then, what he pointed the shooter *at* -- something she called a *teevee* -- generated moving pictures, and quite often he wished he could shoot an arrow at some of those.

Tori taught him how to use the shooter to turn the bigger machine on and off, how to change the kinds of pictures it displayed, and how to adjust the volume. She made it quite clear that spending too much time in front of it would cause terrible damage to his brain, although she claimed the machine *she* worked with presented no such danger. The oddities mounted like discarded bones.

Much like another machine she often used, which played the most amazing music, the teevee would only work if fed shiny flat discs. These bore symbols and pictures he rarely understood, but which helped him distinguish between them nonetheless. The giants called them "movies," and for once the name actually made some sense. One of Tori's favorites featured a vast desert and was the first he ever watched.

According to Tori, someone called "O'Toole" was in it and supposedly displayed his best part. Mato had puzzled over that for most of the time he watched and never did see what she was talking about. The people in the box were at war, and even though they generally appeared much smaller than he and Reyna, they possessed the same kinds of tools the giants commonly used. They even talked!

Alas, they never attempted to talk to him, or Tori. They were only interested in each other. It was like watching people through a window, only the view changed constantly. Sometimes a single face filled the whole area. At other times, he could see crowds. They wore flowing robes and rode on two different kinds of animals. He recognized the horses immediately, but it took some time before he recalled seeing the other animals, ugly beasts and much larger than horses, painted on the walls of the cavern of dreams. No one had ridden those in the cavern, however.

Was this the giants' vision of the dream world? Who were these madmen in flowing robes? Many bore weapons similar to those the giants used to kill game. Mato hesitated to call them hunters, for they did little that required a hunter's skill. Anyone could hide in a tree and wait for an animal. They used their clever killing tools at distances far beyond the reach of any bow Mato had ever used.

Mato had watched them "hunt." A loud sharp noise, in most cases, signaled the death of the giants' prey. They would then climb down from their hiding place to claim the kill. When alone, they often whistled, but if not they uttered boastful words to their companions.

Mato had often wished for a weapon such as the giants used. On the box in Tori's cabin, he watched multitudes of men use the fearsome tools against one another. The ensuing chaos had not bothered Tori. Perhaps she had watched giants kill each other so often, it no longer had any effect on her. Mato thought that terribly sad and hoped he would never become so jaded by death.

Still, the technology -- *that strange word again* -- of the box intrigued him, and he had been eager to demonstrate it to Reyna. They had watched several of Tori's discs before she introduced a new feature: movies which didn't live on the shiny flat discs. Instead they lived within numbered spaces *inside the box!*

In short order, both Mato and Reyna discovered which numbers contained their favorites. Mato found the antics of a cat and mouse most entertaining. Like most pets the giants maintained, they had names: Tom and Jerry. Reyna found Mato's choice childish, and told him so. She much preferred programs Tori referred to as "soaps." Once again, Mato had been mystified by the giants' words. They had such an abundance of them, why must they re-use the most common?

"They are about love and betrayal. These are things I know something about," Reyna had said.

"Love? Yes, of course! You have my love. You always have. But these people you watch-- They cannot decide who they love. Besides, you can't understand more than a few of their words. How do you even know what they're talking about?"

"Women know," she said, crossing her arms with a vengeance.

"Women know nothing," Mato muttered back, but not in a voice she was likely to hear.

In order to honor Tori, and because it gave Reyna more exposure to the giant tongue, they watched Tori's favorite movie several times.

"What causes the great noises?" Reyna asked. "The ground rises in the air with fire and smoke leaving nothing but death and great destruction. What kind of tool does that? Nothing I have ever seen. Tori must want us to see this for a reason. I think we should leave, right away!"

Mato patted her hand, but she pulled it back. "This all

seems like magic, but it's just more of their cleverness. He pointed to the teevee. It's merely a toy. A terribly complex toy to be sure, but a toy just the same. Tori says the movies are not real. No one really is killed. It is like the dance The People do to remember the bravest warriors and the most skillful hunters. They only pretend."

"And the dreadful explosions? They aren't real?"

"Tori called them bombs, and yes, they are real and very powerful. A single such weapon could turn this cabin into a pile of sticks."

Reyna considered his words at length before she responded. "If we could find such a thing, such a bomb... We could use it to destroy the tunnel to the cavern."

Mato nodded. "Provided we first find another way in and out."

"Of course." She snuggled close to him. "We would need to be very careful."

"Indeed. But where would we find such a thing? I've never seen Tori use one."

"The other one," Reyna said. "The one she brought to the cavern. My heart tells me he knows about such things."

Mato had often thought that he played the role of the Trickster when he spent time with Tori. How many times had he plotted to steal her magic, only to have her give it to him freely. Should they attempt the same thing with the one called Nate? "Perhaps we should befriend him. When we have his mag--" He stopped. "--his technology, we can blow up the tunnel *and* the cabin."

Reyna hugged him. "That would make Tori very sad."

"Or angry." He crossed his arms. "But she has already betrayed us, by bringing her friend into the cavern without our permission. Not only that, she told me he would soon return. She said she could not stop him."

"No real warrior would enter the home of a lone woman without her permission," Reyna said. "The giants have no honor."

Though it struck him as terribly sad, Reyna spoke the truth. "We must not appear unfriendly. We must pretend to accept this Nate as a friend of a friend."

Reyna nodded. "Even though we both know he's not."

Unable to mask his regrets, Mato added, "I do not wish to make Tori sad or angry, for she has always been good to us. But this... This she brings on herself."

Tessa hadn't felt comfortable all night, and not just because she'd had to refuse Jarred's repeated advances. If he'd shown half as much interest in the Woodall woman, Tessa's job would have been all but complete. But no -- he needed some "hug me-squeeze me" time. Kissy face, rub-a-dub-dub. *What a complete dork.* The sooner she lifted anchor, the better. She stayed in bed, feigning sleep, while he clattered around the sad little apartment getting his shit together.

He came back into the bedroom and bent to kiss her cheek. She kept her eyes closed.

"I'm going now."

"'Kay. See ya."

"You gonna be all right?"

She gazed at him with one weary eye. "I'll probably survive. I can be resourceful when I have to."

"That's my girl," he said, then sauntered off to save the damned and wounded carried into the hallowed halls of the Brooklyn Bereavement Center, or whatever the hell they called it.

With Jarred finally gone, Tessa rolled out of bed, brushed her teeth and picked up the phone. Information yielded the number for the publisher where Cassy Woodall worked, and Tessa put on a bright, happy voice. It almost made her gag.

"Ms. Woodall's office, please?"

"She's not in yet. I'm her secretary. Can I help you?"

"Oh, thank goodness," Tessa said, slipping into a breathlessness she hadn't felt since someone talked her into trying out for the cross country team in high school.

"I know this will sound like a very strange request, but I just don't know where else to turn."

"Well, I--"

"A few weeks ago, I was in the waiting room at the hospital in Brooklyn-- You know, the big one, with the really amazing Emergency Room?"

"Uh, yeah...."

"Well, I was there because my parents were in the most dreadful accident. I was beside myself with grief. I can't even begin to-- Well, it was awful. Truly awful."

"I'm sorry to hear that."

"Thanks. You're very sweet. But the reason I'm calling is because of one of your authors. She works with Ms. Woodall."

"We can't give out--"

"What I found so amazing is that she traveled all that way just to visit her editor. She must be extremely popular. How many of her authors came to visit? Do you know?"

"Several, I'm sure."

"And how many came all the way from Nevada?"

"Well, none that I know of. One came from Wyoming."

Tessa made herself frown. "No, I'm sure she said

Nevada. I'm positive. Anyway, I just wanted someone there, preferably Ms. Woodward, to--"

"Woodall. Her name is Woodall."

"What? No. It's Woodward, I'm sure."

"There's no one here by that name. When you called, you said Woodall."

"Oh? My goodness. I'm so sorry! I can't believe I got something like that so confused." She paused, dramatically. "You wouldn't happen to know of any editors by the name of Woodward at any of the other publishing houses, would you?"

"Ma'am, this is New York. There are publishers on practically every corner. I have a hard enough time just keeping up with the ones on our payroll."

"I'm sure you do a splendid job."

"I try."

"Well, once again, I apologize if I've wasted your time. You've been most helpful." She dropped the receiver in the cradle and stretched. It was all a matter of pulling the right strings. After all, how many clients from Wyoming could Woodall have? Tessa couldn't keep from grinning like a cat in charge of security for the world's canary supply.

All she needed now was a computer and access to the internet. Cassy Woodall's mysterious savior was about to be revealed.

~*~

Chapter 6

We hold these truths to be self evident.
Well, most of 'em, anyway.

Nate needed help to load everything in his truck including climbing gear, lights and knee pads. In addition to a winch, he brought a generator big enough to produce the kind of power he'd need to raise and lower himself into the crevasse. He also decided to do his best not to expose the Indians, or their fantastic cavern. It wasn't just a matter of wanting to spend more time with Tori, though he would admit, to himself at least, that she certainly had a lot to do with his enthusiasm for the effort.

Southern girls weren't all that different from western girls when you got right down to it. They had a different sense of history maybe, and the accent certainly didn't hurt, provided it wasn't too Hollywood. Movie people disgusted him. When they weren't screwing each other, they were screwing around with everything else.

Just look what they did to western history! Thanks to them, I grew up thinking Billy the Kid was a hero instead of a drunk and a back-shooter. What would they do to Mato and his people? He couldn't let that happen.

Nate tried to put himself in the little Indian's shoes, but it wasn't easy, and that had nothing to do with the size of his feet. While Nate had grown up around nature, Mato had grown up *in* nature. Hunting because you liked venison was one thing; hunting because you'd starve to death if you didn't was a whole different deal. He doubted he'd ever be able to truly appreciate what it would be like to grow up without the benefit of a single modern convenience.

Josh Langston

He loved the outdoors, especially in Wyoming where the scenery changed every time you went around a bend. Mountains, streams, canyons, green as far as the eye could see, or -- right after the next turn -- the world offered nothing but shades of brown: from light yellow to dark rust, and everything in between. And that, often in layers. You'd think you'd never get tired of it. But then, maybe it'd snow, or get so hot standing up made you dizzy. Then it'd be nice to go indoors, grab a beer and snuggle with somebody like Tori.

What did Mato have? Reyna, of course, and for someone who topped out around his kneecap, she was one hot little momma. But what did "indoors" mean to them? A nice comfy cave maybe, or a teepee hidden in the woods? When Nate went to bed, he didn't have to worry about wolves or mountain lions or bears wandering in unannounced to eat him.

Life for Mato was nothing like anything Nate had ever experienced, and getting to know the little Indian, let alone think like him, would be a tricky project. But, considering what they might be able to teach each other, Nate decided it would likely be good for them both.

Having reached this happy conclusion to his internal debate, the deputy sheriff pulled to a stop alongside Tori's cabin. Shadow greeted him with a single bark and a tongue that seemed to grow longer every time they met.

He knocked on the door, then waited. Other than the sound of the television, he heard nothing. He was about to open the door and go in when he heard a voice behind him.

"Tori go."

Nate spun around and looked down at Mato. *How had he sneaked up on him so quietly?* "Hey there! I guess I should have called before I came out. I just assumed..."

He stopped talking when he realized Mato wasn't paying any attention, a byproduct of his quick scramble into the back of Nate's truck. The Indian rummaged through the assortment of gear, digging into boxes and shoving aside ropes, pulleys and cartons of climbing equipment. Considering how heavy some of the boxes were, Mato managed them with surprising ease. Despite the extent and variety of his cargo, a good two-thirds of the truck bed remained empty. There would be plenty of space for any remains Nate recovered from the cavern.

When satisfied that he'd seen everything in the truck, Mato sat cross legged on top of the portable generator and stared at Nate without any readable expression on his face.

"Find what you were lookin' for?"

Mato ignored him.

"Seriously. If there's something in particular you need, just lemme know."

Mato nodded in the affirmative and climbed down to the ground.

Oh yeah. I can tell we're gonna be tight. Best buds, for sure.

Nate watched Mato settle on the ground in the shade of the cabin. He had an odd assortment of stuff arrayed in front of him, though none of it came from a box or a carton. On his right, what appeared to be porcupine quills were laid out side-by-side in two ordered groups, their distinctive bands of dark and light colors making them look, from a distance, like striped fabric. A closer inspection revealed that fewer than half of the quills were straight; most had a slight curve. Mato clearly preferred the straight ones.

Next to the quills lay a haphazard pile of milkweed pods, sun-dried and split open, though not enough to spill their frothy insides. Mato extracted some of the fluffy, cotton-like filament and shaped it into strands which he wrapped around a quill by turning it in his fingers. He molded the thickening band of filament as he wound it, forming a cone shaped wad an inch or so from the blunt end of the quill. He would occasionally moisten his fingers with saliva as he worked, which helped the filament hold its shape. He hummed a tune Nate found surprisingly familiar: "Sweet Home Alabama." He tried to picture Lynyrd Skynyrd in war paint, but failed miserably.

"What are you up to?" he asked. But before Mato could respond, assuming he'd bother, the radio inside the truck suddenly came to life, spewing words he could neither understand clearly nor ignore. He yanked open the truck door and grabbed the microphone. "Say again, Dolores."

The transmission sounded as if it had rattled around in a canyon or two before it reached him, but he got the essence of it: an approximate location and the fact that somebody, most likely a rancher, was blowing up stumps or beaver dams without a permit.

"I've gotta go," he said as he dashed around to the driver's side of the truck. "Tell Tori I'll be back later." He slammed the door, gunned the engine and made a tight turn around the barbecue rock. He glanced in the mirror and out the side window, but didn't see Mato anywhere. Praying he hadn't run over him, Nate clattered down the drive toward the highway.

Had it been a shoot out or a bank robbery, he might have taken the route from Tori's cabin to the main road with a bit more speed. As it was, he took his time with the deepest ruts and the biggest rocks. There had been another slide since the last time he came out, and the stretch along the steep hillside was thick with boulders.

Fortunately, none of them completely blocked the way.

He hit the road and increased his speed, knowing it would take the better part of a half hour to even get close to the perps. Just thinking the word brought a smile to his face. *Perps.* Right out of "Law and freakin' Order!" One day maybe he'd run into some *real* bad guys. Not that he was in any way eager to trade rounds with desperados, but it'd be nice to do some serious sheriff stuff. Maybe arrest somebody for something more interesting than being a nuisance or a public drunk.

His destination was an area in higher ground where a rancher had dammed a stream and created a modest lake. A generous spillway allowed water to continue on its former course, so nobody downstream had complained too much. He'd fished the lake a couple times, but he preferred streams. *Nothin' like fly fishing to put your mind at ease. Maybe I'll take Tori up to--*

An explosion in the distance jarred him back to reality. Woods and dense undergrowth forced him to park the truck and proceed on foot. He left the big Ford beside an ancient Chevy Suburban which had more dents and rust than a recycling center. By the time he reached the wall of trees, Mato stood in front of him with his hands on his hips, as if he'd been waiting.

"What the hell're you doin' here?"

"Mato help."

"Naw. You get back in the truck. I'll take care--" As quickly as the Indian had appeared, he dropped out of sight. Nate plunged into the woods after him, but Mato had left no trace.

"Damn it, Mato!" He tried not to raise his voice too much and risk giving away the element of surprise in case the perps outnumbered him. *'Course, now I've got Mato on my side, I shouldn't have anything to worry about.*

It came as no great surprise the Indian ignored him.

Josh Langston

That seemed to be his *modus operandi*, or perhaps more accurately: *ignore and annoy*. And Tori wanted them to become buddies? *Fat damn chance.*

Telling himself Mato had a lifetime's worth of practice hiding from big people, Nate tried to focus on the problem at hand. Another explosion convinced him the issue had a better than even chance of being serious.

Staying low and taking advantage of available cover, Nate crept closer to the lake until he reached a good vantage point. Three men in varying states of inebriation were working more or less in concert to kill anything that might be alive in the lake.

One of them sat in a rubber raft with paddles and a net while the other two stood on shore pointing at fish floating in or near him. Nate couldn't tell how many he'd already scooped into the little two-man craft, but it was clearly more than the three of them would ever be able to eat.

He was about to stand up and shout for them to stop when one of the men lit the fuse on a homemade bomb. The device had been fashioned from a glass jar and a Ball Dome Lid, the same kind his mother used for canning. Lord only knew what sort of explosive it contained, though it was most likely black powder. Not exactly C-4, but clearly enough to blow off an arm, or maybe a head.

"Hold it right there," he shouted, a fraction of a second too late.

The lit bomb scribed an aerial arc that terminated a dozen yards from the rubber dinghy. The occupant made a valiant attempt to put his paddles to work, but only managed to throw up a bit of spray which the splash from the ensuing explosion completely dwarfed.

The shore team burst into laughter at their terrorized companion rocking atop the wave they'd just created.

"That's enough," Nate said in his command voice. Though he approached them with his hand on his holstered Glock, they appeared unconcerned until he got within range of the sawed off shotgun the shorter of the two suddenly produced. He leveled it menacingly.

"What d'you want?"

Nate raised his hands. "You boys doin' some fishin'?"

"What's it to you?" asked the man with the shotgun.

With the twin gun barrels occupying his attention, Nate almost missed it when the gunman let go of the weapon with one hand in order to slap at a spot somewhere between his shoulder blades.

"What izzit?" the other asked, a look of deep, alcohol induced concern on his sunburned face.

"Hornet. Damn thing stung me!"

"Holy shit!" yelled the taller one, reaching suddenly for his own back. "How'd you piss 'em off?"

"I din't! Now git 'em off me!" The gunman turned his back so his partner could brush away the stinging insects. Only, there weren't any. What he found was a porcupine quill which had pierced the first man's shirt and embedded itself in his back, midway between his shoulder blades.

"If that stinger came from a hornet, the sumbitch must be the size of a Cessna."

"Pull it out!"

"Hell, I've got one in me, too."

"C'mon, man, hurry!"

Nate, meanwhile, had pulled his service weapon, chambered a round and stepped close enough not to miss if he had to shoot. He tried to keep a straight face as he watched the two "sportsmen" staggering around trying to remove Mato's quills. This they finally accomplished before collapsing against each other for support. The shotgun slipped slowly out of the shorter man's fingers as he looked at Nate for some sort of explanation, his eyes rolling slowly upwards as he went to sleep.

Nate gazed past them to see if Mato had shown himself, but the Indian remained hidden. Nate gestured to the man on the lake. "Bring it in."

"I din' do nuthin'," the man mumbled. "I was just sittin' here when them two buttholes got here. I--" He slapped at the back of his neck, then shouted when he discovered the quill sticking out of the space between his hat and his shirt collar. "What the hell?"

"You got a rope in that thing?" Nate asked, though he doubted the boat's occupant would be able to throw anything across the thirty yards of water separating him from the shore. A minute or so later, he slumped backwards, unconscious.

"I hope you didn't kill 'em," Nate said, assuming Mato was still within earshot.

"Sleep only," the Indian said, once again from a position behind the deputy which he had somehow reached in utter silence. He rested a 3-foot long rod on his shoulder, the end of which sported a hole about the same diameter as the milkweed floss he'd wrapped around the porcupine quills.

Nate acknowledged the blowgun with a nod. "Nice shootin'."

Mato pointed to the two men on the ground, then drew his hand back toward the one in the raft. "You kill now?"

"*What?* No. Hell no! Being stupid isn't a hangin' offense. It probably should be, in some cases, but not this one." He shook his head. "How long will they be out?"

Mato squinted at him.

"How long sleep?" Nate said, mimicking Mato's pidgin English.

"Not long."

Great. It's like asking a prairie dog for the time of day. "I'm going back to the truck for some rope. You-- You can do whatever you want. I don't care."

Mato kicked one of the sleeping figures, a gesture clearly meant to demonstrate his disdain rather than to inflict injury. "Stupid," he said. "Stupid men."

When Nate returned, Mato was gone. The deputy sheriff tied a rock to the end of a line and tossed it into the raft, which he then coaxed to shore. After lugging the inert body of the rafter over to his companions, Nate emptied the dead fish into a large, black plastic bag. There had to be over a hundred of them, and he doubted anything in the water remained capable of swimming. Or breathing.

Damned shame, he thought, then began the task of searching their gear scattered on the shore. He only found one more of the homemade bombs. Stored in a foam drink koozie, it lay inside a small canvas backpack with "U.S." stenciled on it in black. "I'm sure you've made Uncle Sam proud today, boys," he said to the three snoring sinners. "Now I'm gonna have to clean up after you."

Mato was waiting in the truck when Nate brought out the first load of their stuff and shoved it in the back of the Suburban, which someone else would eventually haul away. He was already dreading the part where he'd have to do a fireman's carry and bring the three "fisherman" out of the woods. "How long sleep?" he asked again, but Mato still hadn't mastered the 24 hours in a day concept.

Instead, the Indian pointed to the sun, then traced its probable path until his arm was extended straight overhead.

Nate got it. "'Til noon, then." He glanced at his watch. "A couple hours. Two hours," he said, for Mato's

103

benefit. He held up his first and second fingers. "They'll sleep for two hours."

Mato walked silently back into the woods.

When Nate returned to the scene of the crime, Mato had already rounded up everything Nate had been forced to leave out of the first load. The pile of gear in the Indian's arms went over his head so he had to walk facing sideways in order to see where he was going.

"Need a hand?" Nate asked.

Mato ignored him and continued into the woods on a trail Nate hadn't noticed before. *How'd he find it when I didn't? Little bastard has some serious skills.* He tossed the largest of the three miscreants over his shoulder and carried him back to the truck.

Mato had already deposited his load and was headed back to the lake. They passed each other on the trail, both of them stepping to the side to make room for the other. Have to give credit where it's due, Nate thought. Mato was pitching in to a degree far greater than anything Nate thought him capable of. The little guy was strong, to say nothing of resourceful.

They passed each other again on the trail. Nate was returning for perp number two while Mato carried the bag of dead fish to the truck. That left only the raft and the shotgunner. Nate had pulled the plug on the raft, but the air wasn't flowing out of it as quickly as he'd hoped. That wasn't necessarily a bad thing. It'd give him time to rest after he got the last of his charges in the truck.

Again he passed Mato on the trail.

"You don't have to do any more," he said. "You've already done more than your share."

Mato answered as he always did. With silence.

By the time Nate had his prisoners securely trussed -- to the truck and to each other -- Mato reappeared dragging the partially inflated raft behind him. Once again, Nate found the little guy's strength prodigious, considering his size.

"Looks like I owe you some lunch," he said, gesturing for Mato to join him up front. The Indian tossed his blowgun and a short piece of leather bearing his remaining darts onto the seat and climbed in.

"Lunch?" Mato said, smiling for the first time.

"Yeah. I think we've earned it." *Too bad we've got to make a couple stops before we can eat. I wonder if he likes Chinese?*

~*~

Tessa had been forced to wait until lunch time before she could find an appropriate target and zero in on him. Her goal was a male who worked in marketing for the same publisher as Cassy Woodall. If he wasn't already familiar with the various authors assigned to the company's editors, it wouldn't take him long to look up any one individual. Provocative clothing and a three martini lunch could do wonders to loosen a man's tongue, among other things.

Fortunately, she was only interested in finding out which of Woodall's clients lived in Wyoming. An address would be helpful, but wasn't expected. She had no intention of raising anyone's curiosity to a possibly uncomfortable level. The last thing Tessa needed was for someone to contact Cassy's friend before Tessa did.

She had the name, Victoria Lanier, before the table had even been cleared. More remarkable still, she had a shipping address in some backwater town to go with it, complements of an eager-to-please young executive with a Blackberry and some astonishing database skills. Tessa gave her benefactor a made-up identity and phone number along with the promise of an intimate -- and prolonged -- reward when he called. Then it was off to Poughkeepsie, home of Jerry Bernstein and Bernstein Labs. It was nice to be working again. *Too bad I can't keep doing it alone.*

There was no way around it. She needed a sample of Lanier's blood, but she lacked the skill set to get it herself. Besides, she always got a little queasy around the stuff. The mere thought of willingly making a donation of blood made her head spin. How could people *do* that? It was just... gross.

Fortunately, she recalled the name of the man who'd tried so hard to get her to join the company softball team: Mort Lund. Not just a dork, a master dork. Possibly the model for *dorkus disgustus*, the quintessential King Kong of dorkdom. But one she would have little trouble controlling. Best of all, he was the only licensed phlebotomist at Bernstein Labs. He should be able to draw the required sample without killing or maiming the esteemed Ms. Lanier.

Tessa recalled laughing when she first heard the word -- *phlebotomist* -- but it certainly sounded better than "blood sucker" and undoubtedly secured a certain level of esteem for whomever had a strong enough stomach to learn the trade. As Mort Lund undoubtedly had.

Tessa checked her watch and concluded he would no doubt be sticking his needle into some hapless victim at that very moment. "Mort, old pal, you're about to go on a trip with me. I'll do my best to make it as pleasant as possible for both of us, but if you so much as touch me, I'll sew my initials on your scrotum with your own needle."

She didn't often make herself giggle, but when she did, she liked it. Now she needed to come up with a plausible reason for Victoria Lanier to volunteer some of her blood. Hopefully she didn't share Tessa's views on the subject or she'd have to come up with an alternative means of getting what she wanted. That wasn't always a bad thing. It did, however, almost always slow things down.

~*~

Once she had the groceries loaded, Tori tipped the bag boy and piled into her Nissan, eager to put the town of Worland behind her. Ten Sleep didn't have a grocery store, and she couldn't afford to shop at Caleb's little store. His prices were just too much for her battered bank account. She loved the man like a father, but book sales lately hadn't been spectacular, and Cassy made it clear she wanted to get her hands on Tori's next manuscript.

She decided it had been too long since she spoke with her editor friend. Once she cleared the outskirts of town, she hit the speed dial assigned to Cassy's office.

Her secretary intercepted the call but passed her on when she recognized Tori's voice.

"Cassy! How's it goin?"

"Hi, Tori. I've missed you."

The two exchanged pleasantries for a long few moments, then Cassy took the conversation on a tangent Tori never expected.

"Guess what I did this morning," Cassy said.

"Gimme a hint. Was it legal?"

"Yes."

"Was it moral and ethical?"

Cassy paused only briefly. "Yeah. Only I haven't said anything to my priest yet."

"Good God Cass, did you get yourself knocked up?"

"I think so. At least, I hope so."

Tori's attempt at a joke lay mangled on the concrete, a victim of a long fall from a low place. "You're kidding, right?"

"No. I went to a clinic this morning and had myself inseminated."

"Oh. My. God."

"What?"

"I can't believe it! Do you know anything at all about the... uhm... sperm guy?"

"They're called donors. And yes, I was given a profile. He's healthy and smart."

"What's he look like?"

"I have no idea. And really, I don't care. I'm doing this in memory of Rachel."

"What if you have a boy?"

"I'm not planning on it, but I'm prepared to deal with that if it happens. Besides, what difference does it make? All I want is a healthy baby. I'll name it after Rachel one way or another."

Tori didn't realize she'd been holding her breath while Cassy spoke. She let it out slowly. "Wow, Cass. That's uhm... amazing. It takes guts to raise a child alone. I don't think I could swing it."

"You've got two miniature Indians under your roof, girl. It doesn't get much more committed than that." She laughed. "How's that going, by the way?"

"Fine. Except the local deputy sheriff thinks Mato may have poisoned Shawn."

"So? The bastard deserved it."

"Of course he did, but Nate--"

"Nate? You're on a first name basis with the guy who wants to arrest Mato?"

Tori hesitated to go into any details. "He's really a good guy. And he doesn't want to arrest Mato. He's just trying to make sure I understand all the possible ramifications."

"I thought the case was closed."

"That's what Nate's trying to do. But he has to have a body, or some plausible explanation of what happened to it. Otherwise, Shawn stays on the wanted list."

"And that matters because...."

"I went through all this with Nate and barely got him to agree to keep Mato, Reyna and the cavern out of his report if at all possible."

"He *knows* about them?"

Tori still hadn't gotten over her initial feelings that she had betrayed a trust. "It's complicated."

"Please tell me you aren't sleeping with this guy."

Tori laughed, but she knew it didn't sound convincing. "No. I haven't slept with him."

"Did I hear the word 'yet' in there somewhere?" Cassy asked.

"No, and I don't have any immediate plans to change that."

"How 'bout long range plans?"

"Stop being so nosey!" Tori said with a laugh.

"Actually, I've got something to confess, too. The doctor who treated me when I was recovering from the attack--"

"Did I meet him?"

"I dunno. Maybe. Anyway, he was intensely curious about my rapid recovery. He was pretty insistent on finding out if I had any unauthorized medical treatments."

Tori sucked in her breath. "You mean, like the transfusion?"

"Yeah."

"What'd you tell him? Good God, Cassy, if someone were to find out about that, there's no telling where it might lead."

"I know! I didn't tell him anything. And it almost got -- well, actually, it did get -- embarrassing. But I kept my mouth shut. I swear."

Tori exhaled with a whoosh. "Good. Thank you." She coughed nervously. "I was hoping we could talk about the book," she said, desperate to change the subject.

"You're working on a *book?*" Cassy's sudden switch to sarcasm actually helped, and Tori realized they both wanted to change the subject.

"It's stalled," Tori said. "Again. The story isn't going anywhere, dammit. There's no action. No romance. No mystery."

"I don't believe that."

"I'm going to have to start making stuff up!"

"Perish the thought!" Cassy gasped. "Imagine a fiction author reduced to using her imagination. What's the world coming to?"

"You aren't helping."

"Sorry. Why not try this: sit down in front of that fancy schmancy computer monitor I sent you and write something exciting. Put your hero in jeopardy. Kill somebody off."

"You're a hard woman, Cassy Woodall."

Tori imagined she could see Cassy nodding her head. "But I love ya for it."

"I love you too. Now go. Get busy. Make me proud."

"I'll try."

Cassy groaned. "Don't make me go all Yoda on ya!"

~*~

Chapter 7

Ideas don't take up much space,
until the government gets ahold of them.

Carmine DeLuca stared at the black Lincoln town car pulling into Spaski's DeeLux car wash. *Where the hell did they all come from? How many rich doctors, lawyers and stock brokers were there in the Upper West Side?* He grabbed a cleaning rag and waited for the sleek vehicle to arrive at his work station. He didn't mind the fancy cars, especially the limos, since they often yielded a bonus for diligent workers like himself. He smiled recalling how many times he'd tapped into the booze he found on board. He reasoned the owners could easily afford it, and besides, they probably made their money squeezin' little guys just like him. That would change when Carmine eventually got connected. He had dreamed of being a gangster -- a full-fledged wise guy -- for as long as he could remember.

Quick to point out his ethnic qualifications, Carmine had developed a skin thick enough to withstand the scorn which almost always followed such declarations. One of the many things he needed to make himself more desirable to the mob, was a great nickname. Unfortunately, he'd yet to hit upon one that fit both his physical attributes and his demeanor. He'd tried several, but they never seemed to garner any respect. Having to deal with the wit of the local talent at the DeeLux didn't help.

"Hey, look," said Alvin Jones, an insanely tall black who'd worked at the car wash longer than anyone except the owner. "It's 'Big Time' Carmine, the bad ass gangsta.

Josh Langston

'Sup Big Time?"

"Eat me, Alvin," Carmine said, hoping to project the proper level of belligerence. It was important to show his toughness even though they both knew Alvin could mangle him with ease.

"Spaz wants to see yo ugly ass," Alvin said stabbing a thumb over his shoulder in the general direction of the cramped, windowless room where their boss spent most of his life.

Carmine brightened. "Maybe he wants to give me a raise."

"Maybe he wants *you* to give *him* somethin'."

"Like what?"

"A blow job. If you wanna keep workin' here, that's prob'ly what it'll take."

Carmine tossed his cleaning rag aside, lowered the zipper on his coveralls to mid chest, and sauntered over to the space his co-workers had dubbed "The Hole." Stuart Spaski waited inside.

The juice-stained necktie did little to improve Spaski's appearance. His dark complexion and ample size suggested a Buddha in the sanitation trade. The little room could have used two or three dozen scented candles. Though intensely aware of these things, Carmine knew better than to say anything.

"We got a problem," Spaski said.

"With what?" Carmine asked.

"You." The big man eased back in his chair, causing its support system to register a protest.

"What'd I do?"

"I s'pose that wasn't you drank up all the single malt in councilman Mangano's limo?"

Carmine shook his head vigorously. "Single malt? Like malt liquor?"

112

"No, you moron. Single malt like in Scotch whiskey."

"Wasn't me, man. I hate scotch. Single malt, double malt, raspberry flavored, whatevah."

"You arguin' wit' me?"

"I'm tellin' you the truth."

Spaski looked dubious. "I don't see you and 'truth' spending a whole lotta time together. Ya know what I mean?"

Carmine shrugged. "I can't look through yer eyes. I do my job, is all."

"They tell me you think you should be in the mob."

"It could happen."

"And then what? You gonna try and shake me down?"

"I wouldn't do that." *At least, not on Day One. Day Two, maybe.*

"I don't believe you."

"Why not? I got an honest face."

"You got shit, DeLuca. You're outta here. When ya steal from my customers, it's like you're stealin' from me. I can't have that."

"But, I didn't--"

"You're fired, meatball! Get outta here."

Carmine straightened to his full, five-foot, six-inches. "You owe me for most of a week."

Spaski stared at him. "You got any idea what 40-year-old single malt scotch sells for?"

"I aware'y tol' you, I don't like scotch. How the fuck should I know what it sells for?"

"One shot's worth a helluva lot more than you make in a week. You're lucky I don't charge you for the difference."

"But--"

"G'wan! I'm a busy man."

Carmine walked away. Stripping out of his DeeLux

jumpsuit, he left the garment where it hit the cement floor, in a shallow pool of soapy water.

"See ya' roun', Big Time," Alvin called out from the depths of the car wash.

Not if I can help it, Carmine thought.

~*~

Caleb Jones pulled to a stop in front of Maggie Scott's house in Ten Sleep, a town of about 300 mostly friendly people. A ranger in the nearby Bighorn National Forest, Maggie split her free time between Caleb and a handful of dedicated pinochle players. She came outside when Caleb beeped the horn of his newly acquired vehicle.

"Where'd you get that?" she asked, strolling up to the Dodge minivan crowding her drive.

"My uncle left it to me."

"You had an uncle? I thought your momma found you under a booger bush."

Ignoring her remarks with practiced ease, Caleb motioned for her to come closer while he swung open the driver side door. "Check this out," he said.

She slapped her hands to her cheeks in mock surprise. "Oh. My. God. It's... It's a van!"

"Look closer, woman. It's a van with *hand controls*. I can drive without using my feet."

"As opposed to driving without using your head?"

"Just 'cause you're a hot babe, don't think you can sweet talk your way into getting a ride."

Maggie chuckled. "And why would a hot babe want to crawl into a van with a dirty old man?"

"Ya don't have to use 'em," he said, ignoring her and pointing to the hand controls. "Just slide this doohickey outta the way, lock it down, and it's back to normal. Slick, huh?"

Maggie bent forward for a closer look, rubbed her chin, and laid a hand on Caleb's thigh. "Is there something you aren't tellin' me, Romeo?"

"Huh?"

"Is everything else under the hood in workin' order?"

"What're you-- Oh!" He smiled and gently shifted the position of her hand a few inches closer to his heart. "It all works just fine. But bein' an older model, it's manual, not automatic."

"This is where I register shock and call the authorities to report a sex fiend loose in the neighborhood, right?"

"Or, you could climb in and we could go for a spin. It really is tricked out pretty nice."

Maggie gave him a quick kiss then walked around to the passenger side and got in. "I thought your uncle lived in a tent behind a water tower in Scranton or some other nasty place. How'd he ever afford something like this?" She waved her hand at the fully furnished van with its four captain's chairs, matching drapes, and polished wood interior.

"He wasn't poor; he was frugal."

"Guess it runs in the family."

"And it wasn't Scranton. That's in Pennsylvania. He was a Texan, like me."

"So, what happened to him, and why'd he leave this to you?"

Caleb started the engine. "I was the only family he had after his wife passed. Her name was Mildred. An awful woman. It's no wonder they didn't have any kids." He shifted the van into gear and pulled away from Maggie's house.

"Sometimes a woman's attitude reflects the life she's had, or the person she's living with. Maybe your uncle was a pain in the ass."

"Digger had his faults. But--"

"Digger?"

"He wanted to be a bull rider but never quite got the hang of it. Kept landing on his head. They told him if he kept it up, sooner or later they'd have to dig him outta the dirt."

"Is that how he got hurt?"

"Hurt?"

She pointed at the hand controls. "Yeah. Is that why he needed a specially equipped vehicle?"

"Oh, no. That was for Mildred. I don't know what her problem was. Like I said, she wasn't a lot of fun to be around. Digger had the van modified for her."

Maggie looked at the familiar scenery. "Where we headed?"

"Thought we'd drop by Tori's place. I've been thinkin' 'bout the little guy."

"And his girlfriend?"

"Well, yeah. Kinda hard not to. Anyway, I thought I'd offer to teach him how to drive."

"Teach Mato to drive?"

"Yeah."

She put a hand on his forehead. "You runnin' a fever?"

"I'm fine. I just thought it would be neighborly."

"Neighborly is sharing a batch of cookies, not teaching a two-foot tall Indian how to drive a five-ton vehicle. Besides, where's he gonna go? How's he gonna get a license?"

Cal deliberated before answering. "I just thought it might be a good skill for him to have. The more he knows about how we live, the better off he'll be when the time comes to decide where and how he wants to live. If he had a horse, or some other means of gettin' around, I wouldn't worry about it. But everywhere he goes, he goes on foot. Imagine livin' like that!"

"Did you intend to leave the van with Tori?"

"Well, no."

"Then, how's he going to use it to go anywhere?"

"I figured he could borrow it if he needed it."

Maggie patted his knee. "Cal, you're a great guy. Always thinkin' about other people. But sometimes, you don't think things all the way through. Sometimes you miss the obvious 'cause you're concentrating so hard on what isn't."

"Like teachin' Mato to drive?"

"Right. And like the fact that I'm working today. I don't have time to drive anywhere."

Caleb slapped his forehead. "I knew that!" He slowed the van and prepared to turn around. "Once I got the idea in my head, I couldn't shake it."

"Mato driving?"

"Yeah. I'm still gonna do it. We can tool around on the back roads."

"Back roads are the only kind we've got around here."

Caleb nodded. "I wouldn't put him in the way of any traffic. At least, not until he knows what he's doing. I'm not completely irresponsible."

"Promise me you'll run it by Tori first."

"It's not like he's her child, y'know."

Maggie smiled knowingly. "Actually, that's exactly what it's like."

"I meant it in the legal sense."

"And I meant it in the 'let's not get the poor guy killed' sense."

Cal stopped when he reached her house. "Dinner tonight?"

Josh Langston

"Only if you survive Mato's driving lesson."

~*~

Nate remained mystified by Mato. The man -- for
that's what he was, despite his tiny size -- seemed to have
no fear. Firearms and explosions didn't phase him, though
it wasn't likely he had ever been close to either. Yet, he
threw himself into the fray when it came to the three
drunken "fisherman" and took them all out without
raising a sweat. Abso-freaking-lutely amazing!

And his skill set didn't end with a silent weapon fired
from a hidden position. No, the little guy had insanely
good instincts when it came to sneaking through the
woods or finding game trails that most folks wouldn't
recognize in a thousand years. Nate hoped he'd never
have to try and track him. That would be a completely
lost cause. He could easily see where people would make
assumptions based on Mato's size rather than his skills, or
his heart. *Big* mistake.

Tori had urged him to be friends with the Indian, and
the more he learned about her primitive housemate, the
more he realized such a friendship could be a profound
treasure. Provided, of course, Nate kept his head screwed
on properly and stuffed the bulk of his preconceived
notions in the garbage. Where they belonged. Most of
'em, anyway.

After eliciting a promise from Mato that he'd stay out
of sight in the truck, Nate had dropped his charges off at
the Sheriff's office in Worland, governmental ground zero
for Washakie county. The paperwork dragged on, but he
took a break to deliver a Coke to Mato in one of the tiny
little plastic cups Dolores Mansheer, the radio operator,
kept beside the water cooler. A very thin, long straw

would have worked better, but he had no idea where he might find one.

He smiled thinking of Dolores -- Dee to everyone in the department. Far more than a mere radio operator, she was *ex-officio* office manager, cookie maker and keeper of the peace between peace officers -- a mother figure to all the guys in the department, including the sheriff. Everyone knew her birthday, but no one knew her age. She'd been a fixture before Nate arrived, and would undoubtedly be there when he retired, assuming he lived that long.

"Done with that report yet?" she asked when he dropped back into his creaky desk chair after taking the Coke to Mato. "You look like you could use some lunch. Catching bad guys and knocking 'em unconscious is hard work." She gave him a measured, and fully suspicious, look.

"They passed out, Dee," he said. "I didn't touch 'em."

"You sure? I'd hate to see your good work turned on its ear because you took advantage of those poor boys."

It was his turn to give her a suspicious look. "You couldn't smell those 'poor boys' when I brought 'em in?"

She laughed. "Are you kidding? The guys in the barbershop down the street smelled 'em when you brought them in."

"Then, what's the problem?"

"I dunno. They looked a little too, you know, glassy eyed. Like they're on meth or something."

"You ever seen anyone on meth?"

"Prob'ly. I've been here a long time."

"I meant, knocked out by meth. Or any other hard drug." He shook his head. "Those three are boozers. They'll sleep it off and have really bad hangovers. At least, I hope they do. Could be all they get for their little bomb party."

Dolores put her hands on her hips. "They'll spend a few weeks in jail, at least. Maybe it'll scare some sense into 'em."

"I wouldn't count on it," he said.

"Why don't you go get something to eat? I'll finish your paperwork. Assuming you trust me."

He had already finished writing up the details of the arrest. What remained was largely a case of documenting what he'd taken from the suspects and put in his truck. That was all stacked in the "interrogation" room, a corner of the station once reserved for metal file cabinets. Those had since been moved to an annex built after the most recent bond issue. Nothing but the finest for Washakie's crime fighters.

"You'd do that for me?"

"Sure," she said, smiling.

"There's something else, isn't there?"

She raised her eyebrows in a gesture meant to display innocence. It didn't work.

"Dee? What d'you want from me in return?"

"Nothin' much. It's such a small thing I hesitate to even mention it."

Nate put his head on his desk. He hated paperwork. Almost as much as he hated owing favors. "Please, don't keep me in suspense."

"My grandson is in town."

"Oh? That's nice."

"He wants to go horseback riding."

"Shouldn't be a problem. Just about everyone around here owns riding stock."

"'Cept me," she said, smiling coyly.

"Aw hell, Dee. You know I don't do pony rides. I'm not comfortable around kids, 'specially those who don't know what they're doin'. And that's pretty much all of 'em."

"But that's just it -- *you* know what you're doing. I wouldn't trust anyone else with my little grandson."

"Sorry, Dee. I only have one saddle, and it's designed for an adult."

"Marty can handle it. You can ride bareback." She pointed at a snapshot on his desk. It was taped to the side of the monitor that accompanied his aging desktop computer. The photo showed him smiling as he sat atop an impressive dappled gray horse, sans saddle. "And that's not the only horse you have, is it?"

"No," he admitted. He had two others, but one was strictly a pack animal, and the other was getting old. Nate had resigned himself to its retirement. "Can I think about it and get back to you?"

"Today?" she asked.

He nodded.

"Sure!" She made a shooing motion with both hands. "Now go, lemme finish that report. There's nothing else to do around here."

"Thanks, Dee," he said, sliding quickly out from behind his desk.

"Don't forget to call me!"

"I won't. That's a promise."

"You'll like Marty. He's a good kid, really. Deep down, inside."

So, why sell him so hard?

He heard her voice one last time as he crossed through the door to freedom. "You can't believe much of what they say about him!"

~*~

Despite Cassy's distinctly less-than-sympathetic input, Tori continued to struggle with the new book. Her previous effort -- the only manuscript she'd actually finished, let alone sold -- had been based on the life of a long-dead ancestor. His name was Robert Lanier, and Tori had adopted his last name in her attempts to hide from her deranged ex-husband. In addition to the name change, Tori had moved to Wyoming in search of her old uncle's last known address.

The remains of his ancient cabin, and the property on which it sat, had been on the market for ages. Though located near prime ranching country, Lanier's land wasn't suitable for much of anything, although it did have a killer view with which Tori immediately fell in love.

Rebuilding the dilapidated cabin had yielded an unexpected bonanza: Robert Lanier's personal journal, in which he compiled a translation dictionary between English and a previously unknown Indian dialect, and access to a tunnel beneath the cabin which lead to a cavern decorated with prehistoric cave paintings.

Lanier's journal revealed that he, too, had discovered one of the diminutive Indians, a woman named Sleeping Dove or *Leo Kah Nah* in her language. And there his story seemed to end. The journal detailed some of their time together, but then just stopped.

Tori's first book had been based on Lanier's Civil War adventures, for he had been a successful Confederate spy. Romanticizing his encounters, and spicing up the danger level, had been a fairly easy task, since she knew from the beginning how the story would end. His life in Wyoming, however, was an entirely different matter.

Based on his journal comments, Tori was convinced uncle Bob had developed deep feelings for Sleeping Dove. And while their relative sizes made a romantic relationship impossible, it didn't preclude an intense love for one another. Sadly, Tori couldn't prove it.

"Put your hero in jeopardy," Cassy had said. "Kill somebody off."

Had that actually happened? Uncle Bob couldn't have just disappeared. Something happened to him, and more than likely it involved Sleeping Dove.

Standing abruptly, Tori stepped away from her computer and walked to the cabin door. Since Nate had brought him home, Mato had been puttering around outside, cramming odds and ends into an old army backpack he'd found somewhere. She had no idea what he had collected and reasoned that it would be safer for all concerned if she didn't inquire. She liked Mato immensely, but he was still a long way from being "civilized," and despite his amazing artistic talents -- he could convey more with a few pencil strokes than most artists could manage with a full kit of brushes, paints *and* models -- there was very little gray in his black and white world. If he had a motto it would probably go something like: 'Kill first, and ignore the questions.' He definitely didn't like questions.

"Mato?" she called from the stoop. Nate had dropped him off in mid-afternoon after filling her in on the day's adventure. She suspected his rapid departure had something to do with her frosty response to his retelling of the incident with the "fishermen." Mato had sought out Reyna without making any attempt to listen in on their conversation, so Nate's version of the story was the only one Tori heard. Though she attempted to ferret out any subterfuge by questioning Mato about it, his responses were entirely in line with Nate's story. She might have concluded they were conspiring to hide something, only what they had told her was fully appalling on the face of it. If there were more, she hoped they *had* hidden it from her.

The little Indian poked his head around a corner of

Josh Langston

the cabin. "Hm?"

"Do you remember me talking about my uncle Bob?"

He nodded in the affirmative.

"Do you think you could help me find him?"

Mato shook his head the other way. "He dead. Long time."

"Well, yes, I know, but--"

"Body rot. Stink bad. Coyote, buzzard eat. All gone."

It's always lovely chatting with you. Tori sighed. "I'm just trying to think where he might have gone if, for instance, he wanted to take Sleeping Dove back home."

"Leo Kah Nah not come back."

The way he said the name made her think the three syllables were a single word. Uncle Bob's rudimentary phonetics had contained plenty of similar blunders. "You knew of her?" Tori asked.

"Leokahnah great mato. Drew many dreams. Grandmother to Winter Woman. Grandmother to Reyna."

Tori looked over her shoulder at the young Indian woman inside the cabin quietly embroidering an intricate design in a garment of soft leather. "That Reyna? *Our* Reyna?"

"Mato's Reyna," he confirmed.

The woman in question looked up from her work and called out to her mate. Her rapid fire delivery was more than Tori's limited translation abilities could handle.

"What'd she say?" Tori asked.

"She say giant talk too much."

I love you, too, snotcakes. "I'm just trying to figure out where they went and what happened to them. I know they didn't make it, but if they attempted such a trip, where might they have gone?"

Mato's brows drew downward, forming a deep V. "Cold times? Hot? Leaf times? Flower times? The People

124

go different places."

"Even now?"

He made a face that shrieked disgust. "New places now. Giants everywhere."

That made sense. Mato's tribe had been forced out of the lands now inhabited by her kind, as they had been forced to abandon the lands occupied by the Native Americans everyone knew about: Crow, Cheyenne and Shoshone, at least in these parts. Ute and Arapaho further south. Just how far afield had Mato's people traveled?

"Do your people prefer the mountains or the plains?" she asked.

Mato looked at her with undisguised suspicion. "Both good, if no giants. If Leokahnah bring giant, The People hide. Leokahnah no find."

"Would The People try to hurt uncle Bob?"

He considered the question, then rendered a judgment in a series of extraordinarily defiant grunts. "Giant must stay away, or die."

Had Mato's people killed uncle Bob? The thought jarred her deeply. Uncle Bob was an ally, a protector. Surely Sleeping Dove would have told them that, assuming she had survived the search.

"Do you know the places where The People used to go?"

"The old places?"

It became Tori's turn to nod.

"Mato know."

"Can we go there? Look around?"

"Long walk. Many sleeps."

"We'll take my truck."

"Truck go up mountain?"

"Depends on the mountain."

"Most giants ride horse. You have horse?"

"No," she said, smiling for the first time in hours,

"but I know someone who does."

~*~

"Let me get this straight," Mort Lund said after Tessa explained what she needed. "You want me to go with you to some remote place out west and draw somebody's blood."

Tessa bobbed her head up and down. "That's pretty much it, yeah."

"Wyoming?"

"Yes."

"And we're gonna drive there?"

"Part of the way. We'll rent a car in Billings."

"Montana?"

"That's the only one I know of."

"Why can't we fly right to the place we need to go?"

"Because they don't have an airport, genius. We could charter a plane and parachute in, I suppose. You up for that?"

"Parachute? Uh, no."

"Figured as much," Tessa said. "But now that I think about it, gliding in on a parachute would make for a dazzling entry. Too bad it wouldn't be right for us. We're supposed to be public health workers. We'll have to do a little acting when it comes time to get the blood sample."

"Acting?"

"Yeah. You've done role-playing before, haven't you? Like whenever you come home late and the missus wants to know where you've been."

"That's never been a problem."

She eyed him with utter disdain. "Right. Look, I've already cleared all this with Jerry, er, Mr. Bernstein. He's okay with it as long as we don't spend too much money getting the sample, since there's no guarantee it'll pan out."

"What do I tell my wife?"

"I dunno. How 'bout: 'See ya next week'?" Tessa shrugged. "Tell her anything you like, as long as it's not what we're going to be doing."

"She can tell when I lie," Lund said.

"Because she's had lots of practice, or not enough?"

He looked at her as if she had the plague. "Why should I do this for you?"

"'Cause I'm the only one who knows where we're going."

"I meant, what's in it for me?"

Tessa laughed. "Well, it'll get you out of the house, and the lab. Isn't that enough?"

"I'll have to miss a game."

"I'm sure the Bernstein Bruisers can survive without you for a game or two."

"It's the Bernstein Brains, and I'm a starter."

She tried to smile appreciatively, but it was a struggle. "Sometimes we all have to make sacrifices. Do you know anyone else in the company who's qualified to draw blood?"

He pursed his lips in concentration, then responded simply, "No."

"There ya go. You're it: the man in demand. The guy on the hot seat." She leaned over him and gently placed her palm on his cheek. "I've never had any complaints from my other traveling companions."

"Uh...."

"We'll have to get separate rooms, of course. Got to keep up appearances for the home front."

Was Lund turning slightly pink?

"Separate rooms, right."

"But, of course, they have connecting doors. Very

127

handy for making undocumented visits late at night." *Our connecting door, however, will be locked and bolted 24/7. Count on it.* She gave him an evil smile. "I like an occasional toddy before bedtime. How 'bout you?"

"Absolutely. Brandy, or something. Should I pack some?"

She tickled his cheek as she withdrew her hand. "Bring anything you think we'll need. This trip doesn't have to be strictly business. There ought to be time for a little relaxation, too."

He coughed, unconvincingly. *Got 'im!*

"Our flight leaves day after tomorrow. 10:10 in the morning, from LaGuardia. Don't be late."

"Not a chance."

"When I said to bring everything you'll need, I meant it. Rubber gloves, syringes, test tubes -- anything you lab types need for survival."

Lund looked at her as if seeing her for the first time. "What's wrong with this patient? What are we trying to find in her blood?"

"There's nothing wrong with her, as you'll see. She's as healthy as you or me. Probably healthier, living with all that clean Wyoming air."

He sniffed. "I think I smell bullshit." He sniffed again. "Yeah. No doubt about it."

Score one for the geek. She smiled and slipped into techno-speak, a skill she'd honed while hyping Bernstein Labs products in countless on-line investor chat rooms. "We believe the lady in question has some extraordinary antibodies in her blood. We won't know exactly how extraordinary they are until we get the sample back to the lab and examine it. Then, wonderful things -- possibly *spectacular* things -- could happen. Just how spectacular I can't say. Yet."

"Uh huh. She's not infected with anything?"

"Not that we know of."

"That's not terribly reassuring."

"I thought you were one of those tough types -- a no-jock kinda jock."

"Have you ever heard of necrotizing fasciitis?"

"Not until just now. What is it?"

"The best known form is called MRSA. It's basically a flesh-eating bacteria. Lovely stuff. Not something you want to pick up on vacation."

"Relax, Dr. Frankenstein. Our patient is pathogenically boring. But, she may have something really interesting in her blood. Other than that, she's no different than anyone else you'd meet in the normal course of your day."

He eyed her with less than full confidence. "You promise?"

"I do," she said, smiling like she meant it. "Meet me at the Delta ticket counter. Early. Like, eight o'clock."

"What if I get hung up in traffic or something? How do I contact you?"

"You don't. Plan ahead. Be on time. 'Cause if you screw this up, I'll come looking for you with something worse than a bucket of flesh-eating germs."

When he swallowed, his Adam's apple bounced like a carnival ride. "I'll be there."

"Good," she said and sauntered out of the lab. She gave her hips the full sway of a model's runway walk in case other members of the Bernstein Bombers, or whatever they called themselves, was watching. Boosting Mort Lund in the eyes of his male peers was the least she could do. And, if it helped keep him in line, then it was a win-win deal. Tessa liked winning.

~*~

Chapter 8

*A 1-pound hammer kills a roach just as dead
as a 5-pound hammer.
Either way, the roach won't care.*

Nate arrived early the next morning, his truck bearing the same load as before: climbing gear, an electric winch, gas-powered generator, ropes, pulleys and other odds and ends Tori couldn't name.

"Where's Mato?" Nate asked after he backed the truck to the entrance of the cabin.

"He and Reyna went out," she responded, gesturing vaguely toward the wide open spaces beyond the bluff. It was nice having them out from under foot, and bedspread. Watching Nate work was far more rewarding, though how he would get so much stuff down the rabbit hole leading to the cavern was a mystery. She was about to ask him when he rolled the winch across the planks he'd used to bridge the gap between tailgate and threshold. She followed him inside and observed as he set it up inside the cabin and tossed the end of the steel cable into the opening beneath the hearth.

"How long is the cable?" she asked.

"There's fifty yards on the spool. I don't want to unwind it until I'm over the side of that big split in the cavern floor."

"What if the hole's deeper than 50 yards?"

"That's 150 feet!"

"Thank goodness you're here to handle the higher math," she said, wiping her brow dramatically.

"Sorry. But a hole 150 feet deep is... really deep."

"Profoundly so. And I'm guessing it's gonna be dark, too. Hope you've got a good light."

"I do. But I've gotta tell ya, I'm not excited about doing this alone."

"Thanks for the vote of confidence!"

His lips flattened into a tight line. "What I mean is, it'd be nice to have someone familiar with all this gear to help me. If I get into trouble...."

"I'm sure you'll give me adequate instructions," Tori said. "I'm not completely helpless. I managed to survive out here all by myself for quite a while before you showed up."

"You're right, of course. But I--"

"Give it up, Nate. You're only going to get yourself in a much deeper hole than the one in the cavern." She smiled at him, and he surrendered. They both went back outside.

He gathered up a load to be brought in. "So, you gonna give me a hand?"

They worked together without further discussion and brought most of the contents of the truck into the cramped cabin. Nate secured the winch to the floor and promised he'd patch the holes when the job was done.

"You'll make the floor look as good as new?" Tori asked, innocently.

"No. But I'll make it look as good as it did before I put holes in it."

"Hair-splitter."

"If I were going to do anything here, I'd build a deck."

She gave him a puzzled look. "A deck? Like for entertaining? I don't do much of that."

"A deck for gazing at the stars. For looking at the amazing view. For just... I dunno. Whatever. Sunbathing."

"I *would* like that," she said simply, thinking about the prospects of lying beside him, looking at the stars, and maybe... She shrugged. Who knew where something like that could lead. Better to change the subject before she headed to the lumber yard for building materials.

"Do we need all this stuff down below?" she asked surveying the gear. Mato and Reyna's absence was a huge relief. Tori couldn't imagine trying to convince them that carting so much junk into the cavern wouldn't be an affront to the Spirits. Especially since that's exactly what she thought it was.

"Most of it will probably just sit right here until we load it back on the truck," Nate said. "But, if we need it, we'll need it right away. And, if I'm down in the hole, you're the one who's going to have to come up and get it."

Tori found the pint-sized wagon she'd given to Mato for hauling his paints and brushes through the tunnel. "We can put stuff in here as long as it's not too heavy."

Nate attached a line to the business end of the steel cable, tossed a coil of rope over his shoulder and started down the hole, dragging a canvas bag behind him. Tori followed, pulling Mato's wagon with a leash she'd bought for Shadow. The dog was with the Indians.

Once they reached the cavern, Nate set up lights and took pictures of Shawn's footprints leading to the break in the floor. He then put on a climbing harness and hooked himself to the line that led back to the surface.

"Should I have stayed above to operate the winch?" Tori asked.

"Nah. I've got a remote control. I want you nearby in case I run into a problem." He pressed a button on the remote and backed over the lip of the crevasse, moving slowly.

Tori took a tiny step closer to the edge. Nate might

know his business, but she was still worried. She tried to lighten the mood. "What's the holdup? Was I supposed to pack meals and a sleeping bag?"

"I figured you could just crawl back out for any of that stuff. You're not hungry already, are you? We just got started." All but his head had slipped below the edge.

Tori felt a small stab of concern as his face dropped below her line of sight. "Hey! You okay?"

"Why? You worried?"

"I just don't want to have to haul all this crap outta here by myself."

"Mato might help." His voice was slightly muffled, the wall likely inches from his face.

"See anything yet?"

"No. But I don't want to twist around until I've gone down a bit more."

"How much more?"

"I don't know, Mom. I'll turn around when it feels right."

Tori struggled to keep quiet and managed for a minute or two. "C'mon, Nate. Talk to me."

"I've only gone about fifteen or twenty feet. Miss me already?"

"Can you see anything, smart guy?"

"The light from above is still pretty good, but there's really nothing to look at. The walls are fairly flat and smooth. Nothing to grab. Your ex wouldn't have had a chance even if he could've seen what he was doing. Can't imagine how scared he must've been."

She wasn't the least bit troubled by the idea. Mato was undoubtedly right: Shawn went over the edge and died. The little Indian claimed he could smell Shawn's rotting remains, though Tori never did. She wondered how long he would stink. How long until he rotted away to nothing?

The motor on the winch was too far away to hear, but the steel cable scraping on the rocky edge of the crevasse told her Nate was dropping farther down into the abyss. She wished she had the nerve to lean out over the edge and watch his descent, then told herself he'd fuss at her for taking the risk.

She tried to occupy her time by examining the ancient cave paintings, but her gaze kept going back to one of the most recent -- an image Mato had rendered of her ex-husband in the moments before he plunged down the very hole Nate was exploring. The look on Shawn's face registered sheer terror. *Sucks for you, asshole.* Not for the first time she marveled at how closely Mato's vision of Shawn came to reality, almost as if he'd modeled the scene from life though there had been no light in the cavern when Shawn went over the side. He'd fallen to his death in utter darkness, and assuming there was an afterlife, he'd likely find the same lighting conditions there.

"How's it going?" she asked.

"It narrows," Nate replied, his voice sounding a little strained. "I'm using my helmet light."

"Promise me you won't do anything dumb."

"Uh, right. Nothing dumb."

"I didn't hear much conviction in that."

"Only 'cause I don't know what you consider dumb."

"Okay then, promise me you won't do anything that might get you hurt."

There was a short pause before he responded. "You make it sound like you care."

"I do!" *That sure came out quick.*

He chuckled, and the sound bubbled up like spring water. "I-- Oh. Crap!"

Fear gripped Tori's heart. "What is it?"

134

He mumbled something she couldn't understand.

"What's the matter?" Several scenarios burst through her brain. All bad. All fatal. She lowered herself to the cavern floor and inched toward the edge. Would there be enough light to even see him?

"My gum," he said.

"You're gun? What do you need a gun for? Where is it?" *What the hell was going on?*

"Not gun, gum. Chewing gum. I left it in the truck."

Gum? Tori began looking for rocks she could send over the edge. With any luck, she'd connect with a few, maybe knock some sense into him.

"My throat gets dry. The gum helps. This is hard work."

"And it's going to get lonely if you keep that up."

"What?"

"Scaring me like that!"

"Sorry," he said. "Normally I don't have to worry about that sort of reaction."

"Because all the guys you work with are jerks? Like you?"

He was chuckling again. She could picture the way his eyes narrowed and the creases multiplied when he smiled. She loved that. "I think I hate you," she said.

"Why?"

"'Cause you're laughing at me for caring about you."

Silence. Then, a moment later: "Well. Just damn."

"What now, forget your lip balm? Suntan lotion? *TV Guide?*"

More silence.

"Nate? What is it?" *Stay calm.* Even if he's done something stupid. Even though--

"I'm outta cable."

"All 150 feet?"

"No, I'm holding another thousand in reserve."

Smartass. "Well, can you see anything?"

"As a matter of fact, I do."

"It's Shawn, right?"

"Well, it's a body. Kinda hard to tell who it is."

Tori looked up at Mato's painting on the ceiling. "Can you see a sweatshirt?"

"Yeah."

"Shawn's was red, with a University of Alabama logo on the back. Oh, and he wore jeans."

"Everybody out here wears jeans," Nate said. "Goes with the territory."

"And the sweatshirt?"

"There's a red one on this body."

"Can you reach it?"

"Not without another hundred feet of cable, and even then I'm not sure I could get a body basket through the narrow opening I passed about fifty feet back."

"Then you're calling it a day?"

"Didn't say that. I'd like to try another thing or two."

Tori could imagine him disconnecting and trying to scale the sheer walls to recover the dead body of someone who wasn't worth thinking about, much less recovering. "Don't you dare unhook yourself from the cable," she said, her voice rising along with her fear.

"Not a chance," he said. "I have no desire to stay down here. I was hoping you'd pop back topside and get the grappling hooks for me. I think I might be able to snag him from where I am."

Tori glared from the edge of the crevasse to the path leading back to the surface. It was a long crawl, and she had been dreading it. Now he wanted her to "pop back up to the surface." That would mean not one more trip through the tunnel, but *three*. "You want me to *crawl* back up and fetch some grappling hooks?"

"Yeah. I'll wait. But please hurry. The smell is pretty bad down here."

Well, she thought, that's some consolation at least.

~*~

"Yo, Carmine!"

The mob wannabe drew his head down into his shoulders at the sound of Lawrence Peevy, the building manager. "Hey, Larry. What's up?"

"The rent is up, that's what. You got it?"

"I need a couple more days."

"You said that the last time. When's yer payday? Friday?"

Carmine had no intention of admitting he had just joined the ranks of the unemployed. Peevy was not exactly the sympathetic type. "It's gonna be awhile. I'm thinking of, uh... switching to a different line of work."

"Like boosting hubcaps or mugging old ladies? You know, classy mob stuff."

Carmine felt himself rising to the bait. "That ain't all of it. They protect people, too."

"Yeah, for a price." Peevy poked Carmine in the chest with a grubby index finger. It went with his sleeveless T-shirt and the half-smoked cigar clamped in his yellowed teeth. "Your rent is already late. Pay me tomorrow or your stuff goes into the alley, and I make room for a new tenant."

"Listen Larry, I--"

"No, Carmine. You listen. Pay your rent or get out. It's that simple."

"Where'm I supposed to go?"

Peevy squinted at him. "Do I look like I give a shit?"

~*~

The grappling hooks didn't work. After multiple attempts, Nate managed to snag Shawn's sweatshirt, but the hook didn't hold. It became readily apparent that the deceased's remains were in a serious state of deterioration. Nate told Tori he feared that further attempts to hook the body would hasten the process. She might have been more aggravated about her wasted efforts crawling through the tunnel if Nate hadn't been so angry at himself.

"Shawn will just have to stay as he is, where he is," she said.

Clearly, Nate didn't like the idea. He'd used the winch to haul himself back up to the edge and sat beside her. "I could feel the winch bind on the way up. There's something wrong with the guide on the take-up spool. If the cable doesn't rewind evenly across the reel, it'll jam before it takes up all 50 yards. I had to do some hand-over-hand to get back up, and that's a pain."

"So we need a bigger winch?"

"That'd be nice, but I don't know where I'd get it. We'll have to settle for what we've got. I'll just rappel down there, put the remains in a body bag and haul it up."

"You're going to rappel down the side of a sheer wall?"

"Folks do it all the time," he said with a puzzled look. "You know anything about rappelling?"

"It's something sane people don't do. I hoped you were in that group."

"It's completely safe," he said. "I've done it many times."

"Recently?"

"Well...."

"Nate?" She gave him her gravest stare. "How

138

recently?"

"It's been a year or so, but it's no big deal. I can handle it."

"And what if you can't?"

He shrugged. "Call the office. Tell 'em I won't be coming in."

"Stop it, Nate. I'm serious."

"I am, too. I've gotta get that body outta there. It's the only way to close the case -- the only way you'll ever get any peace and quiet for Mato and Reyna."

"How 'bout if we call Caleb?"

"Have him crawl through that tunnel? With his bad knees? I don't think so. Now, here's how this is gonna work."

Nate explained how he would connect a separate line to a device with a pulley and clamp arrangement. He'd use the winch to lower himself as far as he could go, then rappel the rest of the way. Shawn's remains were wedged at the bottom of the crevasse, where the ground formed a sharp V. Nate would free the remains and load them into the body bag. Then he would climb up as far as he rappelled down, and use the winch to get out of the hole.

"The worst part will be hauling the body up without a winch."

"And then we go for a drink?"

"Then we go for dinner, drinks, and a movie," Nate said. "And maybe--"

"Maybe we could get building supplies for my new deck?" Tori smiled brightly.

Nate chuckled as he prepared for his second descent. "I might need a little rest before I start working on a deck."

"Rest? Nah," Tori said. "You just need a different kind of exercise, and I know just the thing."

Nate's eyes sparkled, reflecting the floodlights. "I

hope it doesn't involve hammers and saws."

"I was thinking more along the lines of wine and soft music."

"I could be talked into something like that."

"But only if you don't kill yourself first."

"If you insist."

She kissed him hard on the lips, then stepped back. "Do *not* hurt yourself, y'hear?"

"No ma'am, I won't."

"Okay then." Tori was convinced he meant it, though it did nothing for her confidence.

Carmine packed his stuff before Peevey could throw it in the alley. Going back to his sister's flat seemed to be his only choice now that he was out of work, again. But, he figured, bad news always came in threes, so there was still time for him to be run over by a garbage truck or maybe a tour bus. They could just scoop his dead ass up and toss it in the trash with his duffle bag. He'd be on a barge headed for a New Jersey landfill by nightfall. Travel had always been his fantasy.

He tried to imagine how the gangsters in the movies would react in his situation. It was a tactic he used often, since movie mobsters were as close as he'd ever been to the real thing, so far as he knew. But, since the real ones operated in the shadows, he didn't *expect* to see them. For now, anyway.

Carmine was daydreaming about whacking both Leonard Peevey *and* Stuart Spaski -- line 'em up, just right, and get 'em both with the same bullet -- when his sister stepped out of a yellow cab. She looked as happy as he felt.

"Get in," she said, motioning for the driver to stow her brother's lumpy duffel bag in the trunk.

Carmine tried to think of something clever or, in lieu of that, something a made man would say. He settled for, "Hi, Ronnie. Thanks for comin'."

Though she loathed the very thought of it, Veronica and Carmine were obviously brother and sister. They had been through a lot together. Perhaps too much. Products of New York's child welfare system, they had been housed as a pair for most of their formative years. Neither recalled much about their parents, though Veronica often found ways to disparage them for having the nerve to die in a car wreck before either of them finished grade school.

Ronnie was two years older than Carmine but shared none of his views about the underworld. Her goal, for as long as Carmine could remember, was to marry her way to success. Her husband, the best catch in a long string of premeditated romances, ran a financial "consulting" firm located far from the financial district, both geographically and legally. Veronica had never visited his office.

Benjamin Lykes made *arrangements*. He put people together. Sometimes face-to-face, and sometimes via less easily understood, and much harder to wiretap, means. For Veronica, the most difficult issue involving Ben came well before they were married.

Always a great one for test-driving potential married names, Veronica quickly recognized the unfortunate result of mating her maiden name with Ben's last name. Veronica DeLuca Lyke wouldn't cut it. Period. She jettisoned the family moniker before they reached the altar. Carmine didn't like the idea, but Veronica didn't care. She was, by God, an original, not a copy.

"You know this move is temporary," she said when both were comfortably seated in the cab.

"Sure. I don't like it any more'n you do," Carmine said.

"I seriously doubt that." She looked briefly out a side window. Someone was destroying a sidewalk with a jackhammer. In New York, someone was *always* destroying a sidewalk with a jackhammer. She shook her head, sending a ripple through her chemically enhanced auburn locks.

"The minute I've got a job and enough money to move into my own place, I'm gone."

"I've heard that before," she said.

"I really appreciate you helpin' me out."

"Yeah," she said. "Whatevah."

~*~

Tori's imagination kicked in the second Nate disappeared from view as he lowered himself over the side. He was humming, as if that would set her mind at ease. It wouldn't be long before he was dangling beside the rubber body bag they'd lowered just before he began his descent. Fortunately there was plenty of nylon line available, so she could let out more if the bag didn't reach Shawn's remains.

She was alternately angry, then glad, that she couldn't actually see Nate working. He'd soon be suspended at the end of a 150-foot rope, with another 50 feet of vertical space to cover. Though quick to claim he could easily manage the drop, he'd been rather vague about how he would climb back up.

"You let me worry about that," he'd said.

Right. No problem. I'll just flip my brain into standby mode and sit here, oblivious, while you drop like an albatross turd into the other pile of crap that used to call

itself my husband. What could possibly be easier?
Removing my own tonsils, maybe, or birthing a lawn
tractor.

"Tori?"

"WHAT?"

"Sound carries pretty well down here," he said. "No
need to shout."

"I didn't." *Did I?*

"Oh. Okay. Anyway, I'm on the bottom."

"So soon?"

"I need you to lower the body bag. Just a few more
feet."

She positioned herself behind the clamp and pulley
arrangement. "Here it comes," she said, slowly paying out
the line.

"That's enough," he responded a moment later. "Lock
it down."

She did, then waited. A television monitor focused on
him would have been nice, she thought. She could watch
him work. She thought about his broad shoulders and
strong arms. The fact that he was tending to her dead ex-
husband somehow didn't matter. What did, was the way
he had returned her kiss, the way he pulled her close, the
way he--

"Done!" His voice echoed in the cavern. "Don't worry
about the body bag. I'll pull it up later."

"What do you want me to do?"

"Go back up and keep an eye on the winch. Make
sure it spools evenly. There's a shut-off switch you can
use if it starts to bind. Okay?"

Tori eyed the path leading back up to the world of
sunlight. She'd already made the trip more times in one
day than seemed fair. The moment the thought rose in her
head she shook it off. Nate was taking all the risk. What
kind of person was she to complain? Besides, would she

rather go topside, or stay below, alone, like him?

"Want me to take anything up with me? I'd rather not have to come back down."

"Right. Load the wagon with anything you can haul. I'll bring the rest when I come."

"What if you run into trouble?"

She heard him laughing. "You worry too much."

That set her in motion, her pique driving her to move more quickly than she would have otherwise. It also drove her to put an extra item or two into the wagon that she probably should have left for Nate to haul. But how else could she demonstrate she wasn't just some wimpy skirt?

After a final adjustment to her knee pads, she started up the path to the surface with Mato's wagon in tow. She had a coil of rope over her shoulder as well. Nate would still have his hands full, but he couldn't accuse her of being lazy.

She covered the first half of the route without difficulty though she was breathing heavily and her heart was pounding from the steep ascent. Then the ceiling began to slope lower, forcing her to bend down and eventually crawl through the final third of the tunnel.

The pace slowed dramatically as she plowed through the dark on her hands and knees. She was sorely tempted to contact Nate on the battery powered radio he insisted they carry, but reaching the surface without his input had somehow become a requirement. It went well with the "I'll show him" mantra she had been muttering under her breath since she left the cavern.

She was still breathing it when she crawled out of the depths. The land of trolls and gremlins lay behind her, and she liked it that way. In her mind, an image of Nate slowly congealed. It started with hairy hobbit feet. And a shovel. Then a torso. With no shirt. And--

"Tori?" Nate's voice crackled over the radio.

She ripped the handset from her belt. "Yeah, I'm here."

"Tori?" he said again.

"What?" she said, unable to filter the annoyance from her voice.

"Press the 'Talk' button," he said.

What the... Oh. Well, lookie there!

"Sorry," she said, pressing the button. "Took me a second to get the radio off my belt."

"I'm ready to use the winch. You in position?"

"Almost," she said. "Gimme a second."

She got to her feet and climbed back into the cabin, resting briefly before stationing herself beside the winch. Once she'd caught her breath, she keyed the Talk button. "I'm ready. What now?"

"Keep an eye on the take-up reel. If the guide doesn't wind the cable evenly, stop the winch and see if you can line it up. Got it?"

"Right. Now hurry up, deputy. I'm gettin' lonely."

He didn't laugh into the radio, but he didn't have to. She could imagine it easily enough. Lately, she'd spent a lot of time imagining things she could do *easily enough* with Nate. Things she'd never in a million years discuss with her Mom. Or Cassy. Or, come to think of it, anybody else on Earth.

That's when she realized the guide on the take up reel wasn't working. Though monitoring the guide had been the only task assigned to her, Tori had screwed it up. The guide hadn't been guiding, and Tori hadn't been watching. She stabbed the STOP button.

Almost instantly Nate's voice came over the radio. "Hey! What's up?"

"The guide thingy isn't working," Tori said. "What do

I do now?"

"How badly is the cable tangled?"

"It's not too bad, but it will be if we don't do something."

"Okay," he said. "Let it unwind until the cable is evenly distributed."

She did as instructed then grabbed her radio. "I'm ready to start winding again."

"Be careful," he said. "Especially if you have to guide the spooling by hand."

"Don't worry about me. You're the one who's dangling from a rope over a bottomless pit."

"Thanks for the reminder."

"Here goes!" She restarted the winch which dutifully wound the cable around the spool in a single spot. Tori tugged on the line to force it into position. The alleged "guide" was as useless as bifocals on a bat, and the cable was stretched taut. Nate's muscular body evidently weighed more than it did in Tori's fevered imagination. *There's a shocker!*

Pulling hard in short intervals worked as well as keeping constant tension on the line, and the steady rocking lulled her. Pull -- relax -- pull -- relax -- pull. Soon, she had her whole body in the act. Arms straight, butt extended, pull. Let the recoil of the cable bring her back into position. Repeat.

It took considerable strength to shift the line across the spool, but Tori found herself up to the task. She was handling it! Without her, Nate would have to climb the whole way. Without her--

Sudden excruciating pain drained her of coherent thought. Then she screamed. She'd never felt such agony, even when Shawn had stabbed her. What was going on? Why wasn't Nate doing anything about it? Why did her hand hurt so much?

The question didn't require a long answer. Her hand was pinned against the take up spool as the steel cable coiled around it. Nate's weight on the line put enough pressure on her fingers to completely cut off circulation, assuming it didn't simply cut the digits off all together.

She hit the STOP button with her free hand, then picked up the radio. "Nate!" she yelled. "My hand is stuck in the reel!"

There was silence from the other end. It lasted for an eternity -- possibly two seconds.

"Unwind it," he said simply. And calmly.

"It hurts!"

"I know, baby. I know. And unwinding it is going to hurt, too. But you don't have any choice."

"It hurts, Nate! Oh my God it hurts!"

"Unwind the damn winch, Tori. Do it now!"

"But--"

"Now!"

She unwound it, and discovered Nate was right. Unwinding it hurt, too. A lot. Tori screamed her lungs out, and while the application of audio should have helped, the pain in her hand didn't begin to subside until the last bit of cable crushing it against the spool finally unwound.

"Tori?" Nate called, urgency in his voice.

Tori was breathing deeply between howls. A new rhythm evolved: breathe -- groan -- breathe -- groan.

"Tori! Talk to me!"

"I'm okay," she whimpered.

"We'll get your hand checked out as soon as I get topside. Okay?"

"Okay."

"Turn the winch back on."

"I don't think I can guide the cable."

"I don't care. Let the damn thing bind. When it won't take up any more line, just shut it off. I'll climb the rest of the way."

"Listen, I think I--"

"Please don't argue with me, Tori. Okay? I'll be there as soon as I can."

"All right." A moment later, she said, "What about Shawn?"

"He's not going anywhere. Right now, all I care about is you."

She liked the sound of that.

~*~

Chapter 9

*Never argue with a pig. You'll only frustrate
yourself and annoy the pig.*

After spending the morning with Nate in the cavern
and the afternoon with him in the ER at the hospital in
Worland, Tori still wanted more. Fortunately, the cable
had only given her a row of deep bruises across the
fingers of her left hand. Nate, the ER nurses, and a trio of
doctors had gone on at length about how lucky she was
the abused digits were still attached. They all claimed to
have seen the results of similar accidents where the
outcome was much worse. Her hand would heal without
permanent damage; that was the thing that mattered.
Well, that and the fact that Nate felt so guilty about the
affair, she figured she could talk him into almost anything
without really trying. She called him an hour or so after
he dropped her off at home.

"Nate?" she asked, letting her voice go soft into the
phone.

"Yeah?"

"Wha'cha doin'?"

"Fixing dinner."

"Anything interesting?"

"Salisbury steak, according to the package. It comes
with mashed potatoes, corn, and some sort of dessert.
Chocolate, I think. Looks like brown snot."

"Yum."

"What can I say? I'm a gourmet."

"Oh, really?" she asked. "I'd have thought 'gourmand'
would be more accurate."

"Why?"

"It suggests gluttony."

"Should I be offended?"

"Nah. You're too tough to be offended by a Georgia girl."

"You're hardly a girl."

"I beg your pardon. I'm a full-fledged member of GRITS."

"Whazzat?"

"Girls Raised In The South. Be nice to me, or I'll report you."

"To who?"

"Whom."

"Whatever."

"Whomever. Geez, you're hopeless."

"Tori?"

"Yeah?"

"What the hell do you want? This isn't about the deck idea, is it?"

She paused for a moment, then said, "I'd like to learn how to ride a horse."

"Good for you. Why?"

"'Cause living out here in the wild, wild west kinda demands it. Don't you think?"

There was a short silence from Nate's end of the line. "I think too many people get on horses these days. They'd probably be better off keeping their feet on the ground."

"You say that like you're working for the horse's union."

"They don't have one here, yet. You're thinking of New York or San Francisco. The thing is, there's way too many idiots trying to ride nowadays. They all think they're rodeo studs or something until they get thrown, or stepped on. Then they become abused citizens in search of an attorney who'll help 'em sue somebody. I have no desire to become a part of that nonsense."

"Me, either."

"Good. Stick to your car."

"Truck."

"Whatever."

"So, how do I get where my truck won't go?"

"I dunno. Walk?"

Tori exhaled loudly. She was in the early stages of frustration and hadn't anticipated Nate's reluctance. What the hell was wrong with him that he wouldn't want to take her out on a trail ride in the big empty? She'd gladly put stars in her eyes if it'd help bring him around. "I want to trace the route my great uncle took when he tried to return Reyna's grandmother to her people."

This time there was a prolonged silence before Nate responded. "I have no freakin' idea what you're talking about."

"My great uncle knew Reyna's grandmother. Or great-grandmother. Sorta. Mato's people don't really concern themselves with generational issues. Or actual family ties, for that matter. Anyone who grows old becomes a grandparent to the entire clan."

"That's convenient."

"Not for genealogists."

"Pity."

"No shit. Anyway, I've talked to Mato about trying to retrace the steps my great uncle--"

"Uncle Bob?"

"Right. Maybe, if we get really, really lucky, we can find out what happened to him."

"He died."

"That's what Mato said. And pretty much the way he said it. Maybe you should forget what I said about becoming friends."

"Tori, do you have any idea how large Wyoming is?"

151

"Actually, I do."

"And what, exactly, do you hope to accomplish by riding across it?"

"I'd like to know what happened to Uncle Bob. Sure, he's dead. We all know that. But, what happened? How did he die? How close did he get to returning Sleeping Dove to her people?" *C'mon, Nate, help me out here!*

"You know there's almost no chance we'll find anything."

"I'm aware of that. But Mato seems to know where to look. Maybe we'll find a cave or the remains of a sod hut or a cabin or--"

"Have you always been such a dreamer?"

She smiled. He *was* coming around. "Pretty much, yeah."

"Have you ever ridden a horse before?"

"Once. When I was a little kid. Does that count?"

"It depends. Did you enjoy it?"

"I dunno. It was a thousand years ago, at a birthday party. I probably did enjoy it, unless I had to go pee or something and got distracted."

"Before we do any long rides, I want to take you for a short trip and see how you do."

"Sounds good to me. Want me to bring Mato, too?"

"Can't say I'm crazy about the idea."

"I thought y'all were on good terms."

"We are, and I'd like to keep it that way."

"He's going with us when we eventually hit the trail of uncle Bob."

"I'm okay with that," Nate said. "I just don't want to take you out for an extended ride until I know you can handle a horse."

"Will that take very long?"

"That's up to you," he said. "For all I know, it could

take forever."

She ignored the slight. "When can we start?"

"Good Lord," Nate said. "What's the hurry?"

"I'm just eager to learn. And it'd give me a chance to spend a little more time with you. Would that be so awful?" She wished she could bat her eyelids at him over the phone though she suspected he'd be immune. But then, cornball played pretty well out here in the boonies.

"Is tomorrow afternoon too soon?" he asked. "I'm pulling a half shift in the morning, but I'm off the rest of the day."

Evidently, cornball went over extremely *well in the boonies.*

"No, wait. That won't work. Your hand--"

"Will be fine. As long as you help me up on the horse and promise not to make me gallop into the sunset, I'll be okay."

"You sure? That damned winch--"

"Tomorrow afternoon would be wonderful," she said, trying to melt into her cell phone.

"Okay, I guess. I can load the horses in the trailer and be out there by three or so. Only...."

Uh oh. "What?"

"I'd prefer to think I'm not being conned. What's the real reason you're in such a hurry?"

That her attempt at phone seduction failed didn't come as a great surprise. Mostly, she figured, for lack of practice. Under such uncompromising circumstances, she opted for the truth. "I need this for the book, and because I'm worried that Mato won't be around much longer."

"Oh man. I had no idea he was even sick."

"He's not. But he might be heading home soon. With Reyna. I think she's pregnant, though that's not surprising."

"It's not?"

"Obviously, you haven't spent much time around them. They're both horny enough to sprout antlers. And neither has ever heard of safe sex. Or quiet, secluded sex, for that matter."

He chuckled. "How... interesting."

"Only for a while," she said, archly.

"She looked pretty trim when I saw her. And as for birth control, maybe they're using their own methods. What makes you think she's pregnant?"

"She can't keep her breakfast down, for one thing. And when she's not barfing, she walks around humming. And smiling. She's doing embroidery for God's sake. Talk about teeny stitches!"

"So? She sounds like a happy person."

"A happy *pregnant* person."

"Then we should be happy, too. Right?"

"Right," Tori said, sounding far more cheerful than she felt.

~*~

After breakfast Caleb drove his new van -- using the full set of normal controls -- to the parking area beside the big rock which Tori used as a base for her hibachi grill. She stuck her head out the door when she heard him drive in.

"Cal! What a nice surprise. What brings you all the way out here?" She paused to look at the minivan. "I thought you said you were gonna get something practical. Are you and Maggie starting a family?"

"A family? Good God, no. Besides, this *is* practical, and economical. I inherited it." He waved her over, leaving the driver's door wide open. That's when he noticed the bandage wrapped around Tori's hand. "What's that all about?"

"Long story. The gist of it is that I hurt my hand trying to help Nate pull my ex-husband's body out of the cavern. He had to finish the job by himself."

Caleb examined the bandage. "Looks bad."

"Everybody tells me it could've been worse. For now, it just makes it really hard to type." She smiled. "So, what've you got here, a camper?"

"It's way more than that," he said. "Come over here. You've gotta see this."

Tori wandered closer and inspected the linkages mounted beneath the vehicle's steering column. "What is it?"

"Hand controls!"

She looked at him in sudden alarm. "What's wrong? Why do you need hand controls?"

He laughed. "I don't. My aunt did. Anyway, I saw this arrangement, and I couldn't help but think of our boy, Mato."

"I'm not following you," Tori said. "What does this have to do with..." Her eyes went wide. "Cal, you weren't seriously thinking of letting Mato use this, were you?"

"What could it hurt?"

"*Him,* for starters! He doesn't know anything about cars."

"I thought this might be a great way to help him learn. We could drive around out here, where there's no traffic, and he could see that it's just a machine."

"It's a huge machine! He needs to master small ones first, like a coffee pot or a pencil sharpener."

"I thought he didn't like coffee."

"That's beside the point. He could get killed trying to drive this monster. I'm not sure *I'd* want to, especially using hand controls."

Caleb pushed his straw Stetson to the back of his

balding head. "Mato's size is going to make things very difficult for him in our world. He's liable to feel powerless. But he's big enough to use the hand controls on the van. I think teaching him how to drive would help restore his masculinity."

She reacted as if he'd just broken wind during confession. "Mato doesn't need any help with his masculinity, believe me. He and Reyna have been--" She cleared her throat. "Let's just say those two have put the entire bunny rabbit population of the western states to shame."

Caleb chuckled.

"What's so funny?"

"I never thought you'd be such a prude."

"I'm not a prude!" She wrinkled her nose at him. "It's just... They never stop!"

"They have to eat sometimes, don't they? And sleep?"

"Okay, maybe it only seems like they never stop. But, oh my Lord-- And loud? Gasping and groaning. My house sounds like one of those sleazy places where they show porno movies all day."

"No kidding? Can I come in?"

Tori gave him a light shove. "What would Maggie say?"

He shook his head. "An interesting question. Maggie's more into...."

Tori put her hands over her ears and chanted, "Nah-nah-nah-nah-nah. You're talking, but I can't hear you, 'cause I'm going nah-nah-nah-nah-nah."

Caleb smiled. In silence.

"There's *some* information decent folks don't share," she said after lowering her hands to her sides. "What you and Maggie do in the bedroom--"

"Isn't something I'd tell you about," Cal said.

"Good! And I hope it's not because you think I'm a prude."

"Certainly not." He paused, debating whether or not to go on.

"What?"

"Maggie said you were acting sorta like Mato's mother. I think she's right."

"That depends on whether or not she meant it in a nice way." Tori fisted her hands on her hips.

Caleb sucked briefly on his lower lip, then went on. "She meant it in a realistic way. Me? I'm thinking you're trying to shelter him. Them, I mean."

"Have you talked to Nate lately? Did he tell you about Mato helping him arrest some nut jobs throwing bombs into a lake up in the hills?"

"You're kidding!"

"Wish I were. While I was so carefully 'mothering' little Mato, he jumped in Nate's truck and went off hunting bad guys with him. Seems one of 'em pulled a shotgun on deputy sheriff Sheffield, but Mato took him out with a blowgun dart dipped in G'nite juice."

"What kinda juice?"

"G'nite. One drop in your bloodstream, and it's good night."

"Ah. Did any of the bad guys see him?"

"Nope. He had all three of 'em out cold before Nate could do a thing." She crossed her arms over her chest. "I'm not worried about Mato; he can look after himself. But Reyna's a different story."

"She needs someone to watch over her?"

"I guess. I don't really know. We don't talk to each other directly very much. It's mostly through Mato. She hasn't gone out of her way to learn English."

"Unlike the pains you've taken to learn her language?"

157

Tori smiled sheepishly. "Yeah, okay. Point taken."

Caleb patted the hood of the van. "Why don't we ask Mato? If he wants to learn how to drive, I'll be happy to show him."

"Hmm. Not that it matters right now. He's not here."

"I thought he was inside. With Reyna. You know...."

"Oddly enough, no. He left before breakfast. Very unusual for him. Didn't say what he was up to, but he had an old army backpack he found somewhere. Probably from World War I. We're talking really old. And small. He's been loading stuff into it. I have no idea what."

Caleb sighed. "Okay then. Maybe next time."

Tori kissed him on the cheek. "It's always good to see you, Cal. But maybe you should call first before you drive out all this way."

~*~

The flight to Billings, Montana, had been a pain, but at least it was over. Mort appeared reasonably refreshed and ready to go. Tessa had traveled in first class while he had a three-seat row in coach to himself. And, while Mort had slept most of the way, Tessa was forced to fend off the advances of a self-proclaimed cattle baron with more money than tact. When she and Mort finally met at baggage claim, she was the wearier of the two.

"If you'll get the bags, I'll get the car," she said.

"I didn't check anything," Mort said. "I put everything in a carry-on."

"Good for you," Tessa said, wondering what was wrong with him. It wasn't like they were going for an overnight, though she prayed they could get the job done in a day. But she was smarter than that. She planned for contingencies, like cold weather, unscheduled stopovers, and the occasional sucking chest wound. "Then, just get my bag, all right?"

"What's it look like?"

"It's pink."

"I probably should have known that."

"I'll pick you up out front as soon as I've got the car."

Tessa would have preferred to rent the car anonymously, but she lacked the time and connections needed to get fake identification. Instead, she charged the vehicle to Bernstein Labs and took advantage of all the extras, minus ski rack and baby seat. Jerry could easily afford giving her some peace of mind.

"Want me to drive?" Mort asked after he filled the trunk with her enormous pink valise. He wedged his carry-on beside it and lowered the lid.

"No," she said, revving the engine.

Mort piled in, and Tessa left the curb without squealing the tires, much as she'd have liked to. The rental didn't hold a candle to Jerry's aberrantly luxurious Mercedes, but it would do. It was dark blue and made by General Motors. *Yawn.* Just the thing for a bureaucrat, even a faux bureaucrat.

"See if you can find a place called Ten Sleep, Wyoming, on the GPS."

Mort set about the task. Tessa hated reading through instruction manuals or, for that matter, figuring out how anything electronic worked. Perhaps if the documentation was written by career women with the communication skills of native English speakers it would be different. The last time she'd struggled with such instructions they came with a clock radio assembled somewhere in the Pacific rim by people who may have heard of the English language, but certainly weren't conversant with it. The clock and the alleged instructions both ended up in the trash.

Josh Langston

"Got it," Mort said.
"That quick?"
"Easy peasy."
Asshole.

Mort grinned at her, which she found disturbing.
"So," he asked, "we're goin' to Ten Sleep?"

"Yes." The man's perception skills were off the chart.
"How far is it?"

"Depends on the route. Do you prefer interstate
highways, or the usual garden variety with towns and
stop signs? Either way it's going to take three to four
hours."

"I want to get in and out as quickly as possible."
"No time for scenery?"
"None."

"Then stay on this road." He punched a few buttons
and set the GPS on the dashboard. "It'll tell you where
and when to turn." He let the back of his seat slide into a
reclining position. "You sure you don't want me to
drive?"

"Quite."
"Wanna stop somewhere for coffee or something?"
"No."

"Oh my. I know someone who's taken their moody
pills for the day. I thought you'd be feelin' pretty good
after sitting in first class. You got breakfast, right? All we
got in coach was coffee and a snack. Some kinda cookie
thing. I asked for peanuts, but they don't serve them
anymore."

She glanced at him briefly before focusing once
again on the road. "I had to sit next to a jerk who
wouldn't stop talking."

"I hate when that happens. I had to fly to California
one time, it was way before I started working for

160

Bernstein Labs. In fact, I was just outta college. Maybe a
year or two later. Or maybe it was... I dunno. I forget.
Anyway, this--"
  "Mort?"
  "Yeah?"
  "Shut up."

~*~

  Nate drove up to the cabin right on schedule. The
horse trailer behind his big Ford pickup barely made the
turn around the barbecue boulder. The combination of
truck and trailer kicked up enough dust to satisfy the most
discriminating fan of sand storms. Tori and Mato, who
had returned about lunchtime, were content to stay inside
until the tan cloud settled on the ground.
  Meanwhile, Nate backed two horses out of the trailer:
a magnificent gray mare and a smaller, but still handsome
brown gelding. The mare had a tendency to prance. The
smaller horse merely shuffled wherever Nate pushed him.
  Tori watched with admiration as he swapped halters
for bridles and tossed a blanket over the gelding's withers.
He followed it with a western saddle, cinching it firmly.
  Tori had been somewhat less than truthful about her
riding history. As a teen she'd gone through the all-but-
mandatory horse phase so many young girls experienced.
She had even managed to save up enough babysitting
money to pay for a few riding lessons, complete with
English saddle, riding crop, and dressage helmet. The
lessons came to an end about the time she discovered that
teenaged boys were willing to pay for her company at
movies, burger joints, and school dances. The allure of
the riding world faded. The notion to re-trace uncle Bob's
final journey had resulted in a newfound horse sense,
albeit not the usual based-on-reality kind that Nate

undoubtedly favored.

"You ready to go?" he asked. "Mato can ride with me."

"Where are we going?"

"Nowhere in particular," he said, gesturing down the driveway. "I thought we'd just ride toward the main road and back." He wiped his neck with a handkerchief, then stuffed it in a pocket of his faded jeans. Tori tried to think of the last time she'd ever seen anyone actually use a handkerchief, but it wasn't easy since her thoughts kept centering on the backside pocket where he'd stored it.

"I'm ready," she said.

They both turned at the sound of an approaching vehicle.

"Anybody you know?" Nate asked.

Tori shook her head. "But, I confess, I was a little late returning my census form."

"Great. Not only are you anti-social, you're unrepentant. They'll probably stick you in a cell with the Unabomber."

"It gets worse. I didn't mention my roommates, the sex pistols."

"Flopsy, Mopsy, and Cottonballs?"

She looked at him with an even deeper appreciation than before.

~*~

Getting to Tori Lanier's insanely remote cabin had taken less time than Tessa imagined, thanks entirely to the GPS unit she'd rented along with the car. The only problem they encountered was when they missed a turn. They had passed through the "town" of Charm without recognizing it. Thankfully, the GPS was unfazed by such distinctions as missing buildings and/or an accompanying population.

Tessa had no idea towns could be so small. Single digit population signs just felt wrong somehow. Civilization demanded greater numbers, or at least, Tessa's version did.

The driveway had been treacherous, and the car had bottomed out at least a dozen times. There seemed to be a dust cloud preceding as well as following them, which made no sense at all. But then, this was Wyoming, and everything about it was an unknown.

She and Lund had passed through some mountains on their journey south, which had certainly made for pretty scenery. And, Tessa thought, the fact that most of it was green and leafy screamed "normal" to her. Victoria Lanier's property, on the other hand, was mostly beige, the vegetation scraggly and stunted. Mort said it was sagebrush. She had no idea if he knew what he was talking about. All she knew was that it appeared dead and dried up, just like the land all around her.

True, there were mountains in the distance, and the sky was a deep, brilliant blue that reminded her of a tropical ocean. The ground, however, seemed to have sucked the moisture out of everything.

"How much farther is it?" she asked for the tenth time.

"According to the GPS, we passed it."

"Passed what? We haven't seen anything!"

"I suspect the coordinates are based on the address. The number corresponds with where the driveway meets the road. It doesn't correspond to the actual location of a building. It's very literal. Think of it as programmer humor."

"There's no such thing," she growled, but kept driving. It couldn't be that much farther. "Okay, you understand your job, right?"

Lund nodded, just as he had every other time she'd grilled him on the upcoming charade.

"I do the talking. All you have to do is follow my lead. Don't contradict me. Don't make conversation."

"So, I'm like what -- a mute?"

"Yeah! That's it. You're mute." She pretended to thumb the mute button on a TV remote control, but she doubted he got the idea. The mute button was a fabulous invention. Maybe Bernstein Labs could build one that worked on people.

"Shouldn't we be wearing name tags or something? Badges? What if she asks for ID?"

"We're supposed to be from the health department, not the FBI. The woman lives alone. She'll go along. I have a talent for persuasion, remember? That's my job."

Lund didn't respond, though it was obvious he wanted to.

Tessa concentrated on the collection of ruts and cross ruts constituting Victoria Lanier's drive. One section in particular tested her nerves as it seemed to sprout huge rocks where other roads merely coughed up litter or roadkill. Seeing the steep embankment down which those boulders had traveled was unsettling. It made her feel like a bowling pin. The bowling alley, or driveway, was easily the most outrageously misnamed stretch of dirt Tessa had ever encountered. *Positively third world. And this is where an author lives? God save us.*

The cabin appeared in the distance. It sat off center near the middle of a wide bluff overlooking an extensive valley of scrub, sand, and dirt. All browns and tans, like uniforms for the Third Reich. *Charming.* Tessa suspected the nearby town's name came from someone's sense of humor.

"Remember, we're--"

"Public health pukes," Lund said.

"Be nice."

"And quiet."

"Especially quiet."

Beside the cabin stood two adults, a very small child, and two horses. Tessa couldn't take her eyes of the beasts. She and Lund had seen hundreds of them en route to Lanier's little corner of hell, but they hadn't gotten close to any. That was about to change.

"I thought you said she'd be alone," Lund said.

"I thought she would be."

"Great."

"Let me do the talking."

"Be my guest."

They pulled to a stop far short of the horses. During their approach the child disappeared, not that Tessa cared beyond a deep-brained acknowledgment of his/her existence -- an additional random smidgeon of data.

"Out," Tessa commanded. She opened her door, exited, and smiled pleasantly at the female member of the remaining duo. "Good afternoon. We're from the health department."

"Really?" asked the male, who looked as if he'd just stepped out of a Marlboro ad. *Cowboy hat. Jeans. Boots, for God's sake.* She wanted to drag him into the back of the rental car and screw him until they either sent out for food or starved to death. *That's a real man, Mort, you weenie!* Instead, she merely nodded in his direction and concentrated on the woman. "I'm looking for Victoria Lanier." She smiled again. "Is that you?"

"It is," she said.

"Excellent." Tessa held out her hand which the woman accepted in a business-like fashion. "We're here because of recent reports of an outbreak of brucellosis.

Are you familiar with the issue?"

"No," the woman said, clearly puzzled.

"I am," the Marlboro man said. He wasn't smiling.

Crap. "Well, without going into a long, drawn out explanation, we have reason to believe there may be an outbreak in the offing. We're concerned about people living in remote areas who may have been compromised without knowing it."

"You say you're from the *County* Health Department?" the Marlboro man asked.

"*State* Health Department," Tessa said, trusting her ability to fabricate the truth as easily as this yokel might be able to verify it.

"Oh, right," he said.

"We'd like to get a sample of your blood," Tessa went on, smiling at Lanier with the most winsome expression she could muster.

"Why?" the woman asked.

"To see if you've been infected."

"How could she have been infected?" asked the cowboy. "She's never been near cattle."

"We're talking about bison."

"She's never been near a bison, have you, Tori?"

The woman appeared completely baffled. "You mean buffalo?"

"Yes," Tessa said, possibly too quickly.

Lanier looked at the Marlboro man. She was clearly still confused. "Buffalo?"

"Big, shaggy beasts," Lund said.

Tessa tried to silence him with a glare. It didn't work.

"We have reason to believe there's been some cross-contamination between cattle and bison herds," he said. "That's at the heart of the problem. We realize the risk of human contamination is small, but--"

"Do you have any identification?" The Marlboro man made the question sound very official.

"Who wants to know?" Lund asked.

"I do," the man said. "I'm Nathan Sheffield, deputy sheriff of Washakie county, and I haven't heard anything about a supposed brucellosis outbreak. At least, not this far from Yellowstone. So, unless you've got something pretty damned official-looking to back up this nonsense about blood samples, I might have to haul you back to the station until we can get it all straightened out."

"This is outrageous," Tessa exclaimed. "I've never been treated this way in my life."

"Sucks, doesn't it?" the deputy said. "Now, about that ID...."

Lund was slapping his pockets as if they were full of insects. "I, uh... I don't think--"

"We don't carry badges, deputy, as you should know. But then, I see you aren't wearing one either."

"I'm off duty. Are you?"

"Of course not. However, I admit failing to bring proper documentation. I apologize for that. It was an oversight, nothing more."

"Then I suggest you go round up your documentation and bring it with you when you come back. For now, you don't get the time of day, much less a blood sample."

Tessa fixed him with her frostiest stare. "What'd you say your name was?"

"Nathan Sheffield. With two F's."

Tessa told Lund to make a note of it. "You'll be hearing from the director about this."

"I'd like that."

She pushed Lund toward the car and handed him the keys. She raised her voice and said, "All we ever hear about is inter-agency cooperation, and this is what we get."

"Yeah," Lund said, somewhat less than convincingly.

Once they were safely in the car she hissed, "Go! Now, damn it."

Lund slammed the shift lever into reverse and gunned the engine. The car responded instantly, throwing Tessa toward the dashboard.

"Geez," she cried. "Take it easy, will ya?"

"Sorry." He shifted into drive and raced away from the cabin. "What're we gonna do now?"

"I dunno. I'll think of something."

"Like what?"

"I said I'd think of something, and I will." But the question kept playing over and over in her head, and she had no idea how to answer it.

~*~

Chapter 10

Torvald raced on, over hills, through shrubs and around
boulders, mindless of obstacles and confident that
20,000 lemmings couldn't possibly be wrong.

Tori reached for Nate's hand. The two of them
watched the gray car pull away, bouncing and grinding its
way down the hardscrabble escape route to the main road.
"That was just... odd."

"My thoughts exactly," he said.

"What's up with the brucellosis thing?"

"Nothing's up, that's what. It's nonsense." Nate
reached into the cab of his truck and grabbed a
microphone, pulling it close to his mouth as he spoke.
"Dee? You copy? It's Nate."

A moment later the radio came to life. "I know," said
a bored female. "I thought you were takin' the afternoon
off for something personal. Too busy to spend time with
my grandson as I recall."

"I'll take him for a ride tomorrow," Nate said. "I told
you that."

"Oh. Yeah. Now I remember. Tomorrow. So, how is
what's-her-name?"

"Her name is Tori Lanier, and she's fine. But we're
wondering why the state health department might have
sent someone out to see her."

"State health department?"

"Yeah."

"Didn't know we had one."

"I'm sure we do, Dee, but I don't think they use field
agents. At least, I've never heard of one. And yet, two of
'em showed up out here. They were talkin' about some

kind of brucellosis outbreak. You heard anything about that?"

"Sometimes the ranchers get fired up about it, but far as I know it's just hot air. Politics."

Nate nodded at Tori. "Thanks, Dee. That's what I thought, too. If you hear anything new or different, let me know."

"Depends."

"Huh? Depends on what?"

"On how far you and Marty ride."

"C'mon, Dee! I've never even seen the kid. Can he stay in the saddle?"

"'Course he can 'stay in the saddle.' You think I'd let him do anything risky?"

"You know him. I don't."

"He's tough enough to go for a ride."

A smile tugged up the corners of Nate's mouth. "Then, I'll take him for the ride of his life."

"Fine. He needs to be challenged from time to time. It'll be good for him."

"A challenge? What kinda challenge?"

"I'll leave that up to you."

"Great," Nate said, his gaze drifting skyward. "That's just what I need."

"Glad to hear it," Dee said. "Base out."

Nate put the microphone back in his truck as Mato walked out of the cabin dressed in shorts and a T-shirt he had expropriated from Lance. Though the little Indian had no use for the doll, he had grown increasingly fond of his wardrobe and was rapidly becoming a typical American. Only shorter, and more crudely armed. He still carried a knife with an obsidian blade.

Tori was glad Mato hadn't made a big deal out of the bandage on her hand. But, other than give it a cursory examination, he'd ignored it. Reyna's response showed a little more concern until Tori wiggled her injured fingers, then Reyna's interest faded.

"Are you sure you're okay to ride?" Nate asked. "We can put this off 'til your hand's better."

"I'm good. Really."

"Suit yourself. We'll head for the paved road, but if you want to turn around before we get there, just say the word." He looked at Mato. "You're ridin' up here with me, little man," he leaned down and offered his hand.

Tori felt certain she'd seen a glint in Mato's eye just before he leaped from the ground. Going almost straight in the air, he stepped briefly on Nate's booted foot and continued his vertical rise as if gravity had no effect on him. He came to rest standing on the horse's rump, behind Nate with his hands on the lawman's shoulders. Nate twisted in the saddle, and the two were able to look each other eyeball-to-eyeball. Mato grinned. Nate didn't.

"He and Reyna have done more riding than I have," Tori said.

Nate's frown didn't change, though he shifted slightly to face her.

"On Shadow," she explained. "Bareback. It's cute."

"Cute?"

"Yeah."

"Monkeys riding poodles in the circus is cute. Out here--"

"Oh, lighten up. Until one of us get our hands on a pony small enough for them, the dog is just about their only option."

He sniffed in response, but she could tell he was trying not to smile. Reaching backwards with remarkable agility, Nate swept Mato up in one arm and deposited him on the horse's back, about where the saddle horn would have been if Nate had been using a saddle. Mato clearly wasn't happy about the relocation, but Nate wouldn't budge on the issue. "You ride here for now. Later, when I know you won't fall and crack your head open, I might -- repeat, *might* -- let you stand behind me."

Tori had been working on a pithy comment involving seat belts when Nate made a clicking noise which his horse interpreted as a shift into Drive. Grabbing the horn on her own saddle, she slipped her left foot in the stirrup and swung up into the saddle. It wasn't graceful, by any definition, but she'd completed the maneuver entirely on her on. That should have counted for something.

"Wait up," she said as Nate sauntered down the drive, the tail of his big gray horse sweeping majestically from side to side. Tori's horse remained immobile.

"You might have to nudge him a little," Nate said over his shoulder, not bothering to look back.

"A nudge?"

"With your heel."

Ah. Tori tapped once lightly, but the horse still didn't move. She tapped again and got the same result. *Okay, horse. Now you're pissin' me off.* She whacked him hard in the ribs with both heels and the animal moved off smartly, in the wrong direction.

"Damn it!" she yelled. "He's not cooperating."

Nate had come to a halt, watching casually as Tori struggled. "C'mon. Show him who's boss."

"I thought you were!"

"Doesn't work that way," he said. "If he thinks you don't know what you're doing, he'll assume you won't care where you go. He's probably trying to figure out how to get home."

"What do I do?"

"Try using the reins."

"You're a big help."

172

"I'm on the horse's side, remember?"

~*~

The only thing worse than driving to the Lanier
woman's house, was trying to drive away from it.
Quickly. Lund ignored most of the ruts and concentrated
on avoiding the boulders littering the way. Tessa
tightened her seat belt. She had one hand on the
dashboard and the other wrapped around the grip above
her door.

"They aren't chasing us, for God's sake," she shouted
at Lund.

"You told me to go fast. This is fast."

"It's too damned fast. Slow down!"

Lund swerved to avoid a microwave-sized rock Tessa
didn't recall seeing on the way in. She forced herself to sit
back. *Think, damn it!* "Are you sure this is the same road
we took going in?"

"Absolutely. Only one way in; only one way out."

"You're sure?"

He looked at her as if a tentacle or some other
random appendage had sprung from her forehead. "Yeah.
I'm sure."

"Watch the road."

"I am. But maybe I should be watching you instead.
What's your problem?"

Tessa's jaws had begun to ache. She forced herself to
unclench them. Their proximity to the steep canyon wall
had grown even more unnerving on the way out than it
had driving in. And for good reason. While she watched,
a boulder the size of an engine block came unglued from
the earthen wall above and in front of them.

"Oh, my God!" she shouted.

Lund, his eyes locked on the rubble-strewn road,

173

gripped the wheel tighter. "What?"

"Stop!" She couldn't take her eyes of the huge stone as it gained speed. "Stop the damned car!"

In the split second it took Lund to jam on the brakes, Tessa realized the boulder was headed right at them. "No!" she screamed. "Go back, go back!"

Lund turned toward her angrily, his frustration having reached the boiling point. Then, he too saw the boulder. With nowhere to go to the left or right, backing up was his only option. Throwing the shift lever into reverse, he stomped the accelerator.

The boulder bounced crazily as it picked up speed, but continued in their direction. Lund kept going. The boulder bounced again, as if it were driven by some sort of wrathful homing device.

Tessa planted both feet on the floorboard and locked her knees. She crossed her arms in front of her head.

"Aw shit," Lund said, just before the boulder smashed into the car, and the air bags deployed. Tessa's world went dark.

~*~

"Does this animal have a name?" Tori asked. She had finally achieved some level of control over the horse, though she had no illusions about how tenuous that control was. Nate had waited until she pulled even with him in the driveway. Mato seemed oddly unconcerned about her horse handling issues, which attitude Tori assumed he had picked up from Nate.

"Elmer."

"The horse's name is *Elmer?*"

"Yeah."

"Elmer."

174

"What were you hoping for? Widowmaker?"

"It just seems like an odd name for a horse. Does he like to chase after 'wascally wabbits'?" She glanced at Mato who was studiously ignoring them both.

Nate remained silent.

"So," she said, "what's your horse's name? Bugs? Daffy?"

"The name on her papers is Miss Manners." He patted the big gray's neck. "I call her Babe."

"Oh. Well, that's... nice."

The afternoon sun beat down on them, but the low humidity made it bearable. Tori wore a cheap straw cowboy hat she'd purchased at a gas station somewhere. It was every bit as plain as Nate's, but lacked, she felt sure, the kind of character under it that made Nate's look appropriate. If nothing else, it kept a bit of shade on her face, and she could always use it to fan herself. Mato was bare-headed, and happy that way.

"Have you got a gun," she asked after they'd been riding for about twenty minutes.

"With me?"

"Yeah."

"No," he said. Then added, "I figured I could trust you."

"What if we run into a rattlesnake or something?"

He squinted at her from under his hat. "All God's creatures have a place in the world."

"How 'bout flies?"

"Except flies," he said. "And politicians. Though, now that I think about it, they're pretty much one and the same."

Tori was going to ask about state health workers as they rounded a curve in the drive that hugged a steep bank. The dark blue sedan with the undocumented bureaucrats sat unmoving in the drive. The passenger side door was open, but from where they stood it was impossible to see any movement inside the vehicle.

"That doesn't look good," Tori said.

Nate lifted Mato and swung him over toward her. "Take him."

Tori reached out, but Mato, who had his feet on the top of Nate's leg, pushed off and jumped between the two horses. He came to rest lightly on Elmer's rump and gripped the back of Tori's shirt in both hands.

Nate kicked Babe into a run and spent about as much time slowing her down as he had getting her up to speed. He dismounted before she came to a stop and approached the open door in a swirl of dust and controlled mayhem.

Tori kicked Elmer with both heels, but he refused to respond with anything more than a spine-mangling trot. Mato didn't seem to mind, and something from one of her few riding lessons came back to her. She hadn't ridden long enough to master the art of posting, but she remembered enough about the technique to ward off the worst of the jolts Elmer delivered.

"They're both unconscious but alive," Nate said when she reached him. Mato dismounted gracefully. *Show off.* Tori was content to reach the ground without embarrassing herself.

"I don't have a first aid kit," he said. "Not that I think it would do much good. The woman doesn't have any open wounds that I could see, but the guy behind the wheel is a mess. Looks like the air bag saved him from the initial impact, but then the boulder rolled up over the hood and smashed through the windshield. "I doubt he's going to make it."

"What're we going to do?" Tori asked. She'd always felt pretty sure of herself when things in her life went sideways, but in this case, she was damned glad Nate was

176

with her.

"You stay with 'em in case they wake up," he said as he threw himself across Babe's back, then shifted easily into a sitting position. "I'm going back to the truck and radio for help. I won't be long." With that, he touched his heels to Babe's flanks, and they took off as if spring loaded. How he hung on was a mystery.

She approached the driver side door which Nate had forced open. Mato focused his attention on the woman, his actions positively clinical. He lifted her eyelids and stared at her pupils, then put his ear to her chest. He looked at Tori past the horribly bloodied face of the driver. "She live," he said.

She was no expert in medicine, but the prognosis Mato offered sounded good. Moving her hand to the shoulder of the driver, she asked, "How 'bout him?"

Mato clambered over the woman and repeated much of what he'd done to her on the man. In the process, he managed to cover himself in a great deal of the driver's blood. The sight might have been terrifying if taken out of context, and Tori was glad no one else was there to observe him.

"Tori," Mato said, his voice calm, "you want him live?"

"Yes," she said without a second thought. The poor guy might have annoyed her that morning, but the offense didn't rise to the level of capital punishment. Besides, having to work with the woman in the passenger seat would give anyone a bad outlook.

Mato remained grim as he reached for the stone knife at his belt. Tori wondered briefly if she should ask him to wait until Nate came back, then reasoned that a delay was no good for anyone, most especially for the clown behind the wheel.

It wouldn't have mattered; Mato was way ahead of

her. Having taken her response as his cue to begin, he wasted no time making the incisions which would allow him to transfer some of his blood to the driver. Tori hoped they hadn't arrived too late.

~*~

Nate's voice must have carried enough urgency to cut through Dee's usual chattiness. She said nothing while he explained the situation.

"The chopper won't be available for some time," she said. "There was a wreck up near Hyattville. Sport utility vehicle versus cattle truck. Nobody won. Including the beef. They'll probably need to make two trips to haul everybody out."

"Then how 'bout sending an ambulance?"

"Stand by," she said, then came back on the air a few moments later. "Okay, the ambulance is rolling. Wish I could do more."

"You might try praying. One of these two probably won't make it."

Dee paused momentarily before going on. "You know 'em?"

"No. They were posing as state health investigators."

"Ah. That's why you called before."

"Yep. I'll get their IDs when I go back. I'll need you to run 'em."

"No problem. Nate, they aren't dangerous, are they?"

He chuckled. "They didn't look it. Not even *before* they got the crap knocked out of 'em."

"It never hurts to be careful," she said.

~*~

Tessa felt pressure on her chest. Someone was talking. It wasn't Lund.

She opened one eye just enough to let in some light, maybe assess the situation before she admitted to being awake. Her head hurt like the mother of all hangovers, but she knew she hadn't been drinking. Mort Lund had been driving, like a complete idiot, when-- The boulder. *Holy crap!* She almost gave herself away. The pressure on her chest eased to nothing.

Through one squinted eye she watched a child crawl from her lap to the console between the front seats. Who let a kid into the car? And what was he doing to Lund?

There had been two voices. Both female. *No, wait. The kid's a male. What the hell is he doing? He has a knife!*

The temptation to open both eyes and cry out was almost more than she could bear. But something convinced her to maintain the pretense of being unconscious. She recognized the Lanier woman standing beside the driver's door, looking in. Shifting her attention from the woman to the child she came to another shocking realization. The kid was no kid. He was a young man. But he was the smallest fully grown human she'd ever seen. Had they crashed into some sort of freak show?

She watched as the little guy made careful incisions in both Mort's wrist and his own. When he cut himself he didn't even flinch. *And he was using a stone knife! What the hell?* The little man then pressed their wrists together and kept the pressure on. He said something to Lanier, but she wasn't sure what it was. His English was terrible, the accent heavy and hard to decipher.

She had no idea where he might be from. His complexion was dark, but that meant almost nothing. Various nationalities all over the world had varying skin

179

tones. His accent was likewise of no help. For all she knew, he might hail from New York.

That gave her a jolt. New York! It wasn't Lanier who'd given Cassy Woodall the life-saving transfusion. It was this little guy. *This guy right in front of her!* Lanier must have smuggled him into the hospital. Of course! She gave her forehead a mental slap. They'd been after the wrong damned target. She didn't need Lanier's blood -- she needed to tap the midget's supply. *How much blood did he even have? No, wait! It doesn't matter.* Blood is a *renewable* resource! He'd have plenty. He'd have to. There was no way she'd let anyone drain her golden goose.

But now what? How was she going to talk her way out of this wreck, or the lies they told about working for the state of Wyoming? And, she wondered as she looked at the bloody mess slumped beside her, what was she supposed to do with Lund?

As she tried to get a handle on those questions, a new one arose. Where was the deputy sheriff who had been with Lanier when they drove up? Surely he was aware of the crash even if he had no idea what they were up to.

Think, Tessa. Think! The internal command was a familiar one, though the occasions she'd used it had never been quite so dire. You're the one who's always prepared. You're the one who thinks through all the options before you leave home.

C'mon, Tessa. Think!

~*~

Where the hell was Nate, Tori wondered. How long did it take to call for an ambulance? Mato had wasted no time doing his thing for the phony health department guy.

The woman hadn't moved. Nate had said she was okay, but Tori wasn't so sure even though the boulder had smashed through the driver's side of the windshield and not the passenger's. The airbag on her side had done its job, otherwise she'd be just as bloody as the guy behind the wheel.

Tori wandered around the car to the passenger side. The door was still open, so she reached in and tried to feel for a pulse. The woman's wrist was thin, her hand dainty. *Probably wears a size nada.* She wondered if women's sizes would someday hit negative numbers. Tori had no fears she'd ever have to try any on.

When the woman groaned, Tori touched Mato on the shoulder. "Time to go," she said.

Mato nodded. He pulled off his T-shirt, tore it into strips and wrapped the longest around the incision in the driver's wrist. The rest of the shirt he shoved into a pocket.

She wanted to tell him not to -- that tiny shirts like his had to be made by hand; they really didn't come from discount stores. Instead, she sighed, and added, "I don't know where Nate is."

Mato exited the car, then turned in her direction. "Nate come. Mato sleep now."

Tori was going to thank him and suggest he find a hiding place, but he had already disappeared. The woman was coming awake. She gave a long, low moan and began to rub her head.

"You okay?" Tori asked, knowing the question was inherently absurd.

"What happened?"

Before Tori could answer, the woman reacted to the injured driver with a short scream.

"He's going to be okay," Tori said, putting her faith in Mato's blood. "I'm sure it looks worse than it is. Head wounds bleed a lot, that's all. My friend has gone to call an ambulance. We all just need to remain calm until it gets here."

Based on the woman's initial reaction to the driver, Tori expected her to be considerably more agitated. Instead, she adopted Tori's "be calm" advice with uncanny speed. And when Nate pulled up in his truck, she barely reacted at all.

"EMTs are on the way," he said. "Sorry it took so long. Babe wasn't happy about going back in the trailer so soon."

"Tell her I want to finish our ride as soon as we can."

"Will do. How are our health workers?" he asked, leaning into the open passenger door.

Tori looked in from the driver's side.

"May I see your ID now?" he asked.

The woman offered her hand instead. "I'm Tessa Bidford. Bernstein Labs," she said, as if that explained everything.

"And your friend?"

"My associate, Mort Lund."

"Also of Bernstein Labs?"

"Yes."

"I'm still going to need to see your identification," Nate said. "And please, no more bullshit about forgetting to bring it with you. Lying to a lawman is a bad idea. In fact, it's just plain stupid."

"I assure you," Bidford said, "I'm not stupid."

Nate did not appear convinced. "Reckon we'll find out."

The Bidford woman was stunningly attractive, but her looks had no apparent impact on Nate. Tori liked that. "Bernstein Labs," Tori said, almost trying not to sound snarky, "is that part of the state health department?"

Bidford laughed, briefly, then put her hand on her head and made a frowny face. "Ow." She looked cute as a kitten. Tori wanted to drown her.

"Your ID?" Nate said.

Bidford fumbled in her wallet for a driver's license and a business card. She delivered them to Nate with a pouty look Tori had last seen on the face of a lingerie model. She decided to use very cold water for the drowning.

Nate gestured toward Lund. "I'll get his ID when they move him to the ambulance." He produced a notepad and recorded some of the information from Bidford's license, then returned it to her. "May I keep your card?"

"Sure," she said, all but fondling him with her eyes.

Good luck with that, you snot. He'll never fall for it.

Nate returned Bidford's smile. "Mind telling me what you were doing out here?"

Tori watched her squirm, but instead of looking guilty, Bidford's reaction was provocative. "We weren't completely honest I admit, but I didn't expect to be attacked for it."

"I'm not attacking you," Nate said.

"No, of course not. I'm talking about Ms. Lanier. Or rather, her driveway. It's booby-trapped."

"What?" Tori exclaimed. "The only boob around here is--"

"I'll handle this, Tori. Okay?"

Bidford slithered out of the car. Nate backed up. Tori imagined she would've crawled into his lap if he'd been sitting down.

"You're saying the falling boulder was triggered automatically? And on purpose?" Nate asked.

"That's probably a little too strong," Bidford said. "But the fact that the boulder fell, and that it may be responsible for my dear friend's death, is evidence of her negligence." She pointed a shaky finger at Tori, her emotions suddenly overwhelming her previous calm. "What kind of monster are you? That man has a wife and children!"

"I don't recall asking y'all to drop by for a visit," Tori said. She had both Irish *and* Confederate blood in her veins. Backing down and/or feeling guilty weren't in her playbook.

"It all started as a publicity stunt," Bidford said. "Someone in our promotions department thought it would be a simply fabulous idea to collect blood samples from prominent artists and thinkers of the day."

Tori coughed. "Me?"

"The idea was to tie our research into the human genome project."

"What on Earth for?" Nate asked.

Tori felt offended, though she wasn't sure why.

"The plan was to see if we could identify the gene for creativity." She paused to let that sink in. When it became apparent it hadn't, she hurried on. "Once such a gene is identified, there's always the possibly it could be manipulated."

Nate had a blank look on his face.

"Look," Bidford said, "if you were going to have a baby--"

"That'd be a little tricky for me, don't you think?" Nate grinned. "Wrong plumbing."

"If you *and your wife* were going to have a baby... You are married, aren't you?"

"No."

"Oh. Well then, just pretend. For the sake of argument. If--"

"Hang on," Nate said, "I need to check on your dear friend."

"Who? Oh! Of course."

Tori couldn't help but snicker at the woman's pathetic attempts to convince Nate she wasn't up to something suspicious. Surely Nate would be able to see right through her. *Surely*.

Nate returned. "He's still out, but his color seems better. You were saying?"

She rested her hand on his arm. "If you and your wife were going to have a baby, and someone came along and offered to insure that your child had the gift of creativity, wouldn't you jump for it?"

Nate looked at Tori. "I dunno. Is that something we'd jump for?"

She grinned back at him. "Is that a proposal?"

"It's just a question. But you're the only impartial witness I've got handy."

Maybe I should drown you both and run off with the driver. "Oh. Well then, yeah. I guess I'd want my kids to be creative. Sure."

"There you have it," Bidford said. "That's what we were up to."

Nate looked at Tori. Then he looked back at Bidford. He took off his Stetson and scratched his head. "Is that all supposed to mean something to me?"

Tori wanted to kiss him.

"Well, yes. Of course! It's what we're all about. What we're trying to do! We want to get a handle on the future. Make it possible for people to have bright, inquisitive children -- children who won't just struggle for a place in this world -- children who'll have a leg up from the very beginning! Isn't that what we all want for our kids?"

Tori fixed her with an accusative stare. "How many kids do you have, Ms. Bidford?"

"Uh, well--"

Just then, the driver let out a groan like something

from an old monster movie.

"He's comin' around," Tori said.

Nate's expression remained neutral. "He can thank God he's got somebody in his corner."

Bidford may have *looked* like she knew who Nate was talking about, but Tori was certain.

~*~

Chapter 11

It is hard to believe that a man is telling the truth
when you know that you would lie
if you were in his place. ~H.L. Mencken

Lanier danced just the way Tessa expected. When Tessa asked deputy Hunk if she could ride with him to the hospital, Lanier almost lost it. Steering her was child's play.

"Wouldn't you rather ride with your friend, in the ambulance?" Lanier had asked.

This gave Tessa another opportunity to show her feelings for dear dorky Mort. It also gave her a chance to call Bernstein Labs without the knowledge of Lanier or the lawman.

Once the EMTs were satisfied that Lund was stable enough to move, Tessa crept to the rear of the ambulance. As soon as they were under way she dialed Bernstein's office on her cell phone. His secretary tried to run interference for him, but it was a tactic Tessa had seen too often.

"Unless you want Jerry to miss out on the business opportunity of a lifetime -- maybe *all* our lifetimes -- get him on the damned phone."

"But he's--"

"I don't care what he's doing, or who. Interrupt him. Now!"

The secretary caved, as Tessa knew she would, and Bernstein wheezed onto the line a few moments later. "What's so friggin' important?"

"How 'bout a cure for trauma?"

"What?"

Tessa explained. "Let's say you get smashed up in an accident like... well, like Mort Lund--"

"Who the hell is Mort Lund?"

"He works for you. In the lab. Drawing blood."

"Oh. A phlebotomist."

"Yeah. Listen, I don't have much time. I have to make this quick. People will be calling to check out my story." She gave him the gist of her tale about secret efforts to secure blood from famous creative people. "I told them the idea came from our Promotions department."

"You *are* the Promotions department," Bernstein said.

"I may have omitted that detail. But it doesn't matter. You just need to cover for me, and use that story. You can say there were very few people who knew about it. After all, it was a secret."

"It certainly was to me," he said.

"Don't get defensive. Especially if you hope to get your hands on the most important breakthrough in treatment methods for trauma the world has ever seen."

Bernstein exhaled with a whistling sound. Tessa imagined she could see the loose tissue suspended from his neck wiggling like some sort of organic bagpipe. Finally, he inhaled. "You sound like you've fallen for your own hype. That's never a good idea."

"This is on the level," she said. "I've got the testimony of the doctor who oversaw the care of a patient who received one -- are you listening? -- *one* treatment. The patient had been severely beaten and wasn't expected to live. Yet, a couple days later she walked out of the hospital. Walked! We'll see the same thing with Lund, I'm sure of it."

"What does the treatment involve?"

"A blood transfusion. Raw. No blood typing, no preparation. The guy doing it didn't even swab the spots where he made incisions. It was all very... primitive. I still can't believe my own eyes."

"Who's the donor?" Bernstein asked.

"That's where I need to do some more work," Tessa said. "I don't know his name, or anything else about him for that matter. But one thing is absolutely certain: his blood makes people well. I'm tellin' you, Jerry, it works like magic."

"And this guy isn't kept under guard somewhere?"

"Nope," Tessa said. "All we have to do is grab him."

"And I presume by 'we,' you mean me?"

"We'll need someone who isn't associated with the lab at all. Period. Can't take any chances with this. The cops already know I'm connected to Bernstein Labs. If the kid shows up missing--"

"It's a kid? You expect me to arrange for the kidnapping of a child? Are you insane?"

"No, no. I just said that 'cause he's small. Very small. About the *size* of a child."

Bernstein's breathing grew raspy. Tessa could imagine his beady little eyes locked onto something on a shelf in his crap-laden office. A bowling trophy perhaps, or a portrait of his hideous family. His first test tube, bronzed, or a ribbon from his first science fair.

"Kids come in a lot of sizes," Bernstein said. "How big a kid are we talking about? An 8-year-old? Ten?"

"More like a toddler."

"*What?*"

Tessa held the phone away from her head, which still ached from the smack of the air bag during the crash. "I told you he was small. So, you won't need an army to get him. Find someone anonymous. Someone who'll fade away and never be heard from again once we've got our

189

guy."

"First you want me to hire a kidnapper, then you want me to have him killed? What am I now, the KGB?"

"Don't think of this as a kidnapping. It isn't. Not really. It's more like a quarantine. A public service. It's something we're doing for the betterment of society. Once we've isolated and synthesized whatever it is in this guy's blood that causes people to experience such phenomenal recoveries, he can go wherever he wants. A world tour, maybe. Why not? He'd be a freakin' hero. Y'know, we probably ought to put him on the payroll. That'd make it all tidy. And possibly legal."

"And the kidnapper? We give him a bullet in the head? Cement shoes?"

"You've been watching too many old gangster movies. I was thinking more along the lines of buying him a cheap condo in Vegas. Property values there are in the toilet right now. Give him a little money, and he'll probably drink himself to death. We keep our hands clean."

"You scare me, Tessa. You know that?"

"Aw, Jerry. You say the nicest things."

~*~

Mato remained hidden until all the giants departed, including Tori and Nate. Though he considered them friends, in a sense, he had no use for the rest of their race. Their machines were noisy. They smelled bad and usually fouled any area in which they were used. And, Mato found it increasingly frustrating that the machines didn't give up their secrets easily.

He had watched both Tori and Nate operate their trucks, but the two machines had different control mechanisms. Tori's had three foot pedals. Nate's had two. Tori spent a great deal of time moving a long lever which stuck up out of the floor. Nate had no such device. But, since Mato couldn't reach the pedals in either one, his hopes of ever operating a truck were doomed.

Tori once mentioned something about one of her friends, a friendly old giant named Caleb, who had a different kind of vehicle. But she was hazy on the details, and Mato lost interest.

Since giving the transfusion to the injured giant, all he really wanted was sleep. Healing, while important, was not his primary duty. First and foremost, he was a provider, and he felt confident Reyna had no complaints about his efforts to provide for her. She, in turn, would produce offspring which they would raise to become valuable members of The People. Such had been the Way since the Beginning, long before The People angered the Spirits and were condemned to live among giants.

The Old Ones said the Spirits balanced the curse of the giants by giving the dreamers the power to heal. Had such an exchange been offered for consideration *before* the Spirits made it happen, Mato felt sure The People would have rejected it. As a dreamer, he certainly would have argued against it. But that had been decided long ago, and the Spirits were not interested in his opinion.

He would heal those he could. It was a pledge he had taken shortly after it was discovered he was a dreamer. But The People never intended him to heal giants, he felt sure. And for good reason. It was exhausting! Someone his size needed little more than a drop or two of a dreamer's blood. But giants? Like everything else -- they needed much, much more.

When the noise finally died down, Mato slipped out from beneath the rocks where he'd been resting. Still dizzy, he knew his return to Tori's cabin would be undertaken at a much slower pace. Perhaps he would meet Shadow along the way, and the dog could carry him to his destination.

Shadow! The dog had been a revelation. He had seen dogs with giants in the past but never quite understood their relationship. The People certainly had no such animals living among them. The very idea was absurd! Rabbits, yes. They were docile, required little care, and tasted very good when prepared with a spicy sauce. But you couldn't ride one! And a rabbit wouldn't defend you. Wouldn't come when you called, simply to be near you. If only dogs didn't eat so much.

It would not be too much longer before Reyna climbed on Shadow's back and they returned to The People. This time, the dog would not cause quite as big as stir as he had previously. The memory made him laugh. Soon, all the young warriors would want dogs of their own, and they would clamor after Mato until he helped them find some. How they would feed the creatures was their problem.

The important thing was to get Reyna home. Now that she was with child, he had an obligation to remove her from possible harm. Staying any longer among the giants would be foolish if not simply reckless. Once he was rested he would begin the preparations.

His emotions tore at him when he thought of the sacred cavern. Though he had searched as thoroughly as he knew how, he could find no other way in. His original plan had been to blow up the entrance using the bomb he stole from the giants who tried to hurt Nate. But without another entry, he would be denying The People access to their holiest site.

It would have to be left up to the Elders. He would tell them everything he knew. The giants had shared much of their magic, though they didn't consider it such. He and Reyna would pass that along as well. And he wanted to bring some of their machines along, too. He had to be careful not to overload Shadow, and he had to be sure the machines they took would still work once they were in the hands of The People. That issue might require a few extra days of planning -- a few extra days of picking Tori's brain. And maybe a little more time with Nate.

~*~

"Carmine! Just the guy I wanted to see."

Carmine deLuca stared at Ben Lykes, his brother-in-law. In the entire time he'd known Lykes, the man had *never* wanted to see him, even at the wedding. Veronica had insisted that Carmine be a groomsman. "Yo, Ben. What's up?" He couldn't resist taking a step or two backwards. "Hey man, like I tol' Ronnie, I don't plan to be here very long. I'm lookin' for...."

"Work. Yeah, I know." Lykes was smiling, which Carmine found unsettling. Lykes never smiled. At least, not at him.

"Don't look so stressed out. We're family. We gotta take care of each other."

"Right," Carmine said, wondering if he'd fallen into another dimension. That happened in comic books and movies. Maybe there was something to it, for real.

"I think I might be able to help you out, job wise," Lykes said. "But I can't really say much unless you promise to keep it under your hat. This is all very confidential. You understand?"

"Yeah, sure."

"I'm serious, Carmine. If I tell you any of this, it can't get back to Veronica. Not a word."

"I'm cool with that," he said. *Talk to Ronnie? When he didn't have to?*

Lykes put his arm around Carmine's shoulders and ushered him into the kitchen. It was spacious by Carmine's standards, but Lykes acted as if he were ashamed of it. "Have a seat," he said, guiding Carmine toward a straight-backed chair at the kitchen table. "You want a beer?"

"That'd be great."

Lykes twisted the cap off a bottle of something imported from Belgium and handed it to him. He opened one for himself and they clinked the necks of the bottles like old drinkin' buddies.

"So," Carmine said, trying not to sound too eager, "what's this job you got?" The beer tasted like runoff from the Spaski's DeeLux carwash, but he said nothing and pretended to enjoy it.

Lykes wore a Cheshire Cat smile and stretched out the moment before he breached the wall of confidentiality. "This could be your big break, kid. Provided you handle it right."

"Yeah?"

"Oh, *hell* yeah. We're talking huge. The kinda deal I never had a shot at, and I've been hangin' around with these people for a long time." He shook his head. "Shit like this never came my way."

"No kiddin'?"

Lykes took a long pull of his beer, then wiped his mouth on the back of his hand and belched. "This Belgian crap tears me up, y'know?"

"No shit," Carmine said. He wanted to burp, too, but couldn't.

"I got a call from this guy. A friend of a friend, y'know? He needs a special favor, and it's worth a lot of money to him. You listenin'? A whole lotta money."

Carmine was indeed listening. In fact, his attention could not have been drawn any tighter without cutting off circulation to his brain. "I'm with ya."

"Oh, shit," Lykes said suddenly. "I just remembered."

"What?"

"Whoever does this job has to have a car. You don't have one."

"I can get one!"

"You can *drive?*"

"'Course I can drive. How hard is that?"

Lykes stared at him, his eyes boring in like carbide-tipped drill bits. "You really know how to drive? You're not just sayin' it to get the job?"

"C'mon man! I know how to drive. You think I'm retarded or something? It's easy."

"Yeah? You got a license?"

"What? No, I don't got a license. I don't own a car. Why would I need a license?"

"You make my head hurt, Carmine! How in hell you gonna get a car if you don't got a license?"

"I wasn't exactly gonna rent one," Carmine said.

His brother-in-law broke into a big grin. He patted Carmine on the cheek with an open palm. "I like your attitude, kid. You're a little stupid, but ya got heart." He took another long swig of his beer. "Gimme a minute to think this through." He turned to the kitchen's twin windows. The view left much to be desired, but by twisting one's neck, the sky became visible between the surrounding buildings, and there was a garden of sorts on the roof of a neighboring two-story structure.

"Tell you what," Lykes said evenly. "I'll get the car. When you finish the job you can have it as part of your fee."

Carmine was dumbstruck. "You're gonna give me a

car?"

"Yeah. And enough money to move away from here. Far away."

That brought him back to reality. "But, I've always lived in the city."

"Times change," Lykes said. "Besides, once this deal's over, it'll be better for everybody if you have a change of address."

"You talkin' Philly, or what?"

"More west."

"Chicago?"

"Keep goin', Carmine."

"You expect me to be a freakin' cowboy? Is that it?"

"Why not? Plenty of fresh air. Good jobs. Scenery. You hang around here, you're just gonna grow old and die. Or, who knows, maybe just die."

"What the hell kinda job is this anyway?"

Lykes squinted at him, as if he needed to do something to drive home the importance of secrecy. "You don't tell nobody about this, right?"

"Right."

"We need you to grab a kid and bring 'em back."

Carmine squinted at him. "A kid. A little kid? Big kid? What?"

"Little. But, grown up."

"Like a midget?"

"Yeah."

"Oh, man! A fuckin' Oompah-Loompah?" He shivered. "They creep me out. Always have. Ever since-- Ever since *I* was little. We went to the circus once and--"

"Carmine?"

"Yeah?"

"Nobody gives a shit what creeps you out. You take the job, or not. That's it. Capiche?"

Carmine considered what little information he had, but there wasn't much to mull over.

"Okay. I grab this kid, and then what? Bring him back here?"

"You take him upstate. I'll give you the details if you want in."

"I dunno. Kidnapping...."

"It's big money, Carmine. How does twenty large sound?"

"Twenty grand? You kiddin' me? Just to grab a kid?"

"Well, he's not really a kid. He's a small adult. Really, *really* small is what I heard. Shouldn't give you any trouble."

"And then, I leave the city? For good?"

"Pretty cool, huh?" Lykes finished his beer and grabbed another. He opened a second one for Carmine and left it on the table. "Veronica says you've got a thing for the mob. You wanna be a wise guy. That true?"

Carmine shrugged. "I think there could be some advantages. I could go that route." *Twenty grand!*

Lykes laughed.

"What?" Carmine asked.

"Don't believe everything you hear about the mob."

"I don't." Carmine couldn't have been more sincere. "I know they do some shady stuff. Hell, who doesn't? But deep down? Deep down, I think they're okay. Just tryin' to get by. Y'know?"

Lykes palmed Carmine's cheek again. "You're too much, y'know that, Carmine? Too fuckin' much."

"So, do I get the job?"

"We'll see," Lykes said, smiling again. "But if I was you, I'd stick pretty close to home the next day or so. You know what I mean?"

"Yeah," Carmine said. But his brother-in-law's smile still made him nervous.

197

~*~

Tori had never been to Nate's house before. Caleb had given her the directions, and even though the old cowboy grocer had been vague about the street names, finding the address was easy. Ten Sleep may have been many, many times the size of Charm, but it was still a very small town.

"Please stay here," she said to Mato. Lance was sitting between them and staring straight ahead. Mato kept pushing the all-too-lifelike doll in her direction while he pressed against the door. "I won't be long."

She hurried up the short walk to Nate's front door and rang the bell. It had been two days since the incident in her driveway, and she hadn't seen Nate since then. She didn't like the idea of *not* seeing him. At all. *But I should've called first, damn it. What's wrong with me?*

The door opened to reveal a boy almost Tori's height. She guessed him to be about 14, and well into that stage when boys ceased to be interesting as children. From Tori's limited experience, the stage lasted several years and usually ended when the subject either entered college, or got a job.

"Where's Nate?" she asked, pleasantly.

Instead of responding, the boy looked her up and down as if she were a mannequin set up for his inspection.

"I'm looking for Nate," she said. "Uhm, deputy sheriff Sheffield. Do you--"

"He's out back," the kid said.

"Can you tell him he has a visitor?"

"He's busy with his horses."

"Ah. You must be his friend's grandson," Tori said.

"It's Marty, isn't it? Nate mentioned he was going to take you for a trail ride."

"Whoopee do," the boy muttered, his face taking on a pained look. "Wasn't my idea. It's bad enough I have to spend so much time with Gran, but she thinks I need to spend every minute outdoors. She says I play way too many video games. I hate video games. They're for losers and dipshits."

"Even solitaire?"

"*Especially* solitaire."

"I see. Does she know you feel that way?"

"Nah. She's old."

"She doesn't sound old on the radio."

He looked at her as if she had sprouted an ear full of potato salad. "She's way older than you."

"I'm sure she just wants you to have a good time."

"Yeah, right."

"I think I'll just walk around back," Tori said.

"Hey, can I ask you something?" Marty opened the screen door.

"Sure."

"Does Nate have a gun? I'm mean, sure, he's a cop and all. But, I was just wondering--"

"He probably has several," Tori said. "Why?"

"I was hoping maybe he'd let me shoot one."

She shrugged. "You can always ask." She turned away before he came up with anything else, and the screen door slapped shut behind her. Once, she took pride in her ability to read people and get a feel for who they really were. It went beyond mere personality, and in most cases she sized folks up correctly. But this kid wasn't coming through clearly. He didn't *look* like trouble, but something about him definitely gave off that vibe.

It was a short trip to the back of the building. Nate's lawn consisted mostly of dried weeds and dead grass.

Josh Langston

There were a couple trees and some bushes that may not have tasted water since the spring rains. The back yard looked marginally better.

Tori recognized Elmer right away. The ornery creature had his head stuck through the fence and was working on a rare patch of green grass.

"Hey," she said, catching Nate's eye as he put a bridle on the big gray mare. "Your little friend told me you were out here."

He shook his head and looked down at her hand. "Looks like a fresh bandage. Is it any better?"

"A little. I'm just impatient. I want to be able to type using both hands. It's a hassle more than anything." She flexed her fingers and reminded herself to take more aspirin. "I drove in to check on my mail and thought I'd pop in and say Hello. Hope you don't mind."

"Mind? Are you kidding?" Nate pushed his hat to the back of his head. "I'd much rather be talking to you than going on a ride with junior." He stuck a thumb at the house. "What a little sh--"

"Now, now," Tori said. "He's somebody's baby boy. Gotta be nice."

Nate growled something back at her, and she decided it was just as well she didn't understand.

"Wish I'd known you were comin'," he said. "I'd have come up with an excuse not to pick up little Marty, and we could've found something more interesting to occupy our time."

"Like building a deck?"

He appeared only somewhat taken aback. "A deck? Okay, a deck. Yours, I presume."

"All that talk about lying out under the stars really got to me."

"A blanket will serve the same purpose," he said.

"I'll bet your blankets all smell like horses. Besides, I kinda like the idea of being able to step outside, without actually being on bare dirt. The whole elevation thing appeals to me."

"Think you can afford it?"

"I have no idea. What will the labor cost?"

He stepped close enough for her to smell his aftershave. "We might have to work out a deal."

"Like maybe I fix you dinner, or something?"

"Or something."

She put her hands on his chest and looked up into his eyes. "Can I ask you something?"

"Sure."

"Did you put on aftershave for Marty's benefit?"

~*~

Though snuggled into a first class seat, Tessa couldn't relax until the door closed on the airliner and sealed her in. Too wired to read the complimentary newspaper she'd been given when she boarded, she flagged down a flight attendant and ordered a drink.

"We'll be airborne in no time," the matronly airline employee said, her smile seemingly carved into her face.

"Okay. I'll drink fast."

"But, wouldn't you rather--"

"I'd rather not have this conversation," Tessa quipped. "I want Vodka and OJ. No ice. And I'd like to have it before I have to apply for Social Security benefits."

The woman turned to do her bidding and Tessa pulled out her cell phone. She speed dialed Jerry Bernstein and once again streaked past his secretary like a Nazi warplane during the blitzkrieg.

"Have you found someone to retrieve our... uh,

201

research subject?"

"It's all taken care of," Bernstein assured her.

"If something goes wrong, we can't have it coming back on us."

"I'm aware of that."

"Who's going to do it?" Tessa asked, unable to keep her curiosity in check. "Wait. Hang on." Another passenger had arrived and claimed the window seat. The new arrival was a huge man wearing suspendered jeans, snakeskin boots and a shirt straight out of a singing cowboy movie from the 1930's. Tessa dodged out of the way to make room for him.

When they were both settled in, she told Bernstein to continue.

"You don't need to know the details," he said. "But you can relax about anyone tracing any of this back to us. We're at least two steps removed from the hiring, and the guy doing the job won't know who to contact until he's got the subject. That's when he'll get in touch with us, and not before."

"And who's he going to contact?"

"I thought about that for a long time," Bernstein said, "but the answer's simple. The only logical person to handle all this, is you."

Tessa's initial reaction was negative, but then she realized being in charge was in her best interests. No one would follow the issue as closely as she would. No one else seemed to understand the awesome potential. Even though Bernstein had bankrolled her efforts, he seemed to be doing it more to humor her than anything else.

"That's good," she said. "I like that." She could hear him laugh.

"I figured you would."

"I'll be back in the office in a few hours, so--"

"Is Lund flying back with you?"

"What? No. He's still in the hospital."

"How's he doing?"

"Fine. He'll be out soon. Evidently, he wasn't hurt as badly as everyone first thought." She didn't tell him the hospital staff had been amazed by the speed of his recovery. Nor did she mention the tantrums she'd thrown about who was to blame for his injuries. Though the deputy sheriff hadn't been moved by her theatrics, everyone else was relieved when she announced that since her associate was doing so well, she probably wouldn't take anyone to court.

"I've asked around. This Lund character is pretty well liked among the lab people."

"Oh? Great," she said. *So, everyone loved the Prince of Dorkness.* "Listen, when I get back--"

"Yeah, about that. I'd like you to keep a lower profile from now on."

What was he driving at? "I don't understand."

"Think about it. We're getting into some sensitive stuff here, skirting the law so to speak."

So to speak?

Bernstein continued. "I want to completely limit management's connection with the project."

"Limit it how?"

"You're going to be the sole management contact. You'll report to me, of course, but even that will be done off the record."

"What? Why?"

"I must retain deniability," he said. "If something goes wrong, it can't get back to me."

"But you're perfectly willing to throw me under the bus?"

"That's an ugly characterization."

The flight attendant arrived with a white, foam cup.

Steam rose from it, and the aroma of coffee spread through the cabin. She handed it to the immense cowboy. "Irish cream, right?"

"Thank you darlin'," he said.

"You're welcome Mr. Torrence." She turned to leave.

"Actually, it's *Judge* Torrence," he said.

She smiled at him. "I knew that, your honor, but at 35,000 feet, we don't call witnesses."

Tessa poked her sleeve. "Excuse me?"

The flight attendant looked back at her. "Yes?"

"Where's my drink?"

"It's coming."

"Them gals sure stay busy," observed the judge. Or cowboy. Or whatever he was.

Tessa responded with a scowl, then spoke harshly into the phone. "You were saying?"

"This is a risky venture," Bernstein went on. "But with great risk comes great reward."

Was he reading from a goddamn fortune cookie? "I'll pull this off," she said.

"I'm counting on it."

"I presume you'll still let me use the lab's facilities?"

"Oh, absolutely. In fact, I'm having an area set aside just for your project."

"Thanks," she said. *Mighty big of him.* Especially since she was about to deliver the greatest advance in healing the world had ever seen.

"So," he went on, "when you get back, don't bother to come in until we've got the area set up. I'm having your office moved there, too. You'll have a separate entrance. No need to share our little secret with anyone who's not directly connected to the research. Don't you agree?"

"Right," she said. And if he needed to cut her off, he could do it without disturbing anyone else. Like pruning a diseased branch from a tree.

The flight attendant returned and pointed at Tessa's phone. "You'll have to turn that off now. We're about to get under way."

"I'll call you from LaGuardia," Tessa said into the phone, then shut it off. She glared at the flight attendant. "Where's my drink?"

The woman gave her the same plastic smile she'd flashed earlier. "We're fresh out of vodka."

Tessa pointed at the cowboy. "Then I'll have what he's having."

"Sorry. Coffee's all gone, too. I'll brew another pot once we reach cruising altitude."

"But--"

"Bring your seat back all the way up, please."

~*~

Chapter 12

*Stress is nothing more than the confusion
created when one's mind overrides the body's
natural desire to choke the crap out of
some jerk who desperately deserves it.*

Mato watched as Tori spoke to a small giant standing in the doorway. She had told him she was going to stop by the place where Nate lived, and he had grown increasingly curious about it. The only giant's home he'd ever been in was Tori's, and he'd since come to realize her cabin was a far cry from the usual lair of the big people. He wanted to see how Nate lived.

While Tori was occupied with the person at the door, Mato slipped out of the truck and raced to the far side of the house. He turned the corner and saw open windows, just like those in the front of the house. With a short burst of speed, he ran half way up to the window and stretched to his full length. His hands caught on the wooden edge, and he pulled himself up the rest of the way. Pleased with himself, he turned in the window and dropped down to the floor inside.

The room was dark, and it took a moment for his eyes to adjust. He waited, motionless, while the features of the room grew more distinct. When he could see reasonably well, he began his exploration. While Tori's house had one main room and a smaller area set aside for bathing, Nate's house had two rooms solely dedicated to sleeping. A bathing room separated them, and all three rooms shared a hallway which led to an open area with a fireplace.

The arrangement was much less crowded than Tori's home. There were separate rooms for meal preparation and consumption. There were cabinets and shelves almost everywhere he looked. Books, to which he had been introduced by Tori, crowded those shelves along with other objects of interest. More books lay stacked on the floor.

In order to get a closer look at the things on the shelves, Mato climbed onto a wide counter about a third of the way up the wide wooden structure. He had his back to the room, absorbed in his inspection. Without warning, two huge hands clamped down on his shoulders and lifted him in the air.

Assuming Nate had picked him up, Mato made little effort to break free. Then he heard a strange voice.

"Nobody told me about you."

Mato strained to see behind him and realized it wasn't Nate, but the smaller giant with whom Tori had been talking when they first arrived. What had she called him?

"What are you, some kinda leprechaun?"

Mato stumbled over a few words, trying to say something that wouldn't make his situation even worse. His captor was unwilling to wait. *What was his name?* He almost had it.

"Talk!" the giant said, and thrust Mato backwards into a large chair. Mato bounced out, his arms and legs poised for flight when the giant knocked him back and pinned him to the chair with one hand. "What are you?"

"Mato," he said, grudgingly.

The giant thumped Mato's face with his finger. Though Mato wanted to ignore it, the contact hurt, and he could not avoid turning away.

"You like that, Mr. Leprechaun?" The giant thumped him again. "I'm the cat that caught the mouse. I could do this all day. You got a pot of gold, Mr. Leprechaun?"

Mato fixed him with a stare. "Stop," he commanded, finally remembering the name.

The giant laughed. "Or what?"

"Stop now, Marty."

"Oh, so you know my name? You been spyin' on me, dipshit?"

How stupid could this young giant be, Mato wondered. Of course Mato knew his name. Hadn't he just used it? Mato wasn't sure what "spying" meant and so didn't attempt to respond.

Marty flicked him again. "Just 'cause you know my name doesn't mean you can boss me around. You can't. I'm too big for you."

"Boss? What is boss?"

"I'm the boss!" He poked Mato's chest hard as if to drive the point home.

Mato's growing anger helped him ignore the pain of the attack. His mind raced to find a way to escape. "Stop," he said again. "Mato fight."

That brought a peal of laughter. "You wanna *fight* now? You gonna beat me up? Dipshit."

Mato twisted, not because he thought he might get free, but only to shield the movement of his hand when pulling the knife from his belt. He held it by his side, out of his assailant's sight. When Marty curled his finger and pushed his hand forward to deliver another blow, Mato jabbed the blade into his finger with both hands. The point went in between the fingernail and the first knuckle, just to the side of the bone. Mato twisted the handle to make sure Marty felt it.

He did.

The reaction was both loud and satisfying. As the giant screamed and huddled over his wounded finger, Mato regained his feet and launched himself from the overstuffed chair. His target was Marty's nose, and he made contact with the crown of his head.

The giant fell backwards, wailing and carrying on as if he'd been impaled. Mato stood to one side of his now whimpering assailant and whispered in his ear. "You are young *and* stupid," he said, slowly and carefully. "Mato let you live, this time." He paused, then added, "Dipshit."

He had no idea what the epithet meant, but it felt right, and saying it made him feel better.

He could hear someone coming in response to Marty's hysteria. It had to be Nate, and Tori would almost certainly be with him. It seemed like a good time to return to the truck.

Carmine took the job. But the satisfaction he anticipated from having a mission, and the beginnings of a future life someplace new, would have been much easier to enjoy if he could have told someone. Anyone. Even Ronnie. But, of course, that wasn't an option. He went through a mental checklist of his other friends and decided none of them was worthy enough to share his secret. That it was a very short list didn't bother him. He'd never had many friends. Which made the whole idea of leaving the city easier to take, too.

Lykes gave him the keys to a car and suggested that he put anything he wanted to take with him in it. They were sitting in an alley behind the building where Lykes and Veronica lived. The car was a Honda Civic of uncertain vintage. Its formerly royal blue exterior bore rust spots in a variety of sizes. A few of those rust spots surrounded odd-shaped holes. Carmine eyed the vehicle with something a great deal less than enthusiasm.

"I should pack my stuff *now?*"

"Yeah. You're leaving today."

"Geez. That was fast. I just got the car." He looked at it again, as if to assure himself that it was, indeed, a car.

"These people," Lykes said, "they don't like to waste time. Besides, they know it's going to take you a while to get to Wyoming and back."

"Wyoming?" It was the first time he'd heard where he was going.

Lykes stared at him, hard. "What?"

"Nothin'," Carmine said. "Where in Wyoming? It's a big place. Ain't it?" Geography had never been his strong suit.

"There's a map in the glove box," Lykes said. "The route is marked on it. Take your time. No speeding. If you get caught driving without a license... Well, just make sure that doesn't happen. Okay? Don't make trouble. Stay under the radar. You understand?"

"Yeah. Sure, no problem. But, I don't think I should drive straight through. I'll need to be sharp when--"

Lykes handed him a thick envelope. *Just like in the movies.* He hesitated before opening it.

"Go ahead," Lykes said. "Check it out. There's enough cash in there to cover food, gas and motels out there and back."

Carmine resisted the urge to count it.

"Don't go crazy," Lykes said, "but you don't have to do everything on the cheap, either. Just don't attract attention. You're just another tourist."

"I've never been outta the city," Carmine said. "What kinda stuff is there to see out there?"

"Do I look like a friggin' tour guide? It doesn't matter. You won't have time for sightseeing. When this is over, you can go see anything you want: Mount Rushmore, Niagara Falls, the Grand fuckin' Canyon. I don't care."

Carmine straightened. "So, where do I go when I've got the kid?"

Lykes handed him a slip of paper. "Find a pay phone and call this number. You'll get your instructions then."

"You make all this sound like spy shit."

"These people don't want to take chances. None. That means once you grab this guy, you have to keep him under wraps. Nobody -- and I mean nobody -- sees him or hears about him. Ever. You got that? When this job is over, you forget you ever took the trip. You never saw the guy, and you sure as hell don't know what happened to him. We clear on that?"

"Yeah, sure. Only--"

"Geezus, Carmine! Only what?"

"I'm supposed to leave him tied up? The whole time? What if he's gotta, you know...."

Lykes shook his head in exasperation. Carmine hoped he hadn't pushed him too far.

"Look in the back," Lykes said.

Carmine opened the hatchback and found a large wire cage. Some towels had been tossed inside for padding.

"That's a dog cage," Carmine said.

"Yeah. So? There's a padlock for the door. What's the problem?"

"I dunno. It seems kinda...."

"Kinda what?"

"Mean."

Lykes stared at him. "*Mean?* You're gonna fuckin' kidnap someone, and you're worried about being mean? What'sa matter with you? You goin' soft on me now? You, the big mob guy?"

"No! I'm good. Really. I can do this."

"Yeah?"

"No problem. So the guy's in a cage for a couple

days. That's no big deal. Makes sense."

Lykes slammed the hatchback closed. "Damn right. Just keep a blanket over it. The windows are tinted, but there's no reason to take any chances."

"Right," Carmine said, trying to hide his misgivings. Nobody deserved to be put in a damned dog cage. That wasn't right.

"Time to pack up your shit, Carmine," Lykes said.

"Yeah," Carmine said. He shoved the car keys in his pocket. "I'll get right on it."

~*~

Tori was right behind Nate when he responded to the noise from the house. They hurried in through the back door and found Dee's grandson lying on the floor holding his nose.

"Marty! What happened?" Tori asked.

The boy continued to blubber. Deep sobs punctuated his ragged breathing.

"Look at me," Nate commanded.

Marty raised his head, revealing an amazing amount of blood. He had it all over his neck and chin, and some had dripped onto the carpet. Nate carefully gripped Marty's jaw and examined him. There were no obvious cuts. The blood had come from his nose which was pushed sideways.

"Who did this to you?" he asked.

Tori couldn't resist looking for some sign that Mato had been there.

"You'll think I'm crazy," Marty said as his tears mixed with the blood and snot.

"Try me," Nate said as he grabbed a box of tissues from a side table and handed them to the boy.

"It was a little man," he said. "He looked like an Indian, but he was really small."

"What happened?"

"I tried to be nice to him. All I wanted to do was talk, but he attacked me."

Nate's eyebrow dipped. "Just how big was this little man?"

Marty held his hand about waist high.

"Three, maybe three and a half feet?" Nate said, basing his guess on Marty's gesture.

"Yeah. And he was mean. He tried to stab me, but I jumped out of the way, and he only nicked my finger."

Tori forced herself not to sound like a prosecutor. "And then he punched you in the nose?"

"He hit me with something," Marty said. "Felt like a bowling ball."

Tori helped him stand up. "You're a pretty big guy, Marty. How tall are you?"

"Five foot six."

Nate put a waste basket at Marty's feet, but the boy made no effort to gather up any of the bloodied tissues he had already dropped on the floor.

"That would make you at least two feet taller than the guy who attacked you." Tori resisted the urge to cross her arms. She'd heard somewhere that such body language indicated she wished to erect a barrier, which idea she found quite appealing. Instead, she leaned back against a bookcase.

"I coulda stopped him, but I wasn't expecting trouble. He had no reason to hurt me. No reason at all."

Nate patted him on the shoulder. "Guess we'd better have somebody examine your nose. Looks like we'll have to put our ride off 'til later."

Marty clearly wasn't upset by the news. "You gonna find the guy that did this? Arrest him or something?"

213

"I'll be honest with you, Marty," Nate said. "I don't know of anybody who matches the description you've given me, such as it is. It sounds like some little kid got the drop on you."

"He was all grown up, I swear!"

"Three and a half feet tall?"

"Maybe even a little shorter."

"Shorter?" Nate glanced at Tori but didn't say anything.

"Was he wearing curly toed elf shoes," she asked, "or have little wings?"

If looks could strike sparks, the one Nate gave Tori would have burnt her to a cinder. He turned to Marty. "You say he had Indian features?"

"Yeah."

"What kind of clothes was he wearing?"

"Jeans and a blue shirt."

Mato, Tori thought. No doubt about it. In fact, he and Lance were dressed the same way. Intentionally. "Are you sure you didn't provoke him?"

"I didn't do nothin'. Honest," Marty said.

"I'll fill out a police report if you want me to," Nate said.

"Yeah! That'll teach that dipsh-- that guy a lesson."

"But once I file it, everyone will know you got your butt kicked by somebody half your size."

Marty started to say something, then settled for just making a face.

"It doesn't matter to me," Nate said. "I'll write it up as soon as we've run you by the doctor and dropped you off with Dee."

"Do you have to say how little the guy is?" Marty asked.

"It's a pretty important feature, don't you think? If all

I say is the guy looked like an Indian, there wouldn't be enough information to arrest anybody. Now, an Indian only three feet tall--"

"I think maybe he was bigger."

"Oh. Four feet tall?"

"I dunno."

"Five?"

"Just forget the whole thing," Marty said.

"You sure?"

"Yeah."

Tori waved at Nate and the boy. "I'll catch y'all later." She couldn't wait to get Mato's version of the story.

~*~

Carmine learned several things very early during his trip west, some about his vehicle, and some about himself. For openers, the radio didn't work. The built-in cassette tape player, however, did. Fortunately, a casual check beneath the front passenger seat yielded a perfectly good audio tape, several tunes on which he actually liked. The best by far was a Ray Charles number.

In addition, Carmine learned that driving triggered two effects in him personally. First: he had a craving for salted peanuts, which a former co-worker at the DeeLux Carwash insisted on calling "goobers." Second: driving made him sleepy. Sadly, the nuts alone did nothing for his drowsiness. Indeed, more than once he'd jerked awake to find himself thumping along the shoulder of the road with a mouthful of peanut paste. If he had any hope of surviving the drive, let alone the mission, he needed something else to keep him going.

Never having developed a taste for coffee, his primary means of countering sleepiness was yet another discovery: Bang Cola. Touted as the most heavily caffeinated beverage on the planet, Bang did everything the ads promised. And more.

One can of Bang gave Carmine a gentle buzz. Two cans turned him into a one-man hand jive band. Three quick cans of Bang -- any of the four fruity flavors would do -- resulted in world class flatulence. Carmine's digestive system, fully goobered and Banged, could provide cover fire for a marine assault team.

Before long he was roaring west on I-70 -- on the rare stretches in Pennsylvania which weren't under repair -- with the windows down and tears in his eyes singing "Can't Stop Loving You" at the top of his lungs. He'd already lost count of how many times he'd harmonized with the blind crooner, but he sincerely felt their duet was worthy of Carnegie Hall. And, Bang gave him a little something extra on the bass track.

~*~

Mato waited patiently for Tori to return to the car. He had long since gotten over his initial fears about the vehicle. Tori's repeated assurances that it was a machine rather than a magical conveyance finally sank in. Once it did, he looked upon it with a mixture of disdain and envy. It was highly unlikely he'd ever have anything like it. He'd carefully observed as she operated the machine, and realized that unless he could somehow reach the pedals, he'd never be able to drive it himself.

When Tori finally arrived, she got in the car, started it, and said nothing. Mato took that as a good sign. He had begun to smile when she broke her silence.

"Care to tell me what happened back there?"

Mato had expected she would demand an explanation. This was much better. "No," he said.

216

"Why'd you hurt little Marty?"

"Marty not little. Hurt Mato."

"You're claiming self defense?"

He shrugged. Stupid giant words. *Self defense.* Was there some other kind?

"Now he knows about you."

Mato couldn't keep from smiling. "Mato teach. Marty smarter now."

"I think you broke his nose."

"Nose very..." He struggled for the word but couldn't find it. "Nose feel pain good."

"Noses are sensitive," Tori agreed. "And when I said he's little, I meant he's young."

"And stupid."

"At that age, all males are stupid."

They drove in silence. Mato had become adept at pretending to be just like Lance whenever anyone looked at them. He could lock his eyes on something he imagined seeing in the distance. Keeping silent and motionless was a trick he had long ago mastered. Any hunter who wished to avoid starvation did the same.

Tori finished her errands and pointed the car toward home. He could not recall a time when they'd spent so much time together without any conversation. Sometimes Reyna would try to punish him by not talking to him. He did not have the heart to tell her he enjoyed such long periods of silence.

"Tori angry?"

"A little. I'm worried what Marty will tell people. I don't want them to come looking for you."

"Boy say, find little-little man. Little man break nose. Who believe?" It had to be the longest string of words Mato had ever compiled. Tori looked at him with something akin to respect.

"You're awfully talkative," she said. "But, at the heart

217

of it, I think you're right. Anything he might say is going to be taken with a grain of salt."

He had no idea what that meant, and his expression evidently indicated it.

"It means folks won't believe him. Once he realizes it, he's not going to be telling people that someone your size beat him up. My guess is, he won't mention you at all."

"So, why angry?"

"I'm not mad at you," she said. "I'm mad at Marty, the lying little..." She smiled. "He needed someone like you to teach him a lesson." She gently poked his shoulder with her index finger. "But it's good you didn't hurt him seriously."

They had almost reached Tori's drive when Mato broached a subject that had been bothering him since he left Nate's house. "Tori?"

"Yes?"

"What is dipshit?"

~*~

"What d'you want?" barked Lykes on the phone. "You weren't supposed to call me, remember?"

"Yeah, well, we got a little problem," Carmine said. He was standing at the counter of Aldo's Auto Repair in Wheeling, West Virginia, where the Honda had been towed.

"What kinda problem?"

"Remember that world class car you got me? The one with the busted radio and rust spots a cat could crawl through?"

"Aw geez, Carmine! Did ya wreck it?"

"It wrecked itself."

"What kinda crap is that? Damn it, Carmine! You had a simple job to do. And all I wanted to do was help you out. This is how you repay me?"

"The mechanic says the timing belt broke," Carmine said. "He says it shoulda been replaced fifty thousand miles ago."

"What's a timing belt?"

"How the hell should I know? I barely know where to put the gas."

Carmine waited for his brother-in-law to process the information. When Lykes didn't say anything, he went on. "The guy says the engine's got a couple bent valves. Plus, we need to replace the water pump and some other stuff. Problem is, I don't got enough money for all that."

"What's it gonna cost -- for everything?"

"Eighteen hundred," Carmine said, mentally boosting the total by three hundred to cover his inconvenience. God only knew how long it would take to do the repairs.

"Eighteen hundred?"

"Yeah." There was another long pause. "Tell me something," Carmine said. "Is this the car I was supposed to have or did someone buy a cheaper one and pocket the difference?"

"You sayin' I cheated you?"

"I'm just sayin' this is a pretty lousy car to send on an important job. It's almost as old as I am, fer Chrissake. If I hit a good-sized pot hole, the bumpers will fall off. I've probably left a trail of parts from here to Brooklyn!"

"Calm down. I'll figure something out."

"Well then, figure out how to pay for the tow truck, too. When the motor stopped, it didn't just need a rest. It fuckin' *retired*. Right in the middle of I-70. A moving van came so close to hittin' me, I could read the label on the driver's shorts. You don't know what it's like out here!" He cupped his hands around the mouthpiece and lowered

219

his voice. "I'm calling from West friggin' Virginia. They do weird shit to people who're just passing through. I'm tellin' ya, I've never seen so many rebel flags."

"I'll send you some money," Lykes said. "Just don't go off the deep end. Okay?"

"That's easy for you to say."

"Find a Western Union office. They're everywhere. I'll wire you some cash."

"This better not be comin' outta my pay when this is done."

"It won't." Lykes' voice carried not the slightest hint of reassurance.

"Don't think you can screw me and get away with it," Carmine said. The Bang not only gave him gas, it filled him with piss and vinegar. "I don't care if you are married to my sister." Nor did it hurt that Lykes was over 400 miles away.

Reyna sat atop the shoulders of the huge black dog, her bare legs dangling down to either side of his neck. Shadow's thick fur and warm skin made her feel comfortable and secure. By tapping a foot on one shoulder or the other she could guide him wherever she wanted to go. From time to time he would spot a ground squirrel, but she could almost always sense his imminent distraction and grab onto his collar before he dashed off in pursuit.

She wished there were some way to discipline him, keep him going where she wanted to go, but the animal was simply too big to intimidate. And, most likely, too smart. Instead, she carried bits of dried meat in a sling on her back. She would reward him at every opportunity,

A Little More Primitive

and when he did something wrong, she would scold.
Though many times her weight, Shadow would become
contrite during such corrections, a condition that might
last as long as several seconds. He much preferred a
gentle word and a taste of the dried meat. For the trip
home she would need a huge supply.

Over time the two developed a bond. Shadow seemed
to enjoy having her on his shoulders, as if he finally had
someone with whom to share his discoveries. Reyna
figured he just liked the way she scratched him behind
the ears. Whatever the reasons, the two got along
famously, and often went for wide-ranging explores when
Mato was away.

Such was the case that afternoon. Reyna was in need
of a particular plant which, among other things, she
would use to make the sleeping paste that Mato needed
for hunting. Winter Woman had shared the secret of its
making and Reyna was eager to try her hand at it. She
had yet to say anything about it to Mato and looked
forward to presenting him with a new supply. He would
be so impressed! The plant she needed was not easy to
find, but even as rare as it was, the final ingredient was
even harder to get. But, she decided, she would only
worry about it when the time came.

The huge dog and the tiny human had been searching
the end of the valley farthest from Tori's cabin when
Shadow came to a sudden stop, his head cocked to one
side. Reyna strained to hear whatever it was that got the
dog's attention, but all she registered were normal sounds:
wind, a cricket, a pair of birds. Had it been a ground
squirrel, Shadow would already have streaked off in
some random direction, his nose close enough to the soil
to mark his passing. But this was different. Reyna's
senses went on full alert, and while the dog stared,
immobile, Reyna cast her gaze from side to side in a slow

221

sweep that would eventually reveal the cause of Shadow's tightly coiled posture.

Finally, she saw what he saw. A smile lit her face, and she patted the big dog's neck in an effort to calm him. A baby prong buck lay in the brush less than a bowshot distant. The tiny deer, a late birth to be sure, remained so still as to become invisible. Unlike antelope or elk, the tiny ruminant had no spots, and no odor. That Shadow had detected anything spoke to his prowess in the wild. Reyna was impressed. But she had no intention of disturbing the tiny creature.

"Come. We must let the little one grow. If the Spirits decide it should appear on our dinner table, then so be it. For now we will let it sleep. It will need all its strength to survive in this world."

Reluctantly, Shadow gave ground. The prong buck never moved. Even more surprising, neither Reyna nor the dog saw the little animal's mother who was almost certainly hovering nearby. It was just as well. Though Reyna enjoyed prong buck meat as much as anyone, she was content to let her mate track it down and do the killing. It wasn't that she was squeamish; she merely agreed with a division of labor handed down to her after countless generations. Her job was not to change it.

After so much sensory stimulus, they should have been more aware of other threats nearby. But they weren't, and when the rattlesnake struck, its warning short and feeble, Shadow bolted.

~*~

Chapter 13

'Twas a woman who drove me to drink, and I never had the courtesy to thank her. ~W.C. Fields

Jeremiah Torrence sat as his desk carefully reviewing the case files and briefs that had piled up while he was in New York. He loved traveling to the Big Apple because his one and only daughter lived there, and whenever he came for a visit, they took in a Broadway show. It was something his wife, Pearl, had to talk him into, the first time. After that he was addicted, and they made the trip every other month. Because of the expense, he allowed himself no other diversions. When Pearl passed away however, the trips became twice yearly events, and he put all his time and energy into his work.

Though it had been -- thankfully -- many years since Wyoming had its last "hangin' judge," there were plenty of defense attorneys who would insist that Judge Torrence might just be the reincarnation of one. Defendants were certainly treated fairly, but if found guilty of harming innocents they could expect Jeremiah to throw not only the book at them, but the book*case* as well.

They called him "Chuckwagon" when he played defensive end for the University of Wyoming. The team never achieved national fame during his tenure, but there was no denying he left his mark. Repeatedly. His personal goal was to disable at least one player per game, and do so strictly by the rules. He didn't get his nickname because of his capacity for food, though that was certainly prodigious, but because when he ran over someone, they usually felt like they'd been hit by a

Josh Langston

Conestoga and trampled by a full team of large and thoroughly unhappy draft animals.

Torrence administered justice in much the same way. When he read the charges against the three men who'd tried to use gunpowder instead of fishing lures, Jeremiah Torrence was not amused. He not only made sure the trio would be accommodated in his court at the earliest opportunity, he took pains to move some other cases around to get to them just a little bit sooner. For reasons he could not begin to understand, the defendants had requested a jury trial. And, they claimed the arresting officer had drugged them prior to the arrest. The brief their attorney submitted argued that such bizarre and dangerous treatment clearly provided grounds for having the case dismissed.

Judge Torrence couldn't wait to see how things worked out in his courtroom.

~*~

"Somebody beats the snot out of my grandson, and you're not even going to look for him?" Dolores Mansheer's face reflected annoyance as she stared at Nate. It was as close as he'd ever seen her to being simply angry. It was not appealing.

"What would you have me do, Dee, arrest every Indian under five feet tall?" His exasperation had been growing since he checked in for an evening shift a few hours after Dee's grandson had his nose pushed back where it belonged.

"Why not? You could line them up and let Marty have a look at 'em."

"Want to do it here, or at the various elementary schools in the county?"

224

"School isn't even in session," Dee said. "Besides, Marty said it was an adult."

"Right. And how many adults do you know who stand less than four feet tall?"

"You said five feet tall a minute ago."

"I'm being as specific as Marty was," Nate said. "Based on what he told me, our perp is Plastic Sam, the elastic man."

Dee responded with a scowl.

"So, I'm thinkin' it was another kid, and Marty was just too embarrassed to admit it."

"Is that so awful? I mean, he's just a child himself. You can't expect him to have an adult's judgment." She paused to rearrange a note pad, a pen and pencil holder, and a small pair of framed photos. When the objects had been safely shuffled, she said, "Okay, maybe it *was* another kid."

Nate resisted the urge to grin. "And, like you pointed out, the schools aren't in session yet, so we'd have to screen the kids from all of them, not just the one in Ten Sleep."

"I suppose."

"And let's not forget that Ten Sleep is located on a very popular route to Yellowstone. So, we're not just talking about Washakie county residents. Do you know how many people visit Yellowstone every year?"

Dee held her tea cup in both hands. "Quite a few."

"And how many do you suppose drive through Ten Sleep?"

She took a sip of her beverage, then carefully put the cup on the table beside the freestanding microphone she spent so much time talking into. "I get it. But that doesn't make it feel right."

Nate shrugged. "Sorry 'bout that. My gut says there's a chunk of this story we haven't heard."

"Are you suggesting Marty is lying?"

"Suggesting? Gosh, no. I'm saying it flat out. Marty isn't telling the whole story."

Dee stiffened. "He's had a... a difficult childhood."

"I suspect most serial killers have said something like that."

"That's out of line, Nate."

"In the words of a friend of mine, it is what it is."

Her face clouded. "Just who do you think is the victim here?"

"That's a good question," he said. "I'll let you know if I ever figure it out." He slipped his hat on and walked out of the office. Sometimes you just had to let folks cool off on their own. Dee was no exception. He didn't feel good about it, but he wouldn't lose any sleep over it either.

~*~

Reyna pulled hard on Shadow's collar, but the dog kept running. She had no idea he was so deathly afraid of snakes. Not that there was anything wrong with respecting them, but fear was something one should reserve for the unknown. Snakes she knew about.

When Shadow finally slowed to a walk, they were already halfway back across the valley. Reyna figured she might be able to find the snake if they went back, but coaxing the big dog into turning around didn't seem likely. Just because he listened when she talked didn't mean he understood what she said, or that if he did understand he would care. In that respect, she thought ruefully, Shadow and Mato had much in common.

Eventually, he stopped. Dropping to the ground in the meager shade of clumped sagebrush, Shadow let Reyna slide off his shoulders. She inspected him for snake bites,

though she felt sure he had escaped injury, else he would
not have been able to run so far. It was unfortunate she'd
missed the chance to get the snake. Its venom, along with
the plant she had been seeking, were the only ingredients
she still lacked for the sleeping paste. It would have to
wait for another day. She wished she had some water for
the poor dog. He lay panting in the late afternoon heat.
The shade would help, but he needed to cool down. She
was content to wait until he was rested. Nor did she mind
walking the rest of the way to the cabin. It would be cool
there, and Tori would have food and drink.

She still wasn't entirely convinced the food Tori gave
them was safe, but since Tori also ate it, her suspicions
had faded. Giant food consisted of many more flavors
and textures than she was used to. Her diet had always
been simple. Tori's was complex, and virtually everything
went through the great white box which rattled and
buzzed in its efforts to keep the food cold.

When Reyna thought Shadow had rested enough, she
urged him to his feet. He was reluctant to get up, but
when she started walking away, he ambled after her.
They had travelled for perhaps fifteen minutes when she
came upon the plant she had sought earlier.

Though twisted and dead in outward appearance, the
plant's roots were alive. She dug one up, careful not to
disturb any others. The plant would most likely survive
without it. Cutting through the root with a sharp stone
proved tiresome. Winter Woman had made it look easy,
but then, she'd been doing it all her life. For Reyna, the
skill was still in development. Finally, she succeeded and
slipped the root into the sling on her back. The treats for
Shadow were long gone.

"Time to go," she said, stroking the big dog's black
nose. He licked her hand and got to his feet. She smiled
thinking about the machine which kept Tori's house cool.

She would love to find something like that to bring to The People when she and Mato finally returned. But, like so much of what the giants had, it was too big to move. Perhaps there was something inside of it which could be removed and taken home. The thought intrigued her. She would discuss it with Mato at the first opportunity.

"Come," she said. "We've done enough for one day." Tomorrow she would look for a snake.

~*~

Tori answered her cell phone on the second ring. "H'lo?"

"Good mornin', Sunshine." Nate's usually reserved tones were absent, replaced by the chipper voice of a male cheerleader.

"Nate? You okay?"

"I thought you'd like to know that the medical examiner's report arrived a little while ago."

She wasn't sure if she should be wary or not. Nate hadn't said anything about how it might go. But then, he was calling her on the phone and sounded happy. If he needed to arrest someone, he'd be--

"Do you want to know what it says or not?" he asked, his voice back to normal.

"Yes. Yes! Of course."

"Hold on. Lemme find the important part."

She heard the rattle of paper. *C'mon, Nate!*

"Okay. Here it is: 'Though the remains showed evidence of considerable soft tissue decomposition, damage to the skeletal structure was consistent with a fall from a height of approximately 18 to 20 stories.' It goes on to list which bones were broken and where."

"No mention of poisons or other chemicals?"

"The tox screen wasn't exhaustive. It only checked for the usual kinds of things."

"Like?"

"Alcohol and anything related to heroin or cocaine. The main thing is, based on the report, there's no reason to expect foul play."

She cleared her throat. "You seem to have overlooked the fact that Shawn was trying to kill me. Doesn't that constitute foul play?"

"You know what I mean."

"So, I'm off the hook?"

"You and Mato, both."

A feeling of weariness came over her. She hoped it was merely the sudden absence of stress. "So, now you'll be able to sleep better knowing you left Mato out of your report?"

"Something like that," he said. "Although there's this whole business with Dee's grandson. You and I both know who was responsible for that."

"Mato said the kid attacked him. He'd have no reason to lie about something like that."

"I know, but what was he doing in the house in the first place?"

Tori shrugged involuntarily. "Looking around, I guess. What was Marty doing in there?"

"Same thing, I suppose," Nate said.

"The kid asked me if I thought you'd let him fire your gun."

"I hope you said no."

"I told him he needed to talk to you." She paused. "I may have said that I thought you might have more than just the one."

"I do," he said. "But I keep 'em locked up. Well, except for..." It was his turn to pause. "Damn."

"What?"

"When I was a teen my dad bought me a little six-shooter. Single action, .22 caliber."

"So?"

"I leave it in my desk. But the desk wasn't locked."

"Is it still there?"

Nate's voice was anything but chipper. "I sure as hell hope so."

"I'm on my way to Caleb's to get some odds and ends. Want me to swing by your place and check? Is the house locked?"

"How 'bout I meet you there," he said. "Is Mato with you?"

"No, but Lance is."

"Maybe you should leave him in the truck."

~*~

Carmine felt pretty good about the deal he'd made with Aldo. Lykes had wired him two grand, and all but two hundred went for car repairs. Including the air conditioner. Carmine had drawn the line at replacing the radio. Not that it would have cost very much, but he figured once he got west of central Ohio, there wouldn't be anything on the air but country and western stations. And he wasn't ready to cast his lot with shit kickers.

Halfway between Wheeling and Columbus he stopped for gas and restocked on peanuts. He couldn't find any Bang in the first three places he checked and began to worry that he might not be able to find it anywhere once he got further west. But he struck gold on the fourth try, and since he knew he would be returning in a matter of days, he only bought three cases.

With a can of Bang in one hand and a bag of salted nuts in the other, he shoved Ray Charles back into the tape player and continued his mission. He could feel his intestines gearing up for the effort and wondered if, with enough practice, he might be able to fart Benjamin Lykes' name.

~*~

Tori reached Nate's house first. Since he lived slightly beyond the city limits of Ten Sleep, his nearest neighbor was nearly a half mile away. Tori didn't get the impression anyone was watching as she walked up to Nate's front door and sat down on the stoop to wait for him. He arrived a few minutes later and dragged her inside as he made a mad dash to a big desk sitting at the far end of his living room.

She watched him pull open the bottom drawer on the left side and reach in, his face an emotionless mask. Her heart began to sink as he rummaged in the drawer.

And then he smiled.

"It's still here," he said, producing a small, black revolver with walnut grips. It looked like the same kind of weapon any self-respecting cowboy might carry, only smaller.

Nate checked the cylinder to make sure it wasn't loaded, then carried it over to a gun cabinet on the far side of the room and stuck it inside. "I should've kept it in here to begin with," he said.

"No harm done," Tori said. "Guess I didn't need to leave Lance out in the truck after all. But I appreciate your concern for his shyness around guns."

He locked the cabinet and dropped his keys on a coffee table. His hat soon followed. "Are you in a big hurry to get to Cal's place?"

"Not especially. Why?"

"I never got to show you around my house."

"That's true." She pursed her lips. "Come to think of it, you've seen all the secrets at my place."

"Mine doesn't have the same historical pedigree yours has. But it's got something yours lacks."

"Really? What could that possibly be? A deck?"

"A bedroom."

"I have a bedroom," Tori said.

"Yes, but there's a kitchen and a living room in it, too."

"And a pair of horny little Indians." She wasn't consciously aware that either of them had moved, and yet they had their arms around each other.

"Horny isn't always a bad thing," Nate whispered as his lips closed on hers.

She thought, momentarily, about making a witty reply, then settled for, "Mmmmm."

Somehow they levitated into Nate's sleeping quarters. Tori couldn't remember moving under her own power. *But that didn't matter.* Only the flow mattered, and it was inexorable.

The drapes were already drawn, leaving the room comfortably dark. The sheets were smooth and cool on her suddenly bare skin. Had she undressed herself? She couldn't remember, and didn't give a damn. Nate's eagerness and intensity matched her own. She tried to focus on pleasing him, but there was no hope for it. He was everywhere she wanted him to be. Fast, slow, firm, gentle, patient, brusque. But mostly patient.

And diligent.

And thorough.

Oh, God. Was he ever thorough.

~*~

"Tori has asked this one last thing of me," Mato said. "And then we can go home."

"For good?"

When he failed to give her the instant reassurance she sought, he knew he'd made a serious blunder. "How can I answer that? There may come a time when we need to come back." He'd almost said 'want to come back.'

Reyna did not speak for a long time, and Mato hoped she was less upset than she had at first seemed. He was wrong.

"How long will it take?"

"A few days," he said.

"And where will you take her?"

"She thinks she might find the bones of her ancestor near the places where The People used to camp in the winter."

"There are many such places. Would she search them all?"

Mato shrugged. "Who can say what a giant will do?"

"They are not as unpredictable as I once thought."

That took him by surprise. "Oh?"

"They do not have the same gods. Their rules are not like ours. It's not that they do things for no reason; they do things for reasons we do not understand."

Mato thought he knew what she meant. "So, you don't mind that I go with her?"

"Of course I mind!"

"I won't take her anywhere near The People. We will only visit the places they no longer use, places the giants have already ruined. The People would never return to them anyway."

"I'm still afraid," Reyna said. "The dream--"

"Does not have to come true!" he said, putting his arms around her. "Our children will be fine. *We* will be fine."

233

"When must you leave?"

"Soon. Tori has gone to talk with Nate. She wants to use his horses."

"Will he go with her?" Reyna asked.

"I hope so," Mato said. "I might ride with him. He knows what he is doing. But the horse knows more about riding than Tori does. I plan to ride the dog. It's much closer to the ground, and Shadow has more sense."

"Sometimes," Reyna said, smiling. "Mato, my warrior, I have a surprise for you."

He beamed. "You do?"

She produced a small leather pouch much like the one Winter Woman had given him long ago. This one featured extensive bead work, and Reyna was understandably proud of it. She still had not found the snake she needed to finish making the sleeping paste. But she planned to continue her search very soon. She apologized for not having the paste ready but promised to have it when he returned.

"How did-- Who..." Mato stuttered.

"Winter Woman showed me how," Reyna said. "If we are going to have children, then we must work together in everything we do."

Mato clasped her in his arms. He had never felt such pride. When they marched into the camp of The People, everyone would know that he was someone of importance. A man of means. A dreamer, yes, but also an accomplisher. Perhaps they would make him a chief. A good chief needed a wise woman by his side, and he had the best.

He could not wait for his journey with Tori to be over.

~*~

Tori slipped from Nate's bed and grabbed his shirt off the floor. She put it on and went in search of water. She knew he was propped up on his elbows, watching her, but she pretended not to notice. *Be casual. Be cool. Don't overreact.* It was easy to say to herself, but what she really wanted to do, once she'd slaked her thirst, was to dive back under the covers and spend the rest of the day making love.

Sadly, when she returned to the bedroom, he was out of bed. He had a satisfied smile on his face as he zipped up his jeans.

"That," he said, emphatically, "was amazing."

Tori plunked down on the bed and crossed her legs, heedless of the open shirt. "Yeah."

"You want to get some lunch?"

She smiled. "Actually, I'm feelin'... a little full just now."

"Dinner, then," he said. "Tonight. Right here in town. Okay?"

"Okay."

"And afterwards... Well, we'll just have to see."

"I have a favor to ask," Tori said.

"Sure. Anything."

"I had another talk with Mato about looking for my uncle Bob."

"Oh? What'd he say?"

"He's willing, but he's also eager to take Reyna back home. She's been giving him a pretty hard time about it. So, if we don't get moving soon, I may not get another chance."

"And you want to borrow my horses."

Eyelash batting had never been one of her great talents, but Tori tried it anyway.

"Got something in your eye, darlin'?"

235

"What? Uh, yeah," she said, digging her finger into the offending orb.

"You know you're not ready to ride anywhere on your own," he said.

"That's the part that bothers me, too. Ya think Caleb might be willing to go with me?"

"I'm sure he would," Nate said. "But there's someone else who might not be too thrilled with that idea."

"Maggie?"

"Me," he said. "Geezus, Tori. We just made love. My head is drifting around somewhere in the goofus-sphere. I won't be able to think of much else besides you for I don't know how long, and suddenly you're talking about going on a trail ride with some other guy?"

"That 'other guy' is old enough to be my daddy."

"I don't care if he's old enough to be your *daddy's* daddy."

She started giggling.

"Stop that," he said, "I'm trying to be jealous."

"You're doin' okay. Keep it up. I'm curious to see where this ends up."

"You know damn well where it'll end up!"

"Nope," she said, wagging her head from side to side. "You'll have to tell me."

"I'm going with you."

She leaped to her feet and hugged him. He slipped his hands inside the open shirt and caressed her back. *Don't stop!* "Do you mean it? Can you get time off that easily? When can we leave?"

"Easy now," he said, holding her at arms length, his big hands fitting easily into the narrows above her hips. "I've got some vacation time coming, although I think I may have burned up a little of that this morning. I hope Dee hasn't been looking for me."

"Well, she can't have you," Tori said. "I found you first."

He kissed her full on the mouth. "You go get your gear together. Tell Mato to pack whatever he thinks he'll need. Have you any idea which direction we'll be going in?"

Tori shook her head again. "He won't tell me anything. Says it wouldn't make any sense."

"I doubt he's spent any time using our roads, but surely we can get close to a starting point and eliminate some of the riding. We'll take the trailer as far as we can, then saddle up and ride from there."

"Can we start today?" she asked.

"Well, late today. I guess our dinner date will have to wait."

"What? Some cowpoke you are! Can't we cook over an open fire?"

He grinned back at her. "Okay, then. I'll take care of the main course. Steaks or something. You can bring a couple spuds and some butter."

"And after dinner?"

"Dessert."

"What'd you have in mind?"

"Something really low cal. If my blanket's not too smelly, you could share it with me."

"There's a chance I could be talked into that," she said. "And besides, it's probably time Mato got a little taste of his own medicine."

~*~

Carmine had been watching for the signs announcing the distance to St. Louis. It seemed like he'd been observing them for the better part of his life. The number of miles was shrinking, but not nearly as fast as he would have liked.

Lykes hadn't given him a timetable for completing his assignment. He was just to go to Wyoming as fast as he could, sneak up to a particular house in the middle of a very specific nowhere, and snatch a kid. Then, get the hell out and head east. All without raising any suspicions. *In, grab, out. Go home.* Piece of cake, Lykes had said. "No special skills. No need for weapons. No risks."

Carmine slapped his forehead, and not just to stay awake. *What the hell was I thinking?*

It was getting late, and he'd tooted his way -- literally -- across the entire Midwest. He was too tired to think straight. He needed food and beer. After a solid night's sleep he'd be good to go again. He'd reach Denver by the end of the next day, assuming the Honda didn't cough up a lung or a piston or whatever it was that made 'em go. In two days, he'd be headed back home.

He thought about taking a different route for the return trip. It certainly felt like something he should do. *It's what a spy would do.* Suddenly he was Carmine Bond, secret agent. Double-oh-freakin'-eight. Except he didn't have a gun, or a cool car. Or, come to think of it, a hot babe waiting for him somewhere.

He started looking for a place to spend the night. James Bond might not be willing to bed down at a Motel 6, but Carmine wasn't so fussy.

~*~

Chapter 14

Any sufficiently advanced bureaucracy is
indistinguishable from molasses.

Dusk was still a couple hours away when Nate pulled
up beside Tori's cabin. She and the dog came out to greet
him. Shadow found the smells from the horse trailer
intoxicating. Tori considered pulling him away, then just
decided to ignore him.

"What's all this stuff in the back?" she asked.

He got out of the truck and joined her. "Camping gear
and food. I can't stay gone more than three days, so I
packed provisions accordingly."

"But, I've got food inside," she said.

"It'll keep. And if we need to make a second trip,
we'll have everything we need."

"Oh. Well, okay. You've done this before. I haven't."

"I've taken some long trips out where there aren't any
roads," he said. "But I've never tried to find the remains
of somebody who died a hundred years ago."

"That makes two of us."

Mato and Reyna came out of the cabin, holding
hands. Compared to the pile of stuff in the back of the
truck, Mato brought almost nothing. He'd be traveling so
light he might as well have been naked. The only weapon
he carried was his stone knife, and his belt seemed
precious little to keep his breech cloth from pushing the
envelope of local indecency laws.

"Mato," Nate said, kneeling to be at face level with
him, "there's something I need to say."

Mato sauntered closer. Reyna stayed two steps
behind him.

239

Nate removed a small box from his pocket. "The other day I got a little angry at you for going with me when I was on duty."

Mato put his hands behind his back and said nothing.

"Now I realize I made a couple mistakes that day. The first was when I let that guy get the drop on me with a shotgun. That was pure stupidity on my part. But the biggest mistake I made was thinking that because you're not as big as I am, you're not able to take care of yourself. Or anyone else. Especially somebody as big as me."

The little Indian appeared to be struggling to follow Nate's words, but he never asked him to slow down or elaborate. Tori figured he was getting the gist of it. It was obvious, however, that Reyna was utterly lost. She tugged Mato's sleeve for the usual translation, but he ignored her.

Nate kept right on. "Anyway, when the time came, you knew exactly what you were doing. You snatched my bacon right out of the fire, and I never thanked you properly."

He held the little package out for Mato's inspection. "I got this for you as a way to say thanks. I hope you can find a use for it. As for me, I learned a valuable lesson: I'll never doubt you again. That's a promise."

Mato accepted the gift box and opened it. Reyna crowded close to see what was in it. Tori found herself leaning closer, too.

Tori began to smile broadly as Mato unwrapped a very small, very finely crafted pocketknife. Though she recognized what it was instantly, the object seemed to baffle the Indians.

Nate held out his hand. "May I?"

Mato surrendered the knife. Nate took pains to show him how to unfold each of the two blades. Both were extremely sharp, as were the points. "I could probably shave with this thing," he said. "It's the smallest one I could find, but I think it's about the right size for you."

The smile on Mato's face would have lit up any room. Nate showed him how to press the release button in order to fold the blades back into the handle. Mato turned to Reyna and went through his own interpretation of how the knife worked. Then, he gave the knife to Reyna and spoke to her in their native tongue. Tori caught a few words, but not enough to follow the rapid exchange. Finally, Reyna bowed to Mato and then to Nate. She held the knife in both hands, but it was evident she had the muscle to use it.

Mato turned to Nate. "Nate good friend," he said, then frowned. "Mato have no gift."

"You saved my life," Nate exclaimed. "That may not mean much to some people, but it's a big deal to me." His smile was warm and wide. "So, gift-wise, I'm the one's got some catchin' up to do."

Mato grinned back at him, and then explained it all to Reyna. She stepped forward and put her hands on Nate's. "Friend," she said, simply, and Tori had no doubt she was sincere.

All too quickly, Tori felt, it was time to leave. She piled into the cab of the truck with Nate and Mato. Shadow jumped in the back. He stood on his hind legs with his front paws on the roof.

They all waved to Reyna as they drove away, except Shadow, who barked.

Mato did not look happy.

"We won't be gone long," Tori assured him. "She'll be fine."

~*~

Tessa's office wasn't ready yet. Neither was the lab. *Her lab*, technically, if Bernstein had his way, and since he owned the biggest piece of the company, that would certainly be the case. Eager to inspect her new domain, Tessa had waited as long as she could before driving to the corporate campus for a visit. The guard at the front gate seemed to recognize her but refused to let her in. She waved her employee badge in his face, but he merely shook his head.

"I'm sorry, Miss Bidford, but I was given strict instructions about you."

"Oh?"

"That's right. You aren't allowed on the premises until I get notification from Mr. Bernstein himself." He took a moment to review a sheet of paper taped to an interior wall of the guardhouse. "Or his secretary."

"I outrank Mr. Bernstein's secretary," Tessa said, coldly.

"In more ways than one," the guard responded. "But that don't change nothing. You can try again tomorrow."

"To get into my own damned office?"

"Yes ma'am," he said.

She wondered how many proxies she'd need in order to vote Jerry Bernstein out of office. Having been to a Board meeting, she had a vivid memory of the universally old, fat, balding men who attended. She knew what was required to get her hands on their shares, but crawling into bed with any one of them, let alone the entire gang, just wasn't an option. She'd rather give her kidneys to a wino.

~*~

Nate had a great deal of respect and admiration for

Mato. No question about it. That didn't mean, however, that the little primitive didn't try his patience. Often. The latest episode revolved around the need to find the closest spot where a road, paved or not, came into contact with the trail Mato would blaze for them in the quest to find Tori's ancestor's remains. By comparison, finding her late ex-husband's carcass had been a walk on the beach. Mato, it turned out, had no idea what function a map served.

"We're here," Nate said, in what he thought was a patient voice, as he tapped the clearly printed line on the county map.

Mato's expression suggested Nate had recently escaped from an asylum.

"This is my house," Tori said, pointing to another spot on the map. Mato shook his head, obviously pained that the Spirits had deposited not one, but two, clearly deranged people into his care.

Designed and printed especially for the use of Washakie county officials, the map was printed on one side only. Nate folded his copy so that a blank side lay face up. He handed his pen to Mato and asked him to draw a small picture of Tori's house.

Mato's glance suggested suspicion, but he went along with the request, quickly and efficiently doing a small rendering of the cabin.

"Good," Nate said. "Now show me where the big rock is."

"Cooking rock?" Mato asked.

"Yeah. Where Tori cooks sometimes."

Mato dutifully provided a sketch of the rock, complete with hibachi grill.

"Now show me where Tori parks her truck."

Mato drew in the truck as seen from the side, just like the cabin and the rock. All were done from a ground level perspective and yielded three objects standing in a row.

"Imagine you are a bird," Nate said. "Can you do that?"

"Mato bird?"

"Sure. Pretend you're an eagle. A mighty bird. And you're hungry. You're hunting."

The little Indian shrugged. "Bird."

"Now, look down from the sky. Can you see the roof of Tori's cabin?"

"No."

"Pretend!"

Mato looked to Tori for help.

"You can do it," she said. "The cabin is square." She slipped the pen from his hand, turned the folded map to another blank side and drew a simple, four line box shape. She drew a bisecting line to represent the ridge of the roof and then a smaller square in the middle of one side. "Here's the chimney."

"Bird see?" Mato asked.

"Yes! Good. Now, where's the big rock?"

Mato studied the little drawing, then put his finger on the paper where Tori's barbecue rock would be. Nate handed him the pen and Mato sketched a jagged oval.

"The bird sees this," Nate said, pointing to what Mato had just drawn. He flipped the map back to Mato's original drawings. "This is what Mato sees."

Suddenly Mato got the idea. "Here truck," he said returning to the overhead view. He sketched Tori's vehicle parked in its usual spot.

"Where's the road?" Nate asked. "How does the truck get to that spot?"

Mato drew roughly parallel lines to represent the dirt track leading to the house and moved his finger along the two-dimensional road.

"Excellent!" Nate said, unfolding the map to reveal

the printed side. He went back to the section where Tori's property lay. "The cabin is here," he said, drawing a miniature version of the square Tori had drawn.

"Rock here." Mato grabbed the pen and drew a tiny circle near the cabin roof. "Truck here."

"Yes! The main road is here," Nate said, pointing to the dark line representing the paved strip leading to Tori's drive.

Mato stared at the map for some time then drew a tentative line to show the connection between Tori's drive and the highway.

Nate began to realize what a teacher must feel when a student made the kind of breakthrough Mato had just had experienced. It was delicious, something beyond words. He eagerly unfolded the map the rest of the way, covering his own and his passengers' laps in the process.

"This is Ten Sleep. This road goes through the mountains to Buffalo. See the river? It runs the length of Ten Sleep Canyon. Steep, high mountains on both sides. Do you know where that is?"

Mato nodded. "Live here when hot," he said, waving his hand at the mountainous national park property. Maggie had taken Nate to parts of the park that were almost never seen by the general public, and yet he knew there were other huge chunks of it he would likely never explore. In which of those wild, uncharted places had Mato and his people lived? My God, he thought. *They're in there now!*

"Tori, didn't you say your uncle tried to find Mato's people before the winter set in?"

"That was his last journal entry. If he wrote anything else, he used a different book. I doubt he expected to come back. That's why he wrapped his journal in oil cloth."

"What route do you think he would have taken,

245

Mato?" Nate asked. *Get me close to a road, podnuh. Please!*

Mato squinted in concentration. He asked Tori where the sun was and where the mountains at the far end of her valley began. He traced lines representing rivers and asked about landmarks. Nate knew where most of them where, but some of the names Mato used left him mystified.

At length, the little Indian pointed to the southern end of Ten Sleep Canyon. "Trail here. Go cold camps this way." He pointed west, out of the mountains. "Hot camps here." He pointed north, into the wilderness areas of the Bighorn National Forest. In both cases, the destinations were vague. Clearly, Mato wasn't giving anything away.

Nate examined the area and found a park service road that would bring them very close to the spot Mato had designated. "Bless you, my friend. I think you've saved us a couple days of riding."

When Tori hugged the little guy, Nate didn't feel the slightest bit of jealousy.

~*~

An early start brought Carmine to Denver in time for dinner. He'd seen a wide variety of restaurants to choose from when it occurred to him that he hadn't really taken advantage of the cash available to him. Lykes had said he didn't need to find the cheapest rooms. Gas prices had actually been fairly reasonable, and he'd been quite frugal when it came to meals. Since he would be taking on an additional passenger the very next day, his last evening alone was at hand.

If he wanted to do anything fun, this was likely his last opportunity to do it on someone else's tab. So he started looking for a strip club. He'd been to a couple in New York, but always managed to exhaust his funds before he wore out his libido. This time, he had Lykes' money in his pocket.

Finding just the right place took more time than he thought it would. After driving around for an hour without success, he returned to his motel. There he discovered an establishment on the adjoining property which featured "the finest in gentlemen's entertainment." It was spelled out in neon lights easily visible from the interstate highway, if not from the parking spot outside his motel room.

Still in his car, he counted out five hundred dollars which he put in an envelope in the glove box. That would cover his expenses on the return trip. The rest -- a respectably thick collection of tens and twenties -- would keep him in booze and babes for the entire evening. With his imagination working overtime, he left the Honda behind and hiked the short distance to the club. He had no doubt that when he returned, he would be in no shape to drive anything anywhere.

Carmine hit the bricks with a smile on his face, cash in his pocket, and lust in his heart.

~*~

"I've only got a couple days I can devote to the search," Nate told Tori. "'Terrible' Torrence has moved up the trial date for the three idiots I arrested who went fishing with hand grenades. I have to be available to testify."

"I'm glad they're going to trial," Tori said.

"I'm *amazed* they're going to trial," snorted Nate. "Their lawyer should have gotten them a deal. No one goes to trial these days unless there's the possibility of acquittal. DAs only want to go to court if it's an election year, and even then they want cases so solid the verdict is guaranteed."

Tori smiled at him from her perch atop Elmer who was reluctantly plodding along beside Babe. Both of them were following Mato who sat astride Shadow and appeared so comfortable he might have been a part of the dog. "That's pretty cynical, even for you."

"I suppose. But plea bargaining is pretty common. It's quicker and cheaper than a trial, and you don't have to drag folks in to serve on juries. People can be funny about that, and juries can be downright vindictive at times. Which is what amazes me about these three Einsteins. Can you imagine anyone around here who'd give 'em a pass for using explosives that way? You can't turn around in this county without tripping over a hunter or a fisherman, and I guarantee none of them will be happy to hear that some half-wit blew up all the trout in somebody's favorite fishin' hole."

"Now I get it," Tori said. She couldn't help but laugh thinking about Mato's role in the affair. "You don't suppose those guys saw Mato, do you?"

"Hell, *I* didn't even see him," Nate said, "and I was looking for him."

"I'd hate for--"

"Nobody's going to mention him, even if they knew about him. Which they don't. And even if they did, how do you think bringing him into the case would make things any better for anyone? The DA certainly isn't going to boast that three brutal outlaws were subdued by a two-foot tall Indian armed with porcupine quills and a hollow tube. And I rather doubt the defense attorney would try to plead excessive force given those same circumstances." He reached out and patted Tori's leg.

"Don't give it another thought. Okay?"

She let her eyes slowly scan upward from his hand on her leg to his eyes. "Don't be startin' anything you can't finish."

His grin was as wicked as her aside. "You don't think I can *finish?*"

"Not on horseback."

"Yeah," he said, laughing. "You've got a point. How much farther do you want to ride?" They had only been on the trail an hour, but dusk always seemed to come quicker in the mountains.

"You're the boss."

"Well then, we'd better look for a place to camp. I don't mind riding in the dark, but you may not like it. Besides, the idea is to look for traces of Uncle Bob. We're going to need sunlight for that."

"Agreed," Tori said. "Besides, I've been looking forward to your cooking. Steaks, right?"

He gave her a surprised look. "I thought you wanted Beanie Weenies."

Mato looked up from his seat on Shadow's back. "Is food?"

Tori frowned. "Depends on your definition."

~*~

The dancer was a pleasantly short, pleasantly curvy blonde whose stage name was Desiree. She had dimples in all four cheeks, which Carmine found irresistible. Unfortunately, there were two others in her tiny audience who found commenting on her charms equally irresistible. But, while Carmine liked what he saw; the other two ridiculed it.

He suggested they switch to one of the other stages if they didn't like what Desiree had to offer. They suggested he shut up before they punched his lights out.

"Ignore 'em, sweetie," the dancer said as she wiggled her way through a tune Carmine had last heard blaring from Alvin Jones' boom box in the damp, squalid darkness of Spaski's DeeLux. He hadn't liked the song then, but Desiree definitely gave it an appealing interpretation.

The other two spectators began to trade fat jokes aimed at her.

"You guys are really funny," Carmine said when he'd finally had enough. "Do you make up your own jokes, or just steal them from bubble gum wrappers?"

Desiree put a soft hand on his shoulder. "They're just college kids," she said. "They've had a little too much to drink. They're not doing any harm."

"Not so," Carmine said. "They're ruining *my* big night out. That ain't right."

The two offered to ruin more than his "big night out," which label they found hysterically funny.

"I can have the bouncer take care of 'em," Desiree said.

Carmine dismissed the offer. "Allow me." Though he knew his bravado was driven largely by alcohol, it hadn't escaped his attention that the *alleged* college kids, both big enough to play football, were having trouble speaking clearly. He felt nearly giddy when he realized that for them, standing was also something of an accomplishment.

"Time for you to go now," he told them.

They invited him to "step outside" with them, for what Carmine assumed would be the usual beat down such invitations led to. He was not keen on being the center of such attention.

"After you," he said, gesturing toward the exit with

both hands. Once their backs were turned, he grabbed a
pair of Coor's 12-ounce beer bottles and followed them
out.

In his admittedly limited experience, Carmine had
observed that preppy types like these often liked to make
witty remarks to each other before proving their
superiority over ignorant local dumb asses. It thus
behooved the ignorant local dumb ass to strike first,
which is precisely what he did. College boy One dropped
before they cleared the front door. College boy Two
tripped over the suddenly driverless limbs of his
companion, then got a downward assist. Carmine used
the same bottle on both and held the second one in
reserve. It proved unnecessary. Real beer bottles don't
break as easily as the ones in the movies. Besides, the
second one still contained nearly a full ration of Rocky
Mountain lager.

Carmine emptied the second bottle over the two inert
forms and returned to look for Desiree. With any luck,
she'd be finished with her set and would be available for a
private performance.

Reyna woke early the next morning, determined to be
in position before the sun rose very high. She wanted to
catch her snake before it chose a place to bask in the
warmth of a clear day. She gathered everything she
would need, though it wasn't much, and marched out the
door of Tori's cabin.

With any luck, she wouldn't have to travel far. She
knew from what Mato had told her, and from Tori's
attitude in general, that the she-giant did not like snakes.
Perhaps if she knew what valuable things the legless ones
did, she would feel differently. But no matter what Tori

or anyone else might think, Reyna valued the snakes for their venom.

Long ago, before The People had drawn their first painting in the Cavern of Dreams, there were many different kinds of animals in the land. Some large and some small, they lived in plenty if not in peace, for life made demands on all of them. Some had sharp teeth, long claws and a sense of smell to alert them when food wandered nearby. Others had amazing eyesight or the ability to hear the footfall of a hunter even when it stalked. The Spirits did these things so that no single kind of animal could claim superiority over the rest.

Runners, climbers, swimmers -- all had some gift the others could not match. Except for the snake. He had no ears, no voice, and no legs. The Spirits had given him nothing but a noisemaker, and this they attached to the end of his tail. Surely the legless ones had angered the Spirits in the time before time, although no one knew for certain what terrible thing they had done. The Old Ones sometimes played a game when The People gathered around a campfire. They would take turns making up stories about what the snakes had done. Some crimes were trivial; others were too dreadful to contemplate. But all the stories were told with a wealth of feeling and detail that made them seem real. At least to the youngest members of the clan.

Reyna smiled in anticipation of the day -- no longer in the distant future -- when she would hold a child of her own and calm her fears as the Old Ones recounted the snake's ancient crimes. The final part of the game was played by the parents of the young. Their task was to explain that the Spirits eventually took pity on the snake, and even though it was too late to give them ears, or legs, or a voice, they gave them teeth and venom. The People

252

complained that these gifts made the snake much too dangerous, for he had learned to crawl very quietly, and no one would know when he was nearby.

In order to satisfy The People, the Spirits gave the snakes a command which they must forever obey. They did not like it, but such is the power of the Spirits that even to this day, the snakes used their noisemakers to warn their prey before they were allowed to strike.

It was a good game, and the stories of the snakes were some of Reyna's favorites. She recalled when she was little and had asked Winter Woman why some snakes had noisemakers and others did not. How could the Spirits have been so unfair? Winter Woman had pointed out that only those with poison had to give warnings. But, Reyna had protested, what did the other snakes do that was so terrible the Spirits took no pity on them at all?

Reyna smiled again, finally appreciating Winter Woman's wisdom, for she always said the answer to Reyna's question was for another time, another game. But it was a game no one ever played.

Nor would she be playing a game when she found the snake she needed to finish the sleeping paste for Mato. Though she was younger and stronger than Winter Woman, Reyna knew better than to try to deal with a fully grown rattler. They had enough strength to twist and curl and thrash until they broke free. A giant could secure one with a single hand. Reyna would need both hands, her legs, and more than a bit of luck. And that assumed she found one no more than half again her own length. If she had a choice, she would prefer one very young, very short, and a little stupid.

As is often the case with well-made plans, hers failed from the start. She heard her snake before she saw it.

Josh Langston

~*~

Carmine woke with a splitting headache. It felt like someone had pasted his eyelids shut, too. His memory of the previous evening's festivities came back slowly. He wasn't sure if the gaps in his memory were good things or not.

There had been a fabulously beautiful woman involved. Her name was Desiree, or at least it had been when the evening began, and she had been enthralled by his attentions. He also recalled dealing with a couple of jerks whose idea of humor was to say unkind things about the newfound love of his life. If only he could remember her real name. She'd given it to him at some point, but for now it was buried in a mental mist.

Certain parts of the evening came back with greater clarity. For instance, the first encounter with the two stand-up comics had been quite positive. He was sure of it. The beautiful young woman had rewarded him handsomely for being her champion. Or at least, he thought she had. It was the second go-round with the guys in golf shirts that left him groping for details. And at least one tooth.

With the tip of his tongue, he explored the pulpy socket that hadn't been there the day before. Had he done something similar to them? Damned details. He would've shaken his head if doing so didn't threaten to degrade his already delicate condition.

He looked down at his knuckles expecting to find them suitably scraped and bruised. They appeared to be pristine. When he eventually stumbled into the bathroom he discovered that his face had not fared as well. A black eye on the left strove to balance the swollen upper lip on the right.

254

His clothing was only marginally bloody, which suggested he had acquitted himself well. In a sudden and inexplicable epiphany, he remembered the girl's name: Domino. Her real name. *Beautiful, busty, blonde Domino.*

It must've been one hell of a night. He sincerely wished he could remember more of it, especially those parts involving the girl.

He found his wallet next to the TV. There was no cash left in it. His car keys were... *Where the hell were the car keys?* He stumbled to the curtain and yanked it open, exposing himself to blinding daylight which turned him around as neatly as the blast from a high-pressure fire hose. Somehow, he forced himself to reopen his eyes and look for the crappy little Honda which contained not only the rest of his money, but pretty much everything he owned.

It was nowhere to be seen.

Chapter 15

"Pressure is something you feel when you don't know what the heck you're doing." ~Peyton Manning

The rattle *almost* made Reyna freeze. The sound was so distinct, it could not be mistaken for anything else. But despite what the Old Ones said around the campfire, Reyna knew the rattle was the exact opposite of a warning, for it caused the snake's prey to *stop* moving. If she were the hunter, wouldn't she rather her target stand still and wait for the inevitable? She didn't blame the snake for not wanting to engage in a chase. But that didn't mean she would fall for his trick.

Moving away from the sound at an angle, she quickly removed herself from the snake's range. She saw it move, too, undulating out from beneath a rock. Now they faced each other on more equal terms, and for every moment the snake gave her to prepare, the odds shifted further in her favor.

She carried two sticks. The longer of the two was forked at the end, and she had used Mato's new knife to prepare it, carving points on both tines of the fork. She had affixed a stiff, circular piece of leather to the end of the shorter stick. Using Mato's paints, she had drawn large eyes on the leather and would use it to focus the snake's attack.

Once she had the snake in the open she shifted her position until she faced it, jabbing with the leather face. The snake coiled, its rattle giving off an annoyingly loud sound. The snake's tongue darted out and back, its head weaving from side to side as it prepared to strike.

"Come to me," Reyna said, her voice a sing-song mixture of prayer and incantation. "Come now, and give me what I want." She continued to wave the false face, jabbing whenever the snake appeared to hesitate. The snake rattled harder and faster. The attack would come at any second. Reyna's hands began to sweat, but she maintained her grip on both tools.

"Come now!" she shouted, and as if in answer, the snake struck out lightning fast, its mouth stretched wide to engage long, sharp fangs. The pale interior of the rattler's mouth was a blur as it moved. Reyna held the false face steady and let the snake hit it.

The snake bounced off the flat leather face as the surface was too wide to bite and did not yield to the fangs. Reyna kept it between herself and the snake like a shield as she thrust the forked stick down, pinning the snake's head to the ground. The two points sank into the dirt and held the snake's head firmly in place.

Though it writhed and hissed, its body coiling and uncoiling in a frighteningly spasmodic display, Reyna felt no pity for it and simply waited until it exhausted itself. When it was spent, she grabbed it by the neck and forced its jaws open. Using a technique taught to her by Winter Woman, she coaxed the serpent to give up several precious drops of its venom which she captured in a wad of milkweed fibers. These she transferred to a container she borrowed from Tori. There would be more than enough to meet the requirements for the sleeping paste.

Pleased with herself, Reyna released the snake a good distance from Tori's cabin, hoping it would forget the experience. She had no desire for it to come back looking for a reward of some kind. Tori was not likely to appreciate such a thing either.

She had considered keeping the rattler for food, but handling poisonous snakes was always tricky, and she

257

refused to risk the tiny life growing inside her. On the way back to the cabin however, she found another snake, one without fangs and poison -- much easier to handle, and almost as tasty. She hauled the black and yellow snake back to the cabin and looked for a place to store it until she was ready to kill and clean it. Letting it crawl loose wouldn't do as there were simply too many places where it might hide, and she had no intention of hunting it down twice.

Then it came to her, as the blindingly obvious often does, and she tossed the snake in the big white box where Tori stored so much of her own food. The snake would not only be easy to find, but should move much more slowly because of the cold. The People could really use something like the food box, and she renewed her intention to discuss with Mato the idea of removing the cold-making parts to take with them when they went home.

Home, she thought. It wouldn't be long now. How happy the Old Ones would be to see them. Not only would they have the great black dog and other treasures taken from the she-giant, it would not be long before anyone who looked at Reyna could tell she was going to have a baby.

She asked the Spirits to look kindly on Mato and the giants. *Let them find what they're looking for, and send my warrior back to me.*

~*~

Mato rode on Shadow's back for much of the morning, then dropped to the ground and continued on foot. Shadow didn't seem to mind carrying him, but ran and played in obvious joy when the burden was removed.

Tori enjoyed watching them both. Mato for his intensity, Shadow for his unrestrained curiosity. The dog's ability to mark his passing was truly amazing. Even Nate commented on it, wondering if the big canine would ever run dry.

"He's piddling dust," Nate said. "I read a poem about that somewhere."

"Your past is even more checkered than I imagined," Tori said.

He chuckled. "I don't recall hearing you complain last night."

She felt herself flush. It had been an extraordinary evening, despite her misgivings about making love where Mato could hear them.

"I don't think it's possible to embarrass him," Nate had said.

"You're worried about *his* embarrassment?"

At her insistence, they waited until the sounds of Mato's breathing suggested he was asleep. The delay only served to intensify their desire, and both were well sated when they finally stopped molesting each other and stretched out on the air mattress Nate had thoughtfully provided.

Tori liked having Nate's arm around her, even if it restricted her movement during the night. She liked his warmth and the smell of him all around her. Neither spoke of love or commitment, but being together seemed so right, so *comfortable*, that she wasn't worried about it. There was a time when she thought she had something similar with Shawn, but that had been long ago, and she had been terribly young, and undeniably stupid. What she had with Nate, whatever it was, felt real. They would talk about it someday, but until that day rolled around, she was quite content to wait.

"Here!" Mato said, driving an icicle into her thoughts.

259

"What is it?"

Mato pointed at the ground. It didn't seem any different than any of the ground they'd been looking at since dawn, when they started their search. "Old trail here."

Nate slipped lightly from Babe's back and dropped to the ground beside him. The two poked and prodded at the soil like investigators isolating skin cells or suspicious fibers at a crime scene. Whatever they found might be invisible to her, but to her highly skilled tracking team, something interesting had this way passed.

Uncle Bob, you old reprobate, did you mark the trail for yourself?

~*~

Carmine was torn between terror and despair. Neither emotion would result in something positive, but he was too befuddled to think of a way out. Call Lykes? Sure. That would go over like dinner in a dumpster. His dear brother-in-law would call Dial-A-Hit as soon as Carmine hung up.

At least he had the advantage of distance. And invisibility. Lykes didn't know where he was. Granted, he knew Carmine's original route -- he had probably mapped it himself -- so he knew where Carmine was *supposed* to be. But that really didn't mean much now. Lykes wouldn't know that Carmine was reduced to panhandling for his next meal. He'd assume Carmine had hit the road with the bankroll intact, probably headed for Vegas. *Note to self: Vegas is off-limits for the next few lifetimes.*

He glanced at the clock. Almost nine. Check-out in two hours. Fortunately, since he didn't have a credit card, they had insisted he pay in advance when he checked in.

And, he recalled, they'd demanded an additional fifty dollar advance against incidentals. How was he supposed to rack up fifty bucks worth of incidentals? Dirty movies? He glanced at the rumpled bed. *Who needed dirty movies when you had the real deal?* At least, he thought he might've had the real deal. A memory would be nice. Maybe two. *Thanks loads, God.*

Had Domino come back to the room with him? Come to think of it, how *had* he gotten back to the room? That part of the evening, like so many others, was still less than fuzzy. He remembered smiling. A lot. He remembered Domino smiling, too, although he had trouble focusing on much besides her amazing chest. And the dimples. Those were etched indelibly in his brain.

Someone slid a key into the door lock.

Carmine stiffened. Lykes! *Shit, shit, shit!* The bastard already had a contract out on him! Would he hear the shots or would they simply go *pifft, pifft* -- lights out? He dropped to the floor between the bed and the wall, scrambling. Quietly, he hoped.

He heard the door open as he tried to squeeze under the bed, but the support for the box springs was built into the floor. Without a jackhammer or a pound of C4, he had no place to hide. *I'm so screwed.*

Resigned, he assumed fetal position and waited for the *pifft* and the darkness.

"What are you doin' on the floor, sweetie?"

Carmine's eyes popped open. *Sweetie?*

He uncurled and looked up into the big, brown eyes of a round-faced brunette holding a bag of doughnuts. She had dimples just like Domino, and -- he spared a quick glance below her neck -- sure enough, the same stunning architecture. But where was her platinum hair? What happened to those enormous, bright green eyes?

"You okay, baby?" she asked.

261

Suddenly, an inspirational news flash: *I'm going to live!* "Yes," he gasped. "I-- I think so."

"I borrowed your car," she said, putting the doughnuts on the bed. It made crumpled bag sounds: a Krispy Kreme drive-by shooting. She continued, "I figured you wouldn't mind. I didn't get anything to drink, though. I thought we could use the little coffee maker and brew our own."

He desperately wanted to ask her who she was, but she seemed *so* familiar. He didn't want to risk offending her. "No, that's fine," he managed to say. "In fact, that's a great idea." *Or would be, if I liked coffee.*

"I let you sleep in. You looked so cute all curled up, even if your face is a little puffy."

"Oh. Right," he said. "Thanks."

"That was some night."

"No shit."

She sat on the bed as he leaned back against the wall, his knees bent and his feet wedged against the frame for the box springs.

"You sure you're okay?"

"I'm a little hazy on a couple things." *Carmine DeLuca, master of understatement.* There were a couple guys...."

She broke into a huge smile, which drove her dimples vertical. "The two who were giving me such a hard time?"

"Yeah. Did they come back? Or send friends?"

"I doubt those assholes have friends," she said. "And no, they didn't come back. Freddie, our bouncer, said he found them, out cold, clogging up the front entrance."

"What'd he do with them?"

"Usually he drags guys like them out back with the rest of the garbage. You'd be surprised how often that happens." Her tone was completely matter-of-fact, which he found a little unsettling.

"But," she went on, "when you passed out, I told Freddie you deserved better than that. No boyfriend of mine gets laid out in an alley."

He felt a weak smile pushing bravely against his bulbous lip. "Thank you."

"I thought you'd wake up after awhile, but when you didn't, I got Freddie to carry you here."

"Here? How did--"

She held up his room key. A diamond-shaped piece of plastic was attached that proudly displayed the motel name and his room number. He had thought the practice went out of fashion with hoop skirts and muzzle loaders but forgot about it once he'd put the key in his pocket.

"This bouncer guy--"

"Freddie."

"Right. He *carried* me here?"

"He's a big guy." She frowned suddenly. "But he doesn't work for free. He kinda helped himself to what was left in your wallet."

"There was something left?"

"Not much. You spent a lot of money last night," she said, looking happy once again. "And most of it was on me. You're amazing!"

"Domino?" he asked, tentatively.

She was still glowing. "Yes?"

"I could have sworn you were a blonde."

Giggling, she touched his cheek. "Only at work. I wear a wig. Oh, and contact lenses. One of the other dancers suggested it. Kinda like a disguise."

Everything else had to be real, he thought. He'd seen it! He'd desperately wanted to feel it, too, but that was against the rules. He couldn't remember if they were the club's rules, or hers. He looked again at the unmade bed.

"Did I... Uhm, did we...."

Domino, still smiling, wagged her finger at him. "You were a perfect gentleman. Well, perfect the whole time you were awake. You're the nicest guy I've ever met at the club."

"Yeah?"

"No one's ever stood up for me before," she said. "You didn't have to, but you did. And those guys were a lot bigger than you are. I don't think either one of them got in a single punch."

He touched the knot bulging above his eye. "So, how'd I get this?"

"You hit your head on the sink in the men's room when you passed out."

"I did?"

"According to Freddie. He found you."

Carmine ran his tongue from the gap between his teeth to the lump on his lip. "And this?" It came out: "An thith?"

"Freddie said that after the sink, you probably bounced off the edge of the toilet."

"I did?" he asked again.

"You had an awful lot to drink, and champagne can make people do weird things."

"Champagne," he mumbled.

"*You* had champagne," she explained. "I had ginger ale."

"I bought you ginger ale?" His memory hadn't improved much, despite the flood of information she provided. Still, he had no idea why he kept rephrasing everything she said as a question.

"You *paid* for champagne," she said. "But we're not supposed to drink on the job. Besides, I'm underage. Well, for another month anyway."

The surprises just kept piling up. He checked her ring finger to see if they'd gotten married while he slept. Other than a nicely manicured nail, the finger went unadorned.

She walked over to the tiny in-room coffee service and fired up the little two-cup pot. He didn't have the heart to tell her he didn't like coffee.

"I called you Galahad," she said.

That he remembered. Mostly because he wasn't sure what it meant. Though he knew it might seem rude, he looked directly at her face, struggling to remember additional details. And then, he did. "You kissed me."

Nodding, she walked to him and helped him to his feet. "Of course."

"And I didn't-- You know...."

"You didn't what?"

"I didn't make you kiss me?"

"Make me? No, silly. I *wanted* to kiss you. You earned it."

"I did?"

"But there's a rule at the club: dancers aren't allowed to date customers."

"Oh." *What a stupid rule!*

"But you're way more than just a customer," she said.

He certainly wanted to be.

"You're my hero."

Something in Carmine's heart shifted. He'd never been someone's hero. He wasn't sure he'd ever even been someone's best friend. But *hero?* Holy crap!

"Oh, yeah, there's something else. I won't be dancing any more."

"What?" *Had he gotten her in trouble with the club? Damn it! What else could he not recall?* "Why not?"

"Well, mostly 'cause I'm not very good at it."

"Are you kidding? You're a great dancer!"

"You're sweet. But the truth is, last night was my

audition, and it didn't go very well. You're the only one who tipped me or bought me drinks."

That came as welcome news. Very welcome.

"If it had just been a matter of how much money you spent -- on me and on drinks -- I'd be back on stage tonight. But the simple truth is, except for you and those two college jerks, nobody else paid any attention. I'll do okay just waiting on tables. Besides, I don't like working with my clothes off."

"I don't either," he said. "On you. Wait. What I mean is--"

"I know what you mean. You told me last night." Her smile was impish. "You told me a lot of things last night. But I wasn't the only one you talked to."

Awesome. I pledged my undying love to every dancer in the joint.

She seemed to take pity on him and explained. "You called your sister, long distance, to tell her about me. Us, actually."

He definitely liked the sound of the word "us" when she said it.

"It was awful late when you called. I think she might have been asleep."

Now that he thought about it, he did remember calling Veronica, though he had no idea what he might have said. Knowing his sister, she'd almost certainly blown him off from the start. He'd most likely only pretended to have a conversation with her. It wouldn't have been the first time. He much preferred to think about the way Domino said *us*. "So, where do we go from here?"

She blinked at him. Huge, brown orbs of innocence. "What do you mean?"

That wasn't what he wanted to hear. He was hoping

for a well thought-out plan that explained what was in store for them with an easily understood destination and how they would get there. But nothing too detailed.

"I'd settle for getting to know each other better," she said. "Without one of us being snockered."

"One of us," he echoed. She had such a nice way of putting things. "Do you live nearby?"

"A few doors down."

"*Here?* In this motel?"

"It's close to the club, and I don't have a car. I rent by the week which isn't too bad, and sometimes they let me work off the rent by cleaning rooms. I was hoping to find a roommate and maybe get an apartment, but they're so expensive. That's why I decided to audition. Dancers can make a lot of money y'know, and I thought... Well, we know how that turned out."

"And you know what? That's okay. It's great, in fact. Maybe you and I can be roommates. I won't be going back East to live. Maybe--" He paused. "There's something I've gotta do first."

"Can I help?"

He shook his head. "It might be dangerous. I can't let you take the risk."

He had seen the look on her face before. Many times. It said: "Carmine, you're so full of crap."

"You have to trust me," he said. "I have to do this, but I'll be back. Tonight!"

"I have to work tonight."

"Are you sure?"

"Of course I'm sure. I work almost every night!"

"I'll be there," he said. "It might be late, but I'll be there."

She smiled. "You're not just saying that?"

He gripped her shoulders with both hands and looked straight into her eyes. "I swear to you," he said. "No

267

matter what, I'll be back."

"Tonight?"

"Damn right tonight."

She put her arms around him. "Did you mean it when you said you loved me?"

I said that? "Well, yeah. Of course!"

"I thought maybe you were just dreaming, or maybe delirious. That's some bump on your head. We ought to get a doctor to look at you."

"Screw the doctor. I want to be with you."

"Really?"

"Really."

"And this thing you have to do?"

"It's just a job," he said. "I have to go to... I have to do a little travel. But I'll be back."

"You promise?"

"I promise," he said. And he'd never said anything he meant more.

~*~

Reyna finished the sleeping paste and packed it in the leather pouch Mato usually wore on his knife belt. Because of the rattler's generous donation, and the fact she wasn't making it for all the hunters of the tribe, she had a significant amount left over. Helping herself to Tori's collection of storage containers, she put the excess paste in a glass jar and left it on the counter. Tori could find a place to store it when she came home. Though she was a giant and seemingly self-sufficient -- it was unlikely she'd ever have to hunt anything bigger than herself for food -- it never hurt to have something on hand to even the odds against predators. Besides, Mato might run out and need more.

Teaching him how to make his own was out of the question. The People had strict rules about who could make it and who could use it, and she was not about to violate the code.

It had been a good day all around: the temperature remained tolerable; the snakes had presented less difficulty than they could have. The sleeping paste was ready, and she had done it all without morning sickness.

She decided to reward herself with a nap.

Most of the drive from Denver to Ten Sleep was yawn-inspiring. Carmine took Interstate 25 north to Buffalo, and then traveled west through the Bighorn National Forest. After seven hours of driving on the interstate highway, the winding, mostly two-lane road through the Bighorn mountains was a definite challenge. Steep grades and switchbacks were the norm, and everybody but him seemed to have grown up driving the automotive equivalent of mountain goats.

Since he preferred not to roll his crappy little Honda over the edge of a cliff, he maintained speeds considerably less than those suggested on the yellow highway signs, thereby earning him a full range of evil looks, hand gestures, and honking horns. Not that he cared. He just gripped the wheel tighter, gritted his teeth, and took another swig of Bang.

From time to time, however, he pulled over to let the accumulated traffic pass him. There was always the chance some idiot with a cowboy hat and a gun rack would be angry enough to push him over the side. He'd heard all about road rage; he didn't need to incite it.

He had stopped for gas just before heading into the mountains and had learned from the attendant that the trip could take anywhere from one to two hours depending on traffic. He managed it in slightly less than three, and wheeled into "downtown" Ten Sleep with an entirely new respect for the interstate highway system. He never wanted to drive on anything else as long as he lived. Sadly, that option wasn't available just then.

He suspected he might have to cut back on the peanuts and Bang. He couldn't be sure, since he'd also consumed an unaccustomed amount of alcohol the night before, but the combination was playing hell with his digestive system. While occupying the throne in one of Ten Sleep's three restaurants, he consulted the map Lykes had given him.

His target lay way outside of town. According to the notes, the house sat at the end of a long drive, and he was advised to park out of sight and approach the building on foot. Well, whoopee do! Who the hell was Lykes to plan every step of his entire mission? Lykes hadn't just driven through the damn mountains, hadn't dealt with the drop-offs and the sheer cliffs leading to certain doom. *Screw 'im!* Carmine knew what he had to do. Then, as he plotted his next moves, he realized that unless his Honda morphed into an intercontinental ballistic missile, there was no way he'd make it back to Denver in time to see Domino before she got off work.

Once he'd cleared his digestive tract, he called her at the club to explain why he wouldn't be there. The manager answered and made it clear he didn't want his employees spending time on the phone when they could be earning him money, either shaking their tails on stage or to and from the bar. Carmine explained that the gravity of the situation was very close to life and death. He didn't add that it was the manager's life which lay in the balance should he keep Carmine from talking to Domino.

The manager relented with a final advisory, "Her name's not Domino. It's Desiree."

"Yeah, and I'm the crown prince of Alabamastan."

The phone bounced off whatever it landed on, the clatter followed by considerable background noise: loud music with a distinct jungle beat, innumerable conversations, the clink of bottles and glasses, laughter. A door slammed, and the level of background noise dropped. Quick footsteps on bare floor. Sounds of a receiver being picked up. Then, a sweet and familiar voice: "Hello?"

"Domino?"

"Carmine!"

"I've missed you," he said.

"It's only been a few hours."

"Seems like a lot longer," he said, his mountain travails fresh on his mind.

"You're still coming tonight, aren't you?" she asked.

"Actually, that's why I'm calling. I--"

"Yeah, I know..." The disappointment in her voice was almost enough to make him abandon the mission. Almost, but not quite. He needed the money.

"You don't understand," he said. "I had to drive a long way, and--"

"To where, exactly?"

"Wyoming. This is going to sound dumb, but if I want to get paid, I can't tell you any more."

He detected a bit of a tremor in her voice when she asked, "Are you doing something illegal?"

"Sorta."

"Is it dangerous?" The tremor had become more definite.

"No," he said. "Well, not very. It's just that it took me ten hours to get here, and there's no way I can make it back tonight. I didn't want you to think I'm some kinda

271

jerk who breaks his promises. I'll be back tomorrow, no matter what."

"You swear?"

"Absolutely!"

"Good. 'Cause I'm not working tomorrow."

Visions of a day in bed with Domino cleared his mind of residual terror from the mountain passage, along with a few other non-essential brain functions.

"Carmine? Sweetie? You still there?"

"Yeah!"

"I have to go. The boss is already mad at me."

"Tell him to back off," Carmine said, "or I'll rip out his liver."

She giggled. "You'll have to go through Freddie first. You up for that?"

"Sure." He had a vague memory of Freddie, though it may have been a residual image of a lowland gorilla he'd seen on the National Geographic channel. Ronnie and Lykes had cable.

"Drive carefully," she said.

He was getting used to that.

~*~

Chapter 16

*Riding is the art of keeping a horse
between you and the ground.*

Mato felt proud of himself. He'd managed to go the entire day without commenting on what Tori and Nate had been doing when they thought he was asleep. He found their attempts at covert lovemaking hilarious. Why would they try to hide their pleasure at the greatest gift the Spirits had ever bestowed? How stupid! They should have howled like wolves at the pleasure they gave each other. He and Reyna certainly had no troubles when they were thus engaged. Once again, the giants confounded him with their odd notions. But, he was pleased for Tori. She deserved someone's love, and Nate seemed like a worthy mate. He hoped they had many children, preferably somewhere other than in the cabin on top of the entrance to the cavern of dreams. Nate's house would be fine.

Still, he didn't want to spark a commotion, something all too easily achieved when it came to Nate and Tori. He was content to keep up the search for her long-dead relative. That, at least, was something he could understand, for he, too, cherished those who brought honor to The People. He assumed the giants had similar feelings. Tori often spoke of Uncle Bob -- such a strange name -- and Mato finally made the connection. Uncle Bob was one of the Old Ones Tori revered. It made sense. He obviously had great power since he was able to communicate with her long after his death. Tori called it *writing*. It was a clever method of recording words with written symbols. Extraordinary!

273

Mato wished he had the ability to record something more precise than his drawings. Though he was quite proud of his skill at rendering images, he had no idea how to record his thoughts and feelings. How handy it would be to record a message for Reyna. Perhaps something like: "My breech cloth needs cleaning," or "How 'bout a nice fat prairie dog for dinner?"

He would have to talk to Tori about this thing called writing. It seemed to offer more than a little benefit.

~*~

Carmine's drive north on the interstate through eastern Wyoming cut through some of the most empty and desolate terrain he could imagine. What he saw when he reached the far side of Ten Sleep, however, was worse.

On either side of the road stretched unimaginably vast tracts of barren ground. Odder still, most of it was fenced. True, there were some cattle scattered here and there as well as a horse or two, but for the most part, it was just... empty. In the city, it didn't matter where you looked. There was always something: buildings, people, signs, litter. Even in the middle of Central Park you could look above the trees and see skyscrapers in the distance. Here, you might see a house, but you'd have to look hard.

Of course there were the little streams. These were crowded with greenery and trees, none of which he could name. Who cared?

Driving was different, too. Considering that he'd done almost 100 percent of his "training" on divided highways with wide medians, constant speeds, and controlled access, he now found himself facing on-coming traffic that passed within a few feet of him. He'd hit the salted nuts and Bang pretty hard between Denver and Buffalo, but driving through the Big Empty required that he pay *serious* attention. So he cranked up the Ray Charles tape and sang even louder.

The sky was adorned with a pink and orange wash that extended from one horizon to the other. He'd never seen so much sky in his life, and to have it available in Technicolor was something clearly beyond his imagination. He wished he could share it with Domino.

How wonderful it would have been to share the whole drive with her! But, of course, that was insane. For one thing, she might try to talk him out of his mission. He was going to grab a guy and take him to New York. The pay would be enough to give him a whole new start in life, and he fully intended to return to Denver to make Domino a part of it.

He knew what would be in store for him if he screwed up the job. Ben Lykes hadn't been specific about the consequences of failure, but Carmine had seen enough gangster movies to know everything he needed to know about that possibility. It was, he admitted to himself, the downside of being connected. There was no way he'd screw this up. No friggin' way.

Though Domino had been helpful in restoring his memories of their night together, serious gaps remained. He felt sure he hadn't said anything to her about the mission, and she had certainly seemed surprised when he announced he had to make a long trip. She seemed more concerned about whether he was coming back than she was about where he was going, or what he had to do. When the time came, how would he tell her he had to drive all the way to New York? He shook it off. There were more immediate problems to resolve. Like finding the house where the little guy lived.

Even though he followed the directions, he missed

turns. The first was in a place called Charm, which he convinced himself wasn't really big enough to have a name, let alone "Charm." What a joke. In any event, he corrected his mistake and headed out on a narrow strip of pavement which had nothing more going for it than a county road designation. At least it was paved. And free of drop-offs.

He watched the odometer to determine where he would find the turn off to his destination. It came up all too soon. The backs of his hands were sweaty, but he wasn't sleepy; he was far too nervous for that. The prospect of kidnapping a human being finally sank in and began to tickle his conscience.

Lykes had told him over and over that it would be easy. Grab the little guy. Stuff him in the cage. Cover it with a towel. Drive home. What could be easier?

Carmine crept down the dirt driveway at the slowest possible speed. He could do this, he kept telling himself, even though he didn't want to. What would Domino say? How would she react if she discovered he'd kidnapped some helpless midget? What if she demanded he set the little guy free? What would he do then? What could he tell Lykes? Where would he like to be buried?

Get it together, you moron! When it came to screaming at himself, he was an old hand. But then, he'd never been so close to doing something so despicable. He tried to remember the last time he'd gone to confession. It was a dim memory. The priest had been a decent sort, or so he thought. What would he say if Carmine came back asking forgiveness for kidnapping some miniature loser nobody'd ever heard of? A lifetime of Hail Marys wouldn't cleanse his slate.

On the other hand, if he didn't pull off this job, what chance would he ever have for a life with Domino? The trick would be to pull off the job without letting her know anything about it. No problem, he told himself.

No problem at all.

~*~

"Cave here," Mato said pointing to a dark patch in the cliffside behind some trees. Tori wondered if he had some kind of super powers like the characters in the comic books she read as a kid. The Amazing Mato -- sees through impenetrable underbrush, leaps absurd distances straight up, makes love the way Nabisco makes cookies: non-stop.

Nate reined Babe to a stop beside Tori, dismounted and offered to help her down. She declined his assistance and nearly kicked him in the head in her haste to get off Elmer's back. They had been riding all day. "You've been here before?" he asked Mato.

"One time," the Indian replied. "Mato very young." He looked directly into Nate's eyes and added, "but not stupid, like giant boy."

"Y'mean, Marty?"

"Yes. Dipshit Marty."

Tori couldn't keep from chuckling, and she was pleased that Nate did the same.

Mato forged ahead, working his way through the underbrush until he reached the rock wall beyond. "Winter Woman find. Show Mato."

"Is there anything in it?" Tori asked. "Like, oh I dunno, bears?"

Mato sniffed the air and shook his head. "No bear. Coyote. Gone now."

"How 'bout bats?" she asked. "I'm not real big on bats."

Mato didn't know what a bat was, so Tori tried to

scratch something representative in the dirt. Rather than attempt to understand her efforts, he simply wiped the surface smooth with the bottom of his moccasin and continued along the base of the cliff until he reached a slight overhang. The opening was so low, even he had to stoop to get through. If she and Nate were to follow him, they'd have to do so on their bellies. Nate retrieved a flashlight from the pack horse before they began.

He waved Tori ahead of him, and once again she declined. "You first, okay?"

"Bats won't hurt you," Nate said.

"Not if they know what's good for 'em!"

"Follow me then, madam explorer." He dropped smoothly to the ground and crawled into the dark slit under the protruding rock.

Tori made a face at his rapidly disappearing legs, then followed him.

The entrance to the cave was neither as dark nor as steep as the tunnel beneath her cabin. And it was much wider, suggesting a natural origin. She was fairly certain the tunnel had been dug by hand, presumably very small ones.

Once inside, she and Nate were able to sit up. Mato stood, though his head just cleared the ceiling. Nate shined his light on the floor and walls. Other than an assortment of footprints, some of which were human, there wasn't much to see.

Mato insisted that Nate shine his light in one particular direction. There, etched into a flat space on the wall, was a crude drawing of two people, one tall, one short.

"Mato draw," the little Indian said. He tapped the taller of the two people. "Winter Woman."

"And you?" Tori asked.

He nodded. "Mato very young. We go now."

"We just got here," Nate said.

Mato crossed his arms on his chest. "No more to see."

Nate shined his light on the wall opposite the one bearing Mato's handiwork. There was something there, too. He asked about it, but Mato professed ignorance.

They all crawled closer for a better look. The image was quite close to the dirt floor and appeared to have been painted on rather than scratched into the surface, like the work of their companion. The image was of a very small woman and a very large bear, on the verge of something very unpleasant.

"Wait a sec," Nate said, squeezing even closer. "What's that?" He pointed to a tiny symbol scratched into the stone.

"It looks like a feather," Tori said.

"Leokahnah," Mato said.

"She signed her work?" Nate asked, then looked closely at Mato. "Do you sign your work?"

He seemed to be struggling with the concept of sign, so Tori tapped the feather symbol. "Leokahnah." Then she cleared a space in the dirt floor and gestured for Mato to draw something. What he came up with looked like a snowflake.

"That's your sign?" she asked. "Mato's sign?"

"Winter Woman," he said. "Mato, no sign. Everyone know Mato work."

"We know one of them was here, anyway," Tori said. "But it must've been before she and Uncle Bob got together. She still had two legs."

"The bear--" Nate began.

"Yeah," she said. "Uncle Bob kept her alive." She shivered, though the temperature was quite pleasant. "Time to go."

"I agree." Nate rolled onto his stomach. "It's not like

we're terribly comfy in here."

"Besides, I'm getting hungry," Tori said. "And it'll be dark soon."

Mato walked ahead of them and slipped out of the cave.

Tori put her hand on Nate's shoulder, and he stopped. "Do you get the feeling Mato is flaunting his ability to get into and out of tight places?"

"Maybe," Nate said. "The feeling I really get is that Mato likes to be in charge. He sure as hell doesn't like following orders."

Tori responded with a snort. "Who does?"

~*~

After dodging boulders and nearly having his teeth jarred loose going over ruts in the driveway, Carmine eventually got close enough to the cabin to see it. The sun hadn't gone down completely, which probably explained why there weren't any lights on. He was tempted to wait until dark and then sneak up to the place for a better look, but his instructions didn't say anything about waiting.

He backed the car up so that it couldn't be seen from the building, then shut the engine off and climbed out. After a moment's hesitation he went to the rear of the car and pulled out the dog cage. It was big enough to be cumbersome, but small enough to be insulting. He wished he had an alternative, but it seemed as if Lykes was right about it. Just as he was right about approaching the house on foot. It didn't make sense to announce his presence. He'd be lucky if someone didn't take a shot at him by the time he reached the cabin. Maybe two shots. Or more. *Get it together, Carmine!*

With no clear plan for the abduction, he was left with

vague ideas about waiting for his victim to step outside.
If that happened, Carmine could just reach out, grab him,
and stuff him in the cage. Job done. *Look out Denver,
here I come!*

So, he waited. Sitting in the shadow of the cabin
beside the steps to the only door, he listened for any
sounds coming from inside. There weren't any.

After waiting for what seemed like hours, he stood
and stretched, then walked over to a window and peered
inside. Not a single light had come on during the time
he'd been there. There had been no sounds, either. Didn't
these people read? Or watch TV? Or eat? Come to think
of it, he needed to eat, but he'd be damned if he was
going to walk all the way back to the car just for a bag of
nuts and a can of soda. Besides, the Bang would likely
give him away.

He couldn't see much of the cabin's interior and
suffered from a growing fear that no one was home.
Wouldn't that be a handy way to explain failure. "Gee,
boss, I went to the house, but there was nobody there."
Pifft. Pifft. Darkness.

Eager to put the operation behind him, Carmine
walked up the front steps and gingerly tested the door
knob. It turned quietly in his hand.

Here goes nuthin'. He pushed the door open, fully
expecting the kind of creaking noise Hollywood always
used on coffin lids. Thankfully, the door didn't make a
sound. Nor did Carmine as he worked his way into the
cabin. He took his time, letting his eyes adjust to the dark.
Soon he could make out objects more easily. Bed. Table.
Chairs. Computer monitor. Sink. 'Fridge. Another bed. A
very small bed. *And occupied!*

Carmine leaned closer for a better look. Damned if
there weren't *two* bodies in it. Lykes hadn't said anything
about two Oompa Loompas. One of them, a female, was

obviously asleep. The other, a male, was dead -- on his back, eyes open, not moving. Beyond mega-creepy. Carmine sniffed the air, expecting the sicky sweet smell of decayed flesh, but got nothing. He couldn't have been dead for long.

On closer inspection, the dead one seemed to have been shoved off the little mattress. *How cold was that? Geez. What, you're dead? Then move over and gimme the covers, you won't miss 'em.*

Slowly, the realization sank in that he no longer had a target. At least, not one that was still breathing. How would Lykes respond to that? "Here's your guy, Ben. What? Yeah, I know, he's dead as road kill. But, he didn't give me any shit on the way home."

Pifft. Pifft. Darkness.

That, clearly, wasn't an option. What the hell was he supposed to do now? Call in? Get instructions? *Right.* That was the quickest route to becoming a dead messenger. No. Freakin'. Way.

He looked down again at the surviving midget. She was the only option open to him. Fortunately she was all wrapped up in a blanket. If he moved carefully, he could scoop her up, in the blanket, and thereby avoid issues of scratching and biting. Screaming he wasn't worried about since they were in -- approximately -- the middle of fucking nowhere. But at long last, he had a plan.

Creeping as quietly as he knew how, Carmine went back to the door and retrieved the cage which he brought into the cabin and deposited silently beside the bed. Some sort of light would have been nice, but he couldn't take the chance. It also would have been nice if he'd thought to examine the latch on the cage door, which, he discovered with more than a bit of anxiety, wouldn't open.

When he forced the issue, jamming the latch to one

side, the whole end of the cage swung open, squealing and rattling at the same time.

The female's eyes opened.

Carmine's heart slipped into *Oh Shit* mode.

And then she screamed.

Who knew so much sound could come from such a small person?

~*~

Darkness came early in Poughkeepsie, NY. It might as well have come with an audible thump, Tessa thought as she sat in her car contemplating the many different methods she might use to kill the chubby renta-cop preventing her from driving into the company parking lot. How long did it take to look up a stupid employee number?

"Okay," he said after paying homage to something on the clipboard in his hand. "You're good."

"Meaning, it's okay for me to enter the holy parking lot and proceed to my humble office?"

"Yes, ma'am."

"Tell me something--" She squinted at the name badge on his green and gray uniform. "--Mr. Krantz. Are you the sole guardian of this facility?"

"You mean, am I the only one on duty?"

She gave him a grudging nod. "That would be more precise. Or is that information classified?"

"Oh, no ma'am. There are four of us on duty at all times. One here, one in the lobby, and two in the office. They monitor the security cameras and take care of clerical stuff. But, we've all got radios, so we can call in reinforcements if needed."

"In case there's a run on parking permits? Why on Earth would you need reinforcements?"

The question seemed to take him by surprise. "Well, in case someone tried to break in."

"Seems to me four-to-one odds would be in your favor." She looked down at the holster on his belt. "Especially four men with guns."

"They're not real guns," he said. "We--"

"You're guarding a high tech laboratory with toy guns?"

"They aren't toys; they're stun guns." He opened the flap on his holster and extracted the device. It didn't look much like a gun. In fact, it looked more like an electric razor. He touched the business end of it: four metal points, two aimed out and two angled toward each other. When he pressed the trigger, a tiny jagged line of electricity streaked and crackled between the two angled pins. Tessa found the display intimidating. Then he put it away.

"We're only supposed to use them in the event of something extreme."

"Help me out here," Tessa said. "What qualifies as extreme? Somebody taking up two parking spaces? Unauthorized use of company stationery?"

The guard straightened, his face serious. "How 'bout a terrorist attack? That would qualify, don't you think?"

Tessa grunted. Maybe there was more to this joker than she'd originally thought. She shifted into gear and drove into the lot.

Her name had been stenciled on a cement parking barrier at the far end. The space was adjacent to a newly installed door, and the ground outside of it had been dug up to accommodate shrubbery which had yet to be planted. A freshly poured cement walkway connected the parking lot to the building. It wouldn't look too bad when finished. Maybe old Jerry was coming around after all.

She walked up to the building and inserted her badge into the reader. Moments later the lock on the door clicked, and Tessa walked into the building.

Her new building.

Her new home.

~*~

Reyna satisfied her need to scream, though logic would have suggested she attempt some other means to effect an escape. Looking directly into the shadowed eyes of the strange giant, she realized he was as frightened as she was. That, surely, would be momentary. What could someone his size possibly fear from her?

Sure enough, he reached for her with both hands. Though she kicked and struggled to free herself, his grip seemed unbreakable. She couldn't bend close enough to his hands or arms to administer a bite, and she had no other weapons. Only warriors slept with a knife nearby. Reyna, like all sensible members of The People, slept naked.

Her efforts to dislodge herself from the giant succeeded only in dislodging the blanket from her body. It fluttered silently to the cabin floor. The giant held her up, staring at her as if he'd discovered something wondrous. Her pulse still racing, Reyna struck with her feet, one of which landed just under the giant's chin, slamming his open jaws together with a satisfying pop. Unfortunately, the blow was not hard enough to render him unconscious, or even enough to make him let her go.

She continued to scream and kick. Pounding on his hands yielded nothing, so she attempted to gouge him with her nails. He obviously didn't like what she was doing to him, but it was also obvious she wasn't causing him enough pain to release her. Instead, he carried her to a metal cage and thrust her inside.

She gripped the wire mesh of her prison and shook the sides as hard as she could. Neither that, nor her renewed screams, had any effect on the cage or the giant. He did something to secure the door, and while he was thus occupied, Reyna huddled at the far end of the cage. By reaching through the wire bars she was able to grab some of the clothing she'd appropriated from the toy Tori called Lance.

Ignoring his shoes, which were too big for her, she concentrated on finding anything she might be able to use. That's when Mato's new folding knife fell from the pocket of the pants she had been wearing earlier.

The giant looked up at the sound, but Reyna moved much faster than any giant. She had the knife in her lap before he could do anything to stop her. While he watched, she carefully unfolded the longest of the two sharp blades. If he attempted to touch her again, she would make him pay for his trouble in blood.

Evidently, he saw wisdom in the idea of leaving her alone. He made no attempt to take the knife away, and merely watched as she put some clothes on.

He attempted to engage her in conversation, but she turned her back on him. Though her command of the giant's tongue was minimal, she did know a few words. Unfortunately, very few of them seemed useful at the moment.

When the giant reached down to lift the cage, Reyna was tempted to stab his fingers. The blade was long enough to reach his knuckles, but woefully short of anything vital. He put the cage on the table and turned away. What was he up to, she wondered. None of the giants she knew showed any interest in turning her into a meal, and Mato had assured her that despite what the Old

Ones said around the campfire, giants had never eaten any of The People.

Perhaps he was hungry for something else, and merely hoped to find it in Tori's food box. She spotted a prize he knew nothing about: the container she'd borrowed to hold the leftover sleeping paste she'd made for Mato.

Stretching her arm as far as she could, she almost touched the jar. It sat tantalizingly close. There was a chance she might reach it with the blade of the knife, but if the giant saw her he might be able to disarm her before she could react.

What would Mato do?

He certainly wouldn't waste time, she told herself, and stuck the knife toward the jar. Working carefully, but taking every opportunity to ensure the giant wasn't paying any attention, she managed to slide the jar close to the cage. It was far too big to squeeze through the bars. Had they been that far apart, she would have been out of the cage before the giant could lock it. Instead, she was forced to open the container and dip the tip of the knife into it. She wouldn't need much, and she'd have to use it fairly soon as it tended to dry out and lose potency when exposed to the air.

Just as she attempted to reseal the jar, the giant gave a startled yelp and jumped backwards, away from the food box. He banged into the table, knocking it over and spilling Reyna and her cage on the floor.

Cursing and scrambling backwards, the giant acted as if the Spirits themselves pursued him, as well they should. She strained to make sense of his words, most of which were short and spoken with the kind of anger and disdain usually reserved for curses.

One of his words she did recognize, and as soon as she heard it, she smiled. The giant had been frightened by her dinner! Too bad she'd saved the striped snake instead of the rattler.

~*~

Once again, Tori, Nate and Mato camped in the open. Without any artificial light to compete with them, the stars sparkled with an intensity city folk rarely experienced. Mato made no comment, but Tori and Nate whispered to each other for a long time, pointing out constellations and imagining what went through the minds of the people who originally painted pictures with the stars.

"I hope we find something interesting tomorrow," Nate said. "I can't spend much more time out here."

"'Cause of the trial?"

"Yeah. I still can't believe those idiots didn't plead out. If I know Chuckwagon, he'll--"

"Chuckwagon?"

Nate laughed. "Sorry. Judge Torrence. Nobody I know calls him Chuckwagon to his face. Anyway, if I know him, he'll put those three knuckleheads *under* the jail."

"Why? Is he some kind of sportsman?"

"I think he just likes to come down hard on certain people."

"But why those three? There's no law against being stupid."

"I can't speak for the judge," Nate said, "but I suspect he's got a problem with people who don't show any respect for others. For example, anyone foolish enough to give him lip will be cited for contempt. He does that a lot."

"When do you go to court?"

"I've got to be available whenever they need me to testify. It depends on how long the trial lasts. Hopefully, not more than a day."

"You think it could go longer?"

He hugged her. "It wouldn't be the strangest thing that ever happened."

"What is the strangest thing that ever happened," Tori asked. "To you, I mean."

"You can't be serious," he said, glancing at Mato who was sound asleep with his head resting on Shadow's stomach.

"Right," she said, and kissed him good night.

And then she kissed him again. She wasn't nearly as tired as she thought.

~*~

Chapter 17

Artificial intelligence is no match for natural stupidity.

Carmine could handle the idea of living with rats. He had, in fact, done it. More often than he cared to admit. But *snakes?* Nobody in America had to live with snakes. The very thought of a snake was enough to raise goose bumps over his whole body. So, when one of the damn things stuck its tongue out at him from behind a carton of eggs, his natural reaction was to move away. Quickly. And anything that got in the way of his escape was just shit out of luck.

He had no idea what kind of snake lurked in the refrigerator. It nearly caused him to lurk in his pants. What kind of people would do such a thing? Geez! And to think he'd been developing a serious case of sympathy for the chick in the cage. It started when the little blanket she was wrapped in fell off, and he discovered she wasn't wearing anything underneath it.

Sure, she was only a couple feet tall, but she was *all girl* -- with the right parts in the right proportions and the right places. It was hard to look at her and not wish he was three and a half feet shorter. If she hadn't kicked him in the chin, he might not have been able to take his eyes off her.

But she had, and he did, and somehow he'd locked her up in the cage. And that made him feel like crap. People didn't belong in cages unless they'd done something really rotten. But putting live snakes in a refrigerator where they'd scare the shit out of some unsuspecting soul like him... Well, that definitely qualified as something rotten.

"So, lady," he said, staring at her in her freshly donned outfit, "maybe if you'd warned me I'd be willing to talk about letting you out."

She didn't respond, possibly because she'd been banged around inside the cage when he knocked the table over. A jar of something nasty had broken when it hit the floor, but he had no intention of cleaning it up. He had hoped to find something to eat in the 'fridge, but that turned out to be fuel for nightmares, which he'd surely be suffering soon.

The best thing to do, he reasoned, was to load the cage in the car and go back to Denver. Nobody out here knew him, so there was no reason to think they might connect him to the crime. Besides, there wasn't anyone else left to report it. He began to feel safe again and actually smiled.

"Don't worry," he told the little hottie in the cage, "I won't hurt you."

He picked up the wire enclosure by the handle on top and had walked the short distance to the door when he felt a sharp stabbing pain in his middle finger. Instantly, he dropped the cage and grabbed the injured digit. As blood dripped freely from his finger, he examined the top of the cage to see what had jabbed him. There was nothing to be seen. Except for his prisoner. She was watching him very closely, as if she expected him to sprout wings or leafy green vegetables.

"What did you do?" he asked, suddenly feeling lightheaded. When his legs became rubbery, he eased himself to the floor. Shoving the cage with his foot, he wedged the hinged end against the wall.

What was going on? He'd never felt so woozy in his life. He slumped down beside the cage, his face a yard away from his prisoner's. "What'd you..." In an overwhelming wash of warmth, Carmine blacked out.

~*~

Though it was late in the evening, Chuckwagon Torrence remained in his office. He'd cleared off the center of his desk, pushing an accumulation of legal briefs, notes, and law books to one side or the other. He'd then poured himself three fingers of very old, single malt scotch. The time had finally come, and he'd been looking forward to it since his secretary arrived with the daily mail.

He loosened his tie, turned in his chair to a compact but powerful stereo on a shelf behind his desk, and pressed a button on the CD player. Immediately, an ethereal voice flowed from speakers in the corners of the room. The last Broadway show he'd seen with his late wife was "The Phantom of the Opera," and the powerful, haunting strains of Andrew Lloyd Webber's music had become a part of his psyche. Just listening to it brought her back to him. For a little while, anyway.

Swiveling back to face his desk, he looked down at the letter from his little girl. Now a resident of New York, and several years out of graduate school, she was anything but a child. Young? Yes, still young. And ambitious, absolutely.

He took a sip of scotch, settled it in his mouth, the flavors bathing his taste buds, then let it flow slowly down his throat. Like the music, it had a warm, familiar feel. He allowed himself the ritual but twice a week, fearing that more often might somehow sully it. Besides, Elizabeth's letters rarely came more often than twice a month, and he could only read them so many times before he committed them to memory. He refused to allow his compulsion to reach that extreme; he knew himself too well.

His letter opener was a gift from her. Antler-handled and balanced like a throwing knife, she must have paid an exorbitant price for it. But she insisted that since she was finally employed, and in a professional capacity, she had earned the right -- and the money -- to buy him something he'd never purchase for himself.

"That's the sort of thing love makes possible," she had told him.

He had laughed, back then. Now, he merely smiled, and used the tool to open her letter. Had she made any progress? He certainly hoped so. He wished there were some way he could help her.

He took another sip of scotch.

And began to read.

~*~

Reyna wondered at first if she had killed the giant. His breathing was so shallow she could see no movement in his chest at all. Of course, being slumped sideways didn't help. She thought he would drop straight to the floor. He had surprised her completely by pushing the cage up against the wall. She thought, at first, that he had done it on purpose, but the more she reviewed his actions in her mind, the more convinced she became that he had acted out of instinct rather than design. Not that it mattered now. She struggled in her efforts to move the cage far enough from the wall that she could swing the door open, but it simply wouldn't budge.

After straining her muscles to the breaking point, she'd slumped down herself, angry and exhausted. Eventually she noticed that the back edge of the cage was pinched tightly against one of the many uneven floor boards. That, and the door, had served to lock the wire container solidly in place. It may as well have been bolted down. The giant was out of the game, but she was still trapped.

She examined the corners of the cage, and she examined the hinges. There appeared to be no way out unless the giant took pity on her, and that didn't seem likely now that she'd used Mato's knife on him. She kicked her feet on the cruel metal bars in frustration. And fear.

This was not what she had seen in her dreams, those frightening, terrible dreams. Nor had Mato made any mention of it. But it could very easily be the harbinger of her nightmare becoming real.

And unless Mato or Tori came home, there would be no escape. The giant would sleep for a few hours, possibly until morning. Mato said they would be gone no more than three sleeps. This night was the second. She dropped to her knees and invoked the Spirits.

Perhaps they would intervene on her behalf. If not, she would have to consider using Mato's knife on herself.

~*~

Carmine came awake slowly. Bright sunlight streamed through the open cabin door and penetrated his eyelids like laser beams.

His head felt like someone had used it for a bass drum, and he knew for a fact he hadn't had a damned thing to drink. A small pool of blood had accumulated under his finger, though the bleeding had stopped while he slept.

Surprisingly, the stab wound didn't hurt very much. More than a paper cut, certainly, but less than, he guessed, a broken bone. He was more concerned about what had caused him to black out. Fatigue? Lack of sleep? Lack of food? Most likely it was a combination of all three. Thankfully, it was behind him, otherwise he might have fallen asleep while driving.

He dragged a hand to his head and shaded his eyes, then focused them on the cage and its occupant. The girl inside looked directly at him, her expression unreadable.

What a babe, he thought. Her features were bold and dark, very... Indian. She had long, black hair. Very straight, and tied in a knot behind her head. Her clothing was unrevealing, though he clearly remembered the unintended view he'd received the night before. Geez. How was he going to explain her to Domino?

That thought prompted him to sit up and look for something to throw over the cage. Once he got the damned thing back in the car, he didn't want anyone, let alone Domino, to see what was in it.

What the hell time was it, he wondered. He'd never worn a watch. It was an extravagance he couldn't afford. But once he finished this job maybe he would buy one. He'd be a man of means then. Maybe not rich, but way better off than he was when he took the job.

He couldn't find a clock in the cabin. It didn't matter. It was breakfast time, but he knew he wouldn't be stopping anywhere for food until he'd put a lot of miles between this cabin and himself. Therefore, the next step would be to load the micro hottie into the Honda and hit the dusty trail.

As he reached for the handle on the top of the cage, he noticed his captive had a wicked-looking knife, and it was pointed right where he had almost put his hand.

"Oh, snap," he said, mimicking something he'd heard at the car wash. "You've got a knife."

She waved it menacingly.

295

"What if I reached in there and tried to grab it?"

She made a stabbing motion, a totally convincing response.

"Right. Y'know what? I'm cool with you having a blade. If it makes you feel better, that's fine." He looked for a piece of rope but couldn't find one. There weren't any blinds in the cabin either, so he couldn't slice off a handy length of cord. He settled for a dish towel hanging from the door handle on the oven.

Moving cautiously, he threaded the thin fabric through the metal handle and lifted the cage from a distance safely out of range of the knife-wielding Oompah Loompette. The grip was awkward, though much safer than simply grabbing the cage's handle. He took one last look around the cabin, studiously avoiding the dead midget on the floor. That wasn't his fault, thank God. As he turned to leave he spotted a shotgun near the front door. How convenient, he thought as he picked it up and checked to ensure it was loaded. Yep, both barrels. Sweet!

Carrying the cage by the extended handle, he walked straight to the car and dropped it in the back. The hatchback door just barely cleared. He put the shotgun on the floor behind the front seats. He didn't have a blanket to toss over the wire cube, so he used a beach towel from Coney Island. He'd gotten a horrible sunburn there one summer. He was 13. Ronnie was 15 and wore a bikini. He thought she looked stupid.

That was the summer he discovered what virginity was. Ronnie had exchanged hers for a music box. Twelve years later, he still had his.

~*~

"Crawling into everything that looks like it might be a cave is not what I had in mind when we started," Tori said. After two and a half days in the saddle, she was looking more than a little bedraggled, but she still had her smile, and that cut through the dust and the smell of horses and all the rest. That smile was really something, and Nate realized he'd do almost anything to see it.

"Hey! Did you hear me?" she asked.

"Right. Caves. Not my idea of a good time, either. But think about it. If winter was coming on, it had to be a lot colder than it is now, and there were no other shelters available. If they were going to hole up for a night, it's logical to assume they'd be better off in a cave than out in the open."

"I was thinking maybe they'd build a small sod hut or something. People on the prairie did that a lot, didn't they?"

"When you've got lots of grass and no trees, you use what's available. But there's no way they'd take the time to build anything. They had to keep moving to reach her tribe before winter set in."

Tori acknowledged that he was probably right. "At least when we crawl into one of these damned caves, I can give my backside a rest." She stood up in the stirrups and rubbed her butt.

Her smile wasn't the only thing that was still working, he thought.

"Cave here." Mato had said the words so often, they began to sound like a mantra. He dropped lightly from Shadow's back and crawled under yet another rock ledge.

"How can he do that?" Tori asked. "He doesn't check for snakes or mountain lions or anything. He could be eaten so fast we wouldn't even know about it until we crawled in after him."

"He uses his nose," Nate said.

"Maybe he should use his brain, instead."

"I think he can smell predators."

Tori looked genuinely surprised. "You're kidding."

"He's lived close to nature all his life. His senses are attuned to the outdoors the way ours are attuned to TV and radio. We can't even imagine how well defined his abilities are. He sees better in the dark. He can hear things we can't. So--"

"What can he hear that we can't?"

"How am I supposed to answer that?"

"Oh. Right." She winked at him.

"I'm just sayin', if his eyes and ears work better than ours, it stands to reason his nose does, too."

Just then, Mato crawled back out from under the overhang. He waved excitedly. "Come look!"

Nate grabbed his flashlight, then dismounted, taking care to stay out of Tori's way as she swung her leg over Elmer's back during her own dismount. One of these days he'd have to talk to her about that. Hopefully before she knocked his head off.

Stiff from riding, Tori took the time to stretch before she got down on her hands and knees for the subterranean crawl. Nate gave her a little space and went in ahead of her. If there was some sort of wildlife in there that Mato had missed, he intended to get to it before she did.

Like the other underground spaces they'd recently explored, this one was small. There were places where Nate could stand, but the ceiling height varied so much, it was safer to stay close to the ground. He was sitting roughly in the center of a space smaller than the average bedroom when Tori joined him. She slipped in quietly and leaned against him.

"You're gettin' better at this," he whispered.

"It's all the practice."

Mato was crouched against a wall. He had in hand the little LED light she'd given him weeks before, but the batteries were wearing down. The light faded as they watched.

Nate and Tori scooted closer, and Nate brought his own light to bear. What they found etched into the rock made Tori gasp. She couldn't imagine how Mato had even been able to see it since the size was considerably smaller than most of the renderings in the cavern beneath her cabin.

She traced the shallow lines of a drawing which showed two people, one much larger than the other, although the smaller body did not appear to be a child. The two were on their sides and nestled like spoons. The people were fully clothed and the sketch had no sexual overtones.

"They look like they're sleeping," Nate said.

"Or dead. But I like your impression better," Tori answered.

Nate touched the surface. "There are some words here, too." He adjusted his light to better illuminate the letters scratched in the rock.

"Can you read it?" She was behind him, unable to see the text clearly.

The letters were very small. "I don't think so," he said. "But at the end I can make out the initials 'RL' and a date: 1886."

"Aw, for cryin' out loud!" Tori fumed. "He did it again."

Nate turned to look at her, unable to see more than her general shape silhouetted by what little light leaked in via the crawl-through cave entrance. "Did what again? Who? Mato?"

"Those are uncle Bob's initials. RL stands for Robert Lanier. And the date makes sense, too. No one ever heard from him again after that year."

"So, what'd he do *again* that's so bad?" Nate asked.

"He wrote the message in one of his damned codes!"

~*~

His head cleared much faster than it had the night he ran into Domino. Though the alcohol had a profound impact, the effect Domino had on him was much longer lasting. While he still had big gaps in his memory about the night they met, he couldn't get the girl out of his mind.

Her revelation about the blonde wig and green contacts had actually eased his concern, since he felt sure that when she wore them guys would likely be scrambling over each other just to get near her. Of course, she had also been wearing a lot of makeup. Maybe, he thought with a guilty chuckle, to compensate for the lack of clothing. He remembered her that way, quite vividly.

He wasted little time deciding whether to tempt fate by driving back through the mountains to reach the interstate highway. The route south was longer, and the roads were narrower, but the ground was flat. Besides, his confidence in his driving had grown significantly. Not so much that he wanted another go at the mountains, but enough that he wasn't overly concerned about driving across Wyoming on garden variety highways. Anything with pavement was vastly superior to the dirt drive leading to the crappy cabin with its snake infested refrigerator. He was still pretty upset about that.

"I hope you like Ray Charles," he said to the little gal caged in the back of the car. He picked up US 20 in Worland and stayed on it until they reached Casper. He stopped there for food and gas, sharing his lunch with his prisoner, then took I-25 to the outskirts of Denver. The entire drive took just under 8 hours. By the time he reached the Mile High City, he was tired, hungry, and desperate for a shower and shave. But most of all, he was simply eager to see Domino again.

He pulled into the motel and found a parking space close to her room. The number was easy to remember since it was almost the same as the room number he'd had: 123 instead of 132.

Going by the strip club would have been a waste of time; she said it was her day off. Once out of the car, he stretched, then brushed haphazardly at the wrinkles in his clothes. He left the windows open slightly, but it wasn't hot, so he figured his caged passenger would be fine in the car. After combing his fingers through his hair, Carmine headed for Domino's room.

In his mind, an appealing scenario for the evening came together. She would answer his knock wearing something slinky and would drag him to bed, tearing off his clothes. He'd suggest they go out for dinner first, but she would decline, and they'd order something and have it delivered. It would be a night he'd never forget. Indeed, nothing had happened yet, and the memories were already piling up.

He had forgotten to stop at the liquor store on his way back from Wyoming. It was only a few blocks away, and he was tempted to make a quick trip before they found other things to occupy their time. But the lure of those "other things" was too strong. Food could wait. Sleep could wait. Even the shower could wait, although the thought of sharing one with Domino kicked off a whole new fantasy.

Somehow he kept from running down the hallway to reach her door. That gave him a tiny sliver of pride, the rest having sloughed off somewhere north of the

301

Colorado state line.

He knocked on the door.

The soft, sweet voice he'd been waiting to hear responded with an eager, "It's open!"

Resisting the urge to undress *before* he went in, Carmine pushed the door open slowly, romantically. He took a breath and stepped inside.

Ben Lykes smiled at him from his seat on the bed. "Yo, Carmine. What took you so long?"

~*~

"No," Nate said, "it's not in code, it's just damned hard to read."

"Oh." Tori tried not to sound as relieved as she truly was. Deciphering uncle Bob's codes had consumed her for much of her formative years. Having to start over on another one was really more than she could stand. "So, what's the problem?"

"Small letters. Lousy light."

Mato shouldered him aside, a neat trick for someone who weighed only about one sixth as much as Nate. In his hand the little Indian held some dark soil which he smeared over the inscription. At least, Tori hoped it was soil. With Mato, one could never be sure what materials he put to use.

"Wonderful. That'll really help," Nate said, his voice oozing sarcasm. "Now we won't be able to see the letters at all."

Mato glanced at him briefly, then continued working. After rubbing the dark soil into the letters, he used a piece of cloth Tori belatedly recognized as one of her handkerchiefs to wipe the surface clean. He smeared a layer of ashes over that and wiped it again. Then he sat back on his haunches and grinned.

"How'd you get your hands on my handkerchief?" Tori asked.

"I'll be damned," Nate said, shining his light on the letters. "Now I can read it."

Tori promptly forgot about the hankie. "What's it say?"

Nate squinted at the inscription, then read: *"'They do not wish to be found.'"*

"That's it?" Tori asked.

"'Fraid so."

"The date bothers me," Tori said. "According to what I've read, the winter of 1886-87 was one of the worst on record."

"It's legendary," Nate said. "Up in Montana they called it 'The Big Die-Up.' But it was pretty bad here, too. In fact, it was tough all over the west: a dry summer followed by a hard winter."

Tori touched his arm. "You make it sound like you lived through it."

"I don't look that old, do I?"

"Relax," she said. "You don't look a day over 80."

He ignored her and went on. "When I was a kid, my dad used to warble through an old cowboy tune. I didn't understand it, but he said he'd explain when I was older. When the time came, he did."

"Are you going to sing for me?"

Rather than answer, he broke into song. His pleasant baritone was as soft as his touch, she thought, and even Mato paused to listen.

I may not see a hundred,
Before I see the Styx.
But, coal or ember, I'll remember
Eighteen eighty-six.

303

The stiff heaps in the coulee,
The dead eyes in the camp.
And the wind about, blowing fortunes out,
As a woman blows out a lamp.

"Wow," Tori said when he finished. "What a happy song."

"Oh, it's definitely not 'Home on the Range.' Just the opposite. It's about the death of open range ranching. Most of the folks who survived that winter still ended up broke."

"And that was the winter my uncle Bob went looking for Leokahnah's people."

Nate once again bent to inspect the artwork. "Look, here's the feather. I'd say this is genuine."

"That was my thought, too," Tori said. "I need to get some photos of it. Can you help me mark the location on our map?"

"Sure," he said, then quoted the inscription once more, "'They do not wish to be found.' That's one hell of an epitaph."

"I'd like to go home now," Tori said.

Mato perked up. "Home?"

She smiled at him. "Yeah. I've had about as much discovery as I can stand."

~*~

"What are you doing here?" Carmine asked, still reeling from the shock of seeing Lykes sitting in front of him. His first thoughts had been for Domino. Was she all right? Had Lykes done something to her? But she appeared to be just fine. She was all smiles.

"He said he flew in to check up on you, make sure you were okay with your new job. I told him you wouldn't give me any of the details, and he said that was good."

Carmine stared at him. "What do you want?"

"Is that any way to treat your supervisor?" Lykes asked. He waved at Domino. "Would you mind if we stepped outside for a minute? We have some things to discuss."

"Go right ahead," she said. "Or, if you'd rather, I can step outside and--"

"Stay here," Carmine told her. "I'll be right back."

"Okay, hon."

He turned and walked from the room. Lykes followed him out, and Carmine shut the door. He walked far enough down the hall that Domino couldn't hear them. "What's going on?"

Lykes grimaced. "Well, genius, you didn't leave me much choice after you called my wife in the middle of the night to announce you'd fallen in love. And with a damned stripper! What's the matter with you? I send you on a job, and you go looking for bimbos! You got any money left, or did you blow it all on Sweetcheeks?" He jabbed a thumb toward Domino's room.

"She's no bimbo," Carmine said.

"She's a stripper, you moron. That automatically makes her a bimbo."

"Screw you," Carmine said. "I'm doin' the job. You didn't have to come out here."

Benjamin Lykes had several kinds of smiles, and Carmine thought he had seen them all, but he hadn't. The smile Lykes gave him was all venom. Eyes hard, face dark, teeth sharp. The fact that his lips were peeled back exposing those teeth did not mean he felt any mirth. "You need to know that I can reach out and touch your little

305

girlfriend whenever I feel like it."

"What d'ya mean?"

"It's so simple, even you should be able to figure it out," Lykes said. "If you screw up the job, you aren't the only one who'll suffer."

"You wouldn't dare hurt Domino."

"Really? Who's going to stop me? You?" He pushed Carmine backwards with one hand. "I drove past a sporting goods store on the way here. I'm sure they have a nice selection of baseball bats. I like the wooden ones; they feel so much more... solid. And I swing a mean bat. I'm a slugger."

"If you even touch her--"

"Shut up, Carmine. I'll do whatever I want to her, and there's nothing you can do about it. Now listen. Quit thinkin' about strippers and finish the damned job. Deliver the midget, and you'll get your money -- twenty grand, just like we agreed." He paused as if considering something. "Make that twenty G's, *less* the cost of airfare and a rental car. Once you get paid, you can come back here and do whatever you want. I won't care, 'cause I'll never see you again. Got that?"

"Yeah."

Lykes checked his watch. "You almost made me miss my flight."

"How sad."

"Watch your mouth, kid. I gotta go."

"You're so worried about the job, don't you wanna see my uh... cargo, before you go?"

"And let him see my face? No fuckin' way!"

Carmine nodded. "Smart. Wish I'd thought to cover *my* face. You might've mentioned that in your instructions."

"You're old enough to wipe your own ass."

"So, you've covered all the angles? What if I deliver the midget and your pals go to the cops?"

"Not a chance," Lykes said with a smirk. "I've got too much on 'em: documents and recordings. Insurance. Know what I mean?"

"Don't suppose it covers me, too?"

"You think this is a union job? You're an independent contractor. Get your own insurance."

Carmine stared at him. The mob concept had lost the last of its luster. "Don't hurt Domino."

"Threats, little man?" Lykes grabbed him and pinned him against the wall. "Or a suggestion?"

Carmine didn't answer. He was thinking about the shotgun in his car.

Lykes released him and walked away. "Get busy, Carmine. And don't screw anything else up."

He wondered how his sister could have married such a complete asshole and whether or not she would cry at his funeral.

~*~

Chapter 18

*The things that come to those who wait
were probably left by those who got there first.*

Tori had been looking forward to being home. Either hers or Nate's, it didn't matter. But it was obvious Mato wanted to go to the cabin. Nate must have realized that, too, since he drove straight to Tori's place.

They pulled in the drive, and long before they reached the cabin, Mato looked uncomfortable.

"You okay?" Tori asked.

In response, he shrugged.

Oh crap. Picking up on Mato's vibe, Nate drove faster.

"Mind the boulders, darlin'," Tori said.

"Gotta push it, babe. Mato appears ready to blow."

"I noticed."

The little Indian straddled the console of the big Ford pick-up, legs dangling to either side. But he'd locked his eyes on the road. Tori couldn't imagine what had him on edge, but then his radar operated outside the dimension she and Nate occupied. And sometimes, Mato was just plain scary.

With dust swirling all about them, Nate brought the truck and the horse trailer to a stop. All three occupants of the vehicle stared at the cabin's open door. Shadow barked.

"Oh, shit," Tori said.

Nate frowned. "I couldn't have said it better."

Mato didn't wait for either of them to crack a door. He dove through an open window and rolled to a stop at the foot of the steps. He was on his feet in an instant and dashed through the door. Shadow ran right behind him. Tori and Nate followed as quickly as they could.

Inside the cabin they found minor chaos. The kitchen table lay on its side, and the bed Mato and Reyna had made such spectacular use of had been shoved out of its usual position. Lance lay on the floor staring straight up at the ceiling. The word "creepy" popped into Tori's head the way it always did when she looked at the doll. *Should've shipped him back to Cassy the day he arrived.*

"Where's Reyna?" Nate asked.

"Good question," Tori said.

"Giants take her," Mato said. The look on his face was frightening. *God help anyone who earned his wrath.*

Nate dropped into a kitchen chair. "What giants?"

Mato shrugged. "Wear long shirts. White."

Nate and Tori looked at each other. She had no clue what he meant, and Nate obviously didn't either. Blank looks were getting them nowhere.

"We've got to be rational," Nate said. "Use some logic."

"I'm fresh out," Tori said. "I'd rather just shoot someone." The thought prompted her to look for her shotgun, which she'd left by the front door. It, too, was gone. She mentioned it to Nate who just shook his head wearily.

"So where the hell is Reyna?" Tori began to raise the table, and Nate helped her stand it upright. In the process, she noticed a broken jar and what looked like mustard on the floor. When she bent down to inspect it further, Mato intervened.

"No," he said, blocking her path with his arm. "Sleep magic. Very strong. Reyna make."

Tori stood up. "Okay then, you clean it up. My hazmat suit is at the cleaners."

309

"Cute," Nate said. He had been poking through the cabin, opening cabinet doors and peering inside. Tori felt slightly violated.

"Find anything interesting?" she asked.

He was standing next to the open refrigerator. "As a matter of fact, yes."

She strode closer to him.

"You may not like this," he said. "But there's a gopher snake in your 'fridge."

Tori backpedalled as Nate dangled a lifeless serpent between them. "They warm themselves in the sun, y'know. Gopher snakes aren't poisonous, but--"

"Nate?"

He looked at her. "--this one's a goner."

"So I'll hum 'Taps' while you toss it outside. Preferably where I can't see it."

Shadow had an interest in the deceased as well, though he was uncharacteristically timid about sniffing it.

"Please," Tori said. "Get that thing outta my house."

"It's just--"

"Throw. It. Out. Now. Please?"

"Gotcha," Nate said, making no effort to disguise his conviction that she was overreacting.

Tori had no wish to know what was going on in his fertile cowboy head. Moreover, she didn't care. Her focus was on Reyna, and she wanted his focus there, too. Mato had all but shut down. He sat on the top step leading into the cabin. Shadow joined him and put his head in Mato's lap.

"Okay, back to logic," Nate said after disposing of the snake. "Let's look around. What can we determine from the scene?"

"Not a damned thing," Tori said, with far more vehemence than she'd intended. Mato and Shadow looked at her in surprise. Nate ignored her reaction. It was probably a cop thing.

"Reyna's gone," he said. "Somebody's obviously been here. So, we'll operate on the theory that whoever it was grabbed her."

"Blood here," Mato said, pointing to a small stain on the uneven floorboards. "Not Reyna's."

"How could he possibly know that?" Tori asked.

Nate touched his nose. "Sense of smell, remember? I told you he's got sensory powers we can't even imagine."

"Who's blood is it?" Tori asked.

Mato shook his head.

"I'm guessing it has something to do with those phony Health Department workers," Nate said.

Tori agreed. "Can we call somebody and have them busted?"

"Not without some evidence."

"How much?"

"At least a smidge."

"A *smidge?*"

"Technical term."

She looked briefly to the heavens. "Where'd they come from?"

"Somewhere in New York," Nate said. "It's in my report. I'll call Dee. She can dig it up."

"Your buddy, Dee? Marty's grandma?"

"Yeah."

"Good luck with that."

~*~

Carmine tried to explain to Domino that Ben Lykes was a bad guy, despite his good manners and the pleasant conversation she had with him when he first arrived. Moreover, Lykes had threatened to hurt her if Carmine didn't finish the job he'd come all the way from New York to do.

"So, what kinda job is it?"

"A rotten one. I never should've agreed to it, but I thought-- Y'know? It doesn't matter what I thought. I've got to deal with it. Just do it, and get it over with. Keep you safe."

Domino gave a short laugh. "Your boss wouldn't hurt me!"

"He hired me," Carmine said, "but that doesn't make him my boss." He paused, mulling over Lykes' comments about insurance and independent contractors. "And I promise, this is the last job I'll ever do for him, or anyone like him."

"How does he even know you?"

"He married my sister, Veronica. I should've been suspicious when I saw him put up with all her crap. She makes the perfect mob wife: greedy and stupid."

Domino winced. "I was thinking, when you called her, that maybe you two were close."

"Close? No. I was drunk. I had to be; there's no other explanation. Normally, I wouldn't call her unless my life depended on it, and maybe not even then."

"C'mon, she's your sister."

"And she's married to the guy who threatened to hurt you if I don't do what he says."

"So, you will? You'll do what he wants?" Domino's eyes had never looked bigger, or more sad.

"Yeah."

"And then?"

"I've got some ideas."

She came closer and put her arms around him. "Do they include me?"

He gave her a hug. "Some of them."

"Only some?" She captivated him again with her soft, doe eyes.

"Only the pleasant ones."

~*~

"They work for Bernstein Laboratories in Poughkeepsie, New York," Nate said, his voice tinny on the phone. "All we have is a Post Office box number, but I'm sure I can find a street address."

"Dee didn't have one?" Tori asked.

"She's off-duty."

"Probably out raising bail for little Marty."

"It's not her fault he's a jerk."

"And a bully."

"That, too," Nate agreed. "Anyway, I'll make some inquiries. Then, when I'm through with this stupid trial, I'll be able to concentrate on tracking them down."

Tori looked at Mato. He had been pacing all evening while Tori waited for Nate to call. After he left, she had taken a much-needed shower and changed into clean clothes. For reasons she couldn't understand, Mato always seemed to look as fresh as ever, even after three days in the wilderness, crawling in and out of caves.

"We need to do something in the meantime. Mato's going to wear a track in the floor."

"I'm stuck," Nate said. "The trial starts tomorrow, but I can't imagine it'll last very long."

"We're going to New York," she said. Mato wasn't the only one who wanted action.

"I'm not sure that's a good idea."

"Why not? We can scout around and make some inquiries."

"And then go to the local police?" Nate's question hung in the air like a gastric emission at a wedding:

unpleasant, hard to ignore, and not what she wanted to discuss.

"That's out, obviously."

"And how're you going to get there? Fly?"

She looked at Mato. Was she ready to drag him around in public? How would he handle being in an airplane? And then, a weird thought: would she have to provide a child's safety seat?

"Tori?"

"Sorry," she said. "I was just thinking. No. We can't fly, and I'm not wild about taking a train or a bus, either. We'll need a car when we get there, wherever there is. *Poughkeepsie?*"

"It's on the Hudson river, a couple hours north of New York City." There was a pause, as if he were allowing time for the information to sink in. Then he added, "I've never been there."

"Me either. I think Poughkeepsie is where old proctologists go to die."

He went on as if she hadn't said anything. "Actually, I've never been east of the Mississippi."

"Everybody needs to see the Big Apple at least once," she said. "Once is usually enough. It's big. And crowded. There are nearly as many Yankees up there as there are in Atlanta."

"That's... shocking."

"Who knew, right? So, it looks like we drive. Can you be ready to go day after tomorrow?"

There was another pause, even longer than the last one. Tori broke it. "What's wrong?"

"I just spent three days with you looking for your uncle Bob's remains."

"And I'm deeply indebted to you," she said, then lowered her voice. "I tried to express my gratitude in a variety of ways, in case you hadn't noticed."

He coughed. "Oh, I noticed. Believe me. Message received."

"Good. So, what's the problem?"

"I don't have any vacation left."

"You're a cop, right? This is official business. You'll be investigating a crime: kidnapping."

"Nobody's filed a complaint. Sure, I can write up the break in, but that won't help Reyna, 'cause legally speaking, she doesn't exist. And if she doesn't exist, how could she have been kidnapped?"

Tori felt betrayed. "So you aren't going to do anything?"

"I didn't say that."

"Well you'd better say something comforting pretty darn fast! I'm about to hang up and take care of this all by myself."

"Give me a day to work things out. I'll talk to the sheriff. I know I can get an extra day or two."

"Let's see," Tori mused out loud, "that might get us to Chicago and back, provided the traffic's not too bad. But New York? There's no way."

"Cut me some slack, will ya?" Nate pleaded.

"Somebody's got Reyna. Do you think they'll cut her any slack? We've got one lead, and the longer we wait to pursue it, the worse it'll probably get for her. As a lawman, you should know that."

Nate exhaled wearily. "No argument. But give me some time to work things out. I know the judge; maybe I can talk to him, get him to delay the trial."

"Fine," Tori said. "But I'm getting ready for a road trip. I hope my truck can make it that far."

"I worry about you driving to town in that thing. Now you're gonna take it across the country?"

He was worried about her! Cool. Very cool, actually.

But damned inconvenient just now.

"No problem," she said. "I'll just take one of my many other vehicles."

"Very funny."

"Then, may I drive *your* truck?"

"It's not mine," he said. "It's a county vehicle. My own truck is in worse shape than yours."

"Well, congratulations, Nate. You've turned into a bureaucrat."

"It sounds like that, doesn't it? I'm sorry."

"What am I going to do?" she asked, plaintively.

"Call Caleb."

~*~

After a brief argument in which Domino suggested several good reasons why she should accompany Carmine to wherever he was going, he put his foot down. "It's just too risky." He handed her two hundred dollars of the money he had stashed away in the car. "I'll call you if I think you might be in any danger. You can use this to pay your bouncer pal to protect you."

"Do you really think that's necessary?"

"Yes."

"How long will you be gone?"

"I don't know. Hopefully, I can make the drive, get paid and be back here in a few days. A lot depends on Lykes. I'm sure he'll try to screw me when this is all over, but I've got an idea about how to be ready for him."

"Don't do anything stupid."

"For me, that's a tall order," he quipped. "Stupid is my middle name."

She kissed him. "Not any more it isn't. I don't fall in love with stupid men."

"I'll call when I can."

"Not at the club. If I'm not in the room, leave a message. Let me know you're okay."

He left her standing in the motel parking lot as he drove away. It was the hardest thing he'd ever done. So far. But he knew there were harder things to come.

~*~

Mato had listened to the conversations between Tori and Nate with only half an ear. He understood little of what they said and relied heavily on the emotion in their voices. Tori, though far more emotional than Nate, was harder to read since she used humor when faced with adversity. More often than not, her attempts at levity made no sense to him at all.

He did understand, however, that she had an idea where to find the giant who had taken Reyna, and he intended to be ready whenever she decided to leave. To that end he had gathered everything he thought he might need: bow, arrows, spear, blowgun, darts, hunting paste, and the prize he'd claimed from the three giants Nate had loaded in his truck. The prize was a dark green bag made from heavy cloth. It contained one of the exploding jars and a device which created a small but intense blue flame with the touch of a button. Prior to finding the device, Mato had never seen fire that could be directed with such precision. Better still, it gave off no smoke. He kept the bag and its contents out of sight, fearing that Nate would know he stole them.

The knife Nate had given him was nowhere to be found. He prayed that Reyna had taken it with her, perhaps hidden in her clothing. She would need it more than he. If she couldn't use it to protect herself, hopefully she could use it to escape. He knew there was another use she might put the weapon to, but the prospect was too grim to contemplate.

He also inspected the cabin for signs left by her captor. There weren't many. He found the scent of one unknown male, but it didn't tell him what he looked like or where he was.

The giant had taken Reyna outside, then carried her a considerable distance to a vehicle like Tori's. Its smell was not only strong, but distinctive. Giants bathed often, minimizing characteristic odors, but their vehicles retained the scents. This one reminded him of the brown paste Tori put on bread with crushed berries. She called it Peebeejay. Giants, he thought with a sigh. No logic at all.

The footprints left by the attacker were smaller than Nate's but larger than Tori's. The tracks disappeared, and the scent faded just out of sight of the cabin. Mato would have preferred to handle both the pursuit and the punishment alone, but finding one particular giant in a world populated by them would be impossible without help. Sadly, it sounded as if Nate might not be going with them.

~*~

Caleb Jones, retired rodeo rider, rural grocer, and harmonica devotee answered his phone on the second ring. "H'lo?"

"Hey, Cal. It's Tori. I need to ask you a huge favor."

"I'm doing fine," he said. "Thanks for asking."

Tori smacked her forehead. "Sorry, Cal. I'm such a ditz. It's just that the world is caving in on me, and--"

"S'pose I could get you to take a breath and settle down before you bring me up to date?"

"Yeah," she said. "You could." She took a deep

breath, sharing the sound with him over the phone. Oddly, it seemed to help.

"Now," he said, his voice sonorous and slow, "as much as you want to take it outta the gate at Mach two, try and hold back a bit. I'm an old man. I need a little extra time to process particulars."

Tori went on to explain about the cabin break in and Reyna's disappearance, the condition of her truck, and Nate's trial schedule.

"How's Mato?" he asked when she finally wound down.

"He's freaking out."

"I can imagine," Cal said. "So, you want to drive to all the way to New York?"

"Yeah."

"But your little truck ain't up to it?"

"That's what Nate says."

Cal chuckled. "You could do a lot worse than payin' attention to that fella. He's nobody's fool."

You should see him when he's about to orgasm, she thought. What she said was, "That's a fact."

"Let's take my van."

Tori held her breath. "'Let's?' As in, let *us?*"

"Yeah," he said. "I haven't been outta town in ages. Maggie says I'm gettin' stale."

"Let me get this straight," Tori said. "You'd be willing to drive with me and Mato all the way to New York?"

"If you'll have me."

"I could kiss you!"

"I'm ready, darlin'. But I'd appreciate it a whole bunch if you'd make sure Maggie isn't around when you do it. She gets a little funny 'bout that stuff."

Tori laughed. "Relax. Maggie isn't worried about me, Cal."

"So you say. I don't want to mess up a good thing. Know what I mean?"

"I do indeed."

"When do you want to hit the road?"

"Mato's ready now, I think. But Nate asked me to hold off until he knows if he can get some time off. I'd hate to make the trip without him, but if he can't leave in a hurry, we're gone."

"That a fact?"

"Yessir, it is," she said.

"Then sign me up. If Nate can't go with you, I will. But either way, I want you to use my van. It's plenty big enough, and whoever isn't driving can rest. Hell, even Mato can drive."

"That's not very likely," Tori said.

"You might want to find a place where he can practice. Ya never know."

Tori tried not to sound too exasperated about Cal's crazy notion. "I know you mean well, Cal, but putting Mato behind the wheel of a big old van is out of the question. We're facing a crisis, a real live emergency. I don't need to add driving lessons for Mato to the list of things we have to do. So, do me a favor, and don't bring the subject up again, okay? Especially around you-know-who." Mato may have looked like he was ignoring her, but she doubted much went on around him that he wasn't aware of. Especially if it had anything to do with Reyna.

"I read you," Cal said.

"You're a prince, Cal. A gen-u-ine prince. I hope you know that."

"I just hope you won't regret talking me into coming with you."

~*~

Carmine decided his best option was to get to New York before anyone expected him. The timing might throw Lykes off his game and give Carmine an advantage. Besides, he'd given Domino a major chunk of his cash, and if things really fell apart, he'd need some money to get back to Denver.

When he first accepted the job, he thought Ben had actually come through for him. In reality, it was probably just a convenient way to get him out of their apartment. Carmine had slept on a sofa bed in the living room. It sat beside some built-in shelving on which Veronica displayed her music box collection. Most of it was junk -- dime store crap made in China by pitiful laborers in sweatshops who probably couldn't afford to buy any for themselves, assuming they had the bad taste to want them. Veronica, however, wasn't burdened by a lack of money or the presence of good taste.

He remembered the night she came home with her first one. She hadn't wanted him to touch it, which, of course, only made him want to examine it more. Later, when he had the apartment to himself, he gave the device the kind of dedicated attention only a 13-year-old with villainy in his heart can apply. Quite by accident, he discovered it had a secret compartment. That revelation led to another, even more astonishing: Veronica kept a diary.

Carmine studied her most personal thoughts, and the details of her most intimate activities, with an intensity and devotion he never displayed for schoolwork. Reading a textbook would never yield knowledge he could use for blackmail purposes. Ronnie's diary, on the other hand, was a treasure trove of such data. He felt like a modern day Blackbeard!

He had been careful not to reveal too much of what

he learned from the journal, lest she figure out where he got it. By scrupulous use of only certain information, he kept her sufficiently wary of him that she never dared to rat him out about anything. But then, his misadventures never amounted to much while hers, in a comparative sense, were spectacular. Naturally, this unbalance resulted in a certain distance between them. It wasn't that Carmine didn't like Veronica, although he couldn't think of anything about her that was particularly endearing. It was more that she hated him for turning her high school years into a series of mini-extortions from which their relationship never recovered.

In an effort to help himself stay awake, Carmine moved the cage to the passenger seat. The arrangement prompted him to try conversing with his prisoner. She rarely said anything he could understand, though she often berated him in a language he'd never heard before, an oddity for a New Yorker. He figured he'd heard them all. Still, he talked to her. Or, at her. He wasn't sure which, not that it mattered. The goal was to keep his eyes open and his car on the road. And it worked.

He talked about his childhood, his inability to find a decent job, and about Domino. He talked about Ben Lykes and his sister. The fact that Ronnie was so easy to manipulate may have been the principal attraction between them. He felt reasonably certain it wasn't love keeping them together so much as it was the ease with which they could use each other. For them, a perfect arrangement.

Driving like a man possessed, a designation to which he felt entitled, Carmine stopped only for food, gas and the use of a toilet. He bought kiddie meals for his prisoner. He hated not being able to allow her out of the cage to attend to her own bodily functions. At least she didn't try to knife him when he cleaned up after her. And while he doubted she could understand what he was saying, he tried to assure her that the trip would be over soon, and she could look forward to far better conditions.

He certainly hoped that was true, but the closer they came to New York, the less he believed it.

~*~

Nate's hopes that the trial would be brief were dashed early in the proceedings. In his opening remarks, the defense attorney charged that the arresting officer had used "crude and barbaric weapons" on his unsuspecting clients, and that their lives were needlessly endangered because of it. Unable to observe the trial until after he testified, Nate learned of the accusation during a recess when the prosecutor descended upon him in the hallway.

"What the hell kind of weapons did you use on those jokers?"

Nate had no idea what he was talking about, and said so.

"The defense attorney claims you used some kind of poison darts."

Shaking his head, Nate assured him that hadn't happened. "The county allows me to carry a very reliable sidearm. Let's not forget, they pulled a shotgun on me."

"And then they just passed out?"

"Yes sir. I have no idea how much they'd had to drink, but it was substantial. I wouldn't have wanted to light a match near 'em."

The prosecutor didn't smile. "Don't try to be cute when you're on the stand."

"Right."

"If this thing blows up because you used some weird kind of weapon, I won't be happy. The district attorney won't be happy. And, I suspect, Judge Torrence won't be happy, either. And, in case you missed the significance of all that, I can guarantee you won't be happy either. Got that, deputy?"

"Yes sir," Nate said. He got it.

And thanks to Mato, he would very likely get a whole lot more. Quite suddenly, keeping his job received a higher priority than obtaining additional vacation time.

He wondered how he would explain that to Tori without sounding even more like a bureaucrat.

~*~

Reyna had been bracing herself for an attack, but it hadn't come. And that confused her.

Even though she'd stabbed the giant who took her from the cabin, he hadn't made any effort to punish her. She fully expected him to show some sign that he felt the wound, but aside from wrapping it with one of Tori's clever bandages, he'd done nothing.

She had spent a long time in the cage and assumed that she would likely end her life in it, when for reasons she couldn't fathom, the giant had moved her to the front of the car. By standing, she could just see out of the window. In the back of the car, she couldn't see anything but sky.

He even gave her food and drink. Granted, it wasn't very good, a failing she'd noticed in much of the food Tori prepared as well, but he was eating the same kinds of things, so she assumed there was nothing else available.

She had no idea where they were. They traveled at speeds she found frightening, but he seemed quite calm, and eventually she accepted that the danger was not as great as she had thought.

He spent a great deal of time talking to her, too. This had bothered her at first, since she assumed he expected her to converse with him. It should have been obvious that she couldn't, but he kept on talking. After a while, the sound of his voice evolved into something comforting. He often smiled at her and even laughed. But they were not the sounds of someone enjoying her imprisonment.

She had the distinct impression he was laughing at himself. It didn't make her situation any less desperate, but it gave her hope that at some point she might be able to use him to her advantage. She decided to postpone her suicide. At least for a little while longer.

Chapter 19

Always take a good look at what you're about to eat.
It's not so important to know what it is,
but it's critical to know what it was.

Tori drove straight to Charm after Nate's call. She had packed the night before in hopes of an early departure. Mato had loaded his gear, too, and was waiting for her when she finally locked the cabin and put Shadow in the back of the truck.

"Get Nate?" Mato asked.

"No," she said, trying to hold back some of her anger and disappointment. "Nate's not going with us." She didn't bother to try and explain the reasons. She didn't care. He had chosen his stupid job over Reyna's life. And now it was up to her, with the support of a tiny warrior and an old man, to drive clear across the country and effect a rescue. *Hey, no big deal. I'm Tori Lanier. I can leap tall buildings with a single bound.*

"What is New York?" Mato asked.

She dodged a driveway boulder and spared him a quick glance. "I'll stop at the library and see if I can find a picture book for you. I'm not capable of explaining it." Though she doubted he had any concept of what a library was, he seemed to accept her answer at face value. Too bad she couldn't count on Nate to act the same way. At least he volunteered to take care of Shadow. *I hope he craps all over the place. Nate deserves it for abandoning us.*

At Cal's house, they moved everything into his minivan. Shadow was lost in a whole new world of smells. Mato was equally fascinated by the furnishings and immediately set about discovering what was stored in every cabinet and drawer. Most of all, he liked being able to stand up between the two big swivel seats in front and look out the windshield.

Tori gave a fleeting worry to how many seatbelt laws they would surely break during the trip, and then smiled grimly. It would be interesting, if not pretty, to see some poor highway patrol guy attempt to get between Mato and the rescue of his true love.

With their gear stowed, Cal drove to Ten Sleep where they dropped off Shadow to roam in Nate's fenced pasture. Since he had already left for Worland to attend the trial, they went on and made the promised stop at the library. Tori overruled Mato when he said he wanted to go inside. It was a short visit. She couldn't find anything appropriate in the children's section and settled for a travel guide. He would learn plenty about cities as they drove through them. With any luck, they could avoid downtown New York. Sane people didn't drive cars there anyway.

By mid-morning they were on the road headed east, their destination some 2,000 miles away.

~*~

Carmine figured he could make the drive from Denver to Poughkeepsie in just under 30 hours, assuming he didn't fall asleep and smash into something. He had actually begun to rely on his passenger to wake him if he dosed off. She may have been little, but she had already proven she had a great set of lungs.

Instead, she fell asleep. And somewhere just outside of Akron, Ohio, so did he.

Fortunately, he had already pulled off the interstate

and took his nap in a rest area. He woke up a few hours later, not exactly refreshed, but able to see another sunrise. He was satisfied with that.

After taking advantage of the public facilities, he sought out a pay phone and made two calls. The first was to Domino to let her know he was still breathing. The second was to a name and number on the instruction sheet Lykes had given him: Tessa Bidford at Bernstein Laboratories, Inc.

The call to Domino lasted all of twenty seconds and consisted mostly of yawns and endearments. Carmine promised to update her when the job was done. He still had several hundred miles to travel, but was confident he'd make his delivery that same day. He didn't say anything about the other stop he'd planned. There was no point in worrying her.

The second call was all business, and he was put through to Ms. Bidford without delay. He identified himself, per the instruction from Lykes, as simply "the special delivery man."

"Where are you," Bidford asked.

"Ohio," he said. "But I'll be there later today."

"When, exactly?"

"I don't know. I've still got a long way to go, and there's no tellin' what traffic will be like."

"Call me when you cross the New York/Pennsylvania line. You'll only be an hour or so away at that point."

"Right," he said. He was going to ask her if she had his money or if he was supposed to get it from Lykes, but she had already hung up the phone. *Nice gal.* He couldn't wait to meet her. The encounter offered as much enjoyment as a root canal, only without the drugs.

~*~

Mato attempted to pace in Cal's vehicle, but there wasn't quite enough room. He couldn't understand why they had to spend so much time getting to their destination. Tori had given him a book, and he'd tried to show his appreciation by looking at the pictures, but they made little sense.

The buildings appeared to be as tall as mountains, though far less sturdy. In fact, he wasn't sure what kept them from falling over. And so many giants! They looked like termites scattering after a nest has been disturbed. Why would so many people want to live together? Why didn't they starve?

At first, while Cal guided the vehicle through the Bighorn mountains, Mato assumed the book was some sort of fairy tale for children. A scary one to be sure, but the giants had proven many times their inability to think logically. For all he knew, they got great sport from frightening their offspring with pictures like these.

He found the tiny symbols more intriguing than the pictures. Tori called it "writing." The pictures helped him orient the pages properly, but the clumps of various characters mystified him.

Cal and Tori watched him and made comments to each other. He assumed they were talking about him, but didn't care what they were saying. The book and its contents were merely something to occupy him while they travelled. Their destination could not possibly be too much farther, else they'd reach the edge of the world.

Though he'd never seen it -- he didn't know anyone who had -- the Old Ones had told him everything he cared to know about the edge of the world. According to them, it was cold and noisy. Nothing grew there. Death reigned above life, and fear had completely displaced love. No sane person went there, and surely no sane person had ever come *from* there.

Mato closed his eyes and sent another silent prayer to the Spirits that Tori not only knew what she was doing, but more importantly, where she was going.

~*~

Nate had never felt so miserable in his life. His conversation with Tori must've been the shortest on record. Not only had it started badly, but it went quickly downhill from there. In the process, he managed to touch on all the wrong things -- his job, the trial, and vacation time -- instead of concentrating on what she cared about: Reyna's life and their relationship. Worst of all, he realized his error at the precise moment he hung up the phone. Tori then ignored him when he instantly redialed.

Being in love with Victoria Lanier was easy. Getting into a relationship with her had been even easier. Now he was learning that *staying* in a relationship with her, at least as long as Mato and Reyna were in her life, would be damned tricky. No wonder cowboys loved their horses.

He went back to his seat outside the courtroom and waited for the prosecution to call him to testify. Dee walked past him twice, but kept her eyes locked on the hallway ahead. He may as well have been a potted plant. *I should change my name to Phil O. Dendron.* But then, of course, no one would take him seriously. Which, he reasoned, would be the case anyway if the defense prevailed.

With his love life in flames and his career in need of a disposable diaper, what options would he have left? An answer eluded him, and brooding about it hadn't changed anything.

That's when Dee made a third pass.

"Mornin'," he said.

She stopped and looked at him, her face unreadable. "You remind me of Marty."

"Oh?" *Just what I wanted to hear.* "How's that?"

"Whenever he gets caught, he gets this look on his face that says the world is about to screw him for something he didn't do."

"But--"

"And there's usually a 'but' in there somewhere, too."

"So, what do you tell him to do, cowboy up?"

"Something like that." She gave him a one-shoulder shrug and walked away.

He started to stand up and say something. There was always a chance she had buried some nugget of advice or inspiration in their exchange, but he couldn't find it. Maybe he just needed to be humble and ask.

Unfortunately, before he could get the words out of his mouth, the bailiff summoned him to the witness stand.

~*~

Despite her best efforts to remain calm, Tessa's impatience got the best of her. Though ordinarily the last person on Earth to find fault with herself, Tessa knew she had slipped into a zone of unreasonableness with which few others could compete. The bellwether moment occurred when her newly appointed secretary, a Bernstein Labs veteran with two decades of loyal service to the firm, left the office in tears. Tessa watched her departure with a mixture of loathing and relief. What the future held for her, and the company, would require strong stomachs and the ability to ignore a string of indignities Tessa couldn't imagine having to suffer herself. But then, she was management.

She had reviewed the blueprints of the area Jerry provided for her operation. The portion dubbed, "Donor's suite" had originally called for an expensive array of amenities including a wide screen television, custom furniture (scaled appropriately), and luxury touches to make a long-term residence more tolerable: hot tub, garden/entertainment space, and a fully stocked gym with size-appropriate exercise machines and free weights.

Constructing and furnishing the original plan would have required an additional month or two, to say nothing of the expense. Tessa red penciled all of it. In its place she specified a wire cage large enough to contain a small lavatory, and a tread mill. It wasn't as if anyone would be doing network television interviews with the subject. What mattered was his *blood*. It would be red, she assumed, and chock full of all the wonderful health-generating goodies they wanted, regardless of whether or not the donor's lifestyle was pleasant. Did anyone consult cows about their working conditions?

Due to her revisions to the construction plans, Bernstein Labs would be ready when their special guest arrived. Tessa had some reservations about the man she had spoken with on the phone, but his part of the project was insignificant. What mattered was having the golden goose on site.

She assumed Lund would be back at work in time to take the first sample of the donor's blood. After all, it was his amazing recovery that prompted Bernstein to put even more money into the project, and not just settle for the original fifty thousand he'd paid to acquire the donor. Lund's survival had been seriously in doubt, and the fact he appeared to be in better health than ever spoke to the value of the donor's hemoglobin, or whatever it was in his blood that made recovery from a fatal injury trivial.

She wondered, based solely on Lund's experience, if she ought to have a transfusion. Though she had absolutely no reason to believe there was anything wrong with her physically, she could only imagine what the benefits of such a treatment might be. Perfect skin? Perfect teeth? She'd noticed a bit of dandruff lately; would that be washed away in a flood of phenomenally good health? The more she thought about it, the more she wanted it -- the more she needed it.

And, by God, she *deserved* it!

If only the idiot delivery guy would call and let her know he had finally reached civilization. Not that Poughkeepsie came very close to living up to the definition. But she was willing to make allowances under the circumstances.

Where the hell was he?

~*~

The defense attorney looked like a decent sort. Not tall, not short, not particularly distinguished, but not shabby either. In fact, he was so average in every way as to be virtually invisible. Had Nate passed him on the street, or sat next to him in a bar, he wouldn't have found anything about him worth remembering. And that included his name.

"According to your report, Deputy Sheffield, you were the only one who responded to the call to investigate the explosions at the pond on the southern end of the Bristol property. Is that correct?"

"Yes."

"And what sort of weapons were you carrying at the time?"

"My service weapon is a Glock, 9mm semi-automatic. There's also a shotgun in my truck, which I left in the rack."

"Then how do you explain the odd puncture wounds suffered by my clients?"

"I wouldn't know where to begin," Nate said. "The woods are full of things which bite, sting or stab. By the time I got to those three, they'd had so much to drink I'm surprised they could feel anything at all."

That evoked laughter from the handful of observers, but Judge Torrence quelled it with a stentorian glare. He turned it on Nate and cautioned him not to editorialize.

"You're saying you can't explain those puncture wounds?"

"That's right."

"You have no idea what made them?"

"No."

"How about the poison they carried? Know anything about that?"

Nate shrugged. "The only poison I'm aware of is the stuff they were drinking."

More laughter.

"I warned you once," the judge said. "Don't make me do it again."

"Sorry, Your Honor," Nate said. "I won't let it happen again."

"We've heard testimony that a powerful anesthetic was administered to these men against their will. What do you know about that?"

"Nothing."

"How'd it get into their bloodstreams?" the attorney asked.

"I don't know that any such thing happened," Nate responded.

"One of the defendants found a porcupine quill in the cuff of his pants."

"I didn't put it there," Nate said, then winced in anticipation of another judicial reprimand. Fortunately, the defense attorney jumped back in before the judge could say anything. "A well respected physician has already testified that he found a piece of just such a quill imbedded in the neck of one of my clients. How do you suppose that got there?"

"I can't say," Nate said. He wished Tori could see him attempting to live up to his promise to keep Mato's existence a secret.

"Both of those quills bore traces of a knockout drug. Can you explain that?"

"No sir, I can't," Nate said.

"You didn't use a homemade blowgun on my clients?"

"I have an excellent sidearm, and I'm a decent shot. Why would I use a blowgun?"

The attorney struck a contemplative pose, then continued. "Because in such close quarters, using your handgun might have killed someone."

"The men were drunk," Nate said.

"The men were drugged," said the attorney. "Did you attempt a field sobriety test?"

"No."

"Why not? Aren't you supposed to test those you suspect of drinking?"

"If they're still conscious, sure. But all three of them had already passed out. There were enough empty beer cans up there to start a recycling center."

"Watch it, deputy," Judge Torrence said.

"Don't you find it a little odd that three grown men would all pass out at the same time?"

"I find it more odd that three grown men would throw homemade hand grenades at each other."

"You didn't answer my question."

"I've been to college frat parties where more than three guys have passed out simultaneously."

"We aren't talking about college fraternity brothers," the attorney said.

"Sorry," Nate said. "I thought the similarities were pretty obvious."

"Who really used that blowgun on my clients?"

"What blowgun?"

"The one used to knock my clients out!"

Nate shook his head. "They were drunk. I hauled all three back to Worland and put them in a cell. They didn't wake up for hours."

"Is *that* normal?"

"Yes. We put drunks in cells all the time."

"Is it normal for them to sleep for hours?"

"It's rare when they don't," Nate said.

The exchange continued in a similar manner until the prosecutor complained that the defense was attempting to plow the same ground for a third time. In his cross examination, the prosecutor had few questions for Nate, and he was excused.

Reluctant even to smile while still in the courtroom, Nate felt much better once he reached the hallway. Another trial had also ended for the day, and the area quickly filled with people. Knots of them formed to discuss events and strategies, though Nate wasn't called upon to join any of them. A pair of fellow officers approached him about going out for a beer, but he declined even without any alternative plans. The corridor had nearly emptied before he made the effort to leave it himself.

As he walked toward the exit, the bulk of a towering, silver-haired jurist blocked his way. "Judge Torrence," Nate said, startled.

A Little More Primitive

"Can we talk, Nate?"

"Sure," he said, wondering what he'd done wrong. Or, more likely, which of his lies had been exposed.

~*~

Carmine's second call to the Bidford woman hadn't ended any better than the first. If anything, she was even more brusque, demanding to know what was taking him so long but not bothering to listen to his response. Another Ronnie: stunningly one-dimensional, like a turd in box of Cracker Jack.

He told the little woman in the cage -- he couldn't bring himself to continue thinking of her as his prisoner -- that her release would come soon. He apologized repeatedly for having to keep her locked up, but assured her that once they got to Poughkeepsie, all that would be over.

If she understood him, which he doubted, she didn't take any comfort from his words. If anything, she appeared more frightened than ever.

Following his directions to the letter, Carmine used a succession of roads leading to a heavily wooded area on the east bank of the Hudson. This was no commercial area or business park. Instead of the anticipated warehouses, shipping docks, and parked tractor trailers, he saw mansions and manicured lawns. It had the feel of Central Park, without the surrounding city.

A small sign heralded a turn which led, eventually, to a huge fenced compound. The grounds inside reminded him of photos he'd seen of ritzy golf courses, only with buildings and in one far corner, what looked like a baseball diamond, complete with a bank of bleachers. They had spared less attention to the area outside the fence, though it was neatly mowed. The fence itself was disguised by high shrubbery, possibly to keep the workers from thinking they'd become inmates.

The woman in the cage grew increasingly agitated as they pulled to a stop at a guard station, the only visible access to the facility. As instructed, Carmine kept the cage covered and told the tiny woman inside to be quiet. And though he had no way to enforce the command, she made no sounds. Which served to make him feel even more guilty.

A heavy, motorized, chain link gate remained closed while the guard called to confirm that he was expected. Moments later, as the gate slid open on a track parallel to the surrounding fence, the guard directed him to an entrance at the far end of the main building. It appeared to be the only part of the compound where the landscaping had not been completed. Carmine nodded his thanks, drove to the designated area, and pulled into a space labeled "Visitor."

As he pondered whether to take the cage with him or leave it behind, a slender woman in stylish clothing marched out of the building and directly toward him. Carmine got out to greet her.

"Miss Bidford?"

"Where is he?" she asked, blowing past his outstretched hand to peer into the back of the car.

"Who?"

She gave him a look that could have wilted an old growth forest. "The donor. Where is he?"

Carmine swallowed nervously. "Yeah, about that. There were a couple problems--"

"We didn't pay for problems."

"I haven't been paid anything, yet."

"You want money, talk to your boss. We've paid all we're going to pay."

"But--"

"Please don't waste my time. Where's our donor?"

"On the front seat," he said. "I covered the cage with a towel just like the instructions said."

She stepped away and walked around the rear of the car, careful not to touch it. Carmine couldn't help but admire her tightly sculpted body. She walked like the kind of super hot model who prances around in expensive underwear. His brain having been hijacked by a fantasy, he paid no attention as she opened the passenger door and snatched the towel from the cage.

"What the hell?" she barked.

Carmine's vision burst like a marshmallow in a microwave.

"What kind of game are you playing?" She slammed the car door shut and retraced her steps until she stood nose-to-nose with him. Her dark eyes held a mixture of anger and contempt. He no longer cared what kind of panties she wore.

"I uh... The guy's dead."

"*What?*"

"I tried to tell you I ran into problems."

"You killed our donor? You fucking idiot!"

Carmine stepped back in surprise. "I didn't kill anybody! When I went into that old house to grab him, he was already dead -- lying on the floor, eyes open, staring at the ceiling. He wasn't moving. Wasn't breathing. Wasn't anything."

"So, who's in the cage?"

"I found her right beside him. Asleep."

"*She* killed him?"

Carmine shrugged. "I doubt it. There wasn't any blood that I could see. But it was dark."

"And you didn't bother to look closer?"

"Hell no! All I wanted to do was get outta there." He

339

was tempted to show her the stab wound on his finger, but that would have meant admitting the little gal still had her knife. If she choose to stab Bidford with it, that was fine by him.

"You should have brought the dead one, too."

"Oh, yeah, right. How stupid of me not to load a dead guy into my car for a trip across country. What was I thinking?"

"Bring her inside," Bidford ordered. She turned away and marched back into the building.

He looked at the woman in the cage. "I'm sure it'll be all right. Since you aren't the one they were looking for, they'll probably have someone take you back home." It seemed like a reasonable solution, and he wondered if he should offer to drive her back since he'd be headed that way anyhow.

Threading the beach towel through the handle to keep his fingers out of knife range, he lifted the cage and carried it into the building.

~*~

Mato's patience had thinned to the breaking point. The drive would last forever. Reyna was probably already in the hands of the giants who wanted to do unspeakable things to her, and he was powerless to stop them.

He had arranged and rearranged his weapons, checked the tips of the blowgun darts to ensure they were ready to accept the sleeping paste which made them so effective. He had a half dozen arrows. Less than he would have liked, but probably enough considering how many blowgun darts he had ready. His spear would likely not be very useful. The giants were just too big to be intimidated by it. Stealth and surprise would be his best tactics, silent weapons his best chance for success.

Cal and Tori would often exchange places. Cal would pull the vehicle to a stop and the two would step outside to stretch. Mato occasionally joined them, but he had enough room to roam around without going outside, and Tori insisted it would be better if he stayed out of sight.

What interested him more than the stops, was the difference in driving styles between Cal and Tori. Cal often enabled the controls which allowed him to drive using only his hands. Tori ignored them, but Mato didn't. Once he realized what Cal was doing, he observed everything the man did until he was satisfied he could do it, too. Was there no end to the secrets the giants had? What other things might he learn from them to take back to The People?

The question had far less luster when he considered it was likely they'd never find Reyna. How would he explain that to Winter Woman? Reyna was his responsibility, and he had failed her.

If need be, he would seek vengeance. He had enough weapons, and more than enough determination, to leave a lasting mark on the giant's world. Nor did he care if he survived.

~*~

Reyna shivered in the cold room where she'd been left. The cage she'd been in during the journey had been jammed against yet another, larger cage. The doors to both were open, and Reyna moved from one to the other like a trained animal.

She brought a blanket with her, since it afforded the best opportunity to hide the knife. Better to save it for a time when she might use it to escape than risk the chance

341

of having it taken from her. No one seemed to notice.

The giant who had brought her here looked very sad, which only angered her. He would be able to leave! But, she reasoned, he could have done worse by her. Would she kill him if she had the chance? It was a question worth pondering. By leaving her with the knife, and not telling her new keepers, he had given her hope that she might escape. Although, even if she did, she was so far from home she doubted she'd ever be able to return.

She would bide her time, look for an opportunity to escape, and then kill herself. The giants must not be allowed access to her dead body. Disposing of herself might be a challenge, but she was of The People. They had faced challenges before.

~*~

Chapter 20

Based solely on personal experience, many folks would rather have Boeing deliver the mail than ride in an airplane built by the Post Office.

Judge Torrence waved Nate to a chair in his office. The judge arranged his black robe on a wooden hanger and put it in a closet. He then strolled over to the high-backed executive's chair behind his desk. Nate couldn't help but notice what the judge wore under his robe: a white western shirt, frayed Wrangler jeans, and plain-toed riding boots. He looked more like a rancher than a jurist. It pleased Nate to see that things hadn't changed since he had been a part of the judge's life.

"You doin' okay, son?" Torrence asked.

"Yes sir," he said, then after an awkward pause added, "How's Beth?"

"She's fine. Says livin' in New York is expensive, but worth it."

Nate could picture her saying exactly that. The whole notion of moving to New York had been the wedge that finally put an end to their relationship. Nate couldn't imagine leaving Wyoming, and Beth couldn't imagine staying there. She claimed to be a city girl at heart, though how she managed that, having grown up in Washakie county, remained a mystery to him.

"I had a little chat with the defense attorney," Torrence said. "Poor bastard knows his clients don't have a chance. Anyway, he told me about something one of those fellas claims to have seen, but he thought it was so odd that he didn't want to bring it up in front of the jury for fear they'd want him to change their plea to innocent

343

by reason of mental disease."

"Seems odd he'd mention it to you, then," Nate said, wondering about the ethics of a private conversation with the judge handling one's on-going trial. But he knew better than to say anything.

"He's new at this, so I cut him a little slack."

"You didn't cut me any slack on the stand this morning."

Torrence pursed his lips. "Come on, Nate. I treated you the same way I'd treat any other witness. I couldn't treat you differently. Especially since everybody knows about you and Elizabeth."

"There's not a whole lot to know," Nate said. "We fell in and out of love." He shrugged. "It happens."

"I hear you're seein' that writer gal over near Ten Sleep."

"That's right, but how'd you know?"

"I'll get to that in a minute. First, I'd like your thoughts on what this man claims to have seen."

"Which is what, exactly?" Nate asked.

Torrence leaned back in his big leather chair, and when he did, most of the chair disappeared from view. "He claims you weren't alone when you made the arrest. He says you had some help."

"Is that what he was trying to get me to say on the stand today?"

"I imagine so. But you didn't, so he didn't feel safe carryin' it any farther."

Nate tried not to squirm in his chair, a dead give-away that he was hiding something, but the judge didn't seem to notice. "Who was this accomplice of mine? Did he say?"

"The defendant claims there was a little guy working with you. He was the one who used a blowgun on them, not you."

Nate nodded, unwilling to say anything.

"He claims this little fella was no more than a couple feet tall. Had Indian features."

"I've heard of guys seein' pink elephants when they were drunk, but this is a first."

"That's the sort of attitude the defense attorney feared the jury would have. And, I've got to admit, if I were the prosecutor, that's the way I'd paint such testimony."

"So why mention it to me?"

"Because I was talking to Dolores Mansheer the other day, and she told me something that got a whole lot more interesting after I heard from that attorney."

"Is this about her grandson?"

Torrence nodded. "She claims he was attacked by a tiny Indian in your house when you were gettin' ready to take the boy on a trail ride. Is that true?"

"I have no idea who attacked him," Nate said with a straight face. "Marty's story changed every time he told it. I didn't have enough reliable information to file a report. Dee wasn't happy about it."

"Correct." The judge reached into a bottom drawer of his desk and pulled out a newspaper which sported a big feature article about the music festival in Ten Sleep. A photograph of the crowd in attendance clearly showed Nate and Victoria Lanier sitting together. "Isn't she your writer friend?"

Nate examined the paper. The photo was a good one: Tori looked fantastic, and he didn't look too bad himself. Cal and Maggie seemed to be playing the role of proud in-laws.

The judge reached toward him and tapped the photo. "Who's that sittin' between you two?"

Nate squinted at the photo, praying silently that Mato hadn't come out of hiding like he had when Nate went after the three idiots now on trial. Thankfully, it wasn't Mato. He started laughing.

"What's so funny?"

"That's Lance," Nate said. "Tori calls him an Asian ball-jointed Doll. Very lifelike. Almost scary in that sense. But he's not so lifelike that he could use a blowgun, or beat somebody up."

The judge took the newspaper back and looked at it with a reading glass he'd extracted from his desk. "Why would a grown woman be carrying around something like this?" Then he fixed Nate with a glare. "And why would a grown man hang around a woman like that?"

"Is this about the case," Nate asked, "or does it have something to do with what went on between me and Beth?"

The expression on Torrence's face told him the judge didn't like the question, but he wasn't the kind of man to lord his position over anyone outside the courtroom. "You two were good together, Nate. I just never understood what happened."

"I'm not sure I understand it myself," Nate said. "I guess it just wasn't meant to be."

"You ever thought about going to New York to see her? Or at least, call, to find out if the spark's still there?"

Nate had considered it. Many times. He had the phone number, but two years had gone by, and he hadn't used it. Then he met Tori. "I've thought about it," he said. "It didn't seem like a good idea."

"You two haven't burned any bridges, have you?"

"Not that I know of. It's just... We've both moved on. I imagine Beth's got plenty of male friends in New York. She's not interested in a homebody like me."

Torrence crossed his arms on his broad chest. He didn't say anything for a full minute, then turned back to the newspaper. "A doll, huh?"

"Yes sir."

"And you expect me to believe the rest is all coincidence?"

"Would you rather believe there's a two-foot tall Indian running around shooting people with a blowgun and beating up kids?"

Torrence smiled. "You ever consider taking up the law?"

"I thought I had."

"I meant as an attorney."

Nate smiled. "I think everyone's better off with me doin' what I'm doin'."

"Which is what, exactly?" the judge asked.

"I'm content to be a deputy sheriff. I think I'm pretty good at it."

Torrence rubbed his face with both hands, then stood, the chat done. "I've known you a long time, Nate. You're a good man. If you weren't, I never would've given you Elizabeth's horse."

"Given?" Nate almost choked. "I had to take out a second mortgage to pay for that horse."

Torrence's smile split his fleshy face into two hemispheres. "You got a helluva deal."

"Yeah, I know. She's worthy of a much better rider than me."

"I doubt that," the judge said, walking Nate to the door. "Let me know if you need anything."

"Actually, there is something," Nate said. "I need to make an emergency trip out of town, but I don't have any time off coming to me."

"You want me to talk to the Sheriff? Get you some free time?"

"Would you?"

"You understand we're talking 'free' as in off-the-clock? Unpaid leave?"

"Sure. That's all I'm asking for."

Torrence smiled. "I imagine the sheriff and I can reach an understanding. We go way back, y'know. And it's not like you ask for favors all the time."

"I'd be very grateful," Nate said.

"No problem." Torrence paused. "But I'd like to add a condition."

Nate tried not to look too suspicious. "What would that be?"

"That you call Elizabeth at some point during your off time. Can you promise me that?"

It sounded like something he could live with, especially if he told Beth it was a command performance. "Sure," he said. "I can do that."

~*~

Tessa was glad that Mort Lund had returned to work. She called him into her office, and he arrived quickly. "Welcome back," she said. "Looks like we're going to be working together again."

He eyed her warily. "Together? I've never seen you visit a lab much less work in one."

"I didn't mean 'working together' in the side-by-side sense. More in the 'same project' sense."

"Oh. Swell."

"You don't seem exactly thrilled," she said, surprised by his modest show of hostility.

"Please. I only just recovered from the last time we sorta worked together."

She waved off his response like a bad odor. "That was an aberration. It won't happen again."

"That's a fact," he said, crossing his arms.

"For now, I just need you to take some blood samples. Surely you're okay with that."

"If it's in my job description, I'm okay with it. But beyond that? We'll just have to see."

"Let's get something straight," she said, standing to reach eye level with him. "Your job description is whatever I say it is. For now, I won't ask you to do anything that isn't in the current one, but I expect you to do whatever that is without delay. Or complaints. You signed a confidentiality agreement when you came to work here. That agreement is still in effect. Do your job and keep your mouth shut, and we'll all be happy."

"Or?"

"Or you're gone. And good luck getting another job in the same field."

"You sounded a lot different when you needed my help in Wyoming."

"So?"

"I'm not the same person I was then."

She looked him up and down, making no effort to disguise the appraisal, and discovered he *had* changed. Certainly not in his wardrobe or appearance, which still bore the unmistakable stamp of a dork, but in his demeanor. Mort, it seemed, had grown a spine. She responded with a "Hmpf," then added, "let me introduce you to our subject. Bring whatever you need to draw the samples."

Lund patted the lightweight canvas bag on his shoulder and followed her through an unmarked door into the room where the subject would be living for the foreseeable future. Tessa stepped forward and tapped the lock on the cage. "The combination is the same as my phone extension. If you haven't already memorized it, do so. I may change the number from time to time, so...."

He was staring at the tiny woman in the cage.

"Mort, did you hear me?"

"Yeah."

"What's the problem?"

He swiveled his head to look at her. "Are you kidding me?"

"About what?"

"Her!"

Tessa didn't get it. "She's the donor. We need samples of her blood."

"Can't you see she's terrified?"

Tessa looked at her and verified the accuracy of Lund's remark. "Okay, she's not comfortable with what you're going to do. I can see that. But as soon as she's been through the procedure she'll understand that it's not all that painful. Next time she won't be such a wuss."

"I can't do it," Lund said.

"Why not?"

"Because she obviously hasn't given her consent. Look at her! She's trying to squeeze through the back of that damned cage. And why the hell is she in a cage in the first place? What's going on?"

"Science is going on," Tessa said. "We believe she has something in her blood that could be of vital importance -- possibly the greatest medical breakthrough in history."

"And all we have to do is steal her blood."

"Steal?"

"That's what it's called when you take something from someone against their will."

"She will be more than adequately compensated," Tessa said. "Now, get busy. There's an entire lab team waiting for the samples."

"A team? Right. It's Friday afternoon, and the lab's empty. If not for the note you sent asking me to stick around, I would have gone home too. An hour ago."

She hadn't asked him to stay, she'd told him. "Just get the samples. I'll have the team start working on them in the morning."

"I can't," Lund said.

"Can't or won't?"

"I don't have a small enough infusion set. What I have is for adults, not for... well, for someone her size."

"So get what you need! Quit wasting time."

Mort gave her a look she couldn't quite read, and then left. Obviously unhappy with her, he also seemed disinclined to do his job. She would have no problem firing him, but finding another qualified phlebotomist could take days, possibly longer. Ultimately, she decided she simply couldn't trust him and so followed him back to his work station.

He was digging through the drawers of his desk looking for something when she caught up with him. "What's the hold up?"

"I need a 23-gauge set, but we don't stock them."

"Then use whatever you normally use."

"It's too big."

Tessa rolled her eyes. "I've heard *that* before, and believe me, it's never true."

"I don't want to hurt her."

"How hurt will your wife and family be when you tell them you lost your job?"

Lund's expression was one of pure loathing, as if that alone would induce her to delay the sample taking. As a spineless dork, he would have disguised that look, or saved it for a time and place where she couldn't see it. The new Mort Lund obviously didn't concern himself with such niceties. She found the change in him moderately intriguing, but in the end, she still didn't care what he thought about anything, much less the possibility that the donor might feel some pain.

"Must I hire someone who doesn't have an over-developed sense of compassion?" she asked.

"No," he said. "I'll take care of it."

~*~

The Bidford woman had told Carmine to get his money from his boss. That meant Lykes, which meant another confrontation. *Oh, goody.* In the back of his mind, Carmine had been thinking that he'd get his money from whoever took delivery of the little person. Getting it from Lykes was a whole different proposition, especially since he'd threatened Domino. That wasn't right, and Lykes knew it. As far as Carmine was concerned, Lykes had ceased to be his boss, and now represented nothing but an obstacle. A significant one for sure, but that's all. Not a brother-in-law, not a partner, and certainly not someone whose future he cared about. It wasn't Carmine's fault that Veronica had chosen to curl up with an asshole.

As for the pint-sized babe in the cage, he refused to think of her as a kidnap victim or a prisoner. It put too much guilt on him. Nonetheless, the word "victim" kept creeping into his head. Did she even have a clue what was going on? What little he knew about the business of laboratories came from his usual information source: Hollywood. Laboratories were places where weirdoes did revolting things to innocents -- usually female innocents who just happened to be drop-dead gorgeous. Which definition certainly fit the tiny chick he'd just turned over to the equally gorgeous, but obviously evil, Ms. Bidford.

How would he feel if someone had stuck Domino in a cage and hauled her off for some mad scientist to work on? Is that what he signed up for? Is that what he'd think about the next time he tried to go to sleep? And if he was lucky enough to fall asleep, what would he dream about?

The trip from Poughkeepsie to Veronica and Ben's apartment should have taken no more than a couple hours, but a traffic jam near Yonkers stuck him in a Friday afternoon rush hour. The sun had nearly set by the time he found a parking space and approached their brownstone on foot. He froze when the two of them left their building and headed toward an Italian restaurant across the street. Ronnie had never quite gotten the hang of cooking, not that Carmine was any great chef. But he could make do. Ronnie's efforts amounted to double that: doo-doo. The thought made him grin, and he realized it had been quite a while since he'd had much to smile about.

Knowing that Ben and Ronnie would be occupied for at least an hour -- Friday nights were notoriously busy for good restaurants -- Carmine slipped into the building unobserved. He still had the key his sister had given him when he lost his apartment, so getting in was simple. Now all he needed to do was rob them. And run like hell.

He searched Ben's desk, but found nothing of interest. He searched the closets, the kitchen cabinets, the pantry, and under their bed, striking out each time. Remembering scenes from a variety of films and TV shows, he looked for envelopes taped to the underside of drawers, but came up empty. No keys to deposit boxes or bus station lockers. He checked framed photos and artwork for anything that might lead him to Ben's hidden cash. Which had to exist. And which had to be hidden.

He had already overstayed his self-imposed time limit of 60 minutes. Lykes would never have been made to wait for a table, so Carmine's play clock had just wound down to zero. He found himself hoping they'd try to take in a movie, but instantly recognized wishful thinking. Bitterly disappointed, he prepared to leave, giving the apartment one last look to ensure he hadn't left anything displaced and thereby invite retaliation. As far as he could tell, the place looked exactly as it had when he entered.

Which is when he heard a key in the front door lock.

Reyna had breathed a deep sigh of relief when the giants left her without inflicting the torture she knew was coming. Her dreams had been horribly specific in that regard. Two giants would come for her: a male wearing a long, white coat, and a female whose tone of voice was more memorable than her clothing. The male had a long sharp needle which he would stab into her arm. The female would watch, perhaps to gauge Reyna's screams. What the giants hoped to learn from her remained a mystery. If it was the location of The People, their efforts were doomed to failure. Reyna had her knife, and she had no qualms about using it -- on them if the opportunity arose, and on herself if it did not.

She heard the door open again, and with a sinking heart watched the same two giants re-enter the room. Reyna huddled against the back wall of her prison, the knife hidden behind her back. She had chosen the longer of the two blades, though she knew neither was long enough to inflict a mortal wound. The best she could hope for was a wound deep enough to distract them while she made her escape. If that didn't work, she would plunge the wickedly sharp steel into her breast and join the ancestors. She did not fear for herself, but her heart was laden with sadness for Mato and their unborn child. Life was rarely fair, she knew, but it seemed doubly cruel to offer the great joy of motherhood, and then take it away and dash it on the rocks of despair.

The giants spoke to each other, and it was obvious the male was subservient to the female. He appeared nervous as he approached the cage. In her dream he carried his implements of torture openly, as if he knew the very sight of them would drive her mad with fear. The woman looked on, impervious yet impatient. How could she be so eager to witness Reyna's pain? What drove her?

The man opened the cage.

Reyna pressed herself against the bars opposite the door. She would not submit easily.

The man smiled at her and spoke, his voice low and soothing, as if that alone would be enough to trick her into aiding in her own undoing. *Come closer, giant, and feel Reyna's sting.*

He reached for her, his arm extending into the cage well past his elbow. The door was too small to allow him to reach in with two hands. Reyna took a deep breath and adjusted her grip on the knife.

Though nearly wild with dread, she had examined her pitiful armory after the giants had come into the room the first time. Besides the knife she had nothing but her wits, and a tiny bit of the sleeping paste which she found in a fold of the blanket she'd brought from the cabin. The fold kept it pliable, though it had dried to such an extent that hunters wouldn't use it. Reyna had no choice. It would work, or not, as the Spirits allowed. She hoped they would answer her prayers for further assistance, since it was obvious they had made the paste available in the first place. But she knew the Spirits could be fickle. They might just as easily withhold their favor as dispense it. Relying solely on the Spirits was an act of desperation. Reyna had not yet reached that point.

The giant's arm was now fully extended, and his

companion remained at his side, talking but offering no assistance. Indeed, since entering the room the female had not stopped talking, which served no purpose other than to annoy the male. Reyna had no idea what she was saying, nor did she care. She was waiting until they distracted each other.

Her moment came sooner than expected. A sharp exchange between the two giants caused the male to look away, and in that brief moment, Reyna struck. Wielding the knife with both hands, she stabbed the fleshy spot between the giant's thumb and forefinger. The finely honed blade bit deep, and Reyna hung on for the inevitable reaction. She wasn't disappointed.

The giant roared and yanked his arm from the cage, dislodging the knife in the process. Reyna grabbed the weapon as she bolted for freedom.

The female was yelling and cursing, maybe at Reyna, maybe at her companion. The latter was too involved with his wound to heed the invective hurled by the female. Reyna paused, torn between attacking the female and making a dash for the open door. Both options held considerable appeal, but she choose freedom over revenge. With the female giant still raving, Reyna burst from the room, then turned and shut the door. It closed with a satisfying click. Unlike the door on Tori's house, this one had no knob on the inside. With any luck, that would slow the giants down and give her time to get away.

~*~

Close to panic, Carmine desperately needed to find a place to hide, but instead his eyes locked on a baseball bat standing near the front door. It appeared to have been used for everything but playing games. The voices coming from the hallway belonged to his sister and brother-in-law. With the doorknob turning, he forced himself to scan the room again. The only place that offered the slightest cover was the futon on which he'd slept during the short time they had housed him. He dove for it, sliding on the hardwood floor and coming to rest underneath as the front door opened.

Veronica entered first, her voice in complaint mode: part whine, part wail. The meal wasn't up to her expectations, an irony of monumental proportions considering her limited culinary skills. Ben paid little attention, mumbling an assortment of monosyllabic and utterly non-committal responses. They didn't argue and rarely raised their voices, but neither did they actually engage in conversation. Both spoke, but it seemed to Carmine as if they were addressing someone else in the room, and he prayed it was someone other than himself.

Ronnie then shifted gears and power turned into an endless recitation of why they should buy dining room furniture, even though their apartment had no such room. Ben's responses focused on the need for obtaining a larger television set. The two spoke as if the other was listening, when clearly neither did. No wonder their marriage worked, Carmine thought. They never argue because they're too interested in their own thoughts to hear what the other has to say. They'd probably both wake up one morning having simultaneously concluded that murder was superior to divorce. But despite the vastly entertaining race they would run to claim the baseball bat -- and use it -- Carmine had no desire to stick around and congratulate the survivor.

His sole task was to remain hidden until they trundled off to bed. Then he could either resume his search for Ben's hidden stash or sneak out of the flat empty-handed.

He had plenty of time to ponder his limited options.

The television remained on for the next three hours, but due to the program choices, it seemed much longer. Carmine could hear the audio, though he couldn't see the screen. He was tempted to just drift off but feared he might snore and give himself away or, owing to a drive-induced sleep deficit, snooze quietly 'til morning when he'd be discovered by a refreshed Ben Lykes with an entire Saturday to devote to his demise. Staying awake was infinitely smarter, but considerably more difficult.

His stomach rumbled, which caused him to break out in a sweat. He had laid off the Bang and peanuts for most of the day in deference to his passenger. Now he realized he'd also avoided exposing himself in a truly nasty fashion.

He did a mental review of all the places he'd searched: all the closet shelves and seemingly innocent containers, all the drawers and under-drawers, all the cabinets, all the furniture. That's when he remembered Veronica's music box collection, and more specifically, her very first acquisition.

Momentarily excited when Ronnie went to bed, Carmine immediately suspected the worst when Ben stretched out on the futon to watch the Yankees play an inter-league game on the west coast. A life-long Mets fan, Carmine had little use for the cross town rivals and their excuse for baseball. Like most die-hard National Leaguers, Carmine disdained the designated hitter rule. It just wasn't baseball. It came as no surprise that Lykes supported the best team money could buy.

Another three hours dragged on, and Carmine's bladder had swollen to the size of an asteroid, if not a small moon. But the gods eventually took pity on him, and directed the visitors to hit into a game-ending double play with the bases loaded. Great stuff, that karma. Ben shuffled off to bed, not bothering to brush his teeth or turn off the lights in the living room.

Carmine waited as long as he thought necessary, then slithered out from under the futon. His arms and legs were stiff, and his hips ached from six hours on a hardwood floor. He allowed himself a few moments to stretch, then headed straight for the display shelf where Ronnie kept her collection.

In the middle of the center shelf sat the gaudy music box she'd purchased with her virtue. That she'd agreed to installment payments didn't diminish its importance, though it certainly had an impact on the market value of her charms.

Carmine wasted no time sliding apart the interlocked panels which gave access to the false bottom of the music box. The space where Ronnie once housed her diary had been given over to new occupants: a thick wad of hundred dollar bills and a small plastic case which held a memory chip. As he crammed the cash into his back pockets, the hall light clicked on and a door opened. Carmine froze for the second time that evening.

With his bladder rapidly approaching critical mass, Carmine stuffed the memory chip in a front pocket and began to mentally rehearse what he would say when confronted. He doubted he'd get too far before the *pifft, pifft,* and the darkness, but he wanted to be ready anyway. One never knew.

He heard another door close and the sound of someone using the toilet, but he was out of the apartment and down the hall before they had a chance to flush.

~*~

Chapter 21

He who dies with the most toys
is, nonetheless, still dead.

Tessa stood in the middle of the room, fuming. Lund lay at her feet, sleeping. Or dead. Or about to be dead; she had yet to decide. When the donor -- for whom Tessa needed a better title; "bitch" perhaps -- had closed the door, she'd quite effectively imprisoned *them*. Tessa had just begun to berate Lund for allowing it to happen when he slumped to the floor, unconscious. What a guy! He'd lost about a teaspoonful of blood, and while that was enough to make her queasy, she had no idea he'd pass out because of it. Then she gave the issue a little more thought. The man's profession was all about drawing blood. Seeing it shouldn't have knocked him out. But something did. She wondered if Jerry Bernstein had anything to do with it. She certainly wouldn't put it past him. Glancing slowly around the room, she looked for some sort of secret gas dispenser. But why would it only have knocked out Lund? She needed answers, but it didn't look like she'd get them any time soon. A damned phone would be nice. Or a door knob, or a fire ax, or a bulldozer.

Safely tucked away in the bottom drawer of her desk lay her purse, inside of which rested her cell phone -- bill paid and battery charged. There were no other means of communicating with the outside world. She'd seen to that when she approved the final blueprints for the donor's "suite." Welcome to Friday night at Bernstein Labs where no one else remained on duty, except the alleged security guards, and she had no idea when they made their rounds. Or even *if* they made rounds.

She resigned herself to an evening of door pounding. Whoever released her would earn her gratitude. The rest of the crew, however, might well be looking for work come Monday morning.

~*~

"If we keep going, we can get there by morning," Cal said, folding the road map to expose most of Pennsylvania. Much of the commonwealth's interstate system was also exposed in a sort of public works autopsy performed by road crews who never tired of either pouring concrete or digging it up.

Tori didn't take her eyes from the oft-patched road. "Then we keep going."

Mato had been awake for much of the trip, but finally crashed in one of the broad captain's chairs in the middle of the vehicle. A crumb dusted paper plate lay in his lap. The trio had been living on soft drinks and ham and cheese sandwiches which Tori whipped up in the minuscule on-board kitchen. They were all too focused on their mission to grumble about it.

"You still angry at Nate?" Cal asked.

"Yep."

"Don't suppose you'd care to talk about it."

"Nope."

They sat in silence for awhile, then Cal switched topics. "What did you have in mind doing when we get to this Bernstein place?"

"I'm going to find out if they've got Reyna," Tori said.

Cal, riding shotgun, steepled his fingers but didn't respond.

Tori frowned. "What?"

"You think they're gonna tell you?"

"If I raise a big enough stink."

"Okay," he said, "let's assume you raise all kinds of hell, but they still just tell us to go away. Then what?"

"I'll tell 'em there's been a kidnapping, and anyone who interferes with our attempts to free Reyna will be prosecuted accordingly. Kidnapping is a capital offense y'know."

"And do you plan to flash your badge?"

"What badge?"

"Exactly. Maybe we should have waited for Nate."

Somehow, Tori managed not to growl. "He isn't coming. We already discussed that."

"Oh," Cal said. "I must've slept through the conversation."

Tori pressed her palms into the steering wheel while wiggling her fingers. "We're on our own. I'm not happy about it, but there's nothing I can do about it. We'll just have to play it by ear. Once we get there, I'm sure one of us will think of something. And, if all else fails, we can go to the police and the news media. Somebody will take us seriously."

If they intended to keep the existence of Mato and his people a secret, Cal knew they wouldn't be able to rely on either the law or the media. He looked at Mato, still sleeping peacefully. "I know one guy who already takes us seriously. I'd sure hate to disappoint him."

~*~

Nate drove to the airport in Billings, Montana, not knowing which airline could get him close to Poughkeepsie, or what it would cost. Shadow had his head out the passenger window, delighted to be going anywhere. Nate wished life were that simple for him, too. He had tried to reach Tori several times, but she was either ignoring him or hadn't bothered to charge her cell phone. Cal's phone barely worked in Wyoming, let alone in foreign territory like New York. *Might as well send smoke signals to Mato. But at night?* Nate would be flying in the dark, literally and figuratively.

He'd been careful not to reveal too much to Judge Torrence, but evidently he'd divulged enough to convince the man he needed to be in New York more than he needed to be standing by in case the prosecutor wanted to quiz him again on his apprehension of the fish bombers. Torrence wished him well, and urged him to stay out of trouble. *Trouble? Me? With a hot-headed miniature Indian and an impetuous rebel writer? What could possibly go wrong?* No problem, he told himself, then added: Just quit thinkin' and drive.

Shadow would have to ride in the cargo hold, since he'd never pass for a service animal, and there was no way he'd fit under a seat. His feet might, but there'd be precious little room to spare. Nate prayed he could rent or buy a cage when he reached the airport. He wondered how serious New Yorkers were about leash laws.

~*~

Reyna passed through several doors in her rush to get out of the building, but none of them offered escape. She stumbled into a variety of rooms which seemed to have no discernible purpose. Fortunately, she didn't encounter any other giants as she desperately sought a way out. She doubted her luck would last much longer, and the two giants she'd escaped earlier would surely be after her soon. Did they have dogs? Thus far the only animals she had seen were rats, but there had been an abundance of them, all caged. Despite the positive feelings she had for Nate and Tori, such a thing only served to underscore the bizarre nature of giants. The People ate many things, but rats? Never.

Since none of the doors she opened led to freedom, she started looking for windows that might allow her to go outside. That strategy paid off quickly, and she climbed up on a counter that stretched the length of an entire room. A row of windows offered a view of the surrounding woods at dusk. Before long the sun would be gone completely. No time to waste.

Again, the giants' logic stunned her; the windows had no handles or locks like those in Tori's cabin. Reyna concluded that the giants merely wished to torment themselves by keeping the woods in sight, but out of reach. She searched for something with which to smash the glass. The counter top sported a variety of potential tools, but none seemed heavy enough for the task.

Her frustration turned rapidly into anger as she focused her efforts on finding something to use as a club. She remembered the last room she had traversed. It had no windows since the walls were lined with tall, thin, metal doors. A row of benches ran through the middle of the narrow space, and the whole area reeked of giant sweat. Reyna suspected the giants stored their soiled clothing behind those doors, and if so, perhaps one of them had left a weapon behind, too. It was worth a look.

She returned to the odd room to inspect the enclosures behind the metal doors. Many were locked, but not all. After working her way down one side of the room, she had reached the middle of the opposite wall when she found her prize: a smooth, stout length of wood. Half again as long as she was tall, the club was tapered, the narrow end tightly wrapped with a cloth band. She feared it might be too heavy to wield, but she'd seen nothing else even remotely suitable.

Reyna dragged the club from the sweat room to the window room and propped it against the counter. She clambered up the shelving, then hoisted the heavy weapon to the counter top beside her. She took a moment to catch her breath before standing the club beside a window with the narrow end at her feet. Taking a deep breath, she pushed the club into the glass with all her strength.

~*~

Tired of pounding on the locked door, and hoarse from yelling, Tessa had gone through every scenario she could think of which might offer a punishment suitable for the guards who had to be actively ignoring her. Nothing seemed satisfyingly gruesome enough, which only frustrated her more.

Even more annoying was Lund, who woke up several times only to drift off again, usually while she was chewing him out. She fervently hoped narcolepsy wasn't contagious.

Sometime in the middle of the night, a "security" person finally opened the door. Flashlight in hand, he stood looking at her as if she'd just beamed in from the Starship *Underprice*, or whatever the morons making the space movies called it. The guard would doubtless be able to tell her, provided she allowed him to keep his tongue after she extracted his spleen through his nose.

She brushed past him in her haste to find a phone and call in some real support.

"What's wrong with this guy on the floor?" the guard yelled as she sped away.

"Wake him up and ask," she yelled back, wondering what she had done to deserve such an array of incompetents.

When she reached her desk, she speed-dialed Jerry Bernstein's home phone. Mrs. Bernstein answered, her slumbers having obviously been disturbed. "Ashley?" she mumbled, her voice stuporous, but rapidly developing overtones of alarm. "Are you all right?"

Ashley? One of the Bernstein brats, no doubt. "It's Tessa Bidford," Tessa said. "I need to speak to Mr. Bernstein. It's urgent."

"What's wrong?"

The word "urgent" confounded her? "Lab security breach. I must speak to Jerry. Now!"

She heard more mumbling, a groan, and the sound of bedsprings. Eventually the lab's founder came on the line. "What's the problem?"

"Our donor escaped. Your boy, Mort, let her out. I want his head when he wakes up."

3 AM was clearly not Bernstein's best hour. "Mort did what?"

"Let her escape."

"Who?"

"The donor!"

"I thought the donor was a he."

Perhaps if you spent a little more time at the lab you'd be aware of these things, lard ass. "No, actually, it turns out we got that wrong. The donor is female, but it's not important. What is important, is that we find her immediately, and we can't rely on the Neanderthals you have doing guard duty."

"I don't-- It's-- I'm confused."

"She locked us in her room, and it took your stellar security staff several hours to release us. She's probably halfway to Boston by now, and you know how *those* people are; they'll shelter anybody. If they get their hands on a midget of the minority persuasion, we'll never hear the end of it. If we don't track her down now, we'll have a public relations nightmare on our hands."

"So I'll just call the authorities and--"

"No! You can't call the damned cops! We have to handle this ourselves. If you call the police, I guarantee the media will arrive first. You want our little project plastered all over the evening news?"

"Of course not. I--"

"You're not thinking clearly because you just woke up. I understand. But here's the thing, we need to be clear headed about this right now. There's no time to brew coffee and mull over our options, 'cause we only have one. Find the little bitch. Find her now, and keep everyone involved quiet. That's the only way we're going to get out of this without having it blow up in our faces."

Bernstein remained quiet for several long moments, then gave vent to a protracted sigh. "You're right. We don't have any alternatives. I'll have the security company send more personnel. In the meantime have the staff on hand search the campus, inside and out. I'll be there as quickly as I can."

"Good," Tessa said. "Now you sound like someone who knows what it means to be in charge."

"Do you need anything?"

Are you for real? "A little help would be nice," she said through gritted teeth.

"It's on the way."

She wondered what movie he'd stolen *that* line from.

~*~

Reyna thanked the Spirits as she ran. Not only had

they allowed her to break out of the giants' frightening building, they had given her a moonless night to aid in her escape. She hurried through the grounds until she reached a high fence.

She climbed up the metal fencing with ease, her hands and feet fitting comfortably in the diamond shapes of the crossed wire. But when she reached the top, coils of horribly sharp metal barred the way. Fortunately, she checked the wicked coils before trying to crawl through them. Otherwise, she might have left a bloodless body for the giants to investigate. She couldn't allow that to happen.

Disappointed, but unwilling to admit defeat, Reyna climbed down and searched along the base of the fence for a low spot. She didn't need a large opening, obviously. Something that would accommodate an animal the size of a skunk or a marmot would do nicely, though she doubted any such creatures would wish to enter the giants' compound lest they be caged and eaten like the rats.

Eventually her diligence paid off, and she located a dip in the ground beneath the fence. Someone had tried to block the low opening with a fallen limb. This she removed with relative ease before crawling to freedom, and then worked back into place to disguise her exit.

The woods beyond the fence provided perfect cover -- wild, thick, and free of even the smell of giants. In the distance she detected other smells, those associated with water.

She moved as quickly as possible, and though hindered by the thick undergrowth, managed a sustainable, ground-eating pace. She finally broke through, and the sudden openness startled her.

The last of her energy drained away as she looked out

upon a vast river, much wider than the lakes she knew from childhood. Much wider than any body of water she had ever heard of. And much wider than any river she might ever swim across. This was the giants' final fence, a fence she could never breach. Disheartened and exhausted, she slumped to the ground, and slept.

~*~

Carmine counted the money he'd taken from Ben twice. The total was almost double what he'd been promised for the kidnapping. The look on the little Indian's face when he handed her over to the ruthless bitch at Bernstein Labs still haunted him.

Though played out from lack of sleep, and terrified by thoughts of what Lykes would do if he discovered who had robbed him, Carmine kept thinking about the girl. Could he just abandon her?

On the other hand, the laboratory compound was heavily guarded. The fences had to be ten feet high. He couldn't remember if the guards were armed or not, and had no idea how many there were. Maybe if he had a machine gun he could force his way in and free the girl, drive her back to where she came from, or at least as far as Denver. He slapped his forehead. Stupid! If he didn't take her all the way home, who would?

At least he had the shotgun, and when he got back to Denver, Domino could help him drive the rest of the way. She could drive through the stupid mountains! There was no question she'd applaud his efforts on the little Indian's behalf. After all, Domino herself had called him a hero! The time had come to prove it: he had to rescue the Indian girl and see her safely home.

Then he fiddled with the memory chip. He'd seen one before, in a digital camera Ronnie kept in her purse. She'd bragged that it would hold thousands of photos, though he'd never seen her take a single one. There was a good chance the chip he held in his hand was empty. Or maybe it was a spare, and the one with the pictures was still in her camera.

Or, knowing Lykes, maybe this one contained images they didn't want anyone else to see. Wait! That had to be it: dirty pictures! The revelation was followed by a profound shudder. Who on Earth would want to see Veronica and Lykes naked? Or... worse! There was more to the epiphany. Perhaps Ben would be willing to pay to ensure that no one else saw them. Maybe the way to avoid his revenge was as simple as blackmail. Carmine began to feel better about his own survival.

But even that didn't keep him from worrying about the little Indian girl in the cage. She deserved survival, too. He hoped he had the guts to see that she got it.

~*~

Bernstein arrived before the extra guards did, and after a brief consultation with Tessa fled to his office leaving her in charge of the search. She sent two of the four resident guards back to their office to review security tapes from the exterior cameras while a third inspected the grounds. The fourth would remain in the guard shack, at least until reinforcements arrived.

A hasty search of the building revealed the donor's means of egress: a shattered window. Lund made the discovery having recovered from his bout of unexplained sleepiness. He had drifted in and out for several hours, but claimed he'd never been completely unconscious. Tessa doubted that, but couldn't prove it. Still, it rankled knowing she might have missed an opportunity to yell at him even more than she had. On reflection, she decided she hadn't backed off simply because he couldn't hear her. Ranting made her feel better, and at such times she didn't care if the rantee got the message.

Bernstein called her cell phone when the additional security force arrived. She got on her radio and summoned the three men not assigned to the front gate and told them to meet her in the main lobby -- a short walk for them, a long one for her. When she and Lund got there, Bernstein was already addressing the troops. The force consisted of the three regulars and four reinforcements.

She stared at the newcomers, and then at Bernstein. "You got four additional guards? *Four?*"

Bernstein seemed perplexed. "They said it was the optimum number."

"I'm guessing that's all Walmart had available during their two-for-one sale. Can't you see we have a disaster brewing? We don't need four; we need forty!"

"You're over-reacting," Bernstein said. "Counting you, me, Mort, and the guy at the gate, we've got eleven. That should be plenty. The campus isn't that big."

Tessa was almost too angry to speak, her emotions staying just barely under control. The man had the imagination of a termite. "Do you suppose she might have *left* the campus?"

His expression told her she'd scored a hit. "How?"

"Beats me. Maybe through the gate when the guard wasn't looking, which -- by the way -- he almost never does. Or maybe she tunneled under the fence. She had most of the night to do it. Come to think of it, she might have built a ladder from fallen limbs and climbed *over* the fence. It doesn't really matter how she did it, though, does it? And if she did, well... What then, oh Great Leader?"

"Sarcasm isn't going to make this situation any better."

"Neither is hiding in an office."

She and Bernstein traded lethal looks, then Tessa sent two of the guards back to continue reviewing security tapes while she and Bernstein lead their respective search teams in opposite directions. Lund went with Bernstein and two guards, Tessa took the remaining three guards with her.

~*~

Tori was behind the wheel when they pulled onto the forested drive that would take them to the headquarters of Bernstein Labs. The fact that it was a Saturday didn't deter them. They reasoned it might even be to their advantage since they'd have to talk their way past fewer people on a weekend.

Mato had been strangely quiet during the last hour or so, and while Tori would have liked to see what he was up to, paying attention to the road was more important. Cal had rarely taken his eyes off the map during that time, so neither noticed that Mato had donned war paint and had his entire stock of weapons within easy reach as they pulled to a stop at the entrance to the Bernstein Labs parking lot. Tori had just enough time to order him to stay out of sight. Mato didn't respond.

"We're closed to the public," said a guard, his tone the antithesis of a warm welcome.

"We have business here," Tori said, striving to sound official.

The guard consulted a sheet of paper on a clipboard. "I wasn't notified of any visitors today."

"We're early," Cal said as Tori cut the engine.

The guard frowned. "What're you doing?"

"Parking. And we're not moving until we have assurances that our friend isn't being held captive here."

"Captive? That's ridiculous," the guard said. "No one's being held against their will here. Now, move your vehicle or I'll have it towed."

Cal shook his head. "Arguing with this lady is a bad idea," he said. "Trust me on that."

"Go!" the guard said, pointing toward the road behind them.

Tori unbuckled her seat belt and got out of the van. Cal did the same.

The guard reached for some sort of weapon on his heavy, black belt. "If you don't get back in that car now," he said, "I'll have no choice but to-- Ow!"

Something had flown past Tori's ear and struck the guard's neck. He took a short, quick step backwards as he fumbled to remove whatever it was from the area of his jugular vein. As she watched, his eyes rolled up as if he were inspecting the top of his skull from the inside, and he dropped like the rest of his bones had morphed into chicken noodle soup.

She was still processing what had happened when she noticed Mato standing in the driver's seat. He had just cranked the engine.

"Cal? Did you-- Watch out!" she shouted.

The old rodeo hand scrambled backwards as Mato gunned the engine and guided the van with the hand controls. He rammed straight into the gate and kept accelerating until the whole section of fencing came crashing down, then rolled forward into the almost empty parking lot. Halfway across, he stopped and disembarked.

Tori and Cal jogged after him. "Wait," Tori yelled. "There's a better way!" When that didn't slow him down, she added, "Please don't hurt anyone."

Two guards came running out of the main entrance. Each carried a weapon of some sort, though at first glance they didn't appear very threatening. If anything, they looked like electric razors, without the cords. Mato put his blowgun to his lips and cut loose. Two darts sailed mere moments apart, and both landed with astonishing accuracy, as if they had homing devices tuned to carotid arteries. The charging guards went down in a snarl of arms and legs. Mato had no use for anything the men carried and jogged nonchalantly past their bodies toward the entrance.

"We've got to stop him!" Tori yelled.

Cal didn't respond until after he'd assured himself that the guards weren't dead, then a smile appeared on his face. "Why's that?"

"Well, because-- Because someone might get hurt."

"I 'spect Mato would tell you somebody's already been hurt. Reyna."

Tori wanted to argue, but Cal had turned to follow the little warrior, and she didn't want to be left behind. She wasn't. The front entrance doors had locked automatically after the two guards came through. Mato was on the ground in front of them, but she couldn't see what he was doing.

Cal reached his side first, then turned and ran back the way he'd come, waving his arms and yelling at Tori to get down. Mato sprinted sideways and dodged behind a brick pillar which supported the arched roof above the entranceway. He had left something on the cement in front of the doors.

It had a fuse.

The fuse sputtered, sparked, and gave off a sinister smoky trail.

Cal yelled something about taking plastic cards from

the downed guards which would have unlocked the doors, but it was too late. He sought shelter behind the pillar opposite Mato's.

Tori dropped to the ground and covered her head as an explosion knocked the doors into the building. Stunned by the blast, she could do little more than look up and watch as Mato disappeared into the dark interior.

Carmine heard an explosion as he turned into the road leading to the lab. Rather than race into the unknown, he took a cautious approach, driving slowly toward the security gate. What could possibly have caused an explosion? Had the bastards already done something to the little Indian?

Unlike during his foray into Ben and Ronnie's apartment, Carmine was well armed. And his weapon was substantially more lethal than Ben's stupid baseball bat. He patted the sawed-off, double barreled shotgun in his lap. It might come in quite handy during the rescue, but he had already resolved to return it to the cabin when he brought the little Indian back to Wyoming. He tried to puzzle out how she might be able to even use it, then decided that wasn't his problem.

Pulling to a stop in front of the ruined gate, he glanced at the guard sprawled near the security shed. He couldn't see any blood and wondered if he'd been hit by flying debris from the explosion.

Then he looked at the downed gate. If the blast came from inside the compound, how had the gate fallen *toward* the exploding buildings? His eyes tracked a path toward the front entrance where he saw two more guards on the ground.

What in the world was going on?

He drove the Honda a short distance into the parking area and stopped near the guard shack. He got out of the car and hurried back to have a closer look at the first guard's body. The man was breathing and bore no discernible marks from the blast. Carmine helped himself to the odd-shaped weapon on the man's hip. It fit easily enough in his hand, the grip being suitably sculpted, but the thing was too light to be a firearm even though it had a trigger. He pointed it toward the ground and pulled the trigger, not at all sure what would happen. The device rewarded him with a buzz and the spark and crackle of electricity. *A stun gun -- how very, very cool!* How handy such a thing would have been when he was digging around in Ben and Ronnie's place. *Bring it on, big guy.*

He pulled the trigger again.

Zzzzt!

Finally, he felt properly armed. The shotgun was nice, but he wasn't looking forward to blowing someone away with it. He held it in the crook of his arm. For sheer intimidation, a shotgun was hard to beat. And now, for the close stuff, he had the ultimate in bad guy neutralizers.

He gripped the stun gun tightly and advanced on the building just the way the cops on TV did it, and found himself hoping somebody would jump out at him.

~*~

Chapter 22

A poet is someone who is not only astonished by everything, but is compelled to admit it.

Tessa and her three valiants stayed near the main lab complex and concentrated their efforts on the area near the broken window through which the fugitive donor had escaped. Bernstein, Lund, and their two guards examined the perimeter fence. With luck someone would uncover a clue leading them to the escapee, the operative word being *luck*. Tessa had no confidence in the tracking skills of the "uniformed professionals" working for them, and was actually glad they weren't allowed to carry firearms. The temptation for her to use one on them would have been unbearable.

When they heard the explosion, everyone stopped moving. Bernstein struck a Heisman pose aimed away from the disturbance while Lund and the two guards stood at parade rest, their faces uniformly slack-jawed as they gazed at the smoke cloud rising above the building. Tessa's gang stared at her, demonstrating their profound lack of personal initiative.

She sent two of her guards to investigate the blast and kept the other at her side, in case she needed something to hide behind. Bernstein jogged reluctantly toward her, his face resembling a Greek tragedy mask. Lund was close behind having dispatched their two guards to join Tessa's to find out what just blew up.

"What the hell is going on?" Bernstein asked.

"It may be a diversion," Tessa said. "If so, it means we're up against a pretty savvy opponent."

Bernstein looked at her in surprise. "Opponent?"

"It's just a figure of speech," she assured him. "You might find it easier to focus on the chase if you think of her as an adversary."

"As opposed to what?" Lund asked.

"Oh, I dunno. How about 'prisoner' or 'kidnap victim'?"

Bernstein put a hand to his forehead. "You really are ruthless."

Yeah, well, it beats being spineless. "One of us has to be." She clicked the TALK button on her two-way radio and asked, "Anybody see what caused that explosion?"

Immediately, four voices responded sending a flood of static and nonsense over the airwaves. How she loved working with professionals!

"Let's go," she said.

"Where?" Bernstein asked, his voice almost child-like.

"To see who's trying to blow up your lab." *And my future.*

"Well, you'll have to do it without me," Mort Lund said.

"What?" gasped Bernstein.

"I'm through," Lund said. "I won't have anything more to do with either of you, or this lab."

"Arrest him," Tessa said, shoving the guard at the phlebotomist.

"I'm not a cop," the guard said. "I can't arrest anybody."

Tessa grabbed the stun gun from the guard's holster and advanced on Lund. "Okay, then, I'll arrest him."

Lund laughed. "In case you hadn't noticed, you aren't a cop either."

Tessa jammed the stunner into Lund's upper arm and pulled the trigger. He stiffened and screamed. He tried to move away, but she clung desperately to his arm and continued to shock him.

"Stop!" yelled the guard, but she ignored him.

Lund was thrashing, his eyes wild and his voice an unrelenting groan. Tessa refused to let go until he went slack and dropped to the ground.

"My God, Tessa," Bernstein said. "You've killed him!"

The guard was kneeling beside him, checking his pulse. "He'll be okay," the guard said. "It won't take more than a few minutes for him to wake up, but he'll be groggy for a while."

"What the hell's gotten into you?" demanded Bernstein. He held out his hand. "Give me that damned thing."

Tessa shook her head. "Not a chance. We can still keep a lid on this."

"What about Lund? Are we going to lock him in a cage, too?"

"Of course not. But we can't let him go just yet. We need to get things under control first, then we just fire him. No one's going to believe anything he says. They'll think he's just trying to settle the score. All we have to do is play it straight."

"What about him?" Bernstein asked, gesturing toward the remaining guard.

"You like working here?" Tessa asked him.

"Yeah."

"And can you keep your mouth shut?"

"Maybe. If I got a raise."

"You got it." Tessa looked at Bernstein and smiled. "See? Everything's under control." She nudged Lund with the toe of her shoe. "Even our traitor."

She told Bernstein to keep an eye on Lund and call her when he woke up. Then she grabbed the guard and headed for the lab from which the donor escaped. There had to be a clue there somewhere.

~*~

Shadow sat in the passenger seat of Nate's rented car, his head out the window as they flew south toward Poughkeepsie. They had arrived in Albany before first light, and Nate felt fortunate to have gotten some sleep. He hoped Shadow wouldn't harbor any long term resentment for being caged and stowed in the belly of an airplane, but the dog was so excited to see him when they spotted each other in the baggage claim area, he knew he had nothing to worry about.

Since he had no leash, Nate had pressed his belt into service, looping it around Shadow's collar. As a cheap substitute it couldn't be beat. As an *effective* substitute, however, it sucked. Nevertheless, he got the dog into the car without too much strain, and they were on their way.

The trip seemed to last way too long, and every delay caused him to worry more. And not just about Tori. He'd have to call Beth sooner or later. Later, he decided. She wasn't sitting by the phone pining for the sound of his voice. She could wait. He'd live up to the promise he'd made the judge in good time. For now he needed to focus on the task at hand, whatever in hell that turned out to be.

He tried Tori's cell phone again, but there still wasn't any answer. Maybe she's in a motel somewhere, getting some rest before they try to talk their way into the lab.

And maybe when this was over, he and Shadow could catch a ride home on some flying pigs.

~*~

Tori entered the lobby of the building and tried to determine which of the connecting corridors Mato had taken. Cal seemed equally perplexed. "Got any ideas?"

She shook her head.

"Maybe we should split up," he said. "I doubt there are any guards left. They weren't expecting an assault team."

"We aren't an assault team!"

He smirked. "Did you mention that to Mato?"

"Let's stick together," she said, ignoring his question.

They decided on the hallway with the fewest doors, reasoning that Reyna wouldn't be kept in an office. Labs ought to be bigger than offices, she figured, so there should be fewer doors. The first room they checked was exactly what they weren't looking for. It contained a bank of television monitors showcasing different views of the building and grounds. Two empty chairs sat in front of the screens. Cal concluded their former occupants were on the ground outside, resting -- comfortably or not -- complements of Mato.

"Oh, crap," Tori exclaimed, pointing at one of the monitors. Two pairs of uniformed guards had joined forces in the lobby, and all of them had weapons in hand. "We've got to find Mato."

The ringing in Mato's ears had gradually subsided. He could hear his own moccasined footsteps, even though the soft leather allowed him to move in relative silence. The same could not be said for the giants hunting him. Even if they had not clumped around in heavy shoes, Mato could hear them talking. And if they had somehow managed not to talk, he could still have heard them breathing.

Josh Langston

He found a large earthenware pot containing some kind of plant he'd never seen before. Its broad leaves and long stems provided excellent cover, and he slipped behind it to wait. A corridor was not the best spot for an ambush, since it limited the options for escape, but he decided it would do, especially since the giants would not be expecting an adversary of his stature. He almost pitied them. But then, he also almost pitied the animals he hunted for food. Somehow, the pity always dissipated by the time the dripping fat from the roasting meat hissed into the flames.

Four giants, dressed alike, passed his hiding place without giving it a look. They were "guards," according to Tori and Cal, who said there would likely be many. Mato watched from behind the plant as they turned away. He fired his first dart at the nearest one, hitting him in the back of the neck.

Cursing and reaching for the barb, the guard got the attention of his companions. Mato got the next closest giant in the side of the neck, and he, too, grabbed at the dart while cursing. The two giants farthest away stood, puzzled, and watched their comrades sink, groaning, to the floor. They still hadn't seen Mato, though they turned in all directions and waved their weapons as if that might frighten him. Mato remained motionless, his blowgun having become one with the stalks of the exotic plant.

When the standing giants knelt to check on the men at their feet, Mato got off two more darts. The first was another perfect strike, entering the guard's neck just below and behind his jaw. The second dart missed the mark, and went into the last guard's collar. Mato figured it hadn't touched him, as he'd not made the customary response. Instead, he snatched the quill from his companion's neck, though the sleeping paste had already begun to do its work.

As the third guard slumped down, Mato reached for another quill and in the process brushed against the leaves of the big plant. He may as well have waved a flag. The last guard turned in Mato's direction and, weapon ready, charged.

Mato rolled clear of the plant to take another shot, but tripped on his bow which he'd carried slung over his shoulder. He landed hard on the blowgun, bending the tube and rendering it useless.

The guard surged toward him, his weapon foremost. Mato had nowhere to go, and backed into the plant hoping to squeeze between the pot and the wall. The pot, however, was too heavy.

"What the hell?" said a voice from down the hall.

Mato looked up in time to see yet another giant. He had no room to draw his bow, and there was no way he'd be able to avoid them both.

Pulling his knife from his belt, he passed it quickly through the pouch containing his sleeping paste and waited for them to come closer.

~*~

Tori and Cal entered a huge laboratory. Tables and chairs littered the room along with an array of gear salvaged from a geek's wet dream. The machines crowding the tables were separated by computers, with no two alike, and monitors of various shapes and sizes occupied counter space everywhere. More of the ubiquitous screens hung from the walls.

Tori had expected test tubes and beakers, glass coils and metal trays bearing partially dissected animals with little pins bearing hand-lettered tags identifying parts. But what she remembered from high school biology definitely wasn't the look embodied by a 21st century science facility.

"I have no idea what we're looking for," she admitted to Cal.

"Good," he said. "I was beginning to think I was the only one."

They poked around until they found a broken window. A baseball bat lay on the countertop and bits of glass littered the inside of the window frame. Tori couldn't help but smile when she saw the destruction. "What d'ya 'spose happened here?"

Cal looked as pleased as she felt. "Looks to me like somebody wanted out. Badly."

"Miss Lanier?" asked a voice from behind them.

Tori spun around. Facing her stood the woman who had pretended to be a Wyoming State Health worker. She was accompanied by a heavyset guard wielding a nightstick. The woman held the same kind of stun gun as the guards Mato had neutralized outside. Tori struggled to recall her name. "I know you," she said.

"You should," the woman said. "Since you almost killed me."

"Bidford." Tori expelled the name like something dislodged from between her teeth.

"You're under arrest for trespassing," the woman said.

"I still don't see a badge," Tori responded. "That seems to be a problem for you, doesn't it?"

"If I hit you with this thing," she said, waving the stun weapon, "you won't be seeing much of anything. Would you like to give it a try?"

Though Tori didn't tower over the other woman, she had a couple inches on her and several pounds. For once, such a weight disparity pleased her. She could take this little snot down, stun gizmo or not. She motioned with both hands. "Bring it, bitch." *What would Nate say?*

The smaller woman hesitated. "The last person I zapped is still out cold, and it only took a few seconds." She depressed the trigger and the device gave a crisp electrical response -- a tiny bolt of lightning -- restrained for now, but easily unleashed. "Still interested?"

"This is a bad idea, Tori," Cal said. "You need to think this through. You could get hurt."

Tori kept her eyes on Bidford. "I'm not the only one." She shifted sideways to put Cal in the path of the guard in case he tried to assist her opponent. "Any time, Snowflake."

Bidford moved with astonishing speed, but it was the direction of her attack that left Tori speechless. The smaller woman jammed the stun gun into Caleb's upper arm while at the same time pressing him against a desk. The weapon buzzed, and Cal yelped, but he couldn't get away. Bidford kept pushing the weapon into him, a look of fierce pleasure contorting her face.

Tori finally reacted, and while it felt like she'd been immobile for minutes, in reality it had only been a few seconds. Leaping forward, she grabbed Bidford's weapon arm and tried to pull it away from Cal. Bidford resisted for an additional moment, by which time Cal's cry of pain had devolved into a terrible groan. He slumped to the floor.

Tori pulled her arm back to punch Bidford, but the guard had circled around behind her during the melee and locked her in a bear hug before she could take the swing. Cal lay on the floor, knees bent and both hands on his chest. He continued to groan, and his face had lost its customary color.

"Lemme go," Tori said, struggling to free herself, but the guard held on tight. She stomped down on his foot.

Hard. When he let go, she rammed her elbow into his ample gut sending him backwards in a limping shuffle accompanied by wheezy grunts.

Dropping quickly beside Cal, Tori gently turned his face toward hers. "Cal? Are you okay?" She knew it was a stupid question, but couldn't help asking.

"Chest hurts," he said. "Can't breathe."

"Call 911," Tori yelled as she loosened the top two buttons of his shirt.

"I don't think so," Bidford said.

"He could be having a heart attack."

"Or he could be pretending." She stepped closer and pressed the stun gun into Tori's neck. "Still want to try this thing? It's got a little charge left."

"I don't have time for your bullshit," Tori said, ignoring the threat.

"And I don't have time for yours," Bidford answered. She called to the guard. "Help her get this guy up and moving."

Tori glowered at her. "He doesn't need to be moved. He needs medical assistance."

"You can provide it once we've got you both secured." She motioned for the guard to take them out of the big lab. She followed behind with the stun gun, occasionally pressing it into Tori's shoulder, but not shocking her. The reminder was enough to keep her moving.

They travelled the entire length of the building before arriving at a smaller lab. Bidford walked them into a room which contained a straight-backed chair and a cage. No windows, desk, or phone. Tori and the guard settled Cal in the chair, then he and Bidford backed out of the room.

"That's it?" Tori asked. "You're just going to leave us

here? He needs a doctor!"

Bidford shrugged. "And I need a vacation. Life sucks sometimes."

Then she closed the door.

~*~

Carmine pointed the shotgun at the guard crouched in the hallway. "Don't move."

The man's head swiveled toward him, and he raised his hands which had been poised to grab whoever was hiding behind the big potted plant. Carmine had a pretty good idea who it was, though he couldn't see her clearly. "It's safe," he called. "You can come out now."

"*Safe?* Are you nuts?" the guard asked. "Look around, asshole. Who do you think put those three men down?"

"I'm not worried about them," Carmine said.

"Well I am." The guard straightened briefly, then suddenly leaped sideways, toward the plant.

Carmine yanked one of the two triggers on the shotgun. The ensuing blast startled them both. A hole about the size of a grapefruit appeared in the wall behind and a few feet away from the guard who was now stretched on the floor, his arms reaching toward the plant.

His screams had been briefly masked by the roar of the gun, but they broke through clearly as Carmine turned his attention from the hole in the wall to a hole in the guard's arm. A miniature Indian warrior -- featherless, but in war paint -- looked up at Carmine as he wiped blood from the blade of his stone knife on the guard's shirt. The guard's scream subsided until it became a mere groan.

The Indian stood and stared at Carmine with a look of grim resolve on his face, half of which was painted dark red. Carmine had little doubt what it symbolized.

387

"Hey, we're cool," he said, more than a little confused since he'd been expecting a small, appreciative female rather than a small, angry male. "I'm not going to hurt you."

The little Indian grunted, his disdain unmistakable.

"Seriously," Carmine went on, "we're on the same side. At least, I think we are."

Turning his head slightly to the side, the Indian sniffed the air. Instantly, his features shifted into a look of rage. "You! You take Reyna!" He slipped the knife into his belt and took the bow from his shoulder. The movements were so fast and fluid, Carmine didn't even react until he nocked an arrow and prepared to shoot him.

"Wait!" Carmine yelled.

But the Indian didn't wait. Carmine heard only the whisper of his bowstring.

~*~

Jerry Bernstein came into the smaller lab as Tessa turned away from the room where she'd locked up their visitors. "Where's Lund?" she asked.

"Gone."

"What?"

"I was going to tie him up, but I couldn't find anything to do it with. He was out cold when I left him to find some rope. When I got back, he was gone. I came straight here."

Tessa turned to the guard and handed him the stun gun. "Go. Track him down. Don't let him leave the grounds."

The guard, however, wasn't moving. "About that raise you promised me?"

"Can we discuss this later? Before the whole damn

world comes crashing down around us?"

"Sure," he said. "Just remember who was there when you needed help."

"I will," she said. *You can bet your fat ass on that.* "Now go!"

He went.

"What do we do now?" Bernstein asked, making it clear he'd turned the entire show over to her. No doubt he'd point the authorities at her, too, if it came to that. For now, all she could do was try to regain control of the rapidly deteriorating situation.

"Like I said before, we need more guards. Can you make some calls? Get some people in here who can actually make a difference?"

She didn't wait for him to answer, choosing instead to use her radio to put out a call to find Lund before he went to the police. Or worse, to the press. She keyed the TALK button and gave the order. The only guard to respond was the one who'd just left the lab. The others all remained silent.

"What's the matter?" Bernstein asked, trying to read Tessa's expression.

"Things might be worse than I thought."

Deep creases appeared in his forehead. They matched his scowl. "I can't imagine how."

Possibly because you don't have much imagination to begin with? "You wouldn't happen to have a gun in your office, would you?"

He responded with a sharp intake of breath. "How did you know?"

"Lucky guess," she said. It was high time they had a little luck. "Let's go get it."

~*~

Nate pulled to a stop beside the guard shack in front of Bernstein Labs. He glanced at Shadow. "This doesn't look good." A uniformed body lay on the pavement, and the gate which should have sealed the area had been flattened and either knocked or dragged a great distance from where it belonged. Shadow found the situation highly amusing and wagged his tail in approval.

Nate shook his head. "You've definitely been hanging with the wrong crowd, chum."

Shadow barked.

"Okay, okay. I'll get on with it. Don't get pushy."

He drove into the parking lot and stopped beside Cal's camper which dwarfed Nate's rental car. He walked around to the other side and let Shadow out. The lot was nearly empty, and there was no one in sight. Anybody who didn't like dogs off-leash would just have to tough it out.

Shadow ran straight to the passenger door of Cal's vehicle and started whining. The door wasn't locked, so Nate let him go inside. The visit lasted only long enough for the big black dog to catalog the most recent occupants, then he was back outside with his nose to the ground.

"Find Tori," Nate said, though he suspected Shadow was way ahead of him.

~*~

Carmine looked down at the arrow quivering in the stock of his shotgun. Had he not been holding the weapon across his chest, the missile would have gone straight into his heart. He looked up to see if the little warrior was about to finish him off with a second arrow, but he was the only one in the corridor still standing. The Indian was gone.

A door opened, and Carmine whirled to face the new threat. He had the shotgun lowered and his game face on. Things were getting way too weird.

"Don't shoot!" yelled the man who'd just entered the hallway. He wore a white lab coat and looked disheveled and nervous.

"Don't *move*," said Carmine.

The man raised both arms. "I'm not involved in this, I swear."

"Yeah? Well, we'll see about that." He yanked the stone-tipped arrow from the wooden stock and was about to toss it away when he noticed an odor coming from the chipped flint arrowhead. He smelled it cautiously, the scent familiar. Where had he encountered it before?

"I'd just like to leave," the other man said. "I don't even work here anymore."

"Sit," Carmine said, gesturing toward the floor.

"Please don't shoot me," the man said, staring at the guards scattered before him. He looked like he was going to cry.

"Sit," Carmine said again, "or I *will* shoot you."

The man sat.

Then Carmine remembered the smell. He'd noticed it in the cabin the night he went to grab the girl, the same night he'd passed out suddenly after she stabbed his finger. Looking more closely at the bodies on the floor, he noticed the darts protruding from the guard's necks. *Interesting.*

He addressed the newcomer. "Do you know how to check for a pulse."

The guy wasn't too nervous to let his eyes roll toward the ceiling. "Well duh. I'm a phlebotomist."

"A *what?*" He waved the question off, not wanting an answer. "Check them. I think they're still alive."

The man scooted across the floor and checked each of the bodies, nodding his head to confirm Carmine's guess.

"Serves 'em right," Carmine said. "They shouldn't have tried to interfere."

"With what?"

"The rescue. You didn't see the guy who did this?"

The man's eyebrows dipped in consternation. "I thought you did it."

Carmine shook his head. "I just got here."

"I'm confused," the man said.

"I was on a mission of my own to rescue the little Indian girl these people were going to experiment on."

The man appeared stricken.

"What's the matter?" Carmine asked.

"She escaped."

"When?"

"During the night."

"Where is she?"

The man held out his hands, palms up. "Nobody knows. I got in trouble because I refused to help them track her down. Then the bastards knocked me out with a stun gun." He looked at Carmine as resolve eliminated the last of his fear. "Any chance I could be of assistance?"

"You mean, like helping me find the girl?"

"Or punishing the people who were holding her."

"Yeah," Carmine said. "That'd be great." He held out his hand and introduced himself.

"I'm Mort Lund," the man said. "Follow me."

~*~

Chapter 23

Women and cats will do as they please, and
men and dogs should relax and get used to the idea.
~Robert Heinlein

Tori helped Cal lie down on the floor. She had already loosened a couple buttons of his shirt, and he was alert enough to make a wise crack about her eagerness to get his clothes off.

She shushed him. "You've gotta just be calm, Cal. I know that may be a little hard, but--"

"You think I'm having a heart attack, don't you?"

"I don't know. But I won't bullshit you. I'm scared."

"Yeah," he said, his breathing still shallow. "Me, too."

Tori stood and examined the door again. The knob and the hinges were on the opposite side. The windowless room offered no way out. "I hate to admit it, but we're trapped."

Cal chuckled.

"What's so funny?" Tori tried not to sound annoyed but feared she had failed.

"You are."

"C'mon, Cal. What're you talking about."

"Getting out. Everyone thinks the only way out of a room is through a door or a window."

Tori looked at the ceiling in the hopes of finding acoustic tiles. If they could be pushed aside maybe she could climb up and get away. But the ceiling appeared solid. "I don't understand."

"Use the chair."

She walked over and examined it. The chair was

composed of common metal tubing, the seat and back padded and covered with vinyl. It appeared hopelessly average. Useless. She looked at Cal on the floor and shook her head. "What? I don't get it."

"Smash through the wall," he said. "I'm guessing it's just gypsum board over metal studs. They didn't build this room to be a bank vault."

"Or a prison!"

"That's what I'm thinkin'."

"Cal, I could kiss you!"

"Get us outta here first, okay?"

Tori picked up the chair and looked for the widest section of wall space. "Here goes nuthin'."

~*~

Mato went forward with another paste-dipped arrow at the ready. He had picked up Reyna's scent -- more than once, in fact -- but didn't want to concentrate on tracking her until he'd eliminated anyone who might try to stop him.

He had wasted a precious arrow on the bad-smelling giant, but refused to waste any more time on him, despite his babbling. His attitude had told Mato more than his words, and it was that which caused Mato to let him off with a warning. The giant should be smart enough to know Mato could have sent the arrow into his brain as easily as he'd hit his gun. If the giant got in Mato's way again, the outcome would be different.

And the difference would be permanent.

One last giant presented himself. Another of the guards about whom Tori had cautioned him. He'd opened a door to the corridor, stepped out, and stopped as if turned to stone, like the trees from the very, very old times. Mato took pity on him and sent an arrow into the upper part of his leg. Reyna's sleeping paste worked its magic. The stuff was stronger than that mixed by Winter Woman. He would compliment his mate most enthusiastically once they were reunited.

The guard went down with a soft sigh, collapsing like a tipi when the poles were pulled. Mato stepped over him and entered the room he had just exited. An older man and a young woman stood at the far end, talking. Mato couldn't make out what they were saying, but opted to investigate.

Crouching low, with his bow parallel to the floor, he crept toward them. They continued talking, oblivious of him, then left the big room.

Mato stood, determined to follow them when he noticed a broken window and a heavy wooden club beside it. He ran to the window, his nose rejoicing in Reyna's scent. She was free! The giants no longer held her in their power. He should have known she would find a way out. His lover was clever, resourceful, and determined.

The last thought gave him pause. What would she do with her hard won freedom? She couldn't walk home, even if she understood the incredible distance such a journey entailed. Nor would she allow herself to be recaptured. And that was the most frightening issue of all. If she made sure the giants wouldn't be able to find her -- or her body -- it was highly unlikely he'd be able to find her either.

He had to begin tracking her, and soon. But first, he had business with the man and woman who'd just left the room.

~*~

Nate had been tempted on numerous occasions to break out his cell phone and dial 911. In fact, each time he stepped over a body -- all of which wore security guard uniforms -- he wanted to call an ambulance. And yet none of them appeared seriously injured.

Of course, he recognized Mato's darts, and that set him at ease. The men weren't down permanently so much as they were down *conveniently*. It was an option law enforcement officers needed to look into.

Still, he hadn't found any sign of Tori and Cal. The fact that she wasn't answering his calls had been resolved when he found her pocket book sitting in Cal's van. Her phone was in it, turned off.

Awesome, Tori. Really clever.

Shadow was having a field day nosing around all the sleeping bodies. More than once Nate had felt compelled to warn the animal about lifting his leg on them. "Not nice," he said, and Shadow seemed to get the idea. But only with great reluctance.

They searched the lobby and several offices, but found no trace of anyone he was interested in. At least, not until they reached a room full of video monitors. A placard on the door announced that the room was intended for "Security." So much for secrecy, he thought.

But Shadow found the room to be a source of great excitement. He sniffed with a nearly violent thrashing of his tail. Nate made sure he didn't stand in the big dog's way, and followed him as he raced down yet another hallway.

~*~

Reyna sat on a wide rock near the river's edge. She had been there since she awoke. The sun had been up for some time, and the giants were already busy on the water. Boats moved up and down -- some large, some small, but all noisy. For her, there seemed to be little difference in going upstream or down. Death would find her in either direction, whether at the hands of the giants or by her own. She knew what The People would prefer, but who spoke for her unborn child?

Earlier, she had heard a distant explosion and wondered if it was connected to her captors. She hoped so. Perhaps their evil buildings and vile cages had been blasted by... who, she wondered. Mato had shown her an explosive device he'd stolen from the giants. They had considered using it on the entrance to the tunnel beneath Tori's cabin. If they had found another way into the cavern of dreams, they might have already used it by now.

But how could Mato even know where she was? She had no doubt he would make every effort to find her, but when pitted against a land filled with giants, what chance did he have? What chance, therefore, did she have?

She picked up a handful of pebbles and tossed them, one by one, into the slowly swirling eddy at her feet. Cold and murky, the water bore mute testimony about the giants' disregard for their world. Why did they feel the need to invade hers?

Shrugging such useless thoughts aside, Reyna knew it was time to concentrate on her own life. So very little of it remained, she refused to waste it worrying about things she couldn't control. There were things to be done and prayers to be said.

She would need something heavy to keep her body submerged. And she would need something with which to bind herself to it until her body was reclaimed by the Spirits. They would send animals to finish the task of eliminating her corpse.

She unfolded the longer blade from the handle of the knife Nate had given to Mato. It would come in handy as she prepared for the end.

There was still time, but not much.

~*~

Tori rammed the chair legs into the wall opposite the cage. It took several tries, but she eventually forced one of the legs through two layers of drywall and into the shallow empty space beyond. The minor success fueled her passion for escape, and she continued the process, stopping only to rip at the crumbling drywall standing in her way.

She soon had two metal studs exposed.

"They're built on 16-inch centers," Cal observed from his spot on the floor.

"And that's useful to know because...."

"'Cause it means you can slip between 'em."

"Are you complimenting my girlish figure?"

He smiled. "I'm saying it's a good thing you're thin, or we'd never get outta here."

Thus encouraged, Tori attacked the wall again, this time sending the legs of the chair through the wallboard on the opposite side of the studs. She sincerely hoped she was ruining the carpeting in both rooms in the process.

"Mind the wires," Cal said, pointing to the flexible metal conduit running through the studs.

"No problem," she said. Stepping over the shielded cable would be easy for her, but maybe not for Cal. Could he follow her?

"Once you get out you can come back and open the door," he said, as if reading her mind.

"Right," she said. "I knew that." *No wonder Maggie*

398

likes him so much.

Kicking with the bottom of her foot, she smashed a hole big enough to slip through easily. Except for the studs, she could have made it large enough to jump rope through, once she got the hang of it. She never realized destruction could be so much fun.

After a brief moment of disorientation, she left the supply closet into which she had escaped, and wandered back into the smaller lab to free Caleb. She arrived just as two men entered the opposite end of the room. One of them was armed.

~*~

Tessa followed Bernstein back to his office. Neither could quite believe the body count of downed guards.

"We should check on them," he said. "If any are still alive, we should call for an ambulance."

Tessa shook her head. "Nonsense. We have to find your gun, and then we have to get out of here." She gestured at the inert forms littering the floor. "Do you see any blood?"

He squinted at the panorama of destruction. "No. But that's not conclusive. They could have other injuries."

"Couldn't we all?" She reached for his beefy arm and pulled him along. "There's no time, Jerry. The game has changed. Drastically. We have to deal with it."

"And a gun is going to help us do that?"

Oh yeah, she thought. *Big time.* "We have no guards left, and there's obviously a maniac on the loose in here. Do you feel safe right now? 'Cause I sure as hell don't."

They bustled on, down the main hall, through the lobby, past an outer office and finally into Bernstein's inner sanctum. He dropped into the huge executive chair behind his massive desk, as if that alone offered some sort of security.

"The gun?" Tessa prompted.

"Right." Bernstein dug around in a drawer and eventually withdrew an ancient handgun.

"What the hell is that?" Tessa asked, staring at the ugly, brass weapon. "A blunderbuss?" It looked for all the world like the kind of gun deranged hunters carried in Warner Brothers cartoons.

Bernstein held it up. Proudly. He also held aloft the biggest cartridge she had ever seen.

"Single shot?" she asked.

"Of course. It's a flare pistol," he said. "A Webley Mark 1 to be precise."

"Does it work?"

"It should."

"*Should?* That's comforting. Has anyone used it since Jefferson was president?"

"It was made in the late 19th century and saw service in both world wars," Bernstein said. He sounded as if he was reading from the text of a museum display.

"May I see it?" she asked.

Bernstein handed the weapon to her. It was surprisingly heavy. And ugly. Scary, too. Tessa liked it. She thumbed a lever on the side of the gun which tilted the barrel forward and exposed the firing chamber. The opening was bigger around than her thumb. "Gimme the bullet."

"It's a flare cartridge."

"Whatever."

He passed her the cartridge which she inserted into the gun. The barrel slipped back into firing position with a distinctive click. "How many more flares do you have?"

"Two," he said. "But they burn magnesium. They could easily start a fire."

"Or stop someone in his tracks?"

"I suppose. They're meant to be fired into the air, not at a target. There's no sight."

"That's okay," she said. If she had to use it, she'd damn sure get close enough not to miss. She put the flare gun in her purse which she'd grabbed on the way. "Let's take your car. It's much faster than mine."

He looked confused. "Where are we going?"

"To the airport. You can call and make reservations on the way."

"I don't understand."

"We're going to Europe," she said. "Didn't you tell me you had a friend there who took care of selling your stocks for you?"

"Well, I-- Yes, but--"

"That's where we're headed."

"Together?"

"I wouldn't think of leaving you behind." She patted her purse, noting how much heavier it felt with the flare gun inside. *Leave him behind? Here? No way. There were vastly better places.*

~*~

Carmine and Mort Lund were on their way to his desk in the smaller of the two labs when they saw a woman enter the room from a storage closet.

"Don't I know you?" Mort said to her.

Her attention, however, was riveted on the shotgun Carmine held. He quickly set it down on a counter top and stepped away from it. Only then did she respond to the man in the white lab coat.

"You came to Wyoming," she said, looking at Lund. "You were hurt in the landslide." Her face turned very dark. "Do you realize what you've done?"

401

"Me?" he said, pressing a hand to his chest. "I didn't want to have anything to do with this."

"And neither do I," Carmine said.

The woman stared at him. "Who are you?"

How was he going to explain that he was the one who kidnapped the little Indian woman? "I, uh-- Y'see--"

"He kidnapped the donor," Lund said.

"The *donor?* You mean Reyna?"

"I didn't know her name," Carmine said. "But I know it was wrong. A terrible, stupid thing to do. That's why I came back. I had to get her outta here and take her back home."

The woman opened a door and moved away from them, then reappeared helping an older man, his face pale.

"I'll call for an ambulance," Lund said. "There's a couch in the break room. He can stretch out there."

The man became agitated. "Don't call an ambulance," he said. "Not yet, anyway. We've got to find Reyna first."

"Don't be silly," the woman said.

Carmine nodded. "You don't look so good. You need a doctor."

"And what are they going to say when they see all the bodies scattered around here? You think they'll just step over them and take care of me? No. They'll call the cops. By the truckload. Then what? Forget trying to find Reyna. We don't want anyone else to know about her anyway. Not yet. Not until she and Mato are ready."

"Who's Mato?" Lund asked.

Carmine thought he knew the answer. He'd met the little warrior in the hall. Thankfully, he'd allowed Carmine to live.

"It's his wife you kidnapped," the man said, but the effort clearly took its toll.

"C'mon," Lund said, "let's get him into the break room. He'll be more comfortable."

Carmine had just turned away to help when a commotion from the corridor distracted him. It sounded like someone was trying to knock the door down rather than open it.

~*~

Nate followed Shadow into yet another lab. This one much smaller than the first, but unlike the other rooms they'd visited, this one had people in it. Conscious people. People he knew.

"Tori!" he yelled.

She swiveled around, then ran toward him as if they'd been separated for months rather than days. A few steps short of her destination she took to the air, landing in Nate's arms with a passion and ferocity he'd never before experienced.

And it was wonderful.

"Oh, Nate! I kept hoping you'd show up, but I never really thought it'd happen."

She slipped from his arms and stood up on her own, then dragged him toward the others. Shadow hadn't waited for them. He had already inspected the two younger men and was concentrating on Caleb, who looked like very old pasta. *How could dogs tell when someone was sick?*

Tori picked up a shotgun and brandished it at the youngest of the men. "This is your fault," she said. "I oughta just shoot your ass right now."

"Hold on a second!" Nate shouted.

"No," the younger man said. He appeared to be in his early twenties, not much more than a kid. "She should shoot me. I deserve it."

403

Nate plucked the weapon from Tori's hands, relieved to see she'd left the safety engaged. "Nobody's shooting anybody's ass today. Or any other body part, for that matter."

"What're you, a cop?" the kid asked, though his manner didn't match his tough talk. The question served, however, to remind him that he was not in uniform.

"Actually, I *am* a cop. But I'm a tad hazy about what's been going on around here." That wasn't entirely true, but he'd never been a Boy Scout. And when acting in an official capacity, honesty wasn't always the best policy. Ask any politician. He turned to Tori. "Where's Mato?"

She shook her head. "We don't know. He took off when we first got here, and we've been stepping over bodies ever since. We ran into the Bidford woman and her boss. She locked Cal and me in a little room--"

"The same one they planned to keep the kidnapped girl in," added a man Nate recognized from the rock slide accident: Mort Lund.

"I'm not worried about Mato," Tori said. "Obviously, he can take care of himself. But Reyna's whereabouts scare me. She broke out, and no one knows where she went."

Nate patted Shadow's head. "I know someone who can find her."

"Go," Tori told him. "I'll stay with Cal."

"Yeah, go find the girl," Lund said. "We'll clean up after the little guy. What'd you call him?"

"Mato," Tori said. "But why would you want to help?"

Lund smiled. "You're all decent people. I'd like to think I am, too."

"I wouldn't mind joining that crowd myself," the kidnapper said. "I've spent way too much time with the

404

other kind." The thought seemed to jog something in his memory, and he reached into his pants pocket and extracted a memory chip. He showed it to Lund. "Have you got a camera we can put this in? It might give us a snapshot of the guy who's behind all this."

"Bernstein?" Lund asked. "He's still in the building somewhere."

"I'm talking about the guy who paid me to take the girl."

Nate grimaced. "I'd like to know more about him, too." Then he whistled for Shadow, and the two of them hurried from the room. Nate wished he'd worn running shoes instead of boots.

~*~

Mato stood waiting for the two giants when they left the older one's quarters. He made no effort to hide and merely kept his back to a large window of the outer office which looked out on a pleasant vista of lush green grass and well tended shrubbery. It was the sort of thick greenery he'd only seen previously in the mountains.

"Where Reyna?" he asked when they reached the middle of the room. He had an arrow in place, though he aimed it toward the floor to avoid frightening them.

The female appeared surprised to see him, and not simply because of his size. Mato recognized her, although her scent was different. Why female giants would want to disguise their signature odor was a mystery to him, like much of what giants did.

"I thought you were dead," she said.

"Who's this?" asked the male.

"He was supposed to be our donor."

"Where Reyna," Mato asked again, raising his bow.

"She's not here," the woman said. "She ran away

405

Josh Langston

before we could explain the program to her. She was
going to have the best job on Earth. You should see the
plans we have for her accommodations. I've got the
blueprints. You might be interested, too. Why--"

"Where Reyna *now?*" Mato shouted. It took a great
act of will not to send these two in search of their
ancestors immediately. Their incessant chatter had driven
him to the brink of madness, but if Reyna had been
harmed, his madness would be the least of their worries.

"I have something here," the female said, digging in a
cloth bag she carried by a shoulder strap, "which ought to
clear things up."

She produced an odd-looking gun which she held in
both hands and pointed directly at Mato.

Without waiting, Mato let an arrow fly. It dug into
the female's shoulder. She turned to one side in shock and
fired the huge gun. The blast wasn't as loud as the one
from the kidnapper's gun, but it was just as startling. So
was the destruction to the big window. Whatever had
come from the weapon left a dark, smoky trail which
hung in the air and marked its passage.

The female giant was already reacting to the sleeping
paste Mato had smeared on the arrowhead. The male was
moving backwards, his hands raised in supplication
before he turned and lumbered back into his quarters.

Mato walked after him, a fresh, paste-tipped arrow
nocked and ready.

The big man was struggling to open a window behind
his enormous chair. If Mato had the time to spare he
would have watched the giant try to crawl through the
relatively small opening. Sadly, that wasn't an option, so
Mato simply launched his last arrow into the big man's
butt.

As the man yelped, then groaned, then slipped away

from the window and toward the floor, Mato bolted past him and raced through the opening to the fresh air beyond.

Now he could look for Reyna. The two giants he left behind would still be asleep when he returned. Just how they died would depend entirely on whether or not he found Reyna, and whether or not he found her alive.

~*~

Nate took Shadow outside by the shortest route he could find: through the broken laboratory window. Making it through had required some modifications to the structure, but two desk chairs and a variety of scientific gear of an appropriate weight and size had sufficed to enlarge the opening. The paraphernalia littered the ground outside the building and caused some momentary concern when Shadow leaped past the carnage to begin tracking their missing friend.

As an actor might have said in some corny old Sherlock Holmes movie, the chase was on. Nate's confidence in Shadow's ability to sort through olfactory stimuli was tempered by history. Shadow was too easily distracted to ever be a hunting dog. He loved anything that produced an odor, and wasn't picky about any of them. If anything, his tastes ran more to the "well-rotted" than "simply rancid" side of the stink scale. And Nate knew it.

In any case, his job was to follow the dog as best he could. Fortunately for Nate, Shadow adopted a wide-ranging approach to smell detection, slaloming back and forth across the Bernstein Labs grounds. Nate could thus walk in a relatively straight line until the dog connected with an odor to his liking. Shadow headed for a spot in the fence marked by a thick branch which someone had jammed under the chain links. The dog was digging at it furiously when Nate arrived. He grabbed on and yanked the offending limb free. Howling with impatience, Shadow dug frantically until the opening was wide enough, then squeezed under the fence and raced into the thick brush beyond.

Nate didn't even bother calling to him. It wouldn't have done any good.

~*~

Mato heard a dog's frantic barking almost as soon as he landed on the ground outside the old giant's quarters. He couldn't see anything as the angle of the building blocked his view. Had the giants given dogs to their hunters? Did they not have the slightest shred of compassion? How did they think Reyna would react when she realized they had set dogs loose in order to find her? Did they even care about the level of terror they would generate?

Seething with anger, Mato prayed that some giant would get in his way as he sought to find his love. They wouldn't stand a chance, even if he had to kill them bare handed. And if he died in the attempt, so be it.

With his rage thus stimulated, and his fear and anger twisted into a white hot weapon of revenge, Mato raced around the corner of the building. The sound of the dog blotted out everything else. The only weapon he still had was his knife, and it was already in his hand. He had never pushed himself so hard, had never run so fast, nor for such a great cause.

The sound of the dog suddenly trailed off into the distance. The animal had obviously broken through the damnable fence which surrounded the grounds. And then he saw him. There! A giant knelt at the base of the fence which appeared no different than any other, save for the dirt scattered on the ground around him. The hound had been at work. And this giant would soon be following him into the woods beyond.

Unless Mato stopped him.

~*~

Chapter 24

Be on your guard against a silent dog and still water.
~Latin proverb

Carmine and Mort worked well together. All his previous jobs, other than the kidnapping assignment, had required that he remain wary of coworkers. Screw ups meant unemployment, and the easiest way to avoid them was to shift the blame to someone else. But here, when Mort lost his grip on an unconscious guard, no one was looking over his shoulder. "Oops" meant, simply, oops.

They collected all the guards, stretching them side-by-side in the Security Office. It seemed only fitting. Lund carefully removed the blowgun darts and stored them in a test tube he'd brought from the lab. They found Bernstein and Bidford in the lab chief's office and left them there rather than add them to the crowd in the security office. Carmine had suggested it since management and labor should never be found sleeping together.

Lund explained his theory about why they were unconscious and not dead. "There's something on the tips of these weapons. It's made from a gland found in poison tree frogs." He held up a blowgun dart and the arrow they'd removed from Bernstein's posterior. "I saw a program on TV that explained it." He paused to scratch his jaw. "As I recall, the poison they used was lethal. But maybe that only applies to frogs from the rain forests of the Amazon." Carmine had roughly the same degree of knowledge about Amazon rain forests as he did about celestial navigation, but it didn't matter. He reveled in the chance to work with a real, live *professional*. He couldn't wait to tell Domino.

"So, you think the little Indian girl will be okay?" he asked. The question had been on his mind constantly, though he'd hesitated to voice it. He knew most of the blame for her predicament belonged to him.

Lund shook his head slowly. "I dunno man. I sure hope so. I only saw her for a minute or two, but she was one scared little lady."

Carmine pressed his palm to his forehead. He felt like shit. "I've never done anything so rotten in my life. I'm such a loser. That lady was right. She should have just shot me. I'm not worth the time it'd take to flush me down a toilet."

Lund grabbed him by the shoulders and gave him a shake. "That's bullshit! You're here, aren't you? If you didn't have a heart, you'd be somewhere else, havin' a good time. But you're not. You're working with me, trying to clean up this mess. Granted, you were partly responsible, but you didn't run and hide. You didn't try to blame somebody else. You stood up. You acted like a man."

Carmine couldn't quite believe what he was hearing. Somebody thought he was doing the right thing? Somebody thought he was acting like a decent human being? Oh, God. What he would have given to have Domino hear that! But more importantly, *he* heard it. No, he *felt* it. Carmine DeLuca was a decent guy. A good guy! Not -- emphatically *not* -- a wise guy.

When they finished sorting the guards and their bosses, all of whom continued to sleep peacefully, Carmine once again brought up the issue of the memory chip and the camera.

"We've got a great camera here in the lab, but we don't need it," Lund said. "We can scan the chip on my

411

computer."

Carmine followed him back through the building to his lair. Lund didn't have a private office; he had a cubicle composed of half walls surrounding a PC, a length of countertop, and some shelves. He had added some personal touches, including a trophy of some kind. Trophies were very cool. Carmine knew several guys who had them. A trophy meant you had accomplished something.

"We just slip the chip into the card reader slot in the keyboard," Lund said, "and open it up like any other memory device."

Carmine had no clue what he meant, but nodded as if he did. "So, where are the dirty pictures?"

Lund examined several screens of data before responding. "There aren't any."

Carmine felt his heart sink. He was all but officially dead. Lykes would remove his internal organs -- one by one -- and toss them off the boardwalk at Coney Island while Veronica played her stupid music box. He'd never see Domino again, never have a life, never father children, never--

"Dude, this is much, much better than sleazy photos."

"Huh?" Carmine DeLuca: master of the monosyllable.

"These are recordings. Of phone calls probably, or other private conversations."

Carmine resisted the urge to scratch his head, a la Stan Laurel.

"Your pal, Lykes, has recordings of people offering him money to do stuff. Probably bad stuff." Lund looked at him with a sad smile. "Really, really bad stuff."

Swallowing hard, Carmine asked, "Is there anything in there about me?"

"You mean about the kidnapping?"

"Yeah."

"I would imagine so," Lund said. "How 'bout if I erase it before we make a copy for our friend the deputy sheriff?"

Carmine stared at him. "You'd do that for me?"

"I think you've earned a little break."

Carmine felt the weight of the world float up off his shoulders. Life was suddenly sweet again.

"But you know what? This whole idea of dirty pictures inspires me."

"You said there weren't any."

Lund smiled the way only very, very sneaky people ever smiled. "There aren't any *yet*."

~*~

Reyna stood near the water's edge. It wasn't deep, by giant's standards, but it was more than deep enough for her needs. She had checked the depth with a tree branch. A nearly square chunk of stone lay at her feet. One last time she checked the vine she had used to tie it to her leg. The vine was secure. It wouldn't come loose by itself, and would resist any efforts she might make if her courage wavered at the last moment.

She took a moment to settle herself before she stepped off the rock into the river. The sky was an amazing shade of blue. The trees and plants all around her almost seemed to glow with life and vitality. Everything was green. Verdant. Lush.

Reyna put a hand on her belly. Inside her, a tiny life struggled simply to exist. She felt a tear roll down her cheek as she tried to find the right words for an apology to her unborn child. If only there were some way to leave a message for Mato... But that was an impossibility. It

413

was something only giants could do. And she was through with them. They had brought her -- and her child -- to this point, this sad and unnecessary point.

It was time.

She knelt beside the rock and put both hands firmly against its cold, hard surface. A simple shove would send the rock into the water. The vine would pull her in after it.

She shoved, hard.

The rock slid to the edge and stopped. A bird seemed to take notice. It chirped as if in warning. Or lament.

Reyna pushed again, grunting with the effort.

And the stone tipped over the edge, pulling her with it.

~*~

Nate heard nothing except the sounds of his own digging. Even Shadow's howls had faded to silence. A worry crept to the center of his attention, edging out the need to dig deeper and faster. Would he even be able to find Shadow once he'd made a space under the fence big enough to let him pass? He wished he had a shovel. Was there a maintenance shed around here somewhere? He turned to look, only to see Mato flying through the air in his direction.

He had no time for words, no time for anything but a hearty grunt. Thankfully, it was enough to break the killing spell which seemed to grip the little warrior. While still in the air, he released the knife and visibly shifted to a less rigid posture.

Nate caught him in both arms as Mato plowed into his chest, knocking them both to the ground.

"Holy crap! You tryin' to kill me?"

"No," the little Indian said as he scrambled to his feet and retrieved his knife, a product of Neolithic period technology. "Kill giant, not friend."

Nate brushed himself off. "You might want to consider firing a warning shot or--"

Mato wasn't paying any attention. His nose quivered in much the same fashion as Shadow's when the dog caught Reyna's scent. "This way," he said, and dived into the freshly enlarged gap beneath the fence.

"Hang on," Nate said, crawling after him. *Tunnels to caves, ditches under fences, what the hell was next, freestyle burrowing?* He wanted to say something to Mato, but the Indian hadn't waited to exchange banter. It was just as well. Nate had no hope of keeping up with him anyway.

He prayed that between the huge dog and the bantam warrior there would be enough of a trail for him to follow. He would be content if he could find them eventually. In terms of speed, little else on Earth could match the pair searching for Reyna now. Anyone else would just get in the way. He rubbed his chest where the hard-bodied Mato had landed.

He pitied any giants the little guy might stumble into.

Carmine followed Lund's lead, but he wasn't comfortable with it. Returning to Bernstein's office, they stripped the two slumbering management types down to their underwear. They both worked up a sweat arranging the ponderous body of Bernstein and the petite form of Bidford so that they appeared to be living out some demented fantasy. Or at least, a fantasy for Bernstein; it would have been a nightmare for Bidford, which is what made it so perfectly fitting. Lund called it "apropos," a word Carmine assumed he'd learned in phlebotomy school. Carmine preferred "gross."

Lund took the photos, directing Carmine to lift this or that, shift his or hers, and otherwise make the resulting piles of pale flesh appear to be engaged in the nastiest sorts of activities. It wasn't easy. In fact, it took considerable imagination. Fortunately, whatever had caused the sleepers to slumber also gave their muscles a bit of plasticity. The bodies could therefore hold a given pose briefly, but long enough for Lund to capture it.

They experimented with molding facial expressions, but the only one that looked real on Bidford was a sneer. Bernstein's "smile" might have been driven by a troublesome bowel movement, but it was close enough to ecstasy to serve their purpose.

"Once they know we've got these," Lund said, patting the camera, "there's no way they'll try to bully us or bother our little Indian friends." That made Carmine feel much better. He wasn't sure Domino would approve, but she would certainly agree that something had to be done to protect the truly innocent. This was simply the best they could think of on short notice.

"I really wish I could be here when they wake up," Lund said as he loaded copies of the photos into a screensaver program on Bernstein's desktop computer. The resulting slideshow struck Carmine as not merely sleazy, but depraved. Lund pronounced it hysterical.

Carmine found the antique flare gun on the floor and held it up for Lund's inspection. "When they wake up, it'd probably be best if this weren't here."

Lund agreed. They took the flare gun with them when they were done.

They left Bidford and Bernstein, clad in their skivvies, locked in an amorous embrace. Then closed the door to give them a bit of privacy.

~*~

As the rock hit the water and the vine around her ankle yanked tight, Reyna felt time begin to stretch. She would soon be dead, and the realization drove her senses to a state of hyper awareness.

A splash from the rock.

Brilliant blue sky.

Bird sounds.

A last gulp of air.

Icy water.

Then she was looking up, through the murky liquid toward a sky she would never see again, a sun which would never give her warmth. And a dog.

A huge, black dog.

Thrashing canine legs churned the water above her. The great bulbous nose swished back and forth in a frantic display of animal despair. Shadow was afraid of the water!

Reyna reached for him. Reached *up*. How could she help him if he was above her? More thoughts raced through her mind. If Shadow was here, then Mato was, too. The rock! She had to get loose from the rock.

Fumbling at the clothing which billowed and swirled around her in the water, Reyna struggled to find the pocketknife. And then she had it. Her fingers nearly numb from the cold, she worked at unfolding the blade. Why couldn't giants make knives the way everyone else did? Why make things so difficult?

There! She had it.

And then she dropped it.

The knife went straight down. The water at that level was even darker and murkier. She could barely see the

417

rock that held her let alone the knife. But there was no time for lament. No time to curse her ill fortune.

She bent down and reached for the knotted vine around her ankle. The knife would have cut it easily. Refusing to dwell on that, Reyna forced herself to concentrate on the knot. Though she had pulled it tight when she first tied it around her leg, the weight of the rock pulling her down had tightened it still more.

She yanked at it again and again, but with each effort the knot only constricted her limb more.

Her air was almost gone.

Glancing up, she saw poor Shadow still thrashing in the water.

Please don't panic, my friend.

But she knew she had failed him.

~*~

The trail Mato and Shadow left might have suited a rabbit, or maybe a small fox. For Nate, tracking the dog and the Indian through the heavy underbrush seemed like an impossible task. He needed a machete, or a chain saw. A front end loader would've done the trick.

From time to time he broke through the greenery, and while the way forward was invariably restricted with trees, shrubs and vines, he always managed to find it. Sometimes crawling, sometimes climbing, he snaked his way forward. The Hudson River had to be near. He could smell it.

And then, in the distance, he heard something.

Barking?

The sound invigorated him, compelled him, drove him on. Even though he knew something was very, very wrong.

~*~

Mato didn't hesitate when he saw Shadow in the water. Still running from the embrace of the green walls through which he had fought his way, Mato raced across the slab of stone which separated him from the river.

Kicking furiously, he tried to reach for the big dog's collar, but the animal wouldn't cooperate. Was he trying to bite?

"What's wrong with you?" Mato demanded.

The dog barked once, then put his head under water.

Mato felt something touch his foot. He jerked his leg away. The fish in this river could be gigantic. The river was certainly wide enough.

Again, something touched his leg.

Pulling his knife from his belt, Mato flipped over and prepared to face a new threat. Would the Spirits never free him to find Reyna?

~*~

Cal looked bad. Tori had hoped that his condition had somehow stabilized since he no longer complained of chest pains. He hadn't complained about much of anything, but that was likely due to his being unable to breathe enough air to waste any of it on speech.

Where was Cal? Where was Lund and the kid? What was his name? Carmine something. Who names their kid Carmine? It was so New York.

And she longed for her little cabin in Wyoming.

But none of that mattered. Cal was in serious trouble, and she couldn't wait any longer. Either she got him to a hospital, or she got an ambulance to come for him. There weren't any other choices.

419

"How's he doing?"

Tori glanced up to see Carmine leaning through the door, a look of concern on his face.

"He needs a doctor." She threw him Cal's car keys. "Can you bring the camper to the door?"

"Sure," he said, snatching the keys from the air. "I'll get Mort. He'll know where to take him." With that, the kid was gone.

Tori put her palm on Cal's cheek. "It's gonna be all right."

He winked at her, but his customary smile had taken flight.

"You'll call Maggie?" he asked, his voice whispery.

"Of course." But it would have to wait until she got back to the van where she'd left her purse and phone.

Lund arrived next, pushing a wheelchair. "Look what I found!"

"Where'd you get it?" Tori asked.

"It was in storage near the locker room. The people on the company softball team may be enthusiastic, but none of us is in very good shape. Fact is, we get hurt a lot." He rolled the chair close to the sofa on which Cal reposed. "This chair gets more use than you might think."

Between them, they got Cal into the chair then wheeled him to the nearest exit. Lund pointed the way. Carmine was ready for them and helped Lund move their patient into the van. If anything, Cal looked even worse. He didn't even try to talk.

Tori turned her phone on and started the engine. Lund rode shotgun and Carmine sat beside Cal in the back.

Following Lund's directions, she left the grounds of Bernstein Laboratories. She glanced at her phone and noted all the messages from Nate. She punched the Dial button to tell him what they were doing. He answered on the second ring.

"We've got her!" he said. The relief in his voice proved contagious. She repeated the words for everyone in the van.

"Is she okay?"

"Yes," he said. "Soaked with river water, but okay. I'll explain when we get back to the lab."

Tori quickly filled him in on Cal's condition, and her fears for him. "I honestly don't even know if he'll make it 'til we reach a hospital. And if he does, then what? Do we sit in an emergency room and wait for someone to check his insurance?"

"They'll drop everything to assist a heart patient," Lund said. "My father-in-law went through it last spring."

"Hey, guys?" Carmine said. "Cal has something to say."

They all went quiet as the old rodeo hand whispered, "Mato."

"What about Mato?" Tori asked.

Cal tried to lift his arm, but the effort seemed too much for him. He managed to whisper one more word: "Transfusion."

"I don't get it," Lund said.

Tori grimaced. "I do. It's what kept you alive after the rock slide."

Lund and Carmine exchanged looks of utter bewilderment.

"Can you get us close to the river? Is there a dock or something? A place to put in a boat?"

"There's a public boat ramp just up the road. But I thought we were going to the hospital."

"There's no time," Tori said, then spoke into the phone. "Nate, can you see a boat ramp anywhere near you?"

421

"It's hard to tell from here."

She turned to Lund. "Is it north of here or south?"

"North."

"Got it," Nate said. "We're on our way. We'll meet you there."

~*~

Lund had been right about the hospital. Once they understood Cal might be suffering from heart problems, they rushed him straight into a treatment room. That left everyone else with little to do but wait. Shadow, having survived a busy morning, lay asleep in the van, his wet coat soaking into one of the plush captain's chairs. Mato and Reyna found a fold-down bed in the van that offered some much-needed privacy.

The others sat in the hospital waiting area contemplating the phone calls they needed to make.

Tori's first call was to Cal's girlfriend, Maggie, who took the news about Cal with stoic grace, just before she broke down. Covering the phone with her hand, and speaking softly, Tori assured her everything would be fine. Mato had been only too happy to perform a transfusion, and Cal had even begun to look better by the time they got him to a hospital.

Then she called her editor, Cassy, to see if she knew of any boutiques that sold clothing for Asian ball-jointed dolls. Reyna's limited wardrobe was in ruins.

"Sure," Cassy said, having recovered from the news about Caleb and her surprise at Tori's proximity. "I know just the place. What does she need?"

"Maternity clothes," Tori said.

Cassy roared with laughter. "I'll take care of it," she promised. "I'm on my way."

Carmine called Domino and did his best to explain what he'd been through. He couldn't decide if he should mention the photos he and Lund had taken of Bidford and Bernstein. There were some things a guy just couldn't discuss with his girl. Unless they got *really* serious.

Lund called home to check in. He couldn't resist telling his wife that he would enjoy full employment for as long as Jerry Bernstein stayed out of prison. And, he added, he anticipated a big raise and a nice promotion. He had copied the recordings from Carmine's memory chip onto disks which he'd given to Nate. As far as he was concerned, that fulfilled his obligation to report to the police. What Nate did with them was up to him.

Nate made the last call.

He dialed Beth Torrence, daughter of Wyoming judge Jeremiah "Chuckwagon" Torrence, and second in command of a New York state task force on organized crime. They didn't waste much time reminiscing as Beth was far more interested in the recordings Nate had mentioned. He couldn't reveal his source, which didn't go over too well, but he promised to mail her a disk as soon as he could. She would have to be satisfied with that.

"It was nice talking with you," she said.

"Yeah. We should do this more often." *Had anything ever sounded more lame?*

His concerns that talking to her might rekindle something from their past quickly faded. Much like his plans to give her the diamond engagement ring his late mother had worn.

He smiled.

His mom would've been pleased by his plans to offer that ring to Tori.

~ The End ~

Josh Langston

About the author:

Josh Langston lives and works in Marietta, Georgia, with his amazing wife and two uninhibited dogs. His prize-winning short fiction has been published in numerous magazines and anthologies. He and Canadian author Barbara Galler-Smith have written a series of best-selling historical fantasy novels. *Druids* and *Captives*, the first two books in the trilogy, are available in print as well as in E-book format. *Warriors*, the final volume, will be out in May, 2013.

Other titles by Josh Langston you might enjoy:

A Little Primitive ** -- The prequel to the book you just finished reading!

Resurrection Blues ** -- A novel of discovery and liberation set in a town that doesn't exist. (Don't miss the sample chapter beginning on the next page.)

Mysfits -- A six-pack of urban (and suburban) fantasies.

Six From Greeley -- Timeless tales from a town that never grew up.

Dancing Among the Stars -- A six-pack of science and speculative fiction.

Christmas Beyond the Box -- Six holiday tales of mystery and magic. (Soon to be available in Spanish!)

The Best Damned Squirrel Dog (Ever) -- A Civil War ghost story.

Books co-authored with Barbara Galler-Smith:

Under Saint Owain's Rock ** -- A contemporary romantic comedy.

Druids -- ** The adventures begin.

Captives -- ** The *Druids* saga continues.

Warriors -- ** The final book in the *Druids* trilogy debuts, spring 2013

**Also available in paperback.
(List last updated on Nov. 29, 2012.)

Connect with me online at http://www.joshlangston.com

Josh Langston

And now...

A sneak peak at the Georgia Author of the Year-nominated novel:

Resurrection Blues

by Josh Langston

Opening Chapter

One good fire is the equivalent of three good moves. -- Wayne A. Langston

Trey opened his door to the first line of a joke: An Indian, a dwarf, and a biker walk into a bar... Except he didn't own a bar, and this clearly wasn't a joke.

"We're lookin' for Trey Bowman," the Indian said.

"As in A. A. Bowman, the third," added the biker.

Trey looked down at the dwarf, expecting her to add something. She didn't. Instead, she stunned him with the sexiest smile he'd ever seen. He dragged his gaze from her face and quickly inspected the other two visitors. They appeared calm, and unarmed. *Always a good sign. Still....*

"He's dead," Trey said.

"Then, who the hell're you?" asked the Indian, "And why are you in his house?"

"Who the hell are you, and why do you want to know?"

The biker looked less likeable than he had before, the morphing process moving him from possible

1

miscreant to probable felon. "It's important we find Trey Bowman. He's not in any trouble. Leastwise, not with us, but if he's dead we'll need to see proof."

"Like a grave?" Trey asked.

"More like a body," said the Indian. "But a death certificate would probably do."

The dwarf continued to smile, but the effect ceased to be sexy. It now seemed morbidly curious-- the sort of smile reserved for really bad traffic accidents, or public executions.

"You didn't answer my questions," Trey said, shifting his foot slightly in order to get more of it wedged at the bottom of the door. "So, again: who are you, and why are you looking for Trey Bowman?"

"Augie sent us," the tiny female said, her voice a delicious tinkling of fine crystal.

"Augie who?"

"Augie Bowman."

"He's still alive?"

"Yeah, but not for long. Doc says he's only got a few days left." The Indian looked down at a photo in his hand, then held it up to eye level and glanced back and forth between Trey's face and the picture. "He sent us to find you."

Trey squinted at him. "Okay, I'm Augustus Bowman."

"The third," said the biker by way of confirmation. "Your grampaw said you go by 'Trey.'"

"I do, but he barely even knows me," Trey said, twisting to see if he recognized himself in the photo. He hadn't seen his grandfather in at least twenty years.

"Why don't you call yourself 'Augustus' or 'Augie?'" the biker asked. "Don't you like your name?"

2

"I like Trey."

"I expected someone more... I dunno, interesting," said the Indian to the biker. "This guy's a geek."

"I am not a geek! I-- I hate computers."

"Relax, sweetie," said the diminutive femme. "He's not talkin' about the kinda geek you're thinkin' of." She looked up at her companions. "I think it's him, but we'd better check his ID just to be sure."

"*My ID?* This is my house, for cryin' out loud. I don't have to produce an ID. You should be showing me yours."

"I'm Warren Lightfoot," said the Indian, pushing his arm between the door and the jamb. "You can call me Bud." He gripped Trey's hand firmly, shook it once, then let go.

"Bud. Right." Trey looked at the biker.

"I'm Dago," he said, keeping his hands in the pockets of his jeans.

"Of course you are," Trey said, utterly clueless. He looked down. "And you must be...."

"The Virgin Mary," she said with an absolutely straight face.

He tried to roll with it. "Would it be okay if I just called you 'Mary'?"

"Sure," she said, relighting her ten thousand watt smile. "I'm not really a virgin."

"Good," he said. "I mean, about your name. Not the, you know--"

"Time to go," said Dago.

Oddly, Trey felt no threat from the bizarre trio. Something about them had the ring of truth, and he felt compelled to go with them. Besides, he'd already made a complete mess of his life, and he clearly had nothing better to do.

3

"You got a car?" Bud asked. "We've got a truck, but somebody'd have to ride in the back."

"Not me!" Mary said. She pushed through the door and grabbed Trey's hand. "You wouldn't make a lady sit in the back of a truck, would ya?" She snuggled up to his thigh, and batted what he suddenly realized were absurdly long eyelashes.

"I've got a car," he said. "I can follow you."

Bud smiled for the first time. "Good, then let's get movin.'"

"Waitaminute!" Trey said. "First things first. How long am I gonna be gone? Do I need to pack some clothes? Leave a forwarding address? Who's gonna feed my parakeet?"

"Good Lord, he's got a tweety," said the Indian. "I told you he was a geek."

"Bring the bird," Mary said. "And throw some clothes in a bag. If you need more later, I'm sure we can find the hole and come back."

"'Find the hole?' What the hell are you talkin' about?"

The biker stared at Mary as if he was contemplating dwarficide.

"It's just an expression," Bud said. "We'll explain later."

Trey looked down at Mary. "I don't really have a parakeet."

"I can get you one."

"No. That's cool. I don't--"

"You like blue or yellow? Green, maybe? I think that's all the colors they come in. But I can check it out." She pulled him after her. "Where's your bedroom?"

Trey hit the brakes. Mary may have been short,

but she had full grown curves. "My bedroom?"

"Yeah. Unless you keep your clothes somewhere else."

"Oh. Right. I thought--"

"You have a dirty mind, Trey." She laughed, and somewhere a shelf full of exquisitely fragile glass toppled onto the floor. "Where's your suitcase?"

He retrieved it from his closet, then paused long enough to look for Mary's companions. "Where are--"

"Outside."

"While we're--"

"In here. Packing." On her tiptoes, she groped blindly in the top drawer of his dresser and withdrew a handful of briefs. "I figured you for boxers." She threw them on the unmade bed, then continued foraging in his other drawers. T-shirts and socks followed the underwear and landed in a pile.

Trey stuffed his clothes into the travel bag as quickly as Mary launched them in his direction. "Jeans and sweatshirts are in the closet," he said, but she had already discovered them. "Will I need a jacket?"

She paused to look at him, curiosity coloring her classic features. "I doubt it. Unless we've slipped into another dimension, this is still summer in Atlanta, isn't it?"

"But I don't know where we're going!"

"West and north, but not far either way."

"That's comforting."

"These are nice," she said, throwing a pair of loafers at him. "Bring 'em."

"Those are my formal sorta shoes. They're a little tight."

"Wear 'em for me, then."

"Okay," he said. "Listen, I'll get the rest of that."

Josh Langston

"No, you won't. We're done. You got that stuff packed yet?"

Very little space remained in the valise. "Uh--"

"Don't forget your hairdryer, razor, and toothbrush."

"Why do I get the feeling you've done this before?"

"I've got six brothers," she said. "Most of 'em are younger than me, but none of 'em know how to pack. It's just not a guy-thing, y'know?"

He nodded. She was right. She was also leaving.

He zippered the case and hauled it out of the room as Mary walked out the front door. With none of his visitors in sight, Trey slipped into the little pantry in his kitchen and reached into the flour container where he kept his emergency fund--a roll of twenties he'd received in exchange for a motorcycle he couldn't afford to keep running. The money was gone.

Trey looked up at a chuckle from just outside the pantry.

Bud held up his cash, still wrapped in a plastic bag. "Lookin' for this?"

"How'd--"

"You'd be surprised how many people hide their money like that," he said, tossing it to him. "You oughta find a safer spot."

"Like the freezer?"

"Nah. I'd have found it there, too."

Trey felt violated. "Where, then?"

"I like banks," he said. "You ready to go?"

"Do I have a choice?"

"Not really."

They left.

~*~

Willard Calcraft had more attaboys and fewer friends than anyone else in the Internal Revenue's regional office in Atlanta. Nicknamed "The Executioner" by some wag who discovered a similarly named 19th century English hangman, Will hadn't actually killed anyone, though it was generally believed his unrelenting zeal for collecting back taxes had caused several clients to come after him.

His wife, Marjorie, had other reasons for wanting him dead. Foremost among them was a tax evader named Anastasia Jones whose profession required the strategic removal of her costume while dancing. Will had racked up some serious overtime on that case.

He had no idea Marjorie was contemplating his demise, but then few of her ideas had ever successfully garnered his attention. His inability to recognize problems of the domestic variety left him free to concentrate on his professional duties, such as the file in his hand.

A single sheet of paper occupied the folder. The name on the neatly typed file tab read: Bowman, Augustus A. The document contained the first clues in the kind of trail Willard Calcraft had followed often. He smiled in anticipation.

There was a "Bowman, Augustus A. " listed as the President of the Resurrection Holding Company, the address a rural route somewhere in Alabama. There was also a "Bowman, Augustus A." listed as the pastor of the Resurrection Free Will Unitarian Universalist Mission. It bore the exact same rural route address as the Resurrection Holding Company. He loved it when tax cheats tried to hide behind religion and considered himself duly constituted to collect that which was due unto Caesar, but not necessarily because he had a thing for Caesar. A final entry showed the results of a search for a personal income tax return for the head of the two organizations: all blanks.

Will swiveled his chair around to face a wall map of his region, Alabama, and quickly browsed through a listing of all the municipalities therein. Few names even came close; a town called Resurrection simply didn't exist. He obtained the zip code for the rural route of the holding company and located the area in the hilly terrain of the state's rugged northern reaches. He hunted for something that may have lent its name to both a trading company and a church. After twenty minutes of close scrutiny, he abandoned the map search without learning anything new. His curiosity growing, Will typed the word "Resurrection" into his favorite internet search engine and came up with an endless array of churches and church-affiliated organizations, but nothing that looked remotely promising from a tax collection vantage.

Rather than antagonize his contacts so late in the day, Will decided to leave the mystery of Resurrection until the next morning. That would give him plenty of time to pay Anastasia a visit before he drove home. He cleared off his desk, made sure he had an ample supply of dollar bills in his pocket, and left.

~*~

Mary rode with Trey as they angled northwest away from Atlanta. She made herself comfortable on top of his travel bag. Trey tried not to stare at the

8

harness strap of her seat belt which neatly bisected her breasts.

"They don't make these damn things for little people," she said. "Driving anything bigger than a bumper car is a real pain in the ass."

"I'd be more sympathetic if I knew where we were going."

"Resurrection, of course."

"Of course," he echoed. He remembered the name, usually spoken under his mother's breath and always referenced in the negative. According to her, Hell was a kinder, gentler alternative. "My mother told me some interesting stories about Resurrection. She wasn't a big fan."

"It's not a place for everyone," Mary said, "but I wouldn't live anywhere else."

"*Have* you lived anyplace else?"

She glanced at him with a slightly pained expression. "I've vacationed elsewhere. Or tried to. Vacation is over-rated. Frankly, I prefer stayin' at home." She pointed at Bud's truck some distance ahead. "Don't lose sight of them."

He increased his speed. "What's so special about Resurrection?"

"It's hard to explain."

"I've got nothin' but time."

"It's something you have to experience. The town isn't much to look at. It's more like your favorite jeans rather than your church clothes."

"I'm not much of a church-goer," Trey said. "None of my family was."

"That's not true. Augie lives next to the church. He's a minister."

Trey felt his eyebrows scrunch together. "Augie

9

Bowman, a preacher? Maybe I'm not your guy after all. My grandfather was--"

"*Is*. He's not dead, yet."

"--is a con artist. According to my mother. As I recall, she also called him a snake oil salesman and a carnival barker. There were some others, too, but those are the ones that stand out."

Mary squinted at him. "Your Mom told you that?"

"Yeah."

"Sure doesn't sound like Augie. She must not have known him very well. Either that, or he's changed. Drastically. The Boss is... The Boss! He's probably one of the smartest men in the world." Mary tried to cross her arms, but the combination of breasts and harness made it tricky. "I don't mean 'smart' like brain surgeon smart. He's smart in practical ways. He makes things work. He's not only a minister--"

"What church would have him?"

"Unitarian."

"Figures."

"He's also the banker."

"The banker?" Trey asked. "You make it sound like there's only one."

"That's all we need."

"A con artist owns the town's only bank?" He chuckled. *These people were deranged.* His mother couldn't have been that wrong about his grandfather, even if she did tend to be a tad over-reactive. "What a set up. He doesn't even have to drive his little lambs to the shed. They line up to be fleeced all by themselves."

"Are you this cynical about everything?"

He shook his head. "Only about cons, and I've gotta tell ya, that's exactly what this feels like."

She looked puzzled. "We're not tryin' to trick

you."

"Right," he said, reaching into the glove box to extract a map. He tossed it in her lap. "Why don't you show me where Resurrection is on that?"

She leaned forward and put the map back. "'Cause I can't."

"You can't read a map?"

"I can't show you where Resurrection is, 'cause it's not on that map. It's not on any map."

"Because it doesn't exist. It's a scam." He slowed the car and looked for a place to turn around.

"What are you doing?"

"Goin' back," he said. "I've got more important things to do than waste my time with lunatics."

"Okay. But what about me? I don't want to go to Atlanta. I wanna go home."

"Fine," he said, flashing his lights as he pulled off the road. The tires crunched in the red clay and gravel of the narrow shoulder. Well ahead of him, the pickup truck slowed, then did a U-turn and sped back toward them. "You can ride back with Dago and Crazy Horse," he said.

"Warren Lightfoot. Bud."

"Whatever."

She frowned at him. "You're a real asshole, you know that? I thought you might be a decent guy, like your grandfather, but I was wrong."

"I am a decent guy," he said. "I just don't like being jerked around, and that's all you've been doing."

The pickup pulled off the road opposite Trey's car. Bud rolled the window down. "What's the problem?"

Mary leaned across Trey and called back, "He wants to go home. He thinks we're tryin' to pull something over on him."

Bud jammed the shift lever into park and killed his engine. His door squealed as he opened it and again when he pushed it shut. He jogged across the road and leaned down to look through Trey's window. "So, you don't want to see your grandfather. He's on his deathbed. It's his last wish, on Earth. But you're too busy to see the old guy off?"

"I think you're trying to pull some kind of scam."

"Like what?"

"I dunno. I'm not the con artist; my grandfather is. And, I suspect, y'all are, too."

Bud pursed his lips and went silent for a long moment. "Why would we bother to scam someone who's broke?"

"Who said I was broke?"

"The Boss."

"I'm not broke!"

"Really? That's odd, 'cause according to Augie, you've been unemployed for almost a year. Your last three checks bounced like Texas Leaguers, and your credit report shows more red ink than black. A lot more. Your bank's going to take your house at the end of the month."

Trey squeaked, "You ran a credit check on me?"

"I didn't. The Boss did. He said he had to wait until you were ready."

"Ready for what?"

"A change," said Mary. "Or would you rather go back to the same old, same old? At least until someone comes along to take it away."

"Now wait just a damn minute--"

"Not us," Mary said, "the bank."

"But--"

"Don't get us wrong," Bud said. "We aren't above trying to pull a fast one on some fat-cat outsider. You're more like family."

"How comforting."

"Don't get drippy on us," Bud said. "Can we go now? I wanna get home before dark."

"Yeah, sure, but I'm not promising I'll stay."

Bud didn't respond. He walked back to his truck, fired it up and gunned the engine through the turn which took him back the way he'd come. Trey pulled out after him.

"No one has to stay in Resurrection," Mary said. "It's not a prison. The people who live there like it there. Give it a chance; you might like it, too. If not, we'll show you the way out."

"I doubt you'll have to show me," he said.

Mary only smiled.

~*~

Marjorie Calcraft propped her chin on her knuckles and blew a strand of limp, blonde hair straight up off her forehead. Her closest friend, Alyson Spencer, topped off her Cosmo, then carefully emptied the shaker into her own glass. "Drink up. The kids'll be home from practice soon."

Marjorie nodded despondently. "It's Tuesday, right? Excitement night."

"You goin' out for dinner?"

"We never go out anymore. Will says it's not cost effective."

"He actually says that?"

Marjorie shrugged. "No, but that's the way he acts. I'm tellin' ya, Aly, I can't take much more."

13

"Then divorce him. You're still a good-looking woman. You could find someone else, someone who'd appreciate you for who you are."

"Oh, right. I'm sure there are loads of handsome, single, well-to-do guys looking for fortyish blondes in size 12 slacks."

"You're a 12?" Alyson asked, the skepticism in her voice barely contained.

Marjorie's lips twisted to the side. "Sometimes. Depends on the label."

"You could settle for less than perfect. Single and well-to-do sounds pretty good. It'd help if they like kids."

"You're the one with kids, not me," Marjorie said. "You make it sound so... mercenary." She swirled the pink beverage in her glass and just barely managed to keep it from sloshing over the edge. She preferred wine glasses, the big, trendy bubble style. The way Alyson made cosmos--half vodka, half cranberry juice, a splash of Cointreau--it only took one to relax her. Two usually put her in a mild state of euphoria. Two, in the bubble glasses, would put her in a coma. That evening, however, she felt nothing but depression. "I think maybe I'll just shoot him."

Alyson grinned. Marjorie knew she liked nothing better than a good conspiracy, especially if nothing ever came of it.

"Could be messy," Alyson said. "Noisy, too. You got a gun?"

"Will does. Somewhere."

"Know how to use it?"

"What's to know? They do it all the time on TV." Marjorie took another sip of her drink. "I could do it. I could lock him outta the house, and when he tried to

14

break in, I could blow his cheatin' little weenie off."

Alyson took a sharp breath. "You think he's cheating? Really? With who? Anyone I know? Wait! I'll bet I know." She gave her head a sympathetic shake. "It's that busty brunette in the house with the pool. What's her name? Sheila something. I've heard she sunbathes in the nude. Can you believe it?"

"It's not Sheila Sonderberg," Marjorie said. "She's at least ten years older than I am. She gives kids piano lessons, fergodsake."

"Well, then, who is it? Anyone I know?"

"Not unless you frequent strip clubs."

Alyson's previous sharp intake of breath failed to compete with her latest. "Are you sure? How do you know?"

"I followed him one night. He's been acting strange lately. Even more than usual, if you can believe it. He gave me some ridiculous story about having to go to the office, but I knew better."

"And he went to a strip club?"

Marjorie nodded, tears welling in both eyes. "It took me fifteen minutes to get there, and I waited for almost an hour. He walked right past me when he came out. Didn't even recognize my car! Never looked in my direction."

"Maybe it was work-related."

Marjorie gave her a look she usually reserved for only the most deserving dumb asses.

~*~

Trey and Mary had driven for about two hours when the pickup in front of them slowed to a stop on the side of the road. Dago hopped out and walked back to Trey's car with the setting sun at his back, framed by a pair of non-descript Appalachian foothills.

"I'll drive from here," he said.

"No thanks," said Trey. "I'm not tired."

"He's not worried about your safety," Mary said. "It's a security thing." She looked into the back seat. "You can stretch out back there."

Trey shook his head. "I'm not stretching out anywhere but right here, behind the wheel. Listen, I promise not to tell anyone where your goofy little town is, if that's what you're worried about."

"We're not worried," Dago said, pressing something cold and hard against Trey's neck.

When he woke, he found himself curled up on the back seat, the sole occupant of the vehicle. He sat up and looked around, expecting some sort of unpleasant side effect from the tranquilizer Dago must have used on him. Instead, he felt surprisingly clear-headed, as if he'd had a good night's sleep.

He felt as though he owed it to himself to be angry at his captors, but he wasn't. Whatever had knocked him out left him feeling awfully good, though he doubted he'd been asleep very long. The sun sat low in the sky, but it was far from dusk. He vowed to settle things with Dago the next time he saw him. And Mary, too. She could have warned him he was about to take a nap.

He exited the car which was parked behind a single, large house, and stretched. The dwelling was no different than a thousand others he'd seen in small towns throughout the South. Someone was in the process of painting the place, but it wasn't a rehabilitation effort. The house had obviously been well kept. A huge dog of indeterminate breed filled the top of the stairs leading to the back door. Trey hoped it was on a chain, though it didn't appear interested in him. It yawned, exposing saurian teeth and a long pink tongue. Trey decided not to venture too far from his car. The thought made him spin around and look at the ignition for his keys. They weren't in sight.

"Trey!" said a gravelly voice from the porch. "How in the hell are you, boy?"

An old man leaned against the porch rail, a smile on his pale face. A great mane of white hair and a full, matching beard gave the man a distinctly Clausian look, although his body would never pass for a jolly old elf.

"Gramp?"

"C'mon up here, boy," said the old man. "Lemme get a look at you."

Trey ambled to the bottom of the stairs but stopped when the gigantic canine lifted its head and stared at him.

The old man waved his arm impatiently. "C'mon up. Tiny won't hurt ya. He's got about as much energy as me, and that ain't sayin' much."

Tiny lowered his great head as Trey climbed the stairs and stepped over him. The dog never even blinked.

The old man grabbed Trey's proffered hand and pulled him into a hug. "God, how I've missed you! I was sorry to hear about your Mom. I wanted to attend the funeral, but the doctor wouldn't let me out of bed."

Pressed to arm's length, Trey examined his grandfather. Though thin and pale, he certainly didn't look as though he'd just crawled from his death bed. "They told me you were, uhm, pretty sick."

"I am. Gonna die soon, they say." He gave Trey a

17

toothy smile.

"You don't sound very upset about it."

He shrugged. "We all have to go sooner or later. No sense worryin' about it." He clapped Trey on the shoulder. "Don't misunderstand. I'm not eager to leave the midway. I'll ride this carousel for a few more turns, but when it's time to climb on the next ride, I'll be ready."

"You think death is just another carnival ride?"

"Isn't it?"

"No! Death is... death. It means everything's over. Done. Endless nothing."

"I like the carnival ride theory better. It's hard to get excited about 'endless nothing.'"

Trey felt suddenly foolish. He slapped his forehead. "I-- I get carried away sometimes and forget when to keep my big mouth shut. I'm sorry."

The old man smiled. "Don't be. You're entitled to your opinion." He motioned toward an open door. "It's cooler inside. You hungry?"

"Actually, I was thinking of maybe drivin' back tonight."

"Then you'll need these," the elder Bowman said, handing him his car keys. "But surely you can stay for dinner."

"You're not going to drug me again, are you?" He still wanted to give Dago a piece of his mind, but the aroma of fried chicken and fresh bread all but overpowered him.

The old man laughed. "I can't promise you won't get sleepy after you eat a big meal, but if you're determined to leave, no one's going to stop you. I'll see to it someone helps you get to the main road."

Trey followed his grandfather through the house

toward the kitchen. All along the way the smells of cooking food grew stronger, and Trey's appetite grew as well. A young woman met them at the kitchen door, then led the old man to a chair at a built-in table. "Have a seat, Boss. Everything's ready."

"Kate, this is my grandson, Trey. The one I've been telling you about."

She smiled and extended a hand. Trey accepted it while examining her face. "You look so familiar."

Kate chuckled. "I understand you spent the afternoon with my big sister. Folks say we look alike."

"Mary's your 'big' sister?"

"Yeah. 'Cept her name's not Mary."

A wave of confusion crested over Trey. It must've shown on his face.

"Her real name's Ethyl. She likes to use a variety of names. Can't say I blame her."

"Ethyl?"

"Yeah, like at the gas station, ethyl or regular."

Trey still didn't understand. He looked to his grandfather for help. He responded while piling chicken on a plate and passing it to Trey by way of Kate. "Ethyl teaches history," he explained. "She was having trouble getting through to some of her students and decided to try something a little unconventional to get their attention."

"This was a couple years ago, and she was getting desperate," Kate said. "There aren't that many folks willing to pay for history lessons to begin with. She couldn't afford to lose any students."

Trey tried to concentrate on what they were saying, but the smell of fried chicken made it difficult. Kate put a fist-sized helping of mashed potatoes on his plate and puddled gravy in the middle. A trickle of the thick, fragrant liquid dripped down one crisp edge of the chicken.

"What'd she do that was so different?" Trey asked.

"They were studying ancient Egypt at the time," Trey's grandfather said. "She came to school dressed like Cleopatra."

"What a shock that must've been," Kate said. "She found a costume from the old show days--harem pants, a skimpy top, lots of jewelry and make-up--then she waltzed into class and introduced herself as the Queen of the Nile. Wouldn't say anything more until the students addressed her properly. Pretty soon they were asking questions and she was giving answers. I daresay those kids learned a lot. Then, when word got out about her skimpy costume--"

"Which took about ten minutes," the old man interjected.

"--a whole bunch of boys signed up for her class. She wouldn't let 'em in unless they agreed to stay the whole year, and paid in advance. She chose one new character a week after that, and just played the roles. I know--I helped her with a lot of the costumes. She got so good at it, and had so much fun doing it, that she let it slide over into her non-school life. She even wears the costumes when she's working at the café. Customers love it."

"I thought you said she was a teacher."

"She is. She's also a business owner. Co-owner, actually. She and a friend run a pastry shop in town."

Trey nodded. "Do you know who she is this week?"

"Wait, don't tell me," said the old man, his food untouched. He clenched his eyes shut in concentration. They all sat in silence until he shook his head in defeat.

"Think Christmas," Trey said.

"Mary! Of course," Kate giggled. "Bet that took you by surprise. 'Course, she's hardly a virgin."

Feeling his role as a southern gentleman had been compromised somehow, Trey said, "I wish y'all wouldn't do that."

"Do what?"

"Tell me you're not virgins."

"Who said anything about me?" Kate asked, as she coolly met his gaze.

Trey chomped down on a fleshy drumstick and chewed to cover his discomfort. He couldn't remember the last time he'd tasted anything so flavorful.

~*~

Resurrection Blues is available now in e-book and paperback formats at your favorite on-line retailer.